"Dale Brown is a superb storyteller."

—W.E.B. Griffin

"A master at creating a sweeping
epic and making it seem real."
—Clive Cussler

"A master of mixing technology and action. He
puts readers right into the middle of the inferno."
—Larry Bond

"Dale Brown is one of the best at marrying high-
tech military wizardry with a compelling plot."
—*Houston Chronicle*

"Brown puts readers into the cockpit. . . .
Authentic and gripping."
—*New York Times*

"The action's relentless. . . . High-tension, all-out
action-adventure . . . Brown out-Clancys Tom."
—*Kirkus Reviews*

DALE BROWN

AND

JIM DeFELICE

ACT OF REVENGE

A NOVEL

wm

WILLIAM MORROW
An Imprint of *HarperCollins*Publishers

This is a work of fiction. Names, characters, places, and incidents are products of the author's imagination or are used fictitiously and are not to be construed as real. Any resemblance to actual events, locales, organizations, or persons, living or dead, is entirely coincidental.

ACT OF REVENGE. Copyright © 2018 by Air Battle Force, Inc. All rights reserved. Printed in the United States of America. No part of this book may be used or reproduced in any manner whatsoever without written permission except in the case of brief quotations embodied in critical articles and reviews. For information, address HarperCollins Publishers, 195 Broadway, New York, NY 10007.

First William Morrow premium printing: February 2018
First William Morrow hardcover printing: January 2018

Print Edition ISBN: 978-0-06-241132-7
Digital Edition ISBN: 978-0-06-241133-4

Cover design by Guido Caroti
Cover photographs © Kletr/Shutterstock (drone), © Tanor/Shutterstock (clouds)

William Morrow and HarperCollins are registered trademarks of HarperCollins Publishers in the United States of America and other countries.

FIRST EDITION

18 19 20 21 22   QGM   10 9 8 7 6 5 4 3 2 1

Revenge, at first though sweet,
Bitter ere long back on itself recoils.

—Milton, *Paradise Lost*
(Book IX, lines 171–72)

ACT OF REVENGE

Data sheet

Important people

Louis Messina—scientist and entrepreneur, proprietor of Smart Metal, deeply religious; lost his hand and his wife in a car accident as a young man; never remarried

Chelsea Goodman—project engineer at Smart Metal; genius at math, young, petite, creative

Johnny Givens—young, athletic FBI agent on Jenkins's task force

Yuri Johansen—veteran CIA officer, in charge of a covert antiterror action group primarily operating overseas

Ghadab min Allah—*nom de terror* of Samir Abdubin, roughly, "God's wrath." More demon than man, with a fetish for knives, especially ornate khanjars, which he uses to slit victims' throats

Shadaa—Ghadab's paramour

Important places

Boston & suburbs—birthplace of freedom, hardscrabble values, great Italian food, and the best baseball team in the world

Palmyra, Syria—city in Syria occupied by ISIS/Daesh, used as sanctuary by Ghadab

Important tech

Bot—Smart Metal slang for robot that can function to some degree on its own, in contrast to mechs and industrial robots designed for specific, stationary tasks such as welding or chip making. Smart Metal constructs all types

Mech—Smart Metal slang for robots that are preprogrammed for specific tasks but retain more flexibility than industrial robots

Autonomy—ability of bot or other entity to "think" or make decisions without direct commands from operator

UAV—unmanned aerial vehicle, commonly referred to as a "drone"; Smart Metal UAVs can operate without direct human guidance

OBSCENITY

———

Flash forward

Boston, Easter Sunday
High noon

LOUIS MASSINA PACED BACK AND FORTH IN THE *small high-security area, worried, anxious, and angry.*

But most of all, impotent. Boston was under attack. The lives of dozens, maybe hundreds, of his friends were directly threatened. One of his closest employees, a young woman with tremendous promise, was among the hostages.

Maybe even dead.

And all he could do, for all his money, for all his inventions—his robots, his drones, his computers, his software—was walk back and forth, trying desperately to suppress what could not be suppressed.

Anger. Rage. The enemy of reason, yet the core of his being, at least at this moment.

There were other alternatives. Prayer, for one.

Prayer is impotence. Prayer is surrender.

The nuns who taught him would slap his face for

thinking that. They held the exact opposite: Prayer was strength, tenfold.

But while in many ways Massina was a man of faith, he had never been much given to prayer. In his mind, actions spoke more effectively than words. Prayers were all well and good, but they worked—if they worked at all—on a realm other than human.

And the action needed now was completely human. Not even the Devil himself could have concocted the evil his city faced.

Light flashed in the center of the far-right monitor.

"They're going in," said the operator watching the hotel where Massina's employee had been taken hostage. The light had come from a small explosion at the side of the building. "They're going in."

Almost in spite of himself, Massina started to pray.

Real time

1

THERE WERE FEW BETTER HOTELS IN BOSTON THAN the Patriot Hotel if you wanted to soak up the city's history: city hall was practically next door, Faneuil five minutes away. You could catch a trolley for the Old Town tour a block or two down the street. Bunker Hill was a hike, but then the British had found that out as well. The rooms were expensive—twice what they would go for at similarly appointed hotels nearby—but money had never been a major concern for Victoria Goodman, Chelsea Goodman's favorite aunt. Victoria had gotten a job as a secretary for

Microsoft very soon after it started, and when she cashed out her stock in the early 1990s, invested in real estate in and around San Francisco, most notably Palo Alto and Menlo Park—the future homes of Facebook and Google. Victoria had that kind of luck.

Despite her luck, and her money, Victoria was especially easygoing, self-assured yet casual. She met Chelsea in the hotel lobby wearing a blue-floral draped dress that showed off toned upper arms and legs that remained trim and shapely despite the fact that she had recently passed sixty.

"Just on time," declared Victoria, folding Chelsea to her chest. "I hope you're hungry."

"I wouldn't mind breakfast," answered Chelsea. "How far did you run this morning?"

"It's not the distance, it's the attitude," replied Victoria. "Only five miles. But it felt wonderful. It's so marvelous running through the city."

"You'll have to try for the Marathon."

"Those days are gone, dear," said Victoria lightly. "I'd never qualify. But thank you for the thought. You didn't bring your young friend?"

"We'll meet her at the Aquarium," Chelsea said. "She had to go to church with her dad."

"Well, it is Easter."

"Actually, they're Russian Orthodox, so it's Palm Sunday. He's a single father, and lately he's been trying to instill religion in her."

Chelsea followed Victoria across the paneled lobby to the restaurant entrance, where a maître d' greeted them with a nod. He had a fresh white rose in his lapel and the manner of someone who'd been looking forward to this encounter the entire morning. He showed the two women to a seat at the far end of the room, then asked if they would care for something to drink while they looked at the menus.

"Mimosas," said Victoria. "And coffee."

"Mimosas?" asked Chelsea.

"Why not? You don't have to work today, and champagne always puts me in the mood for sightseeing."

Chelsea was just about to ask how exactly that worked when a loud crack shook the room. The metallic snap was followed by two more, each louder than the other. The noise was unfamiliar to most of the people in the restaurant, but Chelsea had lately had a singular experience that not only made the sound familiar, but warned her subconscious that there was great danger nearby. She leaped up from her seat, and before her aunt could respond, had grabbed her and pushed her to the floor.

"Someone is shooting!" Chelsea told Victoria as the crack of a fresh round of bullets echoed against the deep wood panels of the room. "We have to get out of here!"

2

Boston, Massachusetts—around the same time

JOHNNY GIVENS COULDN'T HELP BUT BE IMPRESSED. Since coming to Smart Metal, the former FBI agent had seen more than his share of high-tech gizmos and gadgets. The company was the leading manufacturer of stand-alone robots in the Northeast, and its R&D section was beyond anything Jules Verne, Gene Rodenberry, or William Gibson could have imagined. And he himself was an example of its cutting-edge technology—having lost his original legs in an accident while working a case, Johnny now walked on a set of prosthetics designed and manufactured by Smart Metal's Bio-Med division. Yet what he was seeing this morning impressed him even more than his legs. For he was seeing the future of policing.

The Boston Police Department had invited Johnny and his immediate boss, Smart Metal Security Director William Bozzone, to inspect their not-yet-complete Command Center, a veritable Starship *Enterprise* located in a disaster-proof shelter under the Charles River. Besides the normal communications gear one would find in a class-one emergency call center, BCPD Command had dedicated links to a dozen nearby police departments, the Massachusetts State Police, the National Guard, Homeland Security, and even the Pentagon. Police video cameras, set up at every substation, municipal building, and historic site, provided real-time visuals of what was happening around the city. Visual input could also be received from up to twelve helicopter drones, which were piloted from a room within the complex. Commanders could not only speak in real time to any officer on the force, but could "push" data such as video to their devices—phones, tablets, laptops—as well. Sophisticated computers utilized face- and voice-recognition software to ID suspects and present their rap sheets in less time than it would take a police officer to tell them to put up their hands. The center also received status reports on the city's T or subway, buses, electrical grid, and its internet systems. And while still in its infancy, software that integrated all of the available information promised to provide alerts that would make the department far more proactive than imagined even a decade before.

To Johnny, it looked like nirvana: a twenty-first-century tool for law enforcement that would put police officers two steps ahead of criminals. So he was baffled when he noticed Bozzone's frown deepening with every step they took around the center. What had seemed like a quizzical annoyance as they passed through the metal and chemical detectors before boarding the tram at the entrance had blossomed into something that suggested disgust. Bozzone didn't voice it—he was nothing if not disciplined and polite—but having worked with him closely for several months, Johnny realized he was about ready to explode.

Their tour guide, Police Captain Horace Wu, seemed oblivious. Wu, a fifth-generation police officer whose great-great-grandfather had been one of the first Chinese American members of the Boston PD, led them from the Situation Room down a hallway past some as-yet-unoccupied offices to the Galley—a full-service cafeteria that, unfortunately, was not yet manned. Coffee and pastries had been put out on a table; Wu directed Bozzone and Givens to help themselves while he checked on the other groups being shown through the center.

"This is going to kill your diet," Givens told Bozzone, glancing at the array of fruit tarts, jelly donuts, and squares of cheesecake.

Bozzone silently poured himself a cup of coffee and sat down. Johnny helped himself to a Danish and followed.

"Not even tempted?" asked Givens.

Bozzone shrugged.

"What's up?"

"You realize this is Big Brother Central, right?" said the security chief.

"I don't follow."

"The gear here, the coordination, the inputs, and the abilities—it can be used for a lot of things."

"Catching criminals. Sure."

Bozzone focused on his coffee, stirring it slowly.

"Danish is good," said Johnny.

"The problem is balance. And responsibility. Who do we trust with the keys?" Bozzone raised his head and stared at Givens. His expression was somewhere between that of an interrogator and a philosopher, both accusing and pensive at the same time. "Who do we trust watching our every move?"

"It's an extension of the guy on the beat," offered Johnny. "In the old days, a cop would patrol a few blocks, know just about everybody, see just about everything going on. That was community policing."

Johnny, who'd earned a bachelor's in criminal science after his Army service, knew this was an exaggeration, and that in fact it bordered on an idealistic fantasy. But it was the best he could offer at the moment.

He expected Bozzone to counter, but he didn't. Instead, his boss rose.

"Let's get going. I don't really feel like spending all Easter here."

"Good idea," said Johnny. "Otherwise I'll be tempted to grab another Danish."

It occurred to Johnny that their intel shack at Smart Metal, which had been set up to help the CIA complete a mission in occupied Ukraine, had even more capabilities than BCPD Command; Bozzone had raised no objections about that. But this wasn't the place to bring that up. He fell in behind Bozzone, following as he walked back through the hall to the Situation Room, looking for Wu so they could say thank you and take their leave.

They had just spotted Wu across the room with a pair of Massachusetts State Detectives when a buzzer sounded. Givens looked up at the massive LED video panel at the front of the room. A large red banner was flashing across the top of the screen:

Shooting Reported in Old Town District

A systems operator at a console on a raised platform near the back of the room typed furiously, and the image changed from a map of Boston to a bird's-eye view of the area near the harbor. A red marker glowed near a building Johnny recognized as the Patriot, a pricey five-star old-world-style hotel in the center of the city's historic area. The screen divided in half; a video from a police car responding to the scene appeared at the top right, next to the map. Below it was an image from one of the two helicopter drones currently flying above the city.

"Is this a tech demonstration?" Johnny asked.

Before anyone could answer, another banner appeared on the screen, just below the earlier one:

Explosion in Orange Line Station: Back Bay

"Come on," said Bozzone. "Fast."

Johnny followed his boss as he beelined for the exit portal, running to one of the waiting trams. Johnny had barely gotten in when Bozzone hit the Transport button. The magnetic-impulse car shot away from the Command Center toward the facility's guarded entrance.

"We need to get out of here before they go to lockdown," said Bozzone. "Boston is under attack."

"You don't think it's just an exercise?"

Bozzone shook his head. "No way."

3

Near Boston—a short time later

Aₛ ᴀ ᴘʀᴀᴄᴛɪᴄᴀʟ ᴍᴀᴛᴛᴇʀ, ᴍᴏꜱᴛ ᴅᴀʏꜱ, ᴇᴠᴇɴ Sᴜɴ-days, religion did not intrude too greatly into Louis Massina's thoughts, let alone his schedule.

Easter was different.

Easter high mass was a must-attend event; he had not missed one in his memory, which extended back to his days as a toddler. Accordingly, the mass was an exercise in nostalgia as well as devotion. The scent of lilies and incense as he crossed to the narthex from the vestibule returned him to his childhood; by the time he knelt in a pew to pray, he would remember the hard wooden kneelers he'd bruised his knees on as an altar boy. The choir would transport him farther back, to a neighborhood church—boarded now, but at the time crowded with blue-collar parishioners and their prayers. Massina would see his great-aunt, a nun, face beaming as she fingered her rosary beads. He would remember his parents, and the long walk home to the apartment where his mother had hidden their plastic eggs in various crevices.

That was a long time ago, and not just in years.

Conscious of how much had changed, Massina came out of the church in a contemplative mood, and it only deepened when he returned home. If he had been of a different temperament, this contemplation might have led to melancholia, a yearning for the past, and half a bottle of Scotch or some similar beverage. Massina was different: his mood prompted a laundry list of projects he *must absolutely* turn his attention to, things he had to accomplish, projects he had to try. That was his family's greatest legacy—urging him to never be satisfied.

If I can dream it, why can't it be?

A somewhat naive credo, and yet look where it had taken him.

Massina was lost in thoughts of cybergenic prosthetics and autonomous ships when the security system alerted him to the car that had pulled up to the gate.

He was surprised to see that it was one of his company SUVs, driven by Johnny Givens.

"Open gate," he told the system, then went to meet Johnny on the landing to the front steps.

"You have today off," said Massina sharply as his deputy security supervisor got out of the truck. "Why are you here?"

"Terrorists are attacking the city," said Givens tersely. "There's been an explosion in the T, hostages at a hotel downtown, a bombing—"

"Take me to the office."

"Beef wanted you to stay here. It's safer."

"We're leaving now," said Massina. "Do you want to drive or should I?"

JOHNNY GIVENS HAD ONLY WORKED AT SMART METAL for a short time, but he wasn't surprised at all by Massina's decision. He doubted Bozzone would be either.

Getting downtown, however, was not an easy task. The police had cordoned off the area near the Patriot Hotel, and traffic was snarled to the point that they reached a standstill about a dozen blocks from their office. Massina surveyed the situation, sat patiently for about thirty seconds, then unlocked his door and hopped out.

"Mr. Massina!" Johnny shouted. "At least let me come with you."

"Well, come on, then."

"I can't abandon the truck."

Massina shrugged and started away.

They had passed a parking lot a half a block away. Johnny edged his way onto the sidewalk— fortunately empty—then backed all the way to the lot. He pulled into a space, then ran to catch up to his boss.

The inventor was rather short, and Givens had the benefit of appendages that were several times more powerful than "normal" legs. Still, it took him several blocks to catch up. By that time, they were within sight of the renovated factory that housed Smart Metal's offices in the city center.

Two policemen dressed in riot gear stopped them on the next block. Givens prepared himself for an argument, but he didn't get a word out of his mouth.

"Hey, Jimmy O'Brien," said Massina, walking over to the taller of the two officers. "I saw your father at mass this morning. He's looking very well."

"Mr. Massina, how are you?" said the policeman, pushing up the shield on his helmet to see Massina better.

"Not good. What the hell is going on?"

"We're not sure, but the city's on lockdown."

"I'll be at my office," said Massina, already starting past. "If you need anything, send someone around to see Bozzone. We'll send you out some coffee. I'm not sure if there's food, but if so, we'll get you that, too."

"Thank you."

"You know everybody in the city?" asked Givens, catching up.

"Just the important people."

Bozzone met Massina in the entrance hall. "You were supposed to stay at your house."

"You're giving the orders now? What's the situation here?"

"We're secure," said Bozzone.

"How about our people?"

"I don't know where everyone is but—"

"But you're working on it," snapped Massina. It wasn't a question.

"I am."

"Good."

"The police want everyone to shelter in place," said Bozzone.

"Is that wise?"

"Probably."

"Unless they happen to be in a place where the terrorists are," said Massina. "Make sure everyone is accounted for. Update me upstairs in twenty—no, ten minutes."

4

Boston—around the same time

CHELSEA CRAWLED AROUND THE BACK OF THE DINING room toward a door that led to a hallway with storerooms and a bathroom. She could hear gunshots and a commotion at the front of the room, but knew better than to stop and see what was going on.

"Still with me, Aunt Vic?"

"Right behind you," said Victoria.

The lights snapped off just as Chelsea reached the entrance to the hallway. She took her aunt by the hand, then rose and began running down the corridor.

Her first thought was the restroom, but out of the corner of her eye she saw a metal fire door and realized it meant there was a stairway behind it.

"The stairs," she hissed. "Come on!"

She slammed her shoulder against the crash bar as if she were punching into a scrum in a field-hockey game. The door gave way easier than she had expected, slamming against the concrete wall of the stairwell and punching her in the side. Victoria rushed past, ducking to the right as Chelsea pushed the door closed. There was no lock.

"Up the stairs, come on," she told Victoria, though her aunt was already leading the way.

Chelsea expected the older woman to fade as they hit the second flight, but either fear or her daily running exercise—perhaps both—gave her the energy of someone forty years younger. She wasn't even breathing heavily as they reached the third-floor landing.

"How far up should we go?" asked Victoria.

"To the roof!" decided Chelsea.

Unlike the richly paneled and stuccoed walls of the hotel's public areas, plain cement blocks lined this stairwell. Cold to the touch, their solid, no-nonsense, whitewashed surface reassured Chelsea as she climbed. It was a bunker-like womb, a literal stairway to safety.

Or so it seemed until a loud crash reverberated from above. A woman screamed—high-pitched, the sound bounced off the hard surfaces of the walls, vibrating the loose metal of the treads so that the entire stairwell tingled with fear. A deeper sound followed, one even more frightful—it was male, a grunt that turned into a shriek before sinking to a groan, pain mixing with despair. Its echo lingered for only a moment, disrupted by the sound of automatic gunfire, a rapid click and whistle, ricochets dicing the surface of the cement. Splinters began to fall, and a cloud of dust—cement, gun gases, blood—filled the stairwell.

"We gotta get out," Chelsea told her aunt, grabbing her hand and pulling her to the door of the landing they'd just climbed to. The doorknob turned but the door wouldn't open. Chelsea's adrenaline took over. She pulled her aunt with her, descending to the next level down.

Don't panic, she told herself. *Step by step.*

She thought of her trip to the Ukraine, and her training, and how to breathe. She forced herself to slow as she reached the next landing, fighting her adrenaline.

This door also seemed blocked, even though the knob turned.

Oh, for crapsake!

She was pushing, when of course the damn thing opened *into* the stairway.

Calm is better!

Slow is sure. Sure is fast. Slow is fast and sure!

Chelsea closed the door behind them as gently as she could. A fresh shock of gunfire rang from above as the latch closed.

Head leaning forward, arms out as if to catch a fall, Victoria moved in slow motion down the hallway, her head swiveling back and forth.

"Stay close to the wall," Chelsea told her. She put her hand on her aunt's shoulder, gently holding her back so she could take the lead.

"Careful," said a male voice, so loud that she thought it was coming from behind her. She glanced back.

There was no one else in the hall. Chelsea lowered herself into a half crouch and began walking again, her right shoulder hugging the wall. The rooms along the hallway were laid out similarly to the ones in the restaurant—the stairwell at the end, a men's room, a ladies' room. Rather than opening into a larger room, however, this hall led to another passage. Chelsea went down on her knee, peering forward to scan the hall. It was only a few yards in either direction; each end gave way to another hall.

She listened, hoping to hear the voice again. There was strength in numbers.

"Which way do you think?" asked Victoria.

"Right, I think," said Chelsea. "Toward the front of the hotel. Did you hear that voice?"

"No."

"There must be other guests."

"I hope they're on our side."

Chelsea peered around the corner, not sure what to expect. The hall ran for about six feet before giving way to a lounge area that rose above the main lobby. Seeing it, Chelsea knew where she was; the reservation desk was below and to her right. There was a small coffee kiosk around the corner from it. Most of the rest of the lobby area was a maze of low couches and chairs. A bank of elevators lined the hall on the left.

"This is kind of a balcony," Chelsea told her aunt, leaning back. "It's about eight feet wide, and it's over the lobby. The front doors are just over there, and there are a couple of side entrances around that way." She pointed to the section beyond the reservation desk. "It's too high to jump down, but there are stairs at the far end. It's like thirty yards."

"OK."

"The lobby is empty," said Chelsea. She leaned back around the corner, making sure she was right. "Let's go that way while we have a chance."

"Out the front?"

"I think it's our best bet."

"Sneak or run?"

"Run . . . OK?"

Chelsea looked at her aunt's face. Her eyes had narrowed, and while her lips were pressed together, she looked determined.

Chelsea started to get up.

"Wait," said Victoria, grabbing her.

"What?"

"Do you have your phone?"

"Yes."

"We should call and tell someone what's going on."

"God." Chelsea dug into her pocket for her phone. She hadn't thought of that.

But the phone couldn't get a signal. Reception here was always iffy.

"Try yours," she told her aunt.

"I left it in my pocketbook."

"Forget it," said Chelsea. "Let's get out of here. On three."

"On two." Victoria raised her thumb.

Chelsea turned back toward the lobby, leaning forward to make sure the way was clear.

"One, two," she whispered, and then she was

off, flying across the long expanse. The deep carpet muffled her footsteps. The hotel remained eerily silent, without even mechanical noises, let alone people or guns or explosions.

As Chelsea reached the far side of the balcony, she spotted an alcove to the right. A red exit sign lit the corner. She decided that would be a safer route, since they wouldn't be exposed.

"This way, come on," she said, changing direction. She ran into the alcove and stopped at the door.

Just then the lights flickered and the place blackened. Emergency lights tripped on a moment later, casting the hall in a yellowish, almost sepia-toned hue.

"I just need to catch my breath," said Victoria. "What's this? I thought we were going out the front."

"This might go directly outside," said Chelsea. "Better not to be seen."

"Good. Let's go."

But rather than leading to a separate entrance, the staircase came out on the side of the lobby, not far from the reservation desk. Chelsea took a step toward the desk, then quickly retreated as shadows moved across the floor.

She held her breath, waiting. There was no sound, and the shadows were gone.

"Ready?" she whispered to her aunt.

"Yes!"

"We go right to the door," said Chelsea. "When we get outside, run left. I passed a Starbucks there, across the intersection. We'll get help there."

"And lattes," said her aunt.

"Lattes, yes," said Chelsea. "On three."

Though they'd rested for only a moment, her legs muscles had tightened, and Chelsea felt her calves straining as she leaped forward, glancing both ways to make sure the lobby was empty. Heart pounding, she shot toward the row of doors.

A chain linked the bars of the set closest to her. Chelsea ran to the next set—another chain.

They were all chained.

Victoria either didn't see it or didn't quite realize what it meant. She continued past Chelsea and landed both hands on the crash bar. The door budged about an inch and a half before stopping abruptly. Victoria smacked hard against the glass.

Chelsea grabbed her aunt, holding her up.

"That hall," she said. "Come on."

The hallway off the lobby ran parallel to the front of the building. The right side rested against the building's outer wall; the other was lined with offices. Chelsea wondered if people were hiding in some, but decided not to stop or check—they needed an exit, not allies.

There was an external door and a stairwell at the far end of the hall. This door, too, was chained, but the stairway was open. It led to the parking garage, which had several exits and entrances.

"The steps," said Chelsea.

"More steps," said Victoria, her voice resigned but almost comically so, as if they were running a steeplechase or some exercise course, not fleeing for their lives.

The steel doors to the garage were open. Exhaust mingled with fresh air, a good sign, thought Chelsea. She reached the bottom and ran into the garage proper. The ramp to the street was about forty yards away, the gate up, the entrance unblocked. The emergency lights were on, but there was also plenty of light coming from the street and skylights that were incorporated into the garden courtyard in the middle of the hotel.

"Aunt Vic, come on," said Chelsea, helping Victoria as she entered the garage. The older woman was really straining now, and limping—she'd twisted her knee coming down the stairs.

"We're out, we're out," said Chelsea, stooping down to take Victoria's arm and shoulder her out. It was a three-legged race, a lark in the park—an old memory or maybe a dream flitting into Chelsea's thoughts as they half jogged, half hobbled to the entrance.

Thank God! thought Chelsea.

They were maybe ten feet from the ramp when something darted from the left side. It moved quickly, so fast that Chelsea wasn't sure what it was at first. It seemed unworldly, a wraith.

Then she saw it was a man.

Then she saw he held a rifle.

Then she realized the rifle was pointing at her and her aunt.

5

Boston—around the same time

MASSINA LISTENED INTENTLY AS BOZZONE DESCRIBED the situation as he knew it: there had been at least one explosion in the T, a car or truck bomb had detonated on the departure level of Airport Road, a group of terrorists had taken over the Patriot Hotel, another group had taken over the Boston Children's Museum, and a suicide bomber had struck at the Back Bay Police Station. There were reports as well of an attack on a small restaurant in the North End and a disturbance of some sort at a bank on Massachusetts Avenue.

"Those are attacks that are confirmed," said Bozzone. "You're going to have rumors and misinformation, but the bottom line is the whole city is under attack."

"Who?" asked Massina.

"Looks like an ISIS attack, similar to what they did in Paris," said Bozzone. "This isn't just a lone wolf either. This is coordinated."

Massina had reached the same conclusion. But

it didn't matter at the moment who was responsible. The attacks had to be countered.

Revenge would come later.

And they would get revenge. The news of the attacks had awakened a feeling of rage in him, one he knew his city would share.

"What can we do to help?" he asked Bozzone. "Have you contacted the police?"

"I'm not sure they want our help," said Bozzone. "They have their—"

"Nonsense. Offer them our UAVs and bomb mechs for a start. We have ten aircraft just sitting in our warehouse shipping area, ready to go. And probably the same number of mechs. Where's Tommy Blake? Is he at home?"

"No, he's downstairs. He was a few blocks away when he heard the news and—"

"Good. Tell him to meet me in the Box."

"Lou, we really have to leave this to the professionals."

"We're professionals," thundered Massina. "I'll talk to the chief myself. Find the rest of our people. Get them here. Where's Chelsea Goodman?"

"The city is on lockdown."

"Not for us."

TEN MINUTES LATER, HAVING SPOKEN TO THE POLICE chief and the mayor, Massina strode into the "Box," a secure communications facility he had established with the help of the CIA a few months before. He had done so for a mission he considered a patriotic duty. This time, things were different. This was personal: his city was under attack.

Johnny Givens shadowed him, ostensibly as his bodyguard.

"Here," Massina told him, handing him a phone with an outside line. "Call your old boss at the FBI and tell him every asset I have is at his disposal. Tell him we're launching a half-dozen drones in the next ten minutes with infrared and daylight cameras to work with the city police. We can tie them into his network if he wants. I have six bots they can use for bomb disposal. They're on standby until someone needs them."

"You got it," said Givens.

Massina surveyed the row of multipurpose 4K screens sitting on the shared consoles in front of him. Each showed a different news channel. The Box—it was literally that, a large rectangular room sitting in the middle of an open basement space—had dedicated satellite communications and a link to the CIA's Langley headquarters. It also had its own mainframes and a backup power unit independent of the filtered network that powered Smart Metal's own massive arrays.

All these resources, thought Massina. And yet cable news was the go-to source for information.

Bozzone buzzed him on the intercompany talk channel.

"The police department needs a robot to check out a suspicious vehicle on 93 down south of the state police headquarters," said Bozzone.

"Done. Tommy!"

Tom Blake, one of the lead engineers in the

company's mobile robot division, was sitting at a console on the opposite side of the room. Blake had already sent a team of engineers and mechanics to their yard across the river to ready the UAVs.

"Police need a robot on 93. What's the best way to get it there?"

"Use the Lifter. We plop it down nearby."

The Lifter—a two-engined, unmanned helicopter that looked and operated like a flying crane—was still experimental. But Massina didn't hesitate.

"Do it," he said. "Everything we have is in play, experimental or not."

"We need to fuel it," said Blake, his ponytail bobbing. Blake was an old hippie—literally old, at sixty-two, but only figuratively a hippie, given that he was both an aeronautical engineer and a millionaire former entrepreneur whose company Massina had bought for its talent as well as its drone research. "Tell them we'll be in the air in fifteen."

"Make it ten."

"Dig it," replied Blake.

Massina decided that meant yes. He told Bozzone the unit would be on the way.

"One thing," said the security chief. "We're having trouble reaching Chelsea. The cell calls go right to voice mail."

"Get a car over to her house on Beacon Street and get her in here."

"I asked Boston PD to knock on her door. There was no answer."

"Keep looking."

"I'm doing what I can."

"Who's here from AI or general software?"

"Well, you have—"

"Send Chiang and Telakus down." Jin Chiang was a lead engineer on Chelsea's AI team and a former countersecurity expert for IBM—a polite way of saying a hacker—hired to test security systems; his batting average for breaking into systems was higher than Yastrzemski's. Avon Telakus had been a bot developer before going over to Smart Metal's information security systems—their white-hat hacking unit.

"OK."

Johnny waved to get his attention.

"Is it possible to tap into the Homeland Defense information network and supply them with real-time video?" Johnny asked. "The Bureau wants them online, too."

"Absolutely," said Massina. "Let me find a com guy to handle the details. Make sure he's talking to an engineer. Translating'll take all day."

6

Boston—around the same time

CHELSEA GLANCED AT HER AUNT. VICTORIA'S FACE was as white as milk.

The gunman took a step to his right, blocking off their path to the exit. Running would have been foolish in any event; he was holding an AR-15 with a thirty-round clip.

"Back," he said.

Chelsea took a step backward, trying to memorize his face. He was young, with a beard four or five days old. He looked vaguely Middle Eastern, but not like the pictures of terrorists she knew from the television. His lips twitched.

He was nervous.

Not a good thing when he was holding a gun, she realized.

"Let us go," Chelsea said. "We haven't done anything."

"You are a Muslim?" he said, pointing at Chelsea. "Arab?"

She shook her head, worried that he might let her go but keep her aunt here.

"Upstairs," he said, raising his head in the direction they had come. "Both of you."

"She's an old lady," said Chelsea, trying to think of how she might talk her way out of this. "She needs medicine. She could be your mother."

"Go!" The man pointed his gun at Victoria.

"We're going," said Chelsea, taking hold of her aunt's arm. She tugged gently, but Victoria seemed welded to the spot.

"We have to do what he says," Chelsea whispered.

"You look like a good person," Victoria told the gunman. Her voice was stronger than Chelsea expected. "You wouldn't want your mother hurt. You wouldn't hurt anyone. Let us go."

"Back into the hotel," said the man. "Or I shoot."

For just a moment, Chelsea thought of calling his bluff. But that would be suicide.

"Come on," she told Victoria, tugging her gently.

This time her aunt went with her. Chelsea's mind raced as they walked toward the steps. Was there another way out? Was there a car maybe they could steal?

"Is he following us?" Chelsea asked as they started up.

"No," said her aunt.

"That hallway to the right. Maybe there's another door out. Or if there's a room open, we could get out a window."

Chelsea spun right and started sprinting down the hall. The first door on the right was a women's restroom; she decided to try it, pushing inside. Her aunt followed.

There was a window on the far wall, but a thick antitheft screen of wire mesh filled the space beyond the glass. Chelsea pushed up the window and examined the panel. At least a quarter of an inch thick, the diamond-patterned metal remained stout as she pounded against it; her fist didn't even make an indent.

"We'll try another room," Chelsea said.

"I need a breath first," said her aunt.

"We have to keep trying."

"I know, I know. Just a minute. A second."

Victoria exhaled heavily, as if she were blowing out two dozen candles on a birthday cake. She gulped air and pushed it out again.

"Slow breaths, deep," Chelsea told her. "Slow. Try to relax."

You don't give up on a problem, no matter how hard it is.

Her father's voice, in her head, urging her on.

It was his voice she'd heard upstairs. She hadn't listened. Her hesitation had cost them their chance, maybe.

Don't dwell on your mistakes. Move ahead!

"Yes, go," she told herself, answering him.

Victoria thought she was talking to her. "OK."

Chelsea stopped at the door, peeked out, then held it open for her aunt. Out in the hall, they started running again, bypassing the men's room—surely it would have the same window arrangement—in favor of an office a little farther down. The door was locked, requiring a card to open.

"Next one," said Chelsea, already in motion.

She put her fingers on the handle, already calculating that it would be locked and they would have to move on. But by some miracle, the latch sprung open and she nearly tumbled inside.

The room was an office, with a desk, some empty shelves, and a pair of file cabinets. There were two casement windows on the far wall, covered by open blinds but large enough to let in considerable light.

Unlike the windows in the restroom, these opened horizontally, with a hand crank at the bottom. Chelsea flipped the locks open and cranked; the space was narrow but she figured she could pass through. The only problem was the screen separating the room from the outside. There didn't seem to be an easy way to remove it; they'd have to break it down.

"We'll break it with the chair legs," she said, turning back to get her aunt.

She wasn't there. In her haste, Chelsea had left her back in the hall, if not the bathroom.

The door started to open.

Thank God!

"We have a way out," Chelsea said, grabbing the chair. "Come on!"

"You'll come with me," answered the man who entered the room. "Come now or I'll shoot you."

7

Boston—around the same time

BORYA TOLEVI ALWAYS HAD BAD LUCK WITH THE BLUE Line. Always. While many aficionados of the city's subway system rated its trains at the top of the T lines—dubious praise, surely—in her opinion they were the worst. Hers always ran late or was way crowded or smelled beyond human habitation.

Usually all three.

But today was unreal. They were barely out of State Station when the train stopped with a screech.

STOPPED! IN THE TUNNEL!! IN THE F-ING TUNNEL!!!

The lights flickered on and off. Onoffonoffonoff, then full on, then full off, emergency lights coming on, then off and on.

Like bullshit!

Borya looked at her watch. She was due at the Aquarium to meet her friend, mentor, and honorary aunt Chelsea Goodman, along with Chelsea's actual real aunt, in forty-five minutes.

Granted, she had plenty of time to get there—the Aquarium was the next stop—but that required the train moving again.

Maybe it would. Maybe it wouldn't.

In the meantime, she was going to completely gag on the stench wafting from the old men crowding the seats nearby. She was standing in the aisle—easier to avoid perverts that way. But if she had to stand here for two more minutes she was going to either fall over or puke on the floor from the fart-stench wafting her way.

Borya decided her only recourse was to move to another car. She squirmed her way to the door at the end of the car, only to find it blocked by a woman who could have played on the Patriots' front line.

"Excuse me," Borya told her.

"Where you goin', hon?" said the woman. "There's no seats in that car."

"I want to see for myself."

"You're not supposed to ride between the trains," said Fattie. "Or walk between them."

"That's only when they're moving."

"The alarm will sound," she said.

"Alarm? There are no alarms on the doors. What are you, like, a drug addict? Or just from New York?"

Fattie crossed her eyes. Borya thought she might have to poke her to get her to move—the target opportunities were rich—but finally she stepped aside.

As Borya squeezed out onto the minuscule platform between the two cars, she realized that the Aquarium Station was no more than a hundred yards away, a yellowish-red glow down the tracks.

Just as easy to walk.

And why not?

There were a million reasons, death and dismemberment being numbers one and two, with electrocution a close third. But as good at math as Borya was—and she was very, very good—statistics of life and death were not one of her strong points. It took longer—a half second—for her to decide to get off the train than for her to climb up onto the swaying chain gate between the cars and leap onto the narrow ledge next to the tracks. Misjudging the distance, she rebounded back, bouncing off the side of the train car and coming perilously close to slipping between the train and the ledge.

Had the train started to move, she surely would have fallen. What happened next would not have been pretty.

But the train didn't move. Borya bounced to her feet and started along the ledge, steadying herself with her left hand against the train.

It was trickier beyond the subway car, with nothing to help her stay on the ledge. The walkway was barely that, with no rail and a rather slippery surface.

But it figured it would be wet near the Aquarium. *Duh*.

"You! What the hell are you doing!"

The shout took her by surprise. Borya started

to slip but managed to catch herself by falling on her knees.

"Get out of the tunnel! You can't be in the tunnel!"

It was the conductor, shouting through the window at the front of the train. He waved a beam of light at her from his flashlight.

"I'm going home!" Borya yelled back.

It was a lie—a stupid one, but stupid lies were better than nothing, in her experience.

"You'll get killed!" sputtered the conductor. "Get back here! Get back here! Watch out for the third rail! Idiot!"

His words spurred her on. She couldn't run—the ledge was too slippery and narrow for that, and she also worried that he had jinxed her. The third rail loomed large whenever she glanced to her left, monstrously magnified by her imagination.

The station platform was lit by emergency lights. It was deserted.

Had there been a fire? Was there still a fire?

No smoke. The air was—not clean, exactly, but not sulfur-choking, eye-tearing putrid either.

Was the power off all over town? Awesome.

Borya ran across the platform to the turnstiles. Since there were no police, no attendants, and no witnesses, she leaped over the turnstile rather than turning it—she'd always wanted to do that.

She glanced at the ticket booth as she ran toward the exit near the Marriot. The booth was empty, just like the station. The escalator wasn't working either.

Bolting up the stairs, she found a pair of policemen guarding the doorway. "Where'd you come from?" barked one of them.

"I was in the restroom," said Borya.

Another stupid lie: if there was a restroom at that stop, or any in Boston, Borya had never seen it. But the officer didn't call her on it.

"Get inside the building," he told her. "Shelter in place."

"What's that mean?"

"It means get your butt inside the Marriott and stay there."

"What's going on?"

"It's an attack, hon," said the other officer gently. It was a woman—between her uniform and her severe features, Borya hadn't realized she was female. "You want me to take you inside?"

"We gotta stay here," said her partner.

"I'm fine on my own," said Borya.

"All right," said the woman gently. "Just go right up to the main entrance of the hotel. They'll take you in. Everything's going to be all right. Don't worry."

There were four police cars parked outside, and a big green truck that looked like it belonged to the Army. Borya heard sirens in the distance.

A pair of National Guardsmen were in the street, with another near the side door to the Marriott. Borya ran along the front of the building, as if heading for the main entrance. She glanced back to make sure they weren't following her, because the last thing she was going to do was shelter in place.

She had to find Chelsea. But Boston had turned into Zombieland—the nearby streets and sidewalks, which ordinarily would be packed with people, were deserted.

Where would Chelsea be? Her aunt was staying in some hotel, but it *wasn't* the Marriot; she'd mentioned they might take an Uber to get to the Aquarium, which you would never do when you could walk across the street.

So . . .

Where?

Smart Metal. That was the best place to look for Chelsea. That was where she would go when there was trouble. She practically lived there anyway.

The building was back on the other side of the government center.

How to get there?

The subway obviously wasn't working, there was no bus, and it was a long walk.

What she needed was a bike, like the one propped against the wall of the Chart House.

"Sorry. I gotta borrow your bike!" shouted Borya to the air. "I'll bring it back. Promise."

Maybe she didn't shout. But the promise, at least, wasn't a lie.

8

Boston—around the same time

JOHNNY GIVENS PACED BACK AND FORTH IN THE BOX, trying to calm some of the adrenaline building in his body.

It was a lost cause. He needed to be doing something more than just talking to people.

Or worse, listening to other people talk to people.

"I'm in," said Avon Telakus, one of the programming wizards Massina had brought downstairs. Massina had ordered Telakus to hack into the security system at the Patriot Hotel.

Technically illegal.

More than technically. A probable violation of 18 U.S.C. Section 1030 and a whole slew of other laws. But Johnny wasn't working for the FBI anymore.

"They have video?" asked Massina.

"Looks like it."

"Put the cameras on the screen," said Massina impatiently.

"Arraying them up front," said the twenty-something computer whiz.

Low-resolution black-and-white images popped across the monitors at the front of the room.

"Is this the best resolution?" asked Massina.

"It's theirs. The frame rate is choppy beyond belief. They're on backup power—they seem to have cut it at the hotel for some reason."

"I suppose we should be thankful they're not still using videotape," said Massina.

Johnny stared at the screens. The cameras were mostly posted in hallways on the upper floors. At first glance, the place looked deserted.

"Can you move the cameras around?" he asked.

"Negative," said Telakus. "They're all fixed. They have more cameras than we can see here. They have presets operating the mix; this is what was set when they were taken over. I'm going to try to go around it and select cameras individually, but I really need to fiddle—the coding is not exactly world-class, and it looks nothing like the models I've pulled up."

A new set of images popped across the screens. One showed a restaurant. Tables were upended; bodies lay on the floor.

"Looks like we got the right place," said Massina acidly.

MASSINA FOLDED HIS ARMS TIGHTLY ACROSS HIS chest, trying to control the anger he felt. These people had been killed in cold blood for no greater sin than being alive.

I am going to avenge you, he swore. *I am going to reset the balance with these bastards.*

Bozzone buzzed on his intercom. "Borya Tolevi just came in."

"Very good," replied Massina. The feisty kid reminded him a little of himself. "Did her father come with her?"

"No. He's at home. I just talked to him. He's fine. I told him we'll keep Borya here until it's safe. Here's the thing," added Bozzone, his voice rushing as if to keep Massina from interrupting. "Borya was going to meet Chelsea at the Aquarium, but she was way early. She thinks Chelsea was still meeting her aunt at the hotel."

"Not the Patriot."

"Yeah. The Patriot."

9

Boston—around the same time

Chelsea tried to memorize everything she saw, the men especially. They'd need her testimony when they put them on trial.

Counting the one in the garage, she'd seen five. They ranged in height from only a few inches taller than her to well over six feet. Two had full beards, but the others had faces that were simply scruffy, as if they'd forgotten to shave for a few days.

Three wore hotel uniforms—black pants and a blue blazer over a crisp white shirt. The others were in jeans and T-shirts.

All but one looked underfed, even malnourished. They'd hardly be imposing, if not for their guns.

Their guns: AR-15s, civilian versions of the M4 with some slight modifications, some subtly different stocks, a suppressor, and, in one case, a scope.

None of the men wore masks or disguises, as

if they didn't care if they were identified. That wasn't good.

Chelsea and Victoria were led to the Patriot's ballroom, where some fifty other guests and a handful of employees had been taken. Two terrorists stood guard at the back of the room near the main doors; another strutted across the small stage at the front, occasionally waving his gun at the people scattered around the floor.

The prisoners formed themselves into little knots, grouped around acquaintanceships and happenstance. A pile of wallets and purses, handbags and cell phones lay on the floor near the door; clearly these had been confiscated from the people in the ballroom, but the procedure was haphazard—neither Victoria nor Chelsea was searched, and Chelsea still had her cell phone and wallet.

"What do you think they're going to do?" asked Victoria, settling into a spot near the wall, close to a man and woman with three girls, all under seven or eight. "Hold us for ransom?"

"Maybe," lied Chelsea.

She turned her attention to the man on the stage, imprinting him on her brain: his face, brownish, speckled with a few black freckles and a large pimple on his cheek, a bad beard like most of the others, eyebrows far too bushy for the rest of his features. No marks on his brow, no wrinkles, eyes wide open, maybe too far open—it was hard to tell from here.

Khaki pants, a blue T-shirt with some sort of insignia.

A police shield?

Maybe. Some sort of emblem.

Shoes—scuffed brown.

His gun, like the others but with a folded stock. He waved it as if it were a pistol.

Be calm, collect as much information as you can, wait for an opening.

It was her father's voice. He was always with her when she needed him.

Always with me, Daddy.

We'll get through it, kid. Hang in there.

Chelsea turned her attention to the men at the door. One of them was talking into a microphone at his collar.

They were using radios. She hadn't noticed that before.

Analyze it. What does it mean?

They're very organized. They've been planning this for quite a while.

They have money. They're well-funded. Radios. New guns.

They're disciplined.

The man on the stage shouted at a man who was walking around, agitated, near the wall. He told him to sit or he would be shot.

An American accent. Flat. Not Bostonian but native. He was either raised in America or underwent extensive training to get his accent right.

He pointed at someone nearby and told him to get the man to sit.

Definitely native. Not Boston. Not New York either. Not Southern. Flat. Midwest.

He had a little strut. Overconfident.

Were the others American? Or were they foreign?

It suddenly seemed very important to know. She thought of striking up a conversation, talking to them—she could do that, gather information. It might be useful.

She had the cell phone. She could call and give the negotiators little tidbits to help them, intel on where they were, how many, what they were thinking and saying.

There would be negotiators. They would negotiate, even if they weren't going to give in. Buy time until the SWAT team assaulted the place.

Chelsea looked around the room, trying to decide where the assault would come from. There was no way of knowing for sure, but she guessed the back of the room, since it was closer to the exterior.

It would begin with a flash of light and a loud bang: flash-bang grenades, intended to shock everyone inside for a moment, just long enough to get an advantage.

Then gunfire.

A lot of it.

"These bastards," said Victoria. Her voice cracked. She was shaking, starting to lose her composure. "Savages. Who are they? What do they want?"

"ISIS," said a woman nearby.

"Do you know that for sure?" asked Chelsea. "Did they say that?"

"Who else could they be?"

"It's just that, knowing that and suspecting

that are different things," said Chelsea. She was thinking she would pass the information along when she had a chance to use her cell phone—assuming she could get a signal. "The more solid information—"

"It has to be them," insisted the woman.

"Maybe we should pray," said the mother with the children. "We should pray. It is Easter."

Victoria nodded, but didn't join in as the woman began mouthing the words to the Our Father. Two of the girls joined in; the oldest just stared at them.

"All the men will stand up!" shouted one of the terrorists near the door. "Stand and go over to the far wall. Faster!"

The men got up and made their way there, one or two quickly, the others, a dozen and a half, slowly, their shuffle the only way they could protest.

"You and you," said the man on the stage, pointing to two boys barely into their teens. "With the others."

A woman next to one of the boys grabbed him. "He's just a child! Leave him alone."

"I'll kill him, then you," said the man, pointing his gun.

The boy pushed himself away. "I'll be OK, Mom."

One of the men still had his cell phone; it began to ring as they mustered. The man on the stage jumped down in a rage.

"Whose phone?!" he demanded. "Whose phone!"

The men started to separate. Chelsea tensed, sensing they were going to gang up and attack the man with the phone.

What do I do?

She decided she would grab a weapon from one of the men at the door. They'd be so focused on the men they wouldn't notice.

Can I make it?

She'd have to.

No question: I will make it.

She pushed her feet beneath her knees, ready to spring.

"Whose phone!" shouted the terrorist.

One of the men raised his hand. "It's not working," he said, stepping forward with the phone in his hand. "This is just an alarm—"

The terrorist slammed the man to the ground with the butt of his rifle. The cell phone flew to the ground; the terrorist smashed it with his heel.

"Who else? Who else has a phone?"

Victoria looked at Chelsea.

A woman near the front stood and held up her hand.

The terrorist turned on her and began firing.

Chelsea, caught off guard, turned toward the men at the door, but realized she was too far and too late.

"Down!" yelled Victoria, grabbing her as bullets began spraying through the room. "Chelsea!"

Caught off balance, Chelsea twisted down, knocking her chin against the floor so hard she blacked out with the shock and pain.

10

Boston—around the same time

"GODDAMN THESE PEOPLE," SHOUTED JOHNNY, unable to control himself as he watched what was happening in the hotel. The terrorists had just lined up a group of men and mowed them down.

"What's going on inside the hotel?" asked the FBI agent on the other end of the communications line. They hadn't switched in the video yet.

"They're shooting people," said Givens. "It's time to go in."

"The SWAT people are still getting in place. They need those feeds."

"We're working on it." Johnny glanced over at the computer engineers. Telakus was typing furiously; the others stared in horror at their screens.

Sitting here really wasn't going to get those people out of the hotel, Johnny decided.

"Can you find a map or a schematic or something of the hotel?" he asked Telakus. "That would help the SWAT people."

"I've looked. I haven't been able to find anything." The computer whiz shook his head. "Maybe I can break into the architectural archives or something. City hall. The building inspector, whatever. If they're online. But, uh, I probably need Mr. Massina to authorize that."

"I'm sure he will," said Johnny. He turned to his right, expecting to see Massina there. But the boss had slipped out of the room.

MASSINA HAD BORYA REPEAT WHAT SHE'D TOLD Bozzone twice, listening in case there was some detail that he'd missed. But Borya simply had no clue where Chelsea was.

She had to be in the Patriot. Borya didn't know what time she'd been planning to meet her aunt, but if she had left the hotel or not gotten there, surely she would have answered their calls by now.

Or come in to work. *That* was Chelsea.

"Keep looking for her," he told Bozzone. "Keep calling her."

"If we could use the telephone company's GPS system—"

"Good idea," said Massina.

"Can I do something?" Borya asked.

"Stay here in Chelsea's lab, so we know where you are when we need you," he said. "We may need you very soon."

It was a white lie—there was very little a young girl could do—but he wanted to make sure she stayed where she was safe.

"I will."

"Good."

Johnny was ready with a list of what the SWAT team needed by the time Massina returned to the Box.

"Surveillance overhead is great for the grounds and the roof, but real-time surveillance inside would be gold," he told his boss. "Telakus says we could bring one of our computers there, set up a mobile connection, then show them what's going on. It'll be quicker than trying to cobble a connection together."

"That's true," said Telakus. "Time is running out."

"Let's do it," said Massina.

"We need some sort of building diagram," added Johnny. "Can we get somebody to call over to the building inspectors or something like that? Architectural review or—"

"We'll launch a UAV with penetrating radar," said Massina. "Tommy! We need you to set something up."

"Heard ya. Workin' on it. We have a Nightbird outfitted for that mining company and—"

"Do it!" said Massina.

"I want to go with them," said Johnny. "I'll take the computer there."

"Are you sure?" asked Massina.

"Damn sure."

"Good. Because I think Chelsea's in that hotel."

11

Boston—around the same time

CHELSEA OPENED HER EYES, DAZED. VICTORIA PULLED her into her arms, rocking her gently, half sitting, half crouched against the floor. The room smelled of spent gunpowder and blood. People screamed and cried, wailed and moaned in agony. Many of the men who'd been shot were still alive, but the terrorists didn't allow anyone to help them.

"Savages," said Victoria softly, her voice trembling. "They'll kill us all."

"Help will come," insisted Chelsea. "I'm sure. Just stay strong."

"I am."

The terrorist who'd been on the stage earlier began shouting. The women were to move toward the door. A few seconds later, convinced that they weren't moving fast enough for him, he raised his gun and fired toward the ceiling.

A few of the women ran toward the door, but most continued at a slow pace, cringing, unable to force more movement from their bodies. They had entered a fugue state of fear, paralyzed by the certainty that they were going to die.

One of the men near the door stepped forward and began directing them, waving his hand silently as he counted them into groups of five. Chelsea stayed close to her aunt, realizing that they might be split up, but it was no use—the man pointed at her and motioned for her to begin a new group.

Chelsea shook her head.

"I'm staying with my aunt," she said.

Chelsea mustered a death glance as the man stalked toward her. He stared back, eyes locked with hers.

For a moment she thought he was going to shoot her. She stiffened, extending her barely five-foot frame to its full height, and took a deep breath, holding it, waiting for the inevitable— but instead of raising his gun, he grabbed her shoulder with his left hand and hurled her toward the wall.

"You and you," said the terrorist, choosing two other women from the small cluster. Victoria started to join Chelsea, but the terrorist pushed his gun into her chest, nudging at first, then ramming her backward when that failed to stop her.

CHELSEA RAISED HERSELF TO HER KNEES AND watched as her aunt's group was led from the ballroom. Victoria walked with her head down, bent over, undoubtedly hurting from the blow.

Pressure had begun to build behind Chelsea's eyes, a pain that felt similar to eyestrain. She rubbed her temples, then sat back, not wanting to kneel—it was too much like surrender.

The power flicked back on, fans whirring up, lights flooding bright.

The other groups were led out of the ballroom, leaving only Chelsea and the two other women selected with her. They were both about her age, twenties, slim. One looked Latin, the other Irish, with red curly hair. She had a large wet mark in the front of her taupe-colored leggings, running down her leg. The other woman wore a miniskirt and a sleeveless top that revealed well-toned muscles. There was something hard in her face, a kind of frown.

"Up!" yelled the terrorist who'd been on the stage. "Up!"

He waved his gun.

As she walked into the hallway, Chelsea thought of making a run for it. But there was nowhere to go—another terrorist was standing a few yards away.

"That way, right," he said. "Right."

"They're not going to rape us, are they?" asked the girl in the leggings.

"What do you think?" answered the other.

12

Boston—around the same time

THE COMMANDER ON THE SCENE OUTSIDE THE PA-triot Hotel was a police captain whose oversize balding head contrasted sharply with his toned, sleek body: the face of a sixty-year-old above a thirty-year-old's frame. Johnny had met Kevin Smith several times when he was an FBI agent and so wasn't surprised at Smith's blank expression as he detailed the resources he had brought with him from Smart Metal.

"That will all be very useful," said Smith finally, with all the excitement of a man making out a check to the IRS. "Lieutenant Steller is handling intel for the SWAT team, and Percy is in charge of the assault unit. You know Percy?"

"A bit," said Johnny. Johnny thought it best not to give the details; he and Percy had not particularly gotten along.

As in, shouted at each other and nearly come to blows.

"Good." Smith nodded. "This communications specialist—when's he getting here?"

"Any minute," said Johnny. They had biked over, at Ciro Farlekas's suggestion. A fellow security officer who like Johnny had worked with the FBI, Farlekas was an avid biker, to the point of having a Carbondale bike he rode to work every day. Johnny had borrowed something more akin to a tank, but managed to beat him here, thanks to his legs.

The police were working out of a mobile command center—a large, heavily modified van—around the corner of the hotel. Cameras on two police cruisers fed real-time visuals of the building's front. Information on the other three sides depended on spotters who were calling into one of Smith's own com specialists.

"Damn, you're fast," said Farlekas, riding up after being let through by the officers up the block. "Where are we setting up?"

"Right here," said Smith.

"We're gonna fix ya right up," Farlekas told him, his Tennessee drawl unchallenged by Bostonian vowels or idioms. "Jest gimme a few seconds here."

"He's good, don't worry," Johnny told Smith. He didn't know Farlekas really, but everyone at Smart Metal was pretty much the best at what they did. "We're online with their security videos, and we're getting a, uh, drone with radar to map the insides. Do you need mechs?"

Smith tilted his head.

"Mechs are like robots," explained Johnny. All of this had been foreign to him just a few months before; he'd spent several weeks training with them and now could work with them the same way he'd work with a human partner. "They're designed to handle specific tasks, and while they can generally complete that task without detailed instructions, they don't have advanced AI, so they can only do what you tell them to do."

He pulled over the backpack he'd brought with him. "These are small units designed to enter buildings and rubble sites. We can tell them to go somewhere and they'll figure out how to do it."

"They look like little cars without shells."

"More or less," said Johnny. The mechs were tracked, with small claws. They ranged from iPhone to desk calculator in size.

"How do they help us?" asked Smith.

"We can use them to get in," said Johnny. "Kill the power. We come in through a window in the pool area and make our way up the corridors to where the hostages are in the convention rooms."

"How do we know they're there?"

"You'll see when Ciro finishes setting up the link. Should be any second."

Smith picked up the radio. "Percy, come over to the command center," he said. "We're getting fresh intel."

13

Boston—around the same time

Walking ahead of the terrorist with the other
women, Chelsea tried to force fear from her
mind, as if the emotion were a paste that could be
squeezed from a tube. She slowed her breathing,
made her movements more deliberate; she focused
her thoughts on the feel of her hips, her knees,
her neck as she swiveled her head. She told her
heart to slow; she told her glands to stop sweating.

It did almost no good. Her body was slipping
from her mind's control.

Think of a math problem.

It was her father again. She flashed on a scene
from childhood, age eight or nine, talking with
him about a test and how she'd panicked—math,
a simple equation, fill in the x value or some such.
The details of the problem were lost to her, but
his presence, his reassurance, was there, beside
her as she walked.

Her footsteps made no sound on the carpeted
floor. Chelsea was a stride or two in front of the

girl who'd wet her pants; she wasn't sure how much farther back the other woman and the terrorist were.

Lengthening her stride as she neared the end of the corridor, Chelsea began sketching a plan. The hall formed a T with another hallway. She'd turn left and run, run to the emergency exit at the end of the hall.

If there was one. There had to be.

She held her breath as she got closer to the turn.

"Right!" barked the man behind her. "Turn to your right."

Chelsea glanced to her left. There was no hallway there, just four doors to rooms.

She swung her attention back to the right, leaning forward and ready to run. But this hallway was the same—four doors, all rooms.

Now what?

"You, first door."

Chelsea put her hand on the door, expecting it be locked. To her surprise the handle swung down easily.

"Inside."

She went in quickly, looking to see if there was something she could use as a weapon before the others came in.

An iron! The closet.

The door slammed behind her. Chelsea whipped around. No one had followed her inside.

The door locked from the inside; her captor couldn't come in.

Unless he had a passkey. Which naturally he would.

She could open it and go out. But he'd be in the hall, waiting.

How else can I get out?

She went to the window and pulled back the curtains. The glass was fixed in the frame; there was no escape short of breaking it. It looked out on the blank wall of a parking garage; she could wave or pound or even strip herself naked and no one would notice.

Something hit the wall in the room next to her, the one to the right. A crash followed—the TV, she thought—then a scream.

Again. More screams.

Oh, God. Oh, God.

14

Boston—around the same time

"WE HAVE TO MOVE NOW," SMITH TOLD GIVENS. "It's our best chance."

"If you go in like you're planning," Johnny told the commander, "you're dooming the people they've already taken upstairs. The terrorists will just move up and kill them all."

"We'll get to them," said Smith, though his grim expression made it clear he didn't think they'd reach them in time. "If we wait, they'll split the rest and we'll lose them. We already have people in there dead."

Both men were right, which was the tragedy of it—the team didn't have enough people in place to prevent more deaths, but if they waited until they did, more would surely die.

Better to go now.

Johnny nodded, grimly turning his attention back to the monitoring screens. They showed people walking in the hallway, women followed by men with guns.

Chelsea?

Chelsea?

Johnny's breath caught. It was definitely Chelsea, being led into one of the rooms upstairs.

No!

"I'm going to get them upstairs," Johnny told Smith.

"What?"

"I'll bring one of the bots with me and we'll keep them occupied while the team comes up."

"No! No! We need you helping with the robots on the first team and—"

Johnny was already out of the truck.

15

Boston—around the same time

Borya's father, Gabor Tolevi, managed to get nearly to Berkley Street before the traffic became unbearably slow, with cars bunched and not moving for more than a few seconds at a time. There was nothing more frustrating than sitting in a car whose engine could produce 585 horsepower at the twitch of his foot and not being able to use any of it.

Well, there were more frustrating things; he just didn't want to think about them.

He'd told Bozzone that he'd wait until the emergency was over to collect his daughter, but soon realized that would be hours, maybe even days. While he trusted the Smart Metal people and knew his daughter could take care of herself, leaving Borya on her own downtown in the middle of all that chaos bit at his soul. So barely ten minutes after putting the phone down, he set out in his car to get her.

That was an hour ago. At the rate he was inching forward on the street, it would be another six before he reached her.

Tolevi eyed the curb and nearby intersection, balancing his frustration against the potential damage to the underside of his car. Finally, frustration won out: with a jerk of the wheel, he jumped the curb and with one set of wheels on the sidewalk and the other on the pavement, managed to cut the corner just enough to miss both the car in front of him and the no-parking sign. He considered simply leaving the car there, but then saw a driveway nearby. He veered toward it, cringing as the underside of the car scraped against something solid. He managed to angle without seeing sparks; the road in front was every bit as packed as the one he'd just left.

An older woman in a housedress ran down the steps of the house, yelling at him.

"I have to rescue my daughter," he shouted, pulling his wallet out. "I'll pay you twice this when I get back."

All he had were two twenties. He tucked them under the wiper and ran off, ignoring the woman's continued complaints. It wasn't like she was going anywhere whether he parked there or not.

Dodging his way through the bumper-to-bumper jam, Tolevi managed to get to the sidewalk. This was relatively open—a few cars had pulled up onto it, and knots of people gathered on stoops and car hoods, but compared to the streets, the walkway was an open plain. He started to run, passing knots of Bostonians listening to reports on laptops and telephones. The snippets he heard sounded ominous and pushed him faster.

Tolevi was in good shape—he prided himself on his workouts—but it was a long way and he was not dressed for a run, wearing jeans and leather shoes with slick wood soles. Sweat built quickly under his pullover, and the sides of his head began pounding with his rapidly increasing pulse.

But each step also increased his anxiety about his daughter. He had already lost her mother; losing Borya, too, was far beyond what he could bear.

Gravity and heat eventually won. By the time he got to the police barricades a few blocks from the Common, Tolevi's pace had fallen to something between a jog and a fast walk. Practically heaving, he pleaded with one of the policemen to let him through.

"I gotta—get my daugh-ter she—needs—"

"What are you sayin'?" asked the cop.

"Daugh-ter. Meds. Med-cine."

He added the idea of her needing medicine on the spur of the moment. It worked.

"Your daughter's down there?" said the officer. It was clear from the man's face that he had a daughter as well. "Where?"

"Near the river."

"All right. Stay away from the Patriot Hotel."

"Got it."

Tolevi started to run again; energized by the encounter, he entered the Common at a half trot. But he didn't get far before he came to another policeman, who yelled at him to stop and explain what he was doing. Tolevi tried the same tactic, but this time it didn't work: he was shunted to a holding area the police had set up near the Soldiers and Sailors Monument. Several dozen people milled around on the path and the circle; a good hundred or more were sitting or lying on the grass nearby.

"How do we get out of here?" Tolevi asked the first man he came to, a man in his late twenties. He had a bit of a hipster look to him, with a goatee, pale skin, and engineer boots.

"We wait until the police say it's safe to go."

Tolevi moved on. People had their cell phones out, listening to or watching reports. As he moved closer to the west end of the park and approached a police barrier, he decided he would adopt an old but solid tactic—simply walk, eyes straight ahead, a man on a mission.

It didn't work.

"Hey, you—stop," shouted a policeman as he passed.

Tolevi pretended he didn't hear, but there was no way to avoid the two National Guardsmen who turned around near the troop truck ahead.

"You have to go back, sir; I'm sorry," said one of the soldiers.

"What is this, a police state?"

"Don't be givin' anybody a hard time," said a man with a badge swinging from his neck. His Southie accent marked him as a Boston local, though on closer inspection, the badge marked him as a federal marshal. "Get your ass back over with the rest."

Tolevi took a hard right, feinting in the direction of the crowd until he figured he wasn't being watched anymore. He walked along the edge of the crowd until he found a place with only one policeman near the barricade. This time he tried a little subterfuge.

"The Bureau guy with the Guardsman back there wants to talk to you about frequencies or something," he said as he approached. He pulled his wallet out, quickly flipping it as if showing a badge. "I'm with the Marshals Service."

"What about?" asked the policeman, his eyes trailing Tolevi's hand as he slipped his wallet back into his pants.

"The fuck I know. The Bureau people think they are the hottest shit going. I only came down here to help, you know? It's my day off. Hell, I'm supposed to be watching the game by now. I'll take your spot, but come back quick. I need to take a leak ASAP."

Luckily for Tolevi, the officer nodded rather than asking what ball game he was talking about. "Just don't let anybody through, right?"

"Yeah, yeah, don't worry."

Tolevi took off as soon as the man was twenty yards away. Within minutes he was hugging the brick wall of a building on Bruce Place—an alley more than a street—slinking toward his destination.

With downtown and the center of the city

mostly cordoned off, the side streets here were empty, doors and windows were locked tight. Tolevi walked head down, full man-on-a-mission stride; no one who saw him would stop him, or so he thought.

He was on Derne Street, approaching Temple, when he saw two young men duck into the deli on the corner. Surprised that a store was open, he suddenly realized he could do something about his thirst. He went in and hunted for the cooler, still in man-on-a-mission mode; it wasn't until he was taking an iced tea from the shelf that he realized he had clipped all of his cash to the windshield wiper of the car.

He started to put the bottle back when he heard a woman say something in Russian.

The words weren't clear—she was on the phone with someone and hanging up to deal with a customer. But he thought maybe if he spoke to her in Russian, she'd let him come back with the money later. So he took the bottle and started for the cash register. It was only as he turned the corner of the aisle that he realized the two young men he'd seen enter were now robbing the place.

Tolevi reacted instinctively: he threw his right hand forward, smashing the man with the gun in the neck and side of the head so hard with the iced tea that the glass bottle shattered in his hand. As the man went down, Tolevi grabbed his wrist and with a sharp jerk snapped the gun from his hand. It clattered to the floor as its owner rebounded into his compatriot.

For a moment, neither the would-be robbers

nor Tolevi moved. Then all three moved as quickly as they could—the robbers scrambling to leave, Tolevi scooping up the gun. But they were faster: by the time he rose, they were gone. He went to the door; not seeing them, he went back to the counter and examined the pistol.

Cheap Chinese knockoff. Sheesh.

"Babushka," Tolevi called in Russian, not seeing the woman. "Grandma, where are you? It's all right—they're gone."

"Oh, my God, my God, my God," she answered, crawling out from under the counter on her hands and knees. She had armed herself with a sawed-off baseball bat.

Tolevi went around and helped her up.

"Are you all right?" he asked, still speaking Russian.

"Yes, those thieves—you are Russian?"

It was easier to say yes than explain that he was actually a mix.

"You are a good boy," said the woman. Then, with some alarm, she added, "You are bleeding!"

He glanced at his hand. The glass had cut into the palm. It was barely a scratch, but the woman pulled him toward a sink behind the counter and made him rinse it off. He took a wad of paper towels and pressed it against his palm.

"What do you want?" asked the woman, switching to heavily accented English. "Anything!"

"I came in to get something to drink, but—"

"Whatever you want! Free! Take! Take! Wait until my son comes. He will give you a reward."

"I don't need a reward," said Tolevi. "Thanks."

"Don't go. Wait!"

"I have to find my daughter," he told her. "There are terrorists—didn't you hear?"

"I heard, I heard. Go, get your daughter. Go."

"Why don't you hold on to this," he told the old lady, giving her the gun. "Just in case those bastards come back. You know how to use it?"

She mimed the action of pointing a pistol with her hand. "Between the eyes," she said. "Bam."

"Good."

"Then I kick them in the nuts," she added in vulgar Russian. "To be sure."

He gave her a thumbs-up as he left the store.

That's my kind of grandma, Tolevi thought. *I wonder if she's available for babysitting.*

16

MASSINA WATCHED THE SWAT OFFICERS GETTING ready to make their assault. There had already been shooting inside the hotel; they were taking too long.

Too damn long!

"Johnny wants to talk to you," said Telakus, the computer whiz who'd broken into the video system at the Patriot and was feeding data to Givens and the team preparing to enter the hotel.

Massina picked up the handset.

"Chelsea's up on the seventh floor," said Johnny. "I'm getting her."

"What?"

"I saw her."

Massina turned to Chiang. "Check the surveillance feed on floor seven. Get the face-recognition program online—Johnny says it's Chelsea."

"I need to get on the roof. But I want to know what room she's in. Can you use her GPS in her phone?"

"The terrorists are blocking transmissions," Massina told him.

"How about with the UAV?"

The penetrating radar aboard the Nightbird UAV was powerful, but it wasn't designed to identify people inside buildings.

"Maybe if we look at the image," said Massina, though he was doubtful. "We'll try. It's not overhead yet."

"How long?"

"Soon."

"I need help to get on the roof," added Johnny.

"How is the team getting there?"

"It's just me."

Massina rubbed his chin.

"Let me get Blake on the line," he told Givens. "Get to a place where a drone can hover."

CHELSEA HAD ALREADY PUSHED A CHAIR AGAINST THE door when she heard the explosions. They were below her somewhere, two or three together, then a few more.

The assault had begun.

She made sure the chair was as tight as possible against the door panel, then stepped back, looking for something else to block the way. The nightstands flanking the bed were bolted to the floor. The bureau with the TV was either too heavy or fastened as well. The only thing was the chair near the window; she carried it over, lifting it just high enough to get it on the first chair.

She'd taken a step back when the door lock

sprung open, unlocked by the master key of one of the terrorists. Before she could react, the door rammed against the chairs, pushing forward until it was stopped by the bar lock above the handle.

The man outside yelled at her to open the door.

Something warned her what would happen next: she threw herself back behind the wall that separated the bathroom from the bedroom proper. As she hit the floor, bullets flew through the door.

If I'm quiet, she thought, *maybe he'll think I'm dead.*

THE LIFTER WAS DESIGNED TO PICK UP MACHINERY and heavy parts like bridge supports, not people; the grappling claws were metal and hardly gentle as they clamped around Johnny's arms.

He shielded his face as best he could as the twin rotors filled the air with a thick mist of dust and grit. A discarded plastic bag and some pieces of paper flew against Johnny's legs as he was lifted. Blake said something in his earset, but Johnny couldn't hear over the drone's engine.

The UAV took him straight up into the air. Johnny's arms felt as if they would be ripped off his shoulders. He glanced down and immediately wished he hadn't: the ground seemed to be spinning.

It wasn't the ground, it was him: between the motion of the helicopter and the wind, his body twisted and swayed, arcing in a nauseating dance. Blake said something—he was trying to tell

Johnny how to extend his legs to help brake his momentum—but Johnny couldn't make out the words. The UAV slowed and tilted, cutting off some of Johnny's momentum. He forced his eyes open and saw that the roof of the building was to his right, a flat expanse dotted with what looked like sloped aluminum tents—roof shelters for the mechanical equipment. Johnny braced himself as the Lifter darted toward one of the "tents," aiming to deposit him near an access point to a stairwell. The drone slowed abruptly and he swung forward, not quite as wildly as before.

Blake intended on setting him down, but Johnny had had enough: he took a deep breath and let go, falling a good fifteen feet. His legs saved him—the high-tech prosthetics absorbed most of the energy from the fall, leaving him balanced on his feet.

It was his first step that felled him. His head was still dizzy and his stomach reeling. He threw his arms out, cushioning his fall.

Then he threw up.

"You OK?" asked Blake in his ear.

"Ugh."

"Telakus has directions for you. We think we have Chelsea's room."

"Good."

THE MAN AT THE DOOR POUNDED, BUT THE DOOR HELD.

Chelsea heard a scream, then realized it was hers.

I'm losing control!

The door cracked; the lock was giving way.

Desperate, she looked for any cover, any barrier that would slow the demon down, cause him pain or delay or anything—anything was better than surrender.

She reached across to the bed, grabbed the covers, grabbed the top mattress. She pulled it across, over her, as she heard the lock snap off its mounts.

JOHNNY HAD COME EQUIPPED WITH A SMALL PRY BAR in his backpack, as well as a set of lock picks. He needed neither—the roof door was ajar. He dropped to his knee to sling the pack off; opening it, he took out his AR-15 and what looked like a Spalding rubber ball.

Like the assault rifles the police were equipped with, Johnny's gun had a telescoping stock and a laser dot, along with a thirty-round magazine and a spare taped to its side; there were two more in his pack. He checked the gun quickly, made sure he was ready, then tossed the ball into the stairwell.

"It's clear," said Telakus. The "ball" was actually a video-and-audio array ordinarily used for recording experiments, which was now transmitting a signal back to Smart Metal. Software stabilized the images and analyzed them in about a tenth of the time it would have taken a human to simply scan a still picture.

"Johnny, we think there's somebody on her floor," said Telakus. "He's got a gun."

"Right or left off the stairs?"

"Your right."

There was an explosion below. The building shook.

"What the hell?" asked Johnny as he started down.

"One of the bastards in the ballroom blew himself up."

MASSINA LEANED OVER THE CONSOLE IN THE BOX, watching intently as the first wave of SWAT officers followed one of his robots into the building. The bot, equipped with a chemical sniffer as well as a video camera, was looking for explosives, but apparently the terrorists hadn't had time to rig them in that part of the hotel.

Suddenly the screen shook—there had been another explosion offscreen.

"Where?" said Massina.

"The kitchen," said Telakus. "That's number two. They had him cornered. There are only three of them left."

"That's three too many," said Massina.

As AN FBI AGENT, JOHNNY HAD BEEN TRAINED TO deal with hostage situations and had in fact gone through two simulations very similar to this actual situation. But they were buried somewhere deep in his consciousness, pushed away by the adrenaline rocking through his body. He knew he should stop and clear at each landing, but that was impractical now—he needed to get to Chelsea right away; he needed to be there. He really ought to have an entire team behind him; he should have more intelligence, more firepower, more of everything. But the reality was that if he didn't get there now, if he didn't kill the terrorist on her floor, she was going to die.

The ball had bounced against a doorjamb and come to rest on the eighth floor. Johnny grabbed it and went down one more floor, throwing himself against the closed door.

"She still to the right?" he asked Telakus.

"Radar has her there. We can't see the hall. We lost the video from the security camera when the SWAT team went in," added Telakus. "They killed the backup power."

"I'm throwing the ball."

Johnny slipped open the door and tossed the gadget, then, without waiting for Telakus to tell him if it was clear or not, he threw himself out into the hallway, rolling on the floor and then leaping up, an easy target had the terrorist been watching.

"You're clear," said Telakus. "Jesus, wait for me."

Johnny kept moving, scrambling forward. "Where's the room?"

"Fifty feet, on your right, down that little hall—he's going into the room!"

Desperate, Johnny lifted his gun and fired down the empty hall.

CHELSEA FELT THE BEAST ENTERING THE ROOM, plunging past the door, stumbling. She had pulled the mattress over her, and even if there had been light in the room she couldn't have seen him. Yet she knew exactly where he was and what he was doing, what he looked like—five-eight, on the lighter side, scraggly beard, fanatical eyes.

There was gunfire, a burst in the hallway.

Then a boom louder than any she had ever heard before.

A BLAST OF HOT WIND SHOT FROM THE ROOM AS IF A door had opened on hell. Still in the main hall, Johnny fell against the wall, more from shock than anything. He bounced, fell, got back on his feet, and then ran to the hall with Chelsea's room.

Too late. Too damn late.

The corridor smelled of ammonia and steel and blood and something burning. Johnny started to cough. He covered his mouth with his arm, thinking it would make it easier to breathe.

"Johnny? Johnny?"

Telakus called to him from far away. The blast had dulled his hearing.

Rather than answering, Johnny pulled the headset from his ear and unclipped the mic. He stuffed the unit into his pocket: he didn't want anyone to hear.

The door to Chelsea's room had been blown off its hinges. It sat on a slant, propped against mangled furniture. Johnny pushed it to the side, but he couldn't get it entirely out of the way. Squeezing through, he stared at the destruction.

The blast had scorched the far corner of the room and broken the window and drapes, leaving a jagged hole. It had also torn the terrorist into pieces. His legs and the bottom half of his torso lay near the debris at the door. The rest of him had largely disintegrated.

Except for his head. Johnny saw it as he walked into the room. It lay wedged in the corner, red, unrecognizable as anything human, yet somehow obvious.

He went and kicked it. It was like kicking a rotted pumpkin.

Except . . . it moaned.

Johnny jumped back, horrified.

"Help me out of here."

Johnny whirled around. The mattress was moving. Chelsea Goodman emerged from underneath it, face blank, eyes wide, staring up at him.

"Johnny?"

"It's me," he said.

"I'm alive," Chelsea told him. "Oh, my God, I'm alive."

A NEED TO AVENGE

———

Flash forward

Boston—two weeks after the attacks

*M*ASSINA FELT A SUDDEN ATTACK OF NERVES AS HE *was called to the podium. He hadn't expected the President to be here.*

Not that he was intimidated, exactly. Just that he was suddenly aware that this was a very big deal. There were news cameras all over the place; what he said would be broadcast live to the entire world.

Which he wouldn't have minded, except that he hadn't prepared a speech; he hadn't considered what to say. No one had said it would be this important.

Massina took a breath and forced a smile. He remembered the rule one his grammar-school teachers had given him about speaking before an audience: Talk from the heart and you won't go wrong.

"Mr. President, Governor, Mayor, thank you for coming." Massina tilted the microphone down, making sure it was directly in line with his mouth. "Everyone else has spoken about how we'll rebuild,"

said Massina. "We will. And we'll do more than that. Much more."

He stopped talking. It was as if his mind had emptied.

What did he feel?

Something lofty, inspirational?

Hell, no. He felt a need for justice.

Revenge.

Right this wrong.

"I tell you something, from the bottom of my heart, speaking for everyone from Boston, whether you live in town or not," he said. "We're going to get those bastards. We're going to wipe them from the face of the earth. We will. And no one will mess with us again."

The crowd hesitated, then broke into a thunderous applause as he left the microphone.

Real time

17

Six days earlier
Boston, Massachusetts

ONE HUNDRED AND SEVENTY-THREE PEOPLE WERE killed in Boston during the Easter Sunday attacks. Seventeen terrorists also died, but they didn't count as people, at least not to Louis Massina.

Massina attended most of the funerals. The first convinced him to go to them all. It was a service for a young man named Joseph Achmoody.

Massina had met the teenager when he received a limb crafted by Massina's company a year before. He remembered their conversation before the operation: seeking to reassure him,

Massina had showed him his own prosthetic arm, removing the plastic "skin" to let him have a good look at the titanium "bones."

"Yours will be even better than this," he promised. "Lighter, stronger, and it can grow."

"Grow?"

That always got the kids. How could a fake arm grow?

But that part was easy—a simple operation extended the skeleton. Assuming the patient wasn't squeamish—about half were—he or she could even watch.

No, the real art and science were in the way the devices worked seamlessly, or almost seamlessly, with the brain. Translating nerve impulses into actual movement—you could set that out in a formula, and not a particularly complicated one either. But to make it work in the real world, to make it work without a hitch, despite fatigue or something as bizarre as magnetic interference—there was the difficulty. The fact that Massina's scientists and doctors had managed to do it only increased Massina's genuine admiration for the original workings of the human body. To do this all on the fly as it were—to construct life in "real time"— now, there was the magnificence of Nature, and through Nature, God.

As he stood at the back of the church watching Joseph Achmoody's funeral mass conclude, Massina couldn't help but feel immense loss. The unfairness of his death ate at him. The kid had barely entered his teens; most likely he hadn't even had a real kiss yet.

And somehow, the fact that the church was less than a quarter full bothered Massina even more. The kid was a martyr, yet only a handful of people had taken the time to honor him and comfort the family. That, too, seemed wrong. Massina, in a rare and uncharacteristic show of emotion, made a point to go to the mother and father and directly express his condolences.

Walking away, he decided he would go to as many of the others as his schedule permitted, to bear witness, to honor the dead. And he made sure that his schedule permitted the absolute maximum possible.

Today, Benjamin Fallow was being buried in his hometown of Southbridge, Massachusetts. It was in the southern part of the state, a bit far from Boston, and very likely Massina would not have attended this service had it not been for the fact that he had a meeting in Hartford. This was on the way.

Massina stood at the edge of the crowd in the cemetery where Benjamin was being buried. He was forty-five, the father of two children, both in college. There was an article in the local paper giving some brief details about his life; he'd been an insurance salesman. It wasn't clear why he'd gone to Boston that day; the paper only said that he was survived by his wife and sons.

The minister began by reciting Psalm 103, a

verse Massina had heard often over the past several days:

> *The Lord is merciful and gracious, slow to anger, and plenteous in mercy.*
> *He hath not dealt with us after our sins; nor rewarded us according to our iniquities . . .*

Halfway through the prayer, Massina decided he'd had enough—enough funerals, enough sorrow. It was time to move on.

He turned and started walking back to his car. Johnny Givens, who'd accompanied him as an aide and bodyguard, swung around and walked with him.

"Touching service," said a woman near the parking lot. She'd ducked out to smoke; the cigarette dangled from her fingers.

Massina nodded.

"Did you agree?" she added.

The question was so odd, he stopped.

"The choice of the Psalm," she prompted. "Almost like, turn the other cheek. I don't think that's right."

"Neither do I," answered Massina, heading for the car.

18

Libya—a few hours later

Fɪᴠᴇ ʏᴇᴀʀs ʙᴇꜰᴏʀᴇ, Sᴀᴍɪʀ Aʙᴅᴜʙɪɴ ʜᴀᴅ ɢɪᴠᴇɴ ᴜᴘ his family name in favor of Ghadab min Allah— roughly, "God's wrath." In the time since, he had endeavored to live up fully to that name.

He'd done well.

Starting as an apprentice bomb maker, Ghadab had participated in the planning and preparation for no less than twelve "missions" against targets in European cities. Only three of those missions had actually come off, and only one—in Paris, where he had minimal involvement—had resulted in clear victories against the infidels.

Nonetheless, Ghadab was seen as one of the movement's brightest lights, and after fleeing France for Libya, he had planned two attacks, both more spectacular than anything the Caliphate had undertaken before. One was in Rome, the other Boston.

The leadership council vetoed Rome, for reasons Ghadab couldn't fathom. But Boston— Boston had been approved.

It was a grand plan, a simultaneous attack at six carefully chosen locations, each with its own peculiar circumstance. A bombing on the subway, hostage taking in a hotel, a mass shooting in a restaurant—it was the very variety that tormented the nonbelievers. The idea that any place, big or small, might be hit—that was what unnerved them.

And the body count. Over a hundred. The one true God and His holy messenger, praise be his name, would surely be pleased. He'd even managed to keep his contingency strikes on reserve; he could activate them in the future for an even bigger attack if events proved favorable.

Ghadab had one disappointment: he had not been allowed to travel to America to coordinate and witness the attacks. The council had told him flatly that he could not go and had in fact placed him under guard to make sure that he would not disobey. It wasn't a matter of security; they wanted him to plan more attacks and strongly suspected that if he was there he would participate, which necessarily would lead to martyrdom. Instead, one of his lieutenants had been selected to coordinate the operation on the ground. The man, a second cousin of Ghadab's, was now enjoying the fruits of Paradise.

Ghadab did not begrudge him his just reward. He himself had no desire to enter Paradise quite yet. If martyrdom came—and it would—so be it. But before that time, he wanted more than anything to hasten the coming of the end time. The prophecy had to be fulfilled. When the barbarians arrived in force in the Levant, with their armies of devils and the serpents flying above all, then and only then would he be truly comfortable with martyrdom. For that would be the moment of glorious apocalypse. That was the moment the Caliphate was aiming at; that was the goal of the true believers who had pledged themselves to the new order. The new age would be born in that cauldron of fire.

Ghadab's cell phone buzzed with an alarm: it was two minutes before Isha'a, the night prayer. He retrieved his rug and walked out of his room, passing down the long corridor of the ancient building. Built as a castle, it had been converted to an administrative building in the seventeenth or eighteenth century, and completely refurbished and expanded by the old dictator, Gadhafi. Now it was a headquarters for the Caliphate's troops outside of the Levant.

Ghadab had just reached the roof and turned toward Mecca when the first flash appeared on the horizon. He stared at it for a moment, thinking at first that it was a defect in his vision, the product of spending long hours in the desert without proper eyeglasses.

The second flash disabused him of that.

They've come for their revenge.

He threw the rug down quickly, falling on top of it and praying so quickly that he was done even as the formal call to prayers began blaring from the mosque across the way. Ghadab ran to his room and grabbed his small suitcase, then ran to the tunnel as he had rehearsed.

Three of his underlings were already there. Two more followed, and then the bombproof door was closed.

The ground began to shake; the infidels had launched a barrage of Tomahawk missiles at them. They were useless against the massive stones of the castle, and an empty gesture given the depth of the reinforced shelter.

If any of the others thought it strange that Ghadab laughed as the explosions continued, they didn't have the courage to mention it.

19

Boston–a short time later

CHELSEA HAD GONE TO WORK THE DAY RIGHT AFTER the attacks, and every day since. Massina himself had told her she was welcome to take time off; in fact, he practically ordered her to do so. But time off wasn't what she needed. She needed something to occupy her mind, to challenge her thoughts, to keep them busy.

Because without that, without something difficult and intricate and knotted to focus on, she thought about what had happened. How close she'd come, first to being raped, then to being killed.

Chelsea had grown up in a suburb of San Diego, the daughter of a white mother and a black father himself of mixed background. Light-skinned, her ethnicity was hard to pin down— she could plausibly pass for Hispanic, Middle Eastern, even Asian and Sicilian as well as black. Like anyone of African descent in America, she had experienced prejudice and to some degree discrimination, but Chelsea would have been the first person to say she'd had a very easy child-hood, and had found far more acceptance and encouragement than most kids, whatever their ethnicity.

The fact that she was very intelligent didn't hurt. Her parents weren't rich, but they were comfortable; there was never a concern about the basics. Frankly, if it weren't for her mother, Chelsea suspected her father would have spoiled her rotten. Along with his reasoned advice and steady manner, Chelsea's dad had a soft, overly generous impulse, especially when it came to his only child. Mom was the family banker, for good reason, and it was Mom who generally imposed the harsher discipline, or at least enforced it.

All of which was to say that nothing in Chel-sea's childhood had prepared her for the shock of Easter Sunday. Even her experiences in Ukraine, where she had faced down gunmen for the first time in her life, couldn't quite compare. She would have been the first to object if someone suggested she'd been traumatized; on the other hand, even she would admit that the experience had been powerful in the most unwelcome way.

After her initial shakiness, Victoria had re-covered quickly. Talking about how scared she'd been the next day before Chelsea left for work, she'd compared it to the time she'd faced down a boyfriend holding a shotgun on her.

"Not quite as scared as that, but almost," she'd said breezily. "There's so much evil in this world."

To Chelsea, the cliché at the end seemed to

make light of what they'd gone through, and she told her aunt she was trivializing murder.

"Come on, dear," said Victoria. "Of course I'm not trivializing it. We certainly could have died."

Though she loved her aunt, she was happy when Victoria left for home Tuesday afternoon, having changed her plans.

The scratches and bruises Chelsea had suffered during her ordeal were minuscule, the sort she might have gotten from falling while running on a sidewalk. She'd been extremely lucky.

Had the man meant to rape her or kill her? Probably both, she thought.

She replayed the tragedy in the hotel obsessively. It crowded into her thoughts while she tried to work, forced its way into her calculations, even elbowed away her attempts to solve sudoku puzzles. The men being lined up, the kid, the AR-15 . . .

Jin Chiang stuck his head through the open doorway of the lab.

"Chelsea, come down the hall and look at this," said the software engineer, bobbing away. "Hurry!"

Chelsea closed down her workstation and locked the door before following Chiang to his lab. There, rather than finding him and one or two protégés staring at a workstation screen, she saw over two dozen Smart Metal employees watching the oversize presentation monitor at the front of the room.

Just as surprising, it was tuned to a cable news network.

"What's going on?" she asked as she came into the room.

Some shushed her. Chiang pointed at the screen.

What she saw first was nothing—literally, just blackness. As she stared, she could make out some boxy shapes; buildings maybe.

Then there was a flash. Several. White and yellow.

Then a red hand rising. But not a hand—flames.

Words scrolled across the bottom of the screen:

U.S. attacking ISIS cell responsible for Boston attacks

UP IN HIS OFFICE, MASSINA FLIPPED BACK AND FORTH between the different channels carrying the news reports. The U.S. had launched a wave of attacks in Libya against different ISIS cells. Targets in at least three different cities were being hit. The commentator speculated that there were probably a dozen others targeted, but at the moment the military was refusing to comment. All the news reports were coming from people on the scene, mostly via cell-phone uploads to sites like YouTube.

One hearty CNN reporter had climbed onto a roof in Tobruk—shades of Peter Arnett in the First Gulf War—and was giving a live commentary as the missiles struck a building about a half mile away.

"I know that building," he told the anchor back home. "It's just a school. Thank God it's night and all the students are at home."

At that point, the "school" erupted in a series of fireballs as the missiles hit a store of ammunition and explosives.

"I suppose those are their pencils igniting," said Massina caustically.

Bozzone, standing near the desk, laughed.

Massina flipped through the channels again, settling this time on Fox. They were replaying an earlier, extremely shaky cell-phone video from Misrata.

"What do you think?" he asked Bozzone.

Bozzone shrugged.

"At least they're doing something," offered Massina.

"True," said Bozzone. "But how do we know these are the guys? It looks more like they're targeting a guerilla movement. Not that there's anything wrong with that, but it's almost beside the point, at least as far as Boston is concerned. Despite what these guys are claiming."

Yes, thought Massina. It wasn't retribution.

CHELSEA STARED AT THE OTHERS AS THE BROADCAST continued. They were smiling, cheering each explosion.

She felt as if she should be doing the same. Yet for some reason, the explosions didn't make her feel any better. Not that she was sorry for the terrorists who were dying; on the contrary, she

knew they deserved to die, and if she'd been pi-
loting the bombers or commanding the missiles,
or even pointing a gun at one of them, she would
have no hesitation pulling the trigger.

But that wasn't the same as feeling satisfied, let
alone elated.

She didn't feel anything. Not joy, not sorrow.

Pain?

No.

Pleasure?

No.

Satisfaction?

Not even close.

Nothing?

Nothing.

"I'm going back to work," she said, leaving
the lab.

20

Boston–around the same time

Tolevi had just sat down to watch television with his daughter, Borya, when the American assault on the ISIS bases in Libya began. His first impulse was to change the channel, but all that did was bring a slightly less fuzzy image of exploding bombs to the screen.

"Do you want to watch this?" he asked.

"Yes. Don't you?"

"Not particularly. But all right."

"Why don't you want to see it?" Borya leaned forward on the couch, her head tilted slightly, a mannerism he thought she'd inherited from her mother. "Does it scare you?"

"How could it scare me?" answered Tolevi. He was genuinely surprised—what did his daughter think of him?

"Maybe you think the bombs will come here."

"We've already been attacked. This is simply the response." He studied her face, as if there were some clue there that would reveal the secret workings of her teenage mind. "And are you scared?"

"Of course not."

"What about the other day, downtown," he asked. "Were you scared then?"

"No."

He actually believed her. The child had a very high threat tolerance, something that often got her in trouble.

"You would have been scared if one of them had pointed a gun at you," said Tolevi. "Then."

"Has that happened to you? I know it has," she added. "I know people have shot at you. That's why you only have half an ear, right? When you were with Chelsea."

"Only a little was cut off," he said defensively. About a third had been sliced, mostly the lobe, by an overzealous Russian prick of an officer.

"They cut it because you wouldn't give up your friends, I bet."

"Where do you get these ideas?" asked Tolevi, rising. He decided he would have a drink.

"Can you get me some chips?" she asked. "If you're going into the kitchen."

"Potato chips give you pimples," he said. But he got the bag out anyway, and also a glass of orange juice—in his mind a balance to the chips—and was bringing them into the living room for her when the doorbell rang.

"You're not expecting anyone, right?" Tolevi asked.

"I doubt it."

That was a no.

"Stay here," he said, setting down her snacks.

Tolevi went back to the kitchen, out into the hall, and checked the video monitor, which showed the front door.

Maarav Medved. A Russian mobster with whom he occasionally did business. He was alone, the street behind him empty.

"What the fuck now?" muttered Tolevi. He opened the drawer below the security monitor and reached behind the back to get the gun hidden above the panel. He slid the gun into the back of his belt and covered it with his shirt before going down to the door.

"What do you want?" he demanded from behind the locked door.

"Gabor! Is that a way to greet an old friend?"

"I heard rumors you wanted to kill me," said Tolevi.

"Kill you? Never!"

"You're lying."

Tolevi put his eye to the security peephole. Medved was still alone. His arms were wide, palms up.

What the hell was he up to?

"You hurt me more than you know, Gabor."

Tolevi cracked open the door. Medved smiled.

"Come in," said Tolevi, stepping back.

Medved spread his arms out to grab him in a bear hug. Tolevi put up his hand.

"My daughter is here," he said.

"And that is perfect, because I have a gift for her."

Medved reached into the pocket of his sport coat. Tolevi stepped back and pulled his pistol.

"What? A gun on your friend? What is this?" sputtered Medved.

"You tried to get me killed."

"No. Never."

"Don't lie."

"It was not me, and you know it. You had trouble with the Russian service, big trouble." Medved shook his head dramatically. "But many people do, and it passes. You have no trouble now! Of course not! You worked that out. Now, I—I had nothing to do with that. Ask anyone."

Medved seemed genuinely offended, even hurt.

"So what do you want?" asked Tolevi.

"Want? Me? Nothing. I am honored to call you a friend."

This, clearly, is going to cost me something huge, thought Tolevi.

"Can I come in?" asked Medved.

"My daughter is here, as I said."

"And as I said, excellent, because I have a present for her. A new iPad." Medved held out a slim rectangle wrapped in plain brown paper. "They call it a mini."

"She has one."

"And now two. This one is better. I understand she is very good at computers, yes?" Medved took a step inside. Tolevi, puzzled by what Medved might be up to, let him go.

Not much was sacrosanct with the Russian *mafya*, but attacking families, especially children, was generally considered out of bounds. And this sort of attention was meant to convey the opposite, to make up for past wrongs.

Or curry favor.

"Borya! Borya!" said Medved, tromping up the stairs to the kitchen. "A present for you."

Borya, bewildered, emerged from the living room. If she remembered Medved, her expression betrayed no hint of it.

"How much you have grown! I brought you a present."

"Thank you," said Borya hesitantly. She glanced at her father. He shrugged.

"How is school?" asked Medved.

"Do I know you?" asked Borya.

Medved laughed genially. "I work with your dad. You and I met at the Christmas party two years ago. I knew your mother," he added gravely.

The last was a lie, but Tolevi didn't correct it.

"Open the present," urged Medved. "Go on."

Borya ripped off the paper gingerly, revealing an iPad mini. It wasn't boxed and didn't include a plug.

"Uh, thank you," she said, turning it over. "You know, usually these have, like, a wire for charging."

Medved's face fell. "Oh."

"I'm sure I have a spare," she said quickly. "Thank you." Borya winked at her father. "I have homework."

"You better get it done," Tolevi told her, winking back.

"So, what favor is it you want?" Tolevi asked when she left.

"Favor? No favor. In fact, I have a present for you," declared Medved.

He reached into his jacket and took out a thick envelope. "It is a way of saying thank you."

"Thank you for what? What did I do for you?"

"Not for me," said Medved. "Someone more important than me."

That would include 99 percent of the world, thought Tolevi. "Can you give me a hint?"

"You helped a babushka, on the day of the attacks," said Medved.

Tolevi shrugged. The old grandma in the deli. He'd forgotten the incident entirely.

"Let's just say she is the mother of someone very important. He will not forget this. Ever. Anything you need—anything—come to me. Bingo."

"Bingo?"

"Yes, yes. Well, have a good night with your daughter. Family is very important. The most important."

Tolevi showed him to the door. It was only when he had gone that he opened the envelope.

There were a hundred one-hundred-dollar bills.

Borya came into the kitchen as he finished counting. "What was that all about?"

"Looks like I did a good deed," said Tolevi.

"I checked it for a virus," she said, holding up the iPad. "It's clean. Newest specs. Is it stolen?"

"That's anyone's guess," admitted Tolevi.

"Do you think there's a bomb inside?" she asked.

"Not one with explosives."

21

Boston–two days later

Massina's vague sense of unease after the American assaults in Libya only grew in their immediate aftermath. The waves of cruise missiles and standoff munitions launched by American ships, submarines, and aircraft were followed by ground operations conducted by Libyan troops. These were reported to be a great success.

Still, despite claims that they had been launched in retaliation for the Boston attacks, nothing Massina heard or read indicated that the Boston plotters had been brought to justice, or even captured. The Pentagon wouldn't even comment on whether they'd been targeted.

Having given the issue some thought following the attacks, Massina realized that Muslim extremists were a nihilistic pathogen that poisoned countries directly and indirectly. No amount of reason or goodwill could convince them to alter their path toward conflagration. Eventually they, or people they influenced, would get ahold of a nuclear weapon. Maybe this would happen in Pakistan, maybe Russia, maybe even, God forbid, the U.S. Millions would die or be poisoned. The only way to prevent that was to stamp them out, and keep stamping.

Given that logic, the attacks in Libya made sense. And yet they were inadequate at best. And since they didn't directly target the perpetrators in Boston—or if they did, clearly they had missed—they were beside the point. If you didn't punish the people responsible for the attacks, there would surely be more attacks.

The evening of the attack, Massina had met with a friend of his at the FBI and offered to help in any way possible. It was a sincere offer, but he could tell from the reaction that his friend thought it was pro forma, the sort of thing people said in times of crisis.

Which only frustrated him more. Still, Massina was taken off guard when he got a text on his private phone a week and change after the attacks:

Can we meet?—YJoh

Massina almost dismissed it as spam, then realized who "YJoh" was. He replied:

Come to my office

The answer came quickly.

Can't. Café near Fenway?

Now it was Massina's turn to pass.

Can't leave office.

Tonight?

He thought for a moment.

I am going to a cocktail party at Hilton Downtown at 7 p.m. Meet me there.

Johansen didn't respond.
"Must be a yes," Massina told himself.

MASSINA SPENT A GOOD FORTY-FIVE MINUTES AT THE party before Yuri Johansen caught his attention with a subtle wave from the portable bar in the corner. Massina excused himself and ambled over, stopping to say hello to the mayor's wife, who was here alone tonight, her husband being in Washington on business.

"I'm so glad none of your people were hurt," she told him after an air kiss.

"Yes, and it's a miracle that you and your family were OK," said Massina.

"We have good people around us. The bastards tried." The word *bastards* came out of her mouth easily, even though it was a stark contrast to her otherwise dignified, nearly prim, manner. Evelyn—*Mrs.* Mayor to the press—was old-Boston Brahmin, a sharp contrast to her husband. Their marriage was the ultimate proof of opposites attracting.

"Anything that I can do to help us get back

on our feet," said Massina, "you'll let me know. Make sure Bobby knows."

"He does." Evelyn grasped his arm. "Thank you, Louis. Your help means a lot."

Massina nodded. Evelyn let go of his arm, then drifted away.

"You feel very strongly about your city," said Johansen, who'd walked over while he'd been talking.

"Of course," said Massina.

"I'd like to have a conversation."

"Go ahead."

"Needs to be private. Come on."

Johansen led him out of the hotel to a waiting Escalade. As soon as both men got in the back, the Cadillac SUV pulled away from the curb.

They drove up to Atlantic Avenue, continuing north. Massina waited for Johansen to say something—anything.

"Mr. Johansen," he said finally, "if you want my help, you should start by not wasting my time. It's very precious to me."

"We believe the Boston attacks were planned by a man whose nom de guerre is Ghadab min Allah—Allah's Wrath."

"I see."

"He was in Libya. He's gone. Where, we're not sure yet."

"Were the attacks launched against him?"

"Multiple targets. The administration—" Johansen paused. "Politics is a complicated thing."

"I'm glad to hear that someone's trying to get him."

"Yes." The word sounded odd, as if it came from a synthetic voice box, rather than a human being.

Johansen looked back out the window. "I'm putting together an operation."

"You or the CIA?"

"It depends whether we're caught," said Johansen. His voice was too serious for Massina to take it as a joke, though perhaps it was meant as a dark one. "You were of great help in Ukraine. I could use some of those devices. And others."

"What do you need?"

"Surveillance drones. An autonomous information-gathering system—we'd plant the bugs around an area and let the system do the heavy work. I won't have enough people to watch everything and can't risk them in certain areas. Your devices solve both problems."

"I see."

"We haven't pinned down for sure where this guy is," added Johansen. "But assuming it's Syria, which is most likely, the political situation there complicates things. The Russians work closely with the Syrians, and in theory we'd have to work with them if we wanted to do something there."

"But you don't want to."

"Not in a million years. Even if their hearts were in the right place," added Johansen. "Talking to the Russians is in effect talking to the

Syrians, and word inevitably gets back to Daesh. This has to be completely off the books."

"Daesh?"

"ISIL, ISIS, scumbags—Daesh. Technically it stands for the phrase *al-Dawla al-Islamiya al-Iraq al-Sham*—the same as ISIL. But in Arabic, it sounds like slang for a traitor against Islam. That's why people in the administration use ISIL—it's translated as Daesh. It's a silly game," added the CIA agent. "But I guess you get your knives in where you can. They don't like it, which to me is the best reason to use it."

"I see."

"Will you help us?"

Massina wanted to grab him and say of course. But he knew this was more like a business decision—or should be. He struggled to be systematic, to think, to divorce himself from the elation he suddenly felt.

A chance to strike back! You bet I'm in!

"Who operates the systems?" he asked Johansen.

"You train my guys."

"When are you attacking?"

"As soon as we have a definitive target."

"Training your people isn't going to work. It'll take months, and frankly, you're unlikely to have the expertise."

Johansen was silent for a few moments.

"I could take two people," he said. Clearly he'd already considered this a possibility. "They stay behind the lines with me in Turkey."

"Two may not be enough."

"It will have to be. And I have to train them. For survival," added Johansen. "Otherwise they don't come. And volunteers. They have to volunteer."

"Fair enough," said Massina. "We'll work it out."

22

Boston–two days later

AFTER THE ACCIDENT THAT HAD COST HIM HIS LEGS, Johnny Givens had undergone a series of operations and rehabilitation that not only rebuilt his body, but made it measurably better. His prosthetic legs, whose jumping strength alone was three times beyond his "natural" strength, were only the most obvious improvement. (The figure came from comparing his ability in the broad jump with his measurements in high school track events.) The medicine that had helped him recover had bulked up the rest of his body; the drugs that got his nerves ready for the grafts to his legs' controls had accentuated not only the rest of his nerves but his brain's processing as well. He literally thought faster and learned quicker as a byproduct of his recovery.

But these improvements had had an odd effect on his emotional state. Confident in his abilities before, he now wondered how much of him was real.

Assigned a counselor as part of his rehab—

post-traumatic stress was among several fears—he found it impossible to describe precisely how he felt. The counselor, a man in his fifties with a beard that made Johnny think of Sigmund Freud, told him what he was going through was perfectly natural.

"What does that mean exactly?" Johnny asked. "What am I going through?"

"Adjustment."

"Adjusting . . . ?"

"Are you sad?" asked the counselor, stroking his beard.

"I wouldn't say I'm sad. Meh, maybe."

"Meh?"

Johnny shrugged. "Meh."

"Describe it."

But Johnny couldn't. He dropped counseling in favor of more workouts; those seemed far more productive. He ran five miles a day, every morning, and used the Smart Metal gym as well. The facility was outfitted along the lines of a Gold's Gym; what it lacked in muscle-conscious gym rats it more than made up in stat-obsessed health nuts. Computers—yours or a central unit—could track and critique every aspect of a workout, from breathing to posture to sweat content. There were four different personal trainer programs, each customizable for body type and goals.

Johnny eschewed that electronic assistance, but otherwise was one of the gym's most frequent "guests," as the system called them. Mornings from eight to ten tended to be rather busy, but otherwise the gym was big enough that it was easy to work through even the longest sequences without interruption. Johnny was often alone when he started, which could be as early as 4:30 in the morning on nights he couldn't sleep.

So he was surprised when, pushing in at 4:42 A.M., he found Chelsea running on one of the treadmills. He waved, but she had her earphones on and her head down as he passed. He got on a treadmill, did a bit of cardio to warm up before hitting the weight machines. He'd just finished some easy hammer presses, still in warm-up mode, when Chelsea walked over.

"I'm sorry to bother you," she said, "but I have a question about one of the machines."

"No problem," he told her, getting up. "What's up?"

"I want to use the Gravitron, but I don't know the settings."

"Gravitron?"

"I'm following this workout." She showed him her phone.

"OK." Johnny took a look at the routine. "The Gravitron's over here."

He showed her how the machine worked—it was like a pull-up machine, with a counterweight—and then spotted her through a set.

She was pretty. A shorter, stronger Ilana Glazer.

No glasses. A heart tattoo on her shoulder, barely visible beneath her T-shirt and wide bra strap, a lightning bolt on her right thigh.

Well-shaped thigh.

"How do your arms feel?" he asked as she dropped down.

"Good. A little burn in the shoulders."

"Two more sets and see how it feels," he told her. "It should be a bit of burn but you should be able to use your arms."

"I hope so." She laughed.

"Have you worked out before?"

"Not here. I haven't done weight training since college, really. I played field hockey in high school," she added. "But since then, I just run, mostly."

"You like hitting people with sticks?"

"It has its advantages."

Johnny spotted her on the next two machines. She was small, but wiry, stronger than he would have expected.

"Is it always this empty?" she asked.

"This early, yeah."

"You always work out now?"

"It varies, but yeah, a lot. I don't—I haven't needed so much sleep since the recovery period, you know, for my legs. I think it's like a side effect of the drugs."

"I'm sorry."

"Nothing to be sorry about."

Chelsea had been there when his legs were crushed, and though she had nothing to do with it, he knew she had some sort of odd guilt about it. It was stupid and irrational, but he could see it in her face.

She stepped forward and wrapped her arms around him in a tight hug.

"It's OK," he told her gently. "It's really all right."

"I'm so sorry," she said, still holding him.

"Are you all right? The attack on the hotel—"

"I'm fine."

She let go. He stared at her for a moment, not sure what to say, if he should assure her he was fine or probe about her reaction to the attack.

Her oversize, shapeless T-shirt and shorts made her look far more vulnerable than she really was.

"I, uh, I gotta get upstairs," he said, glancing at the clock. "I, uh, am picking up Mr. Massina early, for Beef."

"And I gotta finish," she said, turning back to the triceps dip. "See ya later."

Halfway to the door, he stopped short.

"Maybe we can get a drink sometime," he said, his voice more tentative than he wanted.

Her frown threw him off; he braced himself.

"I'd like that," she said. "Really."

23

Boston—two hours later

TOLEVI SWUNG THE CAR TO THE CURB AND LOOKED over at his daughter.

"Have a good day," he told Borya. "Good luck on the test. Be sure to text Mary when you're on your way home."

If Borya heard any of that, she gave no hint. The car door slammed behind her as she ran to see one of her friends near the school steps.

"I thought girls liked to talk," he grumbled to his steering wheel as he pulled back into traffic.

He had a full agenda today. First stop was the Port of Boston, where he had to meet with the man who was going to drive some of his imports to a distribution center down in New York State. Then he was meeting a food broker to see about buying coffee—a lot of it. Tolevi's recent visit to the Ukraine had convinced him that coffee would sell well on both sides of the border— occupied and "free."

Tolevi tightened his grip on the steering wheel as he passed the restaurant that had been shot up and then burned by the ISIS terrorists. Like many people, he wasn't particularly impressed by the administration's "measured action" in Libya. The news sites were all claiming that three or four hundred "ISIS-affiliated fighters" had been killed or rejected from the country.

Somehow that didn't seem like a proper response. The Libyan government, with help from the Americans and Europeans, had launched a comprehensive offensive to retake the western half of the country from the rebels. All very well and good, thought Tolevi, but in the meantime, cut the balls off the bastards who'd attacked. It was the only way to make a point.

Behead them on Boston Common—that was what he wanted to see. And that was the only sort of thing these pricks would really understand. How dare they kill innocent people? What kind of savages were they?

Sociopaths.

Gut them, feed them their balls, then behead them. That was the way to deal with the fucks.

Tolevi's contact worked at a small cargo operation in the shadow of Conley Terminal, Massport's massive container operation on the harbor. Its smaller size meant it had to scramble; more important, its operators were very understanding, even flexible.

Not that Tolevi intended to break the law in this deal. Just bend it a bit, where necessary.

A truck cab without a container cut in front of Tolevi as he entered the yard.

"Asshole," yelled Tolevi, and he laid on the horn.

If the trucker heard it, he gave no sign. Tolevi continued to the small shack where his contact, Andrew Bastos, worked. Inside, he found Bastos in deep discussion with two crane operators.

It was more monologue than discussion, Bastos chewing them out for some unspecified infraction. The men listened with blank expressions—not frowning, not smiling, not showing emotion of any kind.

"Get out, get out, I call the union," said Bastos finally. He had a thick Portuguese accent; he came from Gloucester up the coast, from a fishing family that had members on both sides of the ocean.

"What do you want, Tolevi?" Bastos demanded, dismissing the others. "I don't have all day."

"Your brother-in-law," said Tolevi. "I need him to take a container down. It should be here tomorrow."

"Humph." The man tapped a button on his computer's touchscreen. "Gonna be here late. Maybe that container doesn't get off until morning."

"It'd be better that night."

"There are costs involved."

This was all purely bullshit—Tolevi had checked earlier in the morning; the ship was due to dock no later than 8:00 A.M., and if anything was running ahead of schedule. But the shakedown was part of the arrangement—Tolevi wasn't so much paying to make sure the cargo came off on time as he was paying for silence if anything went wrong.

"You're moving what?"

"Olive oil," said Tolevi.

"From Argentina?"

"They have a surplus."

They did, in fact, have a surplus. And a good portion of the oil in the container was in fact Argentinian.

Another portion had come from Syria, but that fact needn't be specified. The documents certainly didn't.

"And you need my brother-in-law?"

"If you know someone else dependable, I'm all ears."

"He'll do. Usual arrangements."

"Absolutely," said Tolevi.

As he left the building, he found a burly man blocking his way. Tolevi was by no means short, but the man in front of him loomed over him. His T-shirt strained with his arm and chest muscles; he looked twice the size of a professional wrestler.

Three other men, all as big, stood behind him.

"You were in that car," said the man.

"You're the jerk that cut me off?" snapped Tolevi. It wasn't exactly the most politic answer, but if he was going to get beaten up, he might as well go down with dignity.

"I wanted to apologize," said the man. "I'm sorry, Mr. Tolevi."

Tolevi was sure this was some sort of trick.

One of the men nudged the trucker, and he stuck out his hand to shake.

Doubtful but seeing no other choice, Tolevi extended his own. To his great surprise, the man gripped it gently and they shook.

"I really am sorry, sir," said the trucker.

"It's not a problem," said Tolevi, flabbergasted. "Don't worry about it. It's forgotten. I don't even remember hearing anything, except 'good morning.'"

"Anything we can do for you, Mr. Tolevi," said the man who'd nudged the trucker, "just let us know."

Tolevi nodded, then walked quickly to his car.

24

Boston—later that day

THE CLERK FROWNED. "LET'S SEE THE PAPER."

Chelsea took it from her pocket and slid it onto the counter. The clerk picked it up and examined it closely.

"All right, so you have a gun license," he said. "What do you want?"

"Show me the SIG."

"You'd really probably be more comfortable with something smaller," he said.

"I want stopping power," she told him.

The man's moustache twitched. He was older, midsixties, she guessed. Though that wasn't an excuse for his chauvinism.

"Look, I'm an ex-trooper and gun instructor," he told her. "I've seen a lot of girls—"

"I'm not a girl. Are you not going to even show me the gun?"

"A small automatic—"

"If I wanted that, I'd ask for it."

"Old-fashioned shotguns are the best weapon

for home defense. There's nothing like that sound in the middle of the night."

"I have one. I need something to carry."

The clerk removed the gun from the display. He made sure it wasn't chambered, then handed it to her. Chelsea inspected it carefully, knowing he was watching her.

"A lot of people are worried because of the ISIS attacks," he said gently. "I get it. Believe me. And I'm not trying to give you a hard time—"

"You are giving me a hard time."

"I just want to make sure you're getting the right weapon," he said. "Believe me, I know what I'm talking about."

"You think I'm a woman and can't handle a gun."

"What do you weigh? A hundred pounds?"

"I've used 1911s without a problem. I know it's not a toy. You want to come down the street to the police range and see?"

"I'm just trying to help."

The SIG 226 felt heavy in her hand. Chambered in .40 S&W, it was the same gun used by many police officers and even some special-operations soldiers. It could hold fifteen bullets in its magazine.

"You know, if you like SIGs," suggested the clerk, "you might think about a 229 or even a 224. The 224 is really compact. It would fit easier in your purse."

"I don't carry a purse," said Chelsea.

"There's no manual safety," he said.

"No shit."

Chelsea put the gun down on the counter.

"You want a case?" asked the clerk.

"Absolutely," she said, taking out her credit card. "And three boxes of ammo."

25

Boston—around the same time

Ordinarily, Massina would have blown off the fund-raising reception for the New Millennium Advancement Project. He had no connection to the foundation or its board and plenty of other things to do. But in the aftermath of the attacks, he felt almost obligated to attend. The cocktail party was being held at the Windhaven Hotel, across the street from the Patriot, where so many people had been murdered. Windhaven had opened its doors to its erstwhile rival, providing rooms at no charge to some of the displaced guests following the assaults and even lending its own employees. Attending the reception was a small gesture of thanks—and an opportunity to reclaim some of the area soiled by savages.

In the aftermath of the Easter attacks, there was a general consensus that life had to go on. Amid the sorrow and the cleanup efforts, under the watchful eye of National Guardsmen and state police reinforcements, Boston made an effort to push ahead. The citizens didn't ignore what had happened, let alone hide their grief, but many went out of their way to stick to their old routines. Even with a significant part of the Orange Line closed for emergency repairs, ridership on the T approached record levels, as if residents had decided taking the subway was a good way to give the terrorists the finger. Restaurants were overbooked. If the atmosphere throughout the city wasn't quite St. Patrick's Day happy—a bit too warm for that—it was definitely Boston Proud: *F-U to all and any that messed with us.*

Defiance ran deep, from skin to bones and back. But there were other things beneath the surface: wariness, queasy suspicion, distrust. There was ugliness as well. A handful of Arab Americans had been beaten in the wake of the attacks; there were threats and graffiti.

There was also fear. People glanced over their shoulders as they walked. Many rehearsed what they would do if something nearby exploded.

Massina passed through the security check, then waited for Johnny, who had to explain who he was and why he needed his weapon even though he'd been precleared for the event as Massina's bodyguard. The screener's supervisor came over and gave him a small red pin to wear on his lapel.

"Red Badge of Courage," remarked Massina.

The former FBI agent gave him a confused look.

"Stephen Crane. Book," said Massina, turning to greet one of the board members as she came forward to peck him on the cheek.

He peeked at her name tag, unable to place the face.

"Delilah, how are you?" he asked.

"Fab-u-lous." She was a sketch out of *Saturday Night Live*. "And you, Lou-is?"

"Just looking for a drink," said Massina, excusing himself.

He made his way toward the bar at the far end of the room. Along the way he shook a few hands, received three or four air kisses, and nodded a lot. When he made it to the bartender, he asked for a pair of seltzers. Stuffing a five in the cup, he took the drinks and slid sideways toward Johnny, who was watching the crowd. Bozzone insisted he go everywhere these days with a bodyguard, and aside from Bozzone himself, he felt most comfortable with Johnny.

He handed Johnny the cup. "It's seltzer," he told him.

"Thanks."

Massina passed through the crowd, nodding and smiling, occasionally stopping to chat. He knew a good number of the people at the reception, though he wasn't very close to any of them. The crowd was a bit too artsy for his taste.

A half hour later, he nudged Johnny aside and glanced at his watch. "I think we'll call it a night."

"Your party, boss."

"*Party* is too strong a word."

Massina headed to a side door, smiled at two people he didn't know, and pushed through. He walked down a short hall to a door that opened onto a side terrace. To his surprise, there was a small group of men there smoking cigars. He started to pass through—there was a gate at the far end to the street—when someone called his name.

"Louis, trying to escape?"

Massina stopped. "Jimmy? Hey."

A tall, broad-shouldered man stepped through a cloud of cigar smoke and thrust a beefy hand toward him. It was Jimmy Gorman, former district attorney, former mayor, former party chairman, now just a big muck behind the scenes.

"What the hell are you doing at this soiree?" asked Gorman. He pounded Massina's back so hard he nearly coughed.

"Thought I'd see where they were spending my money."

Gorman laughed. "Want a cigar?"

"Nah."

"How about your friend?" asked Gorman, gesturing to Johnny.

"This is Johnny Givens. He works for me."

"Yeah, I see his pin." Gorman smirked, then turned to introduce Massina to the others he'd been standing with. Two were state senators whom Massina had met briefly in the past; the others were business people—donors, he guessed.

Everyone nodded politely. Massina was about to leave when Gorman pointed his cigar in the direction of the Patriot Hotel across the street.

"You want to go for a look?" he asked.

"What's to see?"

Gorman shrugged.

"Johnny helped rescue the hostages," said Massina.

"No shit." Gorman stepped over and clapped Givens on the back. Johnny gave him a very uncomfortable smile.

"So," said Gorman to Massina, "you wanna take a look?"

"Sure," decided Massina. "Sure."

THERE WERE NO LESS THAN THREE DOZEN POLICE OF-ficers and twice that many National Guards-men scattered around the block, with half a dozen cops blocking the entrance to the Patriot. Gorman tossed his cigar into the gutter and walked up to the sergeant in charge of the hotel detail; the man waved them in.

"How long before it reopens?" asked Massina.

"Don't know. They still have their investi-gators running in and out," said Gorman. He waved toward the bank of elevators. "They do a complete DNA vacuum thing or something in each of the rooms, pulling out all sorts of DNA, you know, hair and saliva and that stuff. Look-ing for any sort of clues. Seems like a hell of a lot of work to me, but they know their business. I'll show you the ballroom."

Massina remembered the hallway from the surveillance video, but it was difficult to map that memory on the wide space he walked through

now. In the video, it was dark and grainy, fore-
boding. Now, even though it was night, the
hall was bright and inviting, the walls a delicate mauve, the sconces polished, the hardware
gleaming.

The doors to the ballroom were open. Gorman
ducked under the yellow evidence tape still
strung across them and walked a few feet in.
Massina hesitated, then followed.

"They took out the carpet and the wallboard
for evidence," Gorman said. "That's where the
massacre took place."

He pointed to the area where the men had
been slaughtered. Studs and insulation were all
that were left.

"That's where I danced with my daughter,"
said Gorman, pointing near the stage. "On her
wedding. Not five years ago."

Massina looked around. He'd been at that
wedding.

"Wanna see upstairs?"

Massina caught a glimpse of Johnny's ashen
face.

"I think this is enough," Massina said. "But
thanks."

"Difficult," said Gorman, leading them out.

He stopped when they reached the front lobby,
pensively retrieving a cigar from his pocket and
cutting it with fastidious precision. Retrieving a silver-shrouded torch lighter, he slowly
warmed the end before setting it afire and
taking a puff.

"Bastards," said Gorman. "We can't let them keep us down."

"They won't," said Massina.

"No. I wonder, Lou—I wonder if maybe you might want to do me a favor."

"What's that?"

"I'm getting together some people to make a statement, public, you know? On a stage. TV. Tell the fuckin' world we're not taking this shit on the chin. I know you don't do this sort of thing, but it would be good for us. People respect you."

"I'll do it. Send my assistant the details."

"You got it, bro." Gorman swatted him on the back.

Bro? thought Massina. *He's getting hip in his old age.*

"HOME, BOSS?" JOHNNY ASKED, CLIMBING INTO THE driver's seat.

"No. I have some things to do at the office."

"All right."

"What'd you think?"

"Think of what?" asked Johnny.

"The hotel. Did it bother you? Being inside again?"

"Nah. Just a place."

"We're going to get them back," said Massina. "This sideshow in Libya, it's got nothing to do with what's really going to happen."

"Really?"

"We're lending the government some gear. I need volunteers to—"

"If there's some sort of action involved," said Johnny, "I'd like to be part of it."

"I was hoping you'd think that way," said Massina. "I'll make it so."

26

EVERYWHERE HE WENT, THEY HAILED HIM AS A HERO.

Even at four in the morning, on a dusty airstrip in eastern Syria, Ghadab was well-known. "Emir!" they called him, bowing their heads and striking their chests. Ghadab, in theory traveling in secrecy, was accorded every honor and luxury the Caliphate's soldiers could afford.

Objectively, this wasn't much—fresh water as he stepped from the plane, a blanket against the cold of the truck, which had sat at the edge of the airstrip for nearly three hours, waiting for the plane. But he appreciated it nonetheless.

Escaping from Libya had been difficult. It wasn't just that the Americans were bombarding everything that had even the slightest connection to the Caliphate. The group that had been sheltering Ghadab split into several factions and began attacking each other, making it dangerous even for Ghadab to travel. He'd had to use his influence with two of the rebels to institute a cease-fire so he could meet the plane to Sudan.

Getting from Sudan to Egypt and then Syria was another odyssey. The Jews had spies everywhere, and he'd had to lay over in a gas station in Abri for five hours, at one point pretending that he was the attendant when some men in suit jackets arrived. They turned out to be Saudi businessmen, but could just as easily have been Mossad or even Egyptian GID, who would have shot him and sold his body to the Americans.

Getting into Syria was easy by comparison: a commercial flight in heavy disguise to Jordan; from there, a private plane deposited him in Syria. The truck ride that followed was long and uncomfortable, but not dangerous—the center of Syria and much of bordering Iraq was Caliphate territory.

Located in central Syria, Palmyra was a sleepy town organized around an oasis that made it possible to grow crops. It had been settled for millennia; monuments to old pagan regimes, an outrage to the true God and all that was good, still stood near the town. Its airfield and barracks abandoned at the start of hostilities, it had been one of the first places taken by the Caliphate and had withstood the infidels' many counterattacks. At the moment, the hostilities there were largely dormant here; the puppet Assad was too busy concentrating on his weaker enemies to the northwest to bother with Caliphate strongholds.

Assad's caution bothered Ghadab. The end

time would never arrive if their opponents were so cautious.

He was especially disappointed in the Americans. True, they had attacked in Libya, and quite fiercely, but they had not brought their army back to the Levant as the Word declared they would at the start of Armageddon. The prophecy implicit in the words of the Koran had not been fulfilled.

They were in sight of the city, close enough to make out its minarets in front of the distant hills, when Ghadab saw the first sign of war: a thin trail of gray smoke rose near the river on the near side. Apparently a structure had been targeted overnight. A missile—Russian or American, it was impossible to know—had destroyed the building. Being empty, it was allowed to burn.

"It was on fire when I left," said the driver, pointing in the direction of the ruins. "Now just the rocks are left to burn."

"Do they hit here often?" asked Ghadab.

"A few times. It's not serious. The Russians attack. With them, there is always some danger, since they never hit what they aim at."

A single bridge crossed from the south directly into the city. It had been damaged by artillery and bombed several times, but each time the brothers had repaired it swiftly, and the infidels appeared to have given up on it. They passed over quickly, speeding past an orchard and heading into the city proper. They took a right at the first intersection, then the next left, passing a mosque and continuing on to an intersection dominated by a large park, which in ancient days had been the grounds of a house so large it was called a castle. No longer standing, it had been home to relatives of the emir.

Bordering the park at the corner was a restaurant and inn. The Caliphate had requisitioned it over soon after taking the town.

A single man stood outside the entrance. Ghadab knew him only as "the African"; he was his liaison to the War Council.

"Ghadab min Allah," said the man as Ghadab got out. "The entire city is honored by your presence."

Ghadab bowed his head. They had first met three years before, serving together in Yemen. The African had apparently been born in Ethiopia, though his accent and features seemed entirely Arabic.

"I am honored to be here," Ghadab told him.

"Work brings us all blessings, brother." The African's Arabic was quick and precise, with the slightest hint of Egypt in its accent.

"I was told I have space to work?"

"A facility has been found, a proper place for you," said the African. "We will tour it tomorrow. Tonight, you must rest."

"I'd feel better working."

"Your people have not even arrived." The African's tone was that of a father chiding a child who wanted to play. "Come, we have arranged something for you."

The African led him around the building to

the back, entering a side gate to a fenced patio before continuing through another gate to the garden. Organized around a desert spring, the grounds were crisscrossed by gravel paths and heavily studded with trees; it was cool, almost cold in the predawn air.

"Your thoughts are far away," said the African as they walked. "Best watch your step."

He led Ghadab to a small rectangular pool near the center of the property. At one point, there had been a statue on the pedestal that stood above the pool; Caliphate soldiers had disposed of it soon after claiming the city.

A man stood on that pedestal, hands bowed, head covered. He was barefoot; his clothes bore the blood and tears of a recent beating.

"Hamas," spit the African. "A spy."

Twelve warriors in black uniforms stood in a semicircle at the eastern end of the pedestal. Each held a Kalashnikov diagonally across his chest. Across from them was a young man in traditional Syrian dress, holding a video camera. A boom microphone extended from the top; the man looked like a tourist, or perhaps a new father waiting to capture his son's first steps.

Nearby was another man holding a curved sword.

"We execute him at the moment of sunrise," said the African. "I wonder if you would like the honor?"

Hearing the words, Ghadab no longer felt tired. "It would be my pleasure."

His distractions stayed behind as he walked

to the man with the sword, who handed it to him reverently. It was a heavy, well-polished and finely sharpened tool, a weapon even the Prophet would be proud to wield. Ghadab swung it around his head, slashing the air.

Oh, yes, this is the pleasure of jihad. The victory over the weak, the profane infidels, the destroyers of the Word and all that is holy!

Ghadab climbed up the pedestal. The apostate spy tried to stand erect, but Ghadab saw that his hands were trembling.

"On your knees, blasphemer!" he commanded.

When the man didn't sink fast enough, Ghadab pushed him down with his left hand. Then he positioned his head slightly forward. The man moved it too far, bowing almost to the stone.

Really, it did not matter. A clean stroke or several hacks—it was all the same to Ghadab. There were blotches of dried blood already on the pedestal. It was a sacred place.

Ghadab glanced over his shoulder. The edge of the earth had a pink line, but there was no glow yet.

Another minute. Perhaps two.

The spy began to mutter something.

"What are you saying!" shouted Ghadab.

Instead of answering, the man continued to mutter, almost singing.

It was a prayer.

"Apostate!" shouted Ghadab. "Blasphemer!"

With that, he slammed the sword down as hard as he could, severing in one blow the man's skull from his body. It was a clean stroke, and it unleashed a flood of blood. The head shot forward, bouncing on the flat stone, and rolling off the pedestal. The body stayed as it was for a full five seconds, blood spouting as if it were a fountain. Then it caved off to the side, bereft.

Ghadab plunged the sword into the dead torso, pushing so hard that the tip went through and struck stone.

Satiated, he went down to the African. A calm fell over him; he was no longer annoyed at the inconvenience of being given new quarters or told not to get to work. He felt tired, but also ready to concede that he needed rest.

"Thank you, brother," he told the African. "I wish to pray now and have a meal before I rest."

27

Boston—the next day

CHELSEA RUBBED HER EYES, BLINKED A FEW TIMES, then forced herself to reexamine the code on the computer screen. It was out of whack—she could see the syntax was messed up, but for the life of her couldn't figure out why.

She got up from her console.

I need a break. Coffee.

Chelsea walked down the hall, heading for the kitchenette at the far side. She put a coffee pod in the single-serve and waited for the French Roast to spritz through. A half-dozen donuts, two glazed, the rest sugar-jellies, sat in a box next to the coffee. She barely noticed them, unnerved by her loss of concentration.

Fatigue.

Cradling her cup in both hands, Chelsea walked back down the hallway, passing her own lab and continuing to Room B4. The lab had been taken over by Chiang, who headed a team assigned by Massina to "explore" the identities and location of the perpetrators of the Boston attacks.

"Come to help?" asked Chiang.

"Just seeing how everyone is."

Massina had asked Chelsea if she wanted to be involved, but she demurred. Her instinct was to get back to what she had been doing all along, to not let the attacks alter her course.

She regretted that now.

"Here's something we're stuck on," said Chiang. "Check it out."

In the immediate aftermath of the attacks, there was a flood of postings and communications on social media. The vast bulk of these were not by terrorists; even those expressing "solidarity" with the bastards were almost always far removed from anything nefarious. Nonetheless, a tiny minority of these accounts could be linked to other accounts that were using high-level encryption programs to send messages. A list of these accounts had been developed by the NSA and shared, through the CIA, with Smart Metal.

Chiang's team—or more precisely, their computer software—had broken the encryption the night before. But the messages themselves yielded no useful information about terrorist operations; the bulk were trivial greetings. Of course, those could be code: "All good here" or "Happy Birthday" could easily be meant as a signal to start an attack or lay low. So Chiang and his team were now sifting through those messages and the accounts associated with them, comparing them to different news events and other intelligence that they had gathered to see what information they might tickle out of the cross-references. Thus far, though, none of the patterns they'd noticed seemed significant.

Except one. But it was baffling.

"We've looked at some Facebook pages with baseball postings that might be interesting," said Chiang, explaining that the subject seemed to be an anomaly—onetime entries by posters who otherwise seemed to have no interest in the sport. "We thought maybe they were targets or messages about meeting places, but it looks like a dead end."

Chiang pulled up one of the pages, then clicked into a window that showed the owner's "friends." A number of the accounts were bots, created to increase hits and ratings. The team had ignored them for the most part; Chelsea asked why.

"They're just kind of noise in the system," said Chiang.

"Do you mind?" Chelsea asked.

"Please."

Chelsea sat at the workstation and began looking at the links associated with the bots. The bulk had been traced to outfits in China and Russia and labeled according to expected intent—propaganda was big with the Russian contacts, which, in many cases, used the links to legitimate commenters. The results tended to cluster, with multiple accounts and interlocking links.

So what was interesting?

Not the links, but the lack of them.

"What about this Croatia website?" she asked Chiang about an hour after sitting down. "What's the story?"

"Tourism," said Chiang. "The Google translation is pretty good."

"The pictures are all taken from other sources."

Chiang smirked. "Welcome to the internet."

"Can we get a list of who looks at the site?" Chelsea asked.

"Well . . ."

Chiang leaned over and hot-keyed up a tool to hack into the server.

It was harder than Chelsea thought it would be, way harder than most of the other sites, on par with the work done by the best Chinese sites.

"I think we should look at this one pretty hard," said Chelsea when they finally reached the folders associated with the site. "That's a hell of a lot of material for a tourist site."

"Yeah," said Chiang, opening a folder and a document at random. It was written in Arabic. "You think they get a lot of tourists from the Middle East?"

28

Boston—two days later

THE FACT THAT JOHANSEN BROUGHT A LAWYER BOTH-
ered the hell out of Massina, and his annoyance
only grew as the lawyer insisted on opening the
meeting with a statement.

"For the record," he intoned, "you are private
citizens, acting entirely out of your own self-
interest, sharing in good faith with us information you have developed."

The only way Massina managed to hold his
temper in check long enough to let the idiot
finish was to focus on the rearrangement of the
gear and furniture. The Box had been reconfig-
ured as more of a conference room than a computing center for the meeting; a large table sat
in the middle of the room. All but four of the
dozen chairs were empty. Besides Johansen and
the legal beagle—Massina had blocked out his
name, Bert Backlash or something—Jenkins
from the FBI had been invited. Massina had decided to present the data himself.

"So, for the record," continued the lawyer, "we are all here with no preconceived commitments and no entanglements."

"No one is making a record of this meeting, as far as I know," Massina said. He had trouble pushing the words out of his clenched teeth. "There is no need for legal bullshit."

"I think we all understand each other," said Johansen, trying to soothe things. "This is simply an exchange of ideas. The source of these ideas is not relevant. That's all."

Massina opened his laptop, which was hooked into the large screen at the front of the room to his right.

"This is a restaurant in Palmyra, Syria. It's supposedly a decent restaurant, or it was. There's a small computer in the storeroom that's used as a server. On first glance, the files on the server appear innocuous. They turn out to be sites on the so-called dark web, which I assume you all understand are addresses that, among other things, don't show up on your standard Google search. I'm not going to take you through the entire process," Massina added, "and won't bore you with everything we've found. But we were able to trace the funding network for an organization associated with Daesh through this site."

"This server is linked to the Boston attack?" asked Johansen.

"A credit card associated with one of the bank accounts that this server is regularly used to access, yes. It's an administrative account; the same credentials were used to set up the file system and a peripheral, so we believe there is a physical presence there."

"In other words," said Johansen, "that's where our bad guy is."

"That's where a bad guy is," said Massina. "Or at least someone directly interested in the Boston attacks and helping fund them. Maybe indirectly," he allowed.

"It's an intriguing connection," admitted Jenkins.

"If it were just that," continued Massina, "you wouldn't be here. Another account linked with this server belongs to an alias used by this man."

"Ghadab min Allah," said Johansen when the face came up on the screen.

"You have definite proof that he's tied into the attacks?" asked the lawyer. "Beyond the rumors, which are popular on the web."

Another screen.

"This card was used to pay for a plane ticket to Canada a year ago. It was also used to rent a car. The mileage on the account shows that it could have come to Boston. The names are here; I assume you can verify in your own data from Immigration if he crossed the border."

"He wasn't here when the attacks occurred," said Jenkins.

"No. He was in Libya."

Massina brought up the next screen, which showed the alias he believed Ghadab had used there: Durban Rahm. He continued sketching out what they had found, laying out the network as they knew it. Every so often he would glance at Johansen, trying to gauge how much of this he already knew. But the CIA officer's face remained neutral—until Massina's presentation shifted from briefing to a plan to deal with what they had found.

"Here's what I suggest be done," started Massina. "First—"

"We've heard enough," said Johansen, rising quickly. "And Bert has another meeting."

"Uh—"

"Thank you for briefing us as a private citizen," Johansen said.

The others were already heading for the door.

Massina watched them leave. He knew this must be some sort of internal politics, but it bothered the hell out of him.

Johansen was waiting in the hall, alone; the others were near the elevator, just out of earshot.

"Why the lawyer?" asked Massina.

"I know." Johansen nodded.

"You know what?"

"Let's get a cigarette."

"I don't smoke."

"Neither do I."

UPSTAIRS, JOHANSEN STRODE QUICKLY FROM THE ELevator, through the lobby and outside. Massina took his time catching up.

Johansen knew bringing the lawyer was a mistake, but his boss had insisted on it. He needed a witness when the shit hit the fan.

Which eventually it always did these days, no matter how much good you tried to do or how right you were to do it.

"I didn't mean to blindside you," he told Massina. "The deputy director—"

"Why are you covering your ass?" demanded Massina. "Am I supposed to take the hit if things go bad?"

"You don't understand the atmosphere in Washington these days, Louis. And this administration—let's just say they don't have our backs. Happy to take credit, though."

"And what happens to me?"

"Nothing. Nothing. You did your civic duty, and you have a witness from the FBI and the CIA—two witnesses—to prove it."

"They're going to accuse me of breaking the law?"

"Did you?"

"I could give a shit."

"Then that's your answer. And, uh, given the FBI's reaction, I'd say you must not have." Johansen shifted uncomfortably. He wouldn't hang Massina out to dry, but he couldn't be sure no one else would either. Still, this had to be done. "Look, we're going to get this guy," he said, changing the subject.

"But if things don't work out, it's not going to be a CIA operation."

"It's never a CIA operation," said Johansen.

Johansen had approached Massina because he wanted Smart Metal expertise and tech, but the company's involvement would also provide a very convenient cover if things went south.

Hey, we didn't do it. It was a private company who funded the thing. Apparently there's no law against that—Congress hadn't thought of making it illegal for upstanding citizens to take revenge on bastard scumbags who blew up their city.

At least not yet.

"Your information parallels ours," added Johansen. "Obviously I couldn't say it inside."

"So I wasted my time."

"No. Not at all. It's always good to have independent validation. And when we take a look, you may have more details. To be honest, I think I trust you more than our people anyway."

Johansen looked over to the corner. The others were standing there, waiting. He took out a cigarette—plausible deniability was important. Nobody could lie, yet nobody could tell the exact truth.

I saw him with a cigarette. I wasn't close enough to hear what he was saying.

Not lies, certainly. But not the entire truth.

"You promised two volunteers to watch the equipment," Johansen told Massina. "I need them in Arizona next week. This thing is moving along."

"You'll have them."

"Who?"

"I'm still deciding."

Johansen considered asking for Chelsea Goodman—she had done amazing work in the

Ukraine, and he knew she wouldn't wilt under pressure, something in his mind that techies tended to do—but he decided not to ask.

"They have to be volunteers, your people," Johansen reminded him. "Even though they'll be behind the lines. Volunteers."

"That part won't be a problem," said Massina.

29

Syria—that day

WORN BY THE FATIGUE OF HIS TRAVELS, GHADAB fell back to sleep after morning prayers and would have missed the noon call had he not felt the presence of someone waking him. He opened his eyes and was surprised to see a young, slender woman kneeling next to his bed.

"Honored sir," she said in Iraqi-flavored Arabic, "time to waken."

"Who are you?" he asked.

"Shadaa." She bowed her head.

Ghadab raised his head, looking around. "You're here alone?"

"I am yours."

Puzzled, he ordered her out of the room. When she was gone, he rose and prayed, then changed the clothes he'd fallen asleep in for a fresh pair of fatigues. He spent some time contemplating the words of the Prophet most honored. He thought of his fate, and how he would fulfill it, and permitted himself a small bit of vanity, considering how deserving he was of the praises the African

had given him on his arrival. They were mean-
ingful, for the African was older than he was, old
enough to be an uncle if not his father.

"You are displeased with me?" asked Shadaa
when he emerged from the room.

Her hands trembled. She stood stiffly at attention, as if a soldier, in the middle of the hall.

"I'm not pleased or displeased," Ghadab told
her. "Who are you?"

"Shadaa. Yours."

"I have work," he said.

She bowed her head. He went downstairs,
looking over his shoulder when he reached the
landing to make sure she wasn't following.

She wasn't. She stood in the same place, ramrod
straight.

Before the city had been liberated, the first-
floor restaurant served a mixture of Western
food—Italian and French, along with a little
Greek. Although the bar had been removed and
the liquor destroyed, there were still traces of
this influence; steak and pasta remained on the
menu, though the first was unavailable and the
waiter frankly recommended against the latter.
Only he remained from the old regime; the cook
was the owner's brother-in-law, which was not a
recommendation.

"We have lamb prepared with mint," suggested the waiter, "and rice with apricots. The
meat is fresh."

"That would be fine," said Ghadab.

"As you desire. Water? Sparkling?"

Another Western touch, thought Ghadab. "Plain water."

The waiter bowed, then sped off to the kitchen.

Ghadab was halfway through his meal when the African arrived. He had two young men with him, soldiers.

"I see you are eating," said the African. "I don't want to disturb you."

"Sit with me," said Ghadab. "We'll have lunch."

"Very generous, brother. But we have already eaten. These are my aides, Amin and Horace."

Amin was a common name, but Horace begged explanation.

"I was born in America," said the young man, whose Arabic sounded Egyptian. "My parents were convinced that they should fit in. They were apostates, worse than infidels."

"And then they returned home," said the African. "They returned to the faith."

"They have no understanding of it," said Horace bitterly. "They practice the motions, but do not know the meaning. Empty bottles that should be filled with pure water."

"Like yourself when you arrived," said the African with some fondness.

"Who is the girl?" Ghadab asked. He gestured toward the second floor.

"Shadaa," said the African. "Yours to do with as you wish. The council has made it clear that all fighters' needs are to be answered."

Ghadab didn't respond.

The African asked if she was not pleasing to

him. "We can find another," he added, "or if you prefer—"

"She'll do," answered Ghadab. "I wanted only an explanation."

"The council is ready for you. At your convenience."

"Let's go now."

THE COUNCIL WAS ONE OF SEVERAL GROUPS THAT steered the Caliphate's affairs. The Caliph himself was selected by the highest council, known informally as the *majlis al-shura* or Shura Council, the highest advisers of the people, learned religious leaders who had a deep understanding of the prophecies. The Caliph—to the West, Ibrahim Awad Ibrahim al-Badri; to his followers, Abu Bakr al-Baghdadi—in turn appointed various aides to assist in governing and in the greater struggle. As an overseas soldier, Ghadab answered directly to a subsection of the War Council that ruled overseas jihad.

Ghadab had met the Caliph only once, and then for only a few moments. He didn't expect to see him today, or anytime in the near future. The Caliph was constantly moving and, in any event, had better things to do than meet with a mere soldier, even one who had recently scored a great victory.

But it was the Caliph who greeted Ghadab when they arrived in the great chamber of the council building, a three-hundred-year-old mosque as yet untouched by the infidels' bombs. Under the massive central dome of the vast prayer room, the Caliph looked smaller than Ghadab remembered, thinner, though still as vigorous. His eyes danced as he spoke, darting back and forth before settling on Ghadab's own. The stare had the firmness of a handshake, and it energized Ghadab beyond even the words the Caliph spoke.

"This is one of our truest generals," declared the Caliph. Behind him, three dozen men milled back and forth, as if jockeying for position. Sunlight flooding through the ruby windows cast reddish sunbeams to highlight their faces. "He has struck the infidels' barbaric birthplace. We expect great things. More great things."

Ghadab bowed his head. Emotion overwhelmed him. He was honored beyond belief, empowered. If he could have died in that moment, he surely would have found bliss. There could not be a greater honor than to be praised by the Caliph, with all these worthies watching.

When he raised his head, only a moment or two later, the Caliph was already walking away, called by other business.

"al-Bhaddahi wishes to talk to you," said the African, nudging him gently toward a set of arches on the left. They entered an ornate room whose walls were enhanced with jewels and thick bands of gold chest-high.

Of the Caliph's deputies, arguably the most important was Abu Muslim al-Bhaddahi, a relative of Abu Muslim al-Turkemani and heir to his position as number-two man in the organization. al-Bhaddahi, kneeling alone in the room in prayer, rose as Ghadab entered.

"My brother!" declared the jihad leader, clasping Ghadab to his chest.

"I am honored" was all Ghadab could say.

al-Bhaddahi talked to him as if they were old friends, complimenting him on his great triumph and asking after several men he knew in Libya, only two of whom Ghadab even knew. Asked to describe his mission, he did his best to tamp down his pride, talking about how he had painstakingly built the team that had struck at Boston. He recounted the toll: fifty-eight martyrs, against the demise of three thousand infidels.

That was his count. The Americans of course suppressed it, claiming much less.

"Of course they play it down," said al-Bhaddahi. "The number is not important, in any event. When will you strike again?"

"I am ready to start preparing immediately," said Ghadab.

"Good. We have found you a very suitable bunker. The African will address your other needs so the mission may be fulfilled."

GHADAB THOUGHT "BUNKER" WAS A FIGURE OF speech, but in fact the place *was* a bunker, entered through a tunnel that slanted so sharply downward that Ghadab worried with each step that he would slip. Located on the northern outskirts of the city, the facility was part of an army base abandoned at least ten years before the war. The surrounding buildings were long gone; small piles of rubble remained, but most of the area had been bulldozed clean.

The bunker's walls were bare when they arrived; furniture still needed to be brought in. But the place was more than large enough, bigger than what he had used in Libya by a factor of three or four. There were twelve rooms of various sizes, along with a galley and two bathrooms, one at either end of the long central hall. A musky odor mixed with the scent of bleach; the air circulated poorly. But the facility had nearly twelve feet of dirt and rock atop a reinforced concrete roof no less than four feet thick. Electricity was supplied by a generator near the entrance; a backup generator was located at the rear, buried in its own vault. Communications were handled by a telephone line that ran to the road, as well as a satellite and cell-phone link back near the highway, reached by a dedicated (and buried) line.

"I have a dozen men at your disposal," the African told Ghadab. "They will help you organize the rooms and do anything you require."

"I only want my people here," said Ghadab.

"Understood. We have furniture and the gear you need on its way."

"Then you can leave me," said Ghadab. "Thank you."

"You are going to stay in an empty bunker?"

"I need to think. There is no better place."

"How will you get back to the city?"

"I will stay here until my men arrive."

"As you wish," said the African, nodding. "Your dedication is truly one of our greatest assets."

"Everything comes from God," said Ghadab lightly.

30

Boston—the next day

CHELSEA POUNDED THE TREADMILL, PUSHING HERself with one eye on the heart meter.

One-ninety-five. Well above her target rate. But she had more in her. She leaned her head forward and threw more energy into her legs.

The workouts were the only breaks she took from work now. Tracking the bastard who'd planned the attack had become everything. She saw encryptions and coding and maps overlaid with Arabic even when she closed her eyes. Pounding her body in the gym was the only way to clear it.

"Hey!"

Chelsea jerked her head and saw Borya standing next to her. She pulled off one of her earphones, but kept running.

"Uh, Mr. Massina wanted to see you," said the intern. "I guess it's kind of important. Mr. Chiang sent me down."

"OK." Chelsea dropped into a trot, cooling down. "You're here early."

"No, it's five. I'm, uh, on my way home."

"Oh."

"Was there something you wanted me to do?"

"I've been neglecting you," admitted Chelsea. "I'm sorry."

"It's good. I got a lot of school work."

"Next week, we'll start on a new project. OK?"

"Deal."

Twenty minutes later, hair still wet from the shower, Chelsea knocked on the clear glass door to Massina's outer office. His assistant buzzed her in. Massina, seeing her, went to his own door and ushered her inside.

"How are you doing?" Massina asked as he slipped into his chair behind his desk.

"Fantastic," Chelsea told him.

"You were in the gym?"

"Yes. It helps me think."

"Something new?"

"I always worked out," she said defensively. It was a lie, or at least an exaggeration, but his tone made her uncomfortable. Too . . . *concerned.*

"Beefy says you're bringing a pistol to work."

"I leave it with security at the front. I have a concealed permit."

"You think you need the gun?"

"I do."

Massina nodded.

"Is that it?" asked Chelsea.

"An old friend of yours was here today," said Massina. "Yuri Johansen. I showed him the information your team developed."

"It's Chiang's team. I just helped."

"Right."

"I want to continue working on it. We can find more out about Ghadab. I've found his family name," she added. "Samir Abdubin. He has a sister in Saudi Arabia."

"Is she connected to his network?"

"I'm not sure yet."

"The government is putting together a team to deal with Ghadab," said Massina. His eyes held hers. "They're going to use some of our gear. I need two people—"

"I want to be one of them."

"Maybe you should wait to hear what it is you're volunteering for before jumping off the ledge." Massina got up from his chair and began to pace around the office. When he spoke, he sounded as if he was talking to himself as much as to her. "I need two people who can handle a variety of things. One would be more on the operational side, watching our stuff and making sure the bots are deployed correctly. The other person has to be a jack-of-all-trades, someone who can code and look after the computers."

"That's me."

He looked at her without speaking.

"I'm going," she insisted. "I was in the Ukraine."

"This is a little different. And the hotel—"

"What happened in the hotel doesn't bother me."

"Not even a little?"

"No."

Massina stopped walking. "You want to get this guy?"

"You know I do."

"So do I. You'd stay behind the lines? Do what Johansen tells you?"

"Of course."

"Be ready to travel Friday. Just personal items. The weather will be warm, and there shouldn't be much rain."

Massina watched Chelsea as she left.

She was happy. Not jumping-up-and-down happy, but determined, set—he hadn't seen her like that since the attacks.

Was he doing the right thing?

There were many reasons she *should* go: she knew the equipment they would need; she was one of the best if not *the* best on-the-fly developers he had; she could code with just about anyone; she'd worked on and invented many of the systems that Johansen needed.

She'd already been exposed to a dangerous job in the Ukraine and handled it without a problem. There was no question that she was motivated.

Extremely motivated.

But maybe *too* motivated.

No. If anyone was too motivated it was him.

The phone buzzed. It was his assistant, telling him he was due downtown, at the event Jimmy had asked him to attend.

"The car is waiting," she said.

"All right," he said, rising. "Call Yuri Johansen. Tell him I have the volunteers lined up."

31

Syria—later that day

By THE TIME THE FIRST OF HIS MEN ARRIVED IN THE
morning, Ghadab had hooked the television
screens to the external satellite, allowing them
to monitor the international news. By nightfall,
they had the command room set up, along with
sleeping quarters and a place for making tea and
reheating meals. The men had been assigned
rooms throughout the city, but Ghadab knew
from experience that they would more often
than not sleep here while work was being done.
The group would gather preliminary intelligence, researching likely targets, potential recruits, and methods. When all was ready—weeks
perhaps, though he would push to be finished
as quickly as possible—they would disperse to
finalize plans and begin arrangements, returning at intervals as the project progressed. While
encrypted and coded messages were important,
the in-person meetings and planning sessions
were vital forums, and Ghadab emphasized that

truly critical information should only be passed in person.

The last of his team—Po, a refugee from Britain who'd studied at Cambridge before receiving the call to jihad—arrived an hour after dark. Ghadab elected to return to the city and the restaurant where he'd been given quarters so they could share a meal.

He was surprised to find it overflowing. The place was popular with the Caliphate elite, and there was a long line outside the door when he and his eight companions showed up.

They were about to turn away when one of the waiters ran to Ghadab and urged him and his group inside.

"The house's special room is at your disposal," said the man. He looked Syrian, but his Arabic was stilted and his accent so difficult that Ghadab suspected the man was some sort of spy.

"Where are you from, brother?" asked Ghadab.

"France, your honor."

"How are you here?"

"To join the struggle." The man beamed. "Today I work as a waiter, tomorrow I will be a soldier, God willing."

"Yes, God willing," said Ghadab.

He waved at the others to follow. The waiter brought them through the dining room to a large back room, dimly lit, where two other men were in the process of pushing small tables together to form one big enough to accommodate Ghadab's group. The room had been used as a private club room under the Syrian imposter; despite the Koran's strictures against alcohol, it had served liquor freely until the arrival of the Caliphate. All of the bottles had been removed, of course, but there was still a long bar at one end. Two large urns, one for coffee and one for tea, had been placed at the center, but these were flanked by glasses in various sizes and shapes, stacked at regular intervals as if they were waiting to be called to action.

A cloth was spread over the table, and chairs assembled. Ghadab's crew found their places as dishes and tableware were set. Before Ghadab could order, trays were brought: bread with tabbouleh and dips, an eggplant dish and some relishes.

"The lamb is being prepared," said the waiter. "It will be ready presently."

The waiters were pouring water when Khalid of Portugal got up to examine the televisions behind the bar. Khalid was a soccer fan and hoped to see some European game, but instead stopped at Al Jazeera news channel, recognizing the video they were showing.

"Boston!" he said.

It was a video showing the immediate aftermath of the attack Ghadab and most of this group had planned. Surely this was a sign—Ghadab rose and led the others to the bar to watch the broadcast.

The video was a compilation of scenes Ghadab had seen in Libya, but that did not lessen its impact.

The images flipped by quickly—the burned-out restaurant, bodies in the street, smoke pouring from the hotel.

"God is great!" shouted one of his men as the montage ended and a newscaster appeared on the screen.

"Hush now," said Ghadab. "Let us hear the infidel."

The journalist said they were going live to Boston, for a press conference with the President and the Governor.

An image of the U.S. President filled the screen. Khalid spit at the television.

"The devils speak!" said another of Ghadab's men.

The camera stopped on a man who was walking to the podium. He was short, dressed in a suit.

Words appeared across the bottom of the screen, English with Arabic below.

Louis Massina, CEO/President Smart Metal

The television announcer explained who he was: an inventor, a man who made robots, prominent in local affairs.

"He lost his right arm as a young man," she continued. "The prosthetic he uses is made by his company. It is just a sideline, but the artificial limbs they manufacture are among the most advanced in the world."

Ghadab looked at the arm with interest. It was

impossible to tell the limb was fake, at least from the television.

The American looked directly at the camera.

"I have a message for the Daesh," he said bitterly. "We are not defeated. We will hunt you down and dispose of you."

A few brothers started to laugh.

"Quiet," commanded Ghadab. There was something about this man, something that angered Ghadab—something dangerous as well.

"We're going to get those bastards," said the American. "We're going to wipe them from the face of the earth. We will. And no one will mess with us again."

The men began to boo.

Ghadab raised his hand. Khalid flipped off the television.

"They have not learned humility," Ghadab told the others. "Clearly they require another dose of education."

He turned to Khalid. "Find out all you can about this one. We'll see how he likes the feeling of his skin peeled off from the inside."

TAKEDOWN

———

Flash forward

Syria—three months after the attack on Boston

*T*HE PLANES WERE *R*USSIAN—AND *R*USSIA WASN'T ON *their side, not today, not any day.*

Johansen grabbed the handset to talk with the team in the field. Chelsea, Johnny, and the others needed to get to safety—now.

How ironic: they'd gotten past the most ferocious murderers on the planet and now were endangered by bozos who couldn't find their target city without a map from the CIA.

Real time

32

Two weeks earlier
Undisclosed location—Day 13

JOHNNY GIVENS FELL OUT OF THE HELICOPTER, HIS balance thrown off by fatigue and a sudden shift in the wind that rocked the chopper backward. He pushed right when he should have gone left, then caught himself, jerking back like a wide receiver running a square-in. Grit kicked up by the helicopter's blades sprayed across his path as Johnny ran toward the rendezvous point some fifty yards ahead.

Something flared ahead.

"Incoming!" yelled the team leader over the team radio.

Johnny pushed harder, increasing his speed. More flares.

OK, hit the dirt.

He slid to the ground, then pulled the small multi-control unit from the thigh pocket on his right pants leg. The flexible organic LEDs unfurled, revealing a screen. Johnny pressed his right thumb on it, bringing the device to life.

"Bird 1, view," said Johnny, talking to a Smart Metal UAV overhead.

A view of the battlefield snapped onto the screen.

"Identify fire."

A grid appeared over the image. A red circle flashed on one of the squares to the right.

"Share data," commanded Johnny. "Destiny, take out the enemy unit in Grid 1-D."

Destiny—a rebuilt Global Hawk Block 30 outfitted with GBU-53/B small diameter bombs—took the target from the smaller drone. Within seconds, a single small-diameter bomb fell from the aircraft.

"Stand by for explosion," Johnny warned the rest of the team.

A second later, a mushroom of smoke bloomed at the eastern end of the target area. The gunfire stopped.

"We're clear!" yelled Johnny, scrambling to his feet.

CHELSEA GOODMAN HAD A STITCH IN HER RIBS AND had twisted her ankle slightly when she got out of the helicopter, but there was no turning back now, no quitting.

You volunteered. Suck it up!

Her dad's voice.

She reached the rendezvous point and tapped Fred Rosen, the CIA paramilitary officer in charge, then moved next to the tail gunner.

"You're late," said Rosen over the radio. "Thought we'd have to do this without you, little girl."

She couldn't think of a comeback.

THEY LINED UP ON THE HOUSE. JOHNNY WAS SUP-posed to stay back with the second group, controlling the drones and communicating with the support units. But three members of the first group had been taken out by the earlier gunfire, and so he handed the control unit over to Chelsea and took a position behind the second breacher.

This was the most dangerous part of the assault. They'd lost any possibility of strategic surprise—the shooting surely woke up the house's inhabitants—and while one could argue that they had tactical surprise in their favor, since they were determining when to make their entrance, in truth, any advantage was razor thin.

Johnny readied his gun. Smashing your way into a house produced an enormous adrenaline flow, but in some ways that energy was the enemy. You had to stay within yourself, act exactly as you'd been trained to act.

"Three—two—"

Boom!

"Go!" shouted Rosen as the charge on the door blew off the lock.

In the next second, the breacher shouldered the door out of his way, bursting inside as a pair of flash-bang grenades paralyzed the jihadist in the front hall.

The second man through shot the jihadist in the head.

Johnny ran past, following the lead man to the staircase. They knew from the Nightbird UAV that there were two more terrorists upstairs, and their "jackpot"—a hostage with information they needed.

Bullets spit down the stairs.

"Shit!" screamed the lead man, flattening himself against the wall.

Johnny took a small, spherical mech from his pocket and flung it up the stairs. It bounced off the wall and came to rest on the landing. Tapping his control unit, Johnny connected to the "ball," viewing the image synthesized from its embedded IR and optical cameras.

"Three guys at the end of the hallway," said Johnny.

"Which one's Jackpot?" asked Rosen.

"Can't tell."

"Taser them all. Can't risk killing Jackpot."

"They all have guns," said Johnny. "Something's not right here."

"Taser them all."

Johnny reached to his back and undid the Velcro straps holding the Taser shotgun to his tac vest. Looking something like a Remington 870 with a drum magazine and a 1950s Buck Rogers Day-Glo yellow back end, the Taser fired a small web of electric charges. Get hit anywhere on your body and the charge put you down within microseconds. It could work through clothes as well, though not as dependably.

Which was why he aimed for the face.

Johnny got off a shot before he was hit. He fired twice more, then rolled back, dazed—a round had hit his vest near his shoulder. Though the ceramic plate stopped the bullet and absorbed a good deal of the impact, the blow nonetheless sent a shock through his body. It was as if someone had flipped an on-off switch, temporarily paralyzing his systems. He gasped for air as if he'd lost his breath.

The other members of the team scrambled past him. The three men at the end of the hallway were all down, disabled by the Taser rounds Johnny and the leader had fired.

"Get the hypos in them, cuff 'em," shouted the leader. "Let's go! Let's go."

By the time Johnny got to his feet, the men were trussed and being dragged into one of the rooms. Johnny got up and tapped the man who was guarding the stairs.

"I got this," Johnny said, releasing him to help the others in the room.

Gunfire stoked up outside.

"We need that resistance cleared so the chopper can come in!" said someone over the team radio.

Cʜᴇʟsᴇᴀ sᴡᴇᴘᴛ ʜᴇʀ ʜᴀɴᴅ ᴏᴠᴇʀ ᴛʜᴇ sᴄʀᴇᴇɴ, commanding a refresh. For some reason the infrared camera on the Nightbird UAV had stopped
working.

"Chopper is inbound!" boomed the voice of
the team leader over the radio. "We need that
resistance suppressed!"

That was her job—command Destiny to bomb
the positions. But without the help of the other
UAV, she had to manually calculate the targets:
Destiny was a dumb bird, incapable of selecting
targets on its own.

She couldn't see the enemy, but she knew the
gunfire was coming from positions some five
hundred yards away, behind trees and possibly a
stone wall. So what she had to do was time two
attacks—one as the helicopter came in, then a
second as it took off.

She looked at the grid on the screen and
mentally calculated their position against the
enemy's.

*We have to move back. We're supposed to be farther
away.*

What's the backup position? Delta or Beta?

Shit!

She keyed her mike. "Team, move to pickup
point, pickup point . . ."

Why was her brain freezing on this, of all
things?

"Move to Delta," said Rosen over the radio.
"Prepare for evac."

Chelsea tapped the right side of the screen,

opening the window that showed the pickup helicopter's com section. A double tap sent an audible message over the encrypted line directing it to Delta.

The helicopter's pilot acknowledged. He was two minutes away.

Chelsea went back to the grid and designated the target area for Destiny, directing a line barrage of attacks with half its remaining missiles.

"Launch attack in thirty," she told it. "Attack in thirty seconds."

She turned toward where the gunfire was coming from and waited.

Red flared in plumes of black against the gray distance. The air popped.

Got him!

Chelsea felt herself being pulled to her feet.

"Hey!" yelled one of her teammates. "You gotta get to the exfil! Here's the chopper!"

THOUGH HE WAS THE LAST ONE OUT OF THE HOUSE, Johnny had to pace himself as he ran, consciously holding himself back so he wouldn't pass the others. His legs were just that—*his* legs, completely part of him, exactly as his "real" ones had been before the accident. The only difference was, these were about ten times stronger, considerably faster, and not prone to cramping, tiring, or even getting a mosquito bite.

Not that they were better. They were just . . . his.

The helicopter appeared in a whirl of dust and

dirt. Johnny turned quickly, making sure they weren't followed.

Something moved in the shadows to his right. He stopped. The night glasses were powerful enough to illuminate even a mouse at a hundred yards, but they couldn't see through solid objects, and his vision was blocked by a wall. He waited a few seconds, unsure if he'd actually seen anything or if it had all been a figment of his imagination.

"Chopper! Chopper!" yelled the team leader. "Count off!"

The others were getting aboard, calling out a number as they got inside.

Johnny waited, covering the others, scanning the shadows. It was his turn to go, past his turn.

Nothing was there.

Go!

He leveled his gun and fired in the direction of the house. He kept firing, emptying the magazine as he walked backward to the chopper. Someone grabbed him, pulling.

"In!"

Johnny turned and threw himself across the deck of the helicopter as it swept sideways and swung into the sky. Chelsea was next to him.

"Hey!" he yelled to her. "Thanks."

In the next moment there was a flash, then a rumble.

They'd been hit by a surface-to-air missile.

33

Undisclosed location—moments later

JOHANSEN SHOOK HIS HEAD.

"All right," he shouted, tapping his clipboard against his leg as he walked around the "crash" site. "Exercise over. Everybody up."

One by one, the "dead" rose.

"I think I would have survived the crash," quipped Charles "Manson" Burgoyne.

"Recovery vehicles are that way," said Johansen. "Breakfast and debrief in twenty."

"I want some serious coffee," said Johnny.

"I'd rather a beer," said Burgoyne.

JOHNNY DIDN'T REALIZE HOW HUNGRY HE WAS UNTIL he went back for thirds, chowing down on the excellent prime rib. He hadn't eaten like this since coming to Arizona to train.

Actually, he hadn't eaten like this in years. The CIA knew how to put out a spread.

He stayed away from the beer, refilling his coffee cup. Walking back from the buffet table, he noticed Chelsea sitting by herself. She'd changed and showered, and was huddled over a cup of coffee.

"Hey," he told her, walking over. "This place taken?"

She looked up glumly, then shrugged.

"What's up?" he asked, putting down his plate.

"I fucked up."

"How?"

"I couldn't figure out where to aim the suppressing fire."

"You took out the first wave," Johnny told her. "That missile that got us came from the hill, outside of the landing zone."

"I didn't see them."

"They made it so we couldn't succeed," said Johnny. "We had shit like this at the Bureau. You see the team getting cocky, so you put them in their place. Relax. We kicked ass."

Johnny reached over gingerly and patted her on the back. Chelsea bristled, and he pulled his hand away.

She'd been very standoffish the entire time they'd been training, avoiding him even.

He told himself it was a male-female thing—she had to appear tough and went out of her way to do it. There was only one other woman on the team, Krista Weather, a former Air Force pararescuer or PJ, and even he realized the atmosphere was pretty macho.

Or maybe this was too much for her. The training sessions were pretty damn extreme, beyond even those he'd been through in the Army or the FBI.

"You OK?" he asked.

"Perfect," said Chelsea, rising with her coffee cup. "Just need a refill."

Johnny noted silently that it was more than half-full.

ALL HER LIFE, CHELSEA HAD BEEN AMONG THE BEST, if not the best, at everything she did. Even field hockey, at least on her high school team.

But now, here, she felt like a failure. She'd screwed up and gotten them all killed.

She'd directed the second attack back at the wall, rather than looking for a wide scan from the backup bird, a surveillance drone supplied by the Air Force. She could have—should have—done that. She knew the procedure. She'd practiced.

In a few minutes, once they did the debrief, everyone was going to know.

Was that what bothered her the most—her ego? Everyone knowing she was capable of screwing up?

No, it was the hesitation itself, the way her brain hadn't worked properly. Her brain hadn't worked properly the entire time they'd been training.

Maybe she shouldn't have volunteered in the first place. This was a hell of a lot harder than she'd expected.

Give up?

Weak. Weakling.

I'm not weak. I'm small, tiny compared to most of these guys. But I'm not weak.

Chelsea topped off her coffee cup and glanced over at Johnny. She was embarrassed to go back over.

Why?

Because he knew how vulnerable she really was. He knew she was mostly bluster and bullshit. He'd seen her vulnerable. And that wasn't who she wanted to be.

"All right," said Johansen, walking to the front. "Everyone full? Ready for a nap?"

One or two of the team members laughed. Everyone else had had their sense of humor pounded out of them on the range.

"This was designed as an impossible exercise," said Johansen. "We kept throwing problems at you, left and right, trying to screw you up. And you held up well. So, good. But there's always room for improvement."

Johansen took a step forward as a screen lowered at the front of the room. He began talking about contingencies and communications, "the two C's."

He was big on axioms.

Why the hell did I volunteer for this? Chelsea asked herself for the millionth time. *Who the hell do I think I am?*

34

Over Arizona—two hours later

MASSINA CHECKED HIS WATCH. THEY WERE ROUGHLY five minutes from landing. Time for one more call, maybe two.

He had at least ten important ones to make.

He decided to go with the first one on the list. It was Jimmy Gorman.

Probably not all that important, he thought, punching the number to redial. But it was too late to hang up.

"Louis, is this you?" boomed Gorman's voice.

"It's me, Jimmy. What's up?"

"The governor is hoping to have dinner with you."

"Are you his social secretary now?"

"I should be so lucky. All that free food? No, he asked me to set it up. He loved your speech. Loves it. Raving about it. Wants to get you to run for office."

"That is never going to happen," said Massina.

"Gotta keep him happy. He'll take away the tax credits on your building if you don't keep him happy."

"I received *no* tax credits for that building." It was a point of honor for him, and even the hint touched a nerve. "We get no special treatment from the government and we want none."

"Joking, joking. Relax. Check your schedule and get back to me. I guarantee he'll be there."

Massina hung up before Gorman could continue.

The screen in front of him showed the next call he should make, with a note from his assistant: Charlie Rose re. show. Loved what you said at event. Wants to talk personally.

That would be a long call, no? He looked at the next name on the list—a business associate from Colorado interested in a joint venture.

That would be an even *longer* call.

"Excuse me, sir," said the steward. "We're about to land. We lose the satellite on approach."

"Thank you." Massina flipped over to his message board, running through it quickly. His assistant had just sent a laundry list of things that he needed to do:

Good Morning America needs an answer.

GM contract ready.

Falco needs—

The screen blinked, and an icon appeared, indicating their communications link had just been jammed.

"Off the grid," he said to himself, turning off the laptop. "Thank God."

Mᴀssɪɴᴀ ᴡᴀs ᴀᴛ ᴛʜᴇ ᴅᴏᴏʀ ʙᴇғᴏʀᴇ Tᴇʟᴀᴋᴜs and Chevy Mangro stirred from their seats; they'd slept nearly the entire flight—a small down payment on nearly a month's work of sleep deprivation.

A pair of Jeep Wrangler Unlimiteds drove up to the Gulfstream's ladder. Johansen hopped out of the first one, moving with a spry energy that he'd never demonstrated in Boston or D.C. Shaded by a baseball cap, his tanned face looked twenty years younger. It was only when you stared that you saw the lines around his eyes.

"Welcome to Never-Never Land," Johansen said. "How was your flight?"

"Fine."

"Not as luxurious as you're used to, I guess," said Johansen.

"I fly commercial."

"Is that wise from a security point of view?"

Massina shrugged. In truth it probably wasn't, at least according to Bozzone, but he reasoned that there were security risks no matter what.

"I'm afraid I'm going to have to ask you for your cell phones and any other electronic devices," said Johansen.

"I left them in the plane," said Massina. He glanced over his shoulder to make sure Telakus and Chevy had complied. They nodded.

"Good. Let's get to it."

Johansen got back behind the wheel; Massina sat next to him, and they drove alone to the "Bunkhouse"—a low-slung building nearly ten miles away that functioned as the facility's nerve center. Dirt furled up behind them as they drove, Johansen managing a good clip on the hardscrabble trail. An occasional building intruded on the view, which otherwise ran for miles to a row of white-capped mountains that looked to be holding up the sky. Neither man spoke until Massina asked Johansen how Johnny and Chelsea were.

"Very well," said Johansen. "She's tough. Stoic. I like that."

"Chelsea," said Massina.

"Yup. She's a hell of a girl."

"I wouldn't call her a girl," said Massina.

"They're all girls and boys to me," confessed Johansen.

"Johnny?" asked Massina.

"He's a natural. But I expected that with his résumé. This was all about team building," added Johansen. "I wanted them involved because I want them to work with the others smoothly. She won't be in danger," he added. "Chelsea will be behind the lines. We won't take chances."

"Of course not," said Massina, though they both knew that was a lie.

35

Syria—around the same time

THE KNIFE WAS CRUSTED WITH DIRT, ITS EDGE DULL. Even so, Ghadab immediately realized its worth.

He picked up the one next to it on the table.

"How much?" he asked the man.

"Two hundred Syrian pounds."

"You use the infidels' money?"

"The government has decreed it lawful," said the merchant quickly. "If you have our holy currency, of course I would prefer that."

"And if I have euros?" asked Ghadab.

"I'm sorry, brother," said the man, looking him over quickly. "I will not be able to help you."

"Are there places where they can be exchanged?"

"I would not want to deal with anyone who is a barbarian," said the man. "I'm sure it's not your intention to sin, and I mean no insult, but the law must be followed."

So perfect an answer he had surely rehearsed it, thought Ghadab. He picked up the knife he really wanted. "How much for this one?"

"A hundred thousand pounds."

A hundred thousand pounds would be roughly a hundred euros. Given the quality and age of the blade, it was a bargain, but Ghadab sensed he could get it for far less.

"It's very old and has to be sharpened," he told the man.

"Let me tell you about this knife, brother," said the merchant. "It is a khanjar. It is very special. Used for ceremonies. Oh, an ancient blade—imagine the great men who held this in their hand. Their honor flows to you. Should you buy it, of course."

"Really? This knife?"

"Do you not know the style? It is distinctive." The merchant continued, giving him some basic information about how the curved blade would cut, then embellishing this particular one with a story of how it was passed down from a former Iraqi prince.

"How did it make it across the border?" asked Ghadab. He suspected the story had been fabricated, but it was a good tale.

"Ah, how does anything cross a border?" said the man. "I'm told it came across with a tribesman in the last war with the infidels, sold for the price of three meals."

"I'll give you three meals for it, then," said Ghadab.

"I am not as desperate as the tribesman."

A bit more haggling, and they reached a good price—fifty thousand Syrian pounds. Ghadab took it across the bazaar and found a man to clean and sharpen it while he watched. Two small jewels were missing just above the hilt, and the gold at the top of the dog-bone-shaped handle was worn off, but the curved blade was pristine, strong, well-tempered, and now razor sharp. The weapon was weighted perfectly; it felt like a claw in his hand, one he'd been born with.

He carried it back to his temporary home above the restaurant. Shadaa was waiting for him when he arrived, standing near the door exactly as he had left her that morning, wearing an abaya and hijab, the black robe too long so that it folded on the ground, and her head fully covered, even though they were inside.

"Master," she said.

"Do not call me that!"

"But—"

Darkness enveloped him. He swung his hand up, the knife blade cutting the air with a loud *whoosh*. Ghadab took a step toward the girl, whose body seemed to shrivel before him.

Rage filled every corner of the room. Ghadab drew his arm back, ready to strike with the knife. The girl closed her eyes. Her lips moved in prayer.

Something pulled his arm back. The blackness turned to gray, and for a moment there was nothing in the universe but Ghadab and the girl given to him as a slave.

He could do whatever he wanted and no one would fault him.

"Tell me about yourself," he said.

She stopped mumbling her prayer and opened her eyes.

"Go ahead," he prompted. "Where were you born?"

"Mosul. Iraq."

"Your tribe?"

"Jubar," she said. "But we are Sunni, my family."

Jubar was a large tribe, and a good portion Shia, as she intimated. He considered quizzing her on her beliefs—clearly she expected he would have some doubts, given the way she answered—but her eyes, rimmed with tears, convinced him she was sincere.

"Why were you made a slave?" he asked.

"My father and brother fought against the Caliphate. It is my great shame."

"Were they brave men?"

She hesitated. "They were."

"Misguided," prompted Ghadab.

She didn't answer. That stubbornness impressed him—she was loyal to her family, a good trait, even in one whose family had sinned.

"I can please you," she offered.

Ghadab laughed. "I don't want to be pleased. I'm going to give you back to the African."

She fell to her knees as if in slow motion. He could guess why—the African would think that she had displeased Ghadab in some way. At best, she would be whipped severely and passed on to another warrior. At worst, death, with unimaginable pain.

Better to slit her throat himself; it would be more merciful.

Ghadab looked at the knife in his hand. "Do you know what this is?"

She didn't answer. He stepped toward her and put the blade to her chin—gently. With a light touch, he pushed her head up to look at him.

"Do you know what this is?" he asked again.

"A knife."

"Not just a knife. The curved blade?"

She shuddered.

"My grandfather ten generations ago was a prince," Ghadab told her. He closed his eyes and saw the prince riding his stallion across the sands. The image, though borrowed from American cinema, was true to history; Ghadab's ancestor had led his people against the Portuguese in a failed uprising.

He was brave, but premature; he did not understand the prophecies as Ghadab did.

Tears leaked from the girl's eyes, though she struggled not to sob. Ghadab edged the blade against her neck, pressing very gently, rocking it back and forth.

So easy to snatch her life.

He withdrew the knife.

"I am going to rest," he told her. "Make sure no one enters."

36

Undisclosed location—around the same time

BESIDES FRESH INTELLIGENCE ON GHADAB AND Daesh, Massina had brought along a few more "goodies"—tools he thought would prove useful for Johansen in his operation. Among them were lightweight bulletproof vests constructed of a carbon-boron compound the engineers dubbed "Bubble Wrap." The nickname was obvious: the inserts, which took the place of traditional ceramic plates in standard armor, looked exactly like the sort of stuff you wrapped delicate china in before giving it to FedEx.

"It'll take a fifty-caliber round to pop them," Chevy quipped, showing them off to the two dozen members of the unit Johansen had assembled. Most were ex-military men recruited as paramilitary operatives by the CIA; all were on contract through a third-party company rather than being regular Agency employees.

Plausible deniability if things went to hell.

"The force will knock you down," continued

Chevy, "and it'll hurt like a sonofabitch, but you'll live."

Sweater thin, the vest was a spin-off from a survivable demolitions mech; Massina brought two of those along as well. Except for the material they were made of, they looked very much like standard bomb-disposal bots—six-wheeled critters with three arms, each optimized for a different task. One arm featured a soldering iron tip on the "finger" of one of the arms; field tests by the Army on an earlier model had suggested this would help the mechs modify bomb wiring to destroy the bomb in place using the bomb's own circuitry.

Far more versatile, though somewhat less durable, was "Peter"—officially RBT PJT 23-A, a bot with autonomous intelligence that Chelsea had led the development on. Unlike purpose-built robots, Peter could be given an assignment—"rescue the little girl from that burning building"—and then decide on his own how to proceed. Though it looked like a walking Erector set—it had four appendages that functioned as legs or arms, depending on the situation—Peter was far closer to humans in his capabilities than any anthropomorphic competitor.

In the Smart Metal lexicon, mechs and bots differed in that the former were designed for a specific task and generally had limited native intelligence; the latter were more versatile and, at least to some degree, autonomous. But the line between them constantly shifted and blurred, and the terms were becoming interchangeable even within the company.

UAVs were the aerial equivalent of the bots and mechs. Besides the ones that had been used in the morning exercise—Destiny, Hum, and Nightbird—Smart Metal had provided an aircraft small enough to be hidden in the palm of a hand. Made of metal, it looked like a boxy, twin-tailed paper airplane, with a micro-sized engine and a small propeller at the rear of the stubby body. Powered by a battery and launched with a heave, it could stay aloft for a little over ten minutes and was designed to provide immediate tactical video, relayed to a personal or central link. They called it "Stubby"—these were engineers, not poets.

The CIA had its own goodies, including the Tasers or "Nerf guns." Johansen would also "borrow" feeds from military assets already in theater—which basically meant Global Hawks, the large UAVs that functioned as spy planes. The team would use a new com system tweaked by Massina's engineers to seamlessly interface with transmissions and feeds in a variety of formats. They had also tweaked a portable Arabic translator, making it small enough to fit into an earbud.

Briefing nearly done, Johansen asked Massina to take the floor.

"I just want you all to know how much we appreciate what you're doing," he said. "All of Boston is behind you. Godspeed."

This is a strange place I've reached, Massina thought as the audience applauded. *Not one I could have imagined a year ago.*

"YOU READY?" JOHNNY ASKED CHELSEA AS SHE rose.

"I'm just going to go to bed."

"I meant for tomorrow. For everything."

"Oh." She shrugged. "Yeah."

"I'm pretty excited," he told her. "I feel like we're really doing something."

She looked at him as if he'd just spoken in tongues and couldn't decipher his meaning.

"I'm going to get some rest," she said. "You should, too."

"Come out with us," he said. "We're going into town."

"Thanks. But no." She squeezed his forearm gently, then walked away.

MASSINA FOLLOWED JOHANSEN DOWN A HALLWAY whose rough stone walls wore the marks of the machine that had bored them. The CIA officer stopped in front of a closed door and put his palm on a glass plate near the handle. A numbered keyboard appeared when he removed his hand; he punched a code and the door slid open, revealing a paneled lounge that would not have been out of place in a fancy hotel. An elaborate bar made of maple and exotic inlays stood along one wall. Tables covered with thick white table-cloths stood at intervals around the room.

"Looks like a nightclub," said Massina.

"We needed a place to entertain the VIPs," said Johansen apologetically, leading Massina to the bar. He reached down and retrieved a bottle of Aberlour Scotch.

"None for me," said Massina.

"Hungry?"

"No thanks."

Johansen filled a highball glass halfway. "We really appreciate your help," he told Massina, swirling the liquor gently. "Everything."

"We'll help in any way we can."

Johansen savored a sip.

"Your unit tracking Ghadab," he said pointedly. "I thought you were shutting that down."

"We are."

"Because we don't want him knowing what we're up to."

"I understand. I want to help you get this bastard," added Massina. "I'll do anything I can."

"You've done a lot. More than enough."

"We can do more."

"Some people in the Agency—" Johansen stopped short, then took another sip of the Scotch.

"Some people what?"

"You've been very outspoken." Johansen was making an effort to keep his voice neutral; Massina felt patronized. "I think it would be better if you just took a step back."

"Why?"

"Just . . . you shouldn't be out front on this. Take it down a notch. Two notches," added Johansen. "Seriously, anything you say—maybe it jeopardizes the mission on the ground."

"How?"

"Back here. It's complicated." Johansen drained the glass.

"You want me to shut up?"

"I wouldn't put it that way."

"How would you put it?"

"Your appearances in the media—they draw attention. You don't want that."

"That's true. I don't." Massina rose.

"Sure you won't have a drink?"

"Positive. I have to go."

CHELSEA ANSWERED THE DOOR IN HER SWEATS.

"I didn't mean to disturb you," Massina said.

"Just studying my Arabic." She held up a tablet. *"Masa' alkhayrsmall."*

"Good evening to you. But you're slurring a bit."

"You speak Arabic?"

"A few words. Business."

"*'Udkhul.* Come on in."

The room was about the size of a typical business-class hotel room, with similar amenities. There were two upholstered chairs on the far end. Chelsea took one, Massina the other.

"I wanted to make sure you were OK," said Massina.

"OK? Sure."

"You can back out. Opt out. No problem."

"Why would I do that?"

"I just want you to know I'm completely behind you, whatever you do," he said. "I know this is dangerous."

"Did Yuri put you up to this?"

"Not at all."

"You don't think I can handle it?"

"No. I just . . . want to make sure."

Massina couldn't find the right words. What were they?

I don't want you hurt.

"I'm going to be way behind the lines." Chelsea's tone was insistent, as if she were announcing that the project she was working on would work, despite early results suggesting the opposite.

"OK. Good." Massina reached into his pocket. "I brought you something. A watch."

It was a Timex knockoff, its main attributes being the ability to show the time in two different time zones and its price: under twenty bucks.

"It doesn't just tell the time," said Massina. "There's a locator in it. If you're ever in trouble, remove the thin plastic at the back. Put it somewhere on your skin. It'll send us a beacon. We'll use it to locate you."

"It's a transmitter?"

"No, it's passive. I don't have the resources to outfit your entire team," added Massina. "I'm giving Johnny one, too. If you're in trouble, alert us. I'll move heaven and earth to get to you."

Neither one of them spoke for a moment,

Chelsea looking at the watch, Massina looking at her. The watch contained a rare isotope that could be detected by a commercial mining satellite; removing the film created an electric charge from the skin strong enough to activate a molecular switch that released the shielding. The isotope was ridiculously expensive, and the satellite's services—only leasable for a full year—exorbitant, but the real roadblock to building more was the switch: it had to be constructed in a specialized lab and took a little more than a week to align properly. Massina had hoped to outfit all of Yuri's team, but there simply hadn't been time.

"Thanks, boss." Chelsea rose from the chair and hugged him. "Thank you."

THERE WERE ONLY TWO BARS IN THE NEAREST TOWN. Massina found Johnny and his friends in the first one he checked.

"Hey, boss," said Johnny loudly. He had to shout to be heard over the blaring country music. "This is my boss," he announced to the others at the table. "Louis Massina."

"Looks like you're all ready for another round," said Massina. "I'll get it."

Johnny came over to the bar with him.

"I wanted to say goodbye," Massina told him as they waited for the drinks. "And give you something."

He handed him a watch. "If you get in trouble, pull the vinyl backing off. We'll find you."

"Do I want to know how it works?" asked Johnny.

Massina laughed. "Probably not. I don't have the resources to outfit your entire team," he added. "But both you and Chelsea have one. So . . ." Unsure what else to say, Massina dropped a hundred-dollar bill on the bar. "I have to get back to the plane."

"You don't want a drink?" asked Johnny as he started to leave.

"I have to get back. Stay safe."

37

THE POUNDING ON THE DOOR WAS SO LOUD IT sounded like peals of thunder. Chelsea cowered on the bed, knowing that any moment the locks would give way.

It didn't happen this way.

This must be a dream.

The terrorist barged through the door. Chelsea tried to get up but couldn't. Arms and legs pinned to the bed, she saw him leaning over, climbing atop her.

Wake up! Wake up!

She screamed, and in that moment the nightmare evaporated.

Alone in the room, embarrassed, Chelsea sat up and curled her arms around her chest. She listened for a long minute, afraid someone had heard her. But there was nothing.

It was only a little after nine at night. Most of the team was probably still out drinking.

"Should have gone with Johnny," she said to the empty room. "Should have gone."

Her sweatshirt was soaked with sweat and needed to be changed. She slipped out of bed, pulling the shirt over her head as she walked to the dresser. As she bent down she remembered she'd already packed; all her clothes except what she was wearing and what she'd wear tomorrow were in the duffel bag by the door.

Naked, she crawled back under the covers, willing herself back to sleep.

38

Palmyra, Syria—five days later

Two weeks into their planning sessions, Ghadab sensed that his team had become complacent, even lazy. Ghadab himself had done the hard work two years before, planting deep agents, arranging for young devotees to infiltrate college programs, getting everyone in place. There was much left to do—security routines to be investigated, money to be moved, sleeper cells to be reactivated—but his team here seemed nonchalant, unfocused. They argued among themselves over petty things. Worse, several were spending inordinate hours at the cafés in town. So far as he knew, none were violating the law—if he had even suspected any of drinking alcohol, punishment would have been swift and final. But they lacked the discipline a successful operation required.

And so he planned an exercise in a desert village a few miles south of Dar al'Abid as Sud. Perched on the lowest slope of the mountains, the handful of buildings were grouped around what in ancient times was probably a river, but now was just an indentation in the scrubland. Government troops had recently moved through the village, setting up outposts along the highway to the east, between the settlement and Palmyra. It was roughly eighty miles away from his bunker, if they could have traveled in a straight line.

That, of course, wasn't possible.

His men assembled at one in the morning, woken personally by Ghadab.

"We are having an adventure," he told the few who dared ask why they were being summoned.

They boarded four pickups commandeered from local citizens. Using Caliphate vehicles would have entailed a requisition and unnecessary questions and even possibly interference, and Ghadab had neither the time nor the inclination to deal with such trivialities. It was far easier to walk up to the owner in the market and tell him that the truck would be returned in a few days, with a full tank of gas as payment.

No one argued. He didn't even have to show his gun, though one or two did glance at his knife—he'd bought a fine sheath for the khanjar and hung it from his belt.

They drove on the highway for an hour, following Ghadab, before he veered off five miles short of the government checkpoint. He drove another ten miles southwest over the desert, doing his best to avoid the worst of the dunes and pits as he followed his instincts and a GPS unit he'd bought at the bazaar. The dim light revealed a succession of landmarks he'd memorized the night before; finally, he came to a wide, flat plain with loose sand and stopped.

The rest of his team gathered in a semicircle around him.

"The village of Hum lies in that direction," he told them as they got out of the trucks, "ten miles. It is filled with apostates and nonbelievers. They are Shia, and they welcomed the blasphemer's army. We will show them what happens to such sinners. Here is a map of the place."

Ghadab unfolded a paper image of the place from Google Earth that he had printed earlier. A pumping station sat at one end of the village; before the war it had supplied water for the modest farms on the southern end of town. "How do we punish these apostates? What are the steps?"

"We cut these power lines first," said Idi the Sudanese. "We take over the police station and secure their weapons."

"Strike the pumping station at the same moment," said Ahmed. He was new to the team, a student from Egypt, but very promising: he had recruited two suicide bombers in Cairo before being called. "But we don't have enough explosives."

"This is a farming area, and there are not enough explosives?" prompted Ghadab.

The question sparked the group. They had been thinking in simple terms—cut power, blow up the obvious symbols of corruption. But now they began to think creatively, to see the possibilities, to appreciate the destruction they could inflict. He sat back quietly as they spoke back and forth, until at last they had an outline of a mission.

"I think it is an excellent plan," he said. "But the proof is in the doing. So let it be done."

39

Southern Kurdistan (Syria)—a few hours later

Ten years before, T'aq Ur had been a small but prosperous village on the Euphrates, dominated by Kurds but very much a part of Syria. The people who lived there, Sunni Muslims mostly, grew a variety of vegetables in the river-irrigated fields. There were pomegranate trees, olive groves, apricots. The most prosperous had goats, primarily for their own or their neighbors' tables. The meat was slaughtered by the local butcher in accordance with practices well over a thousand years old; the farming itself was only slightly more advanced. The tiny town was a place time had forgotten.

But the dictator had not. And in the early days of the revolution, he remembered that a politician who had been born there had once opposed him. The Syrian army shelled the town for a week before coming to pick through the remains.

Then came waves of rebels, some backed by Turkey, some part of ISIS. They took the village after two weeks of sieges. A counterattack by the Syrian government failed. The Russians came and bombed, ineffectively, since most of what was left by that time was rubble. A Syrian platoon backed by Iranian regulars managed to gain a foothold, only to be driven out by a Turkish-backed rebel group that numbered no more than two dozen men. The stones changed hands once or twice again, but by that time, the only inhabitants of T'aq Ur were mosquitoes. Even they soon quit the place—there wasn't enough fresh blood to live on.

The Kurds arrived in January, setting up an outpost with American help. The troops moved on within days, pushing their front farther south. T'aq Ur was finally completely free—and completely empty.

The lack of people was exactly why Johansen had chosen it as his base of operations. They were a good distance from Palmyra—roughly a seventy-minute drive across the desert—but within range of the devices that would help find Ghadab. His teams could stage from here without fear of interference or being attacked by surprise. If they needed help, the Kurds were nearby.

His headquarters was in a bunker complex the Israelis claimed had been part of Syria's clandestine nuclear program. There had been six buildings at one time; one was about the size of a small U.S. elementary school. This was now a pile of rubble; besides the bricks, it contained a number of unexploded artillery shells. The next largest building was a barracks designed to hold about a hundred soldiers. It, too, was wrecked, but it had a usable basement, and it was in the basement that Johansen set up shop.

They moved in at night. The basement was cleared easily enough, with the help of Peter and the two mechs programmed for lifting. While it was dusty and filled with spiders and even a few snakes, the walls and ceiling were sturdy, and there was plenty of room for sleeping bags. Partitions were stretched between the piers that held up the building.

They slept in the space closest to the stairs: if the roof collapsed, they'd have the best chance of getting out from there. The next night they cleared more of the building, reinforced the ceiling, then divided the area into living and working quarters.

Prep work nearly done, Johansen sent out patrols in pickups to get a feel for the area. Everyone wore nondescript fatigues; if anyone checked the labels, they'd find they came from China. As much gear as possible had been sourced from outside the U.S.; even the vehicles that had taken them there were Japanese.

Not that the charade would fool anyone.

The agency would use Massina's newly minted public profile as an antiterror firebrand to imply he was behind it all: a self-made billionaire unleashing a private army to revenge his city.

There were precedents, most notably the mission launched by Ross Perot to rescue his people kidnapped by Iran in the late '70s. The media would have a field day drawing parallels between the two men.

Johansen had lied about the Agency wanting Massina to take a lower profile. As far as they were concerned, the louder the better. He, on the other hand, worried the inventor was making himself too much of a target.

Johansen couldn't worry about that now. There were too many other things to fret about.

CHELSEA SPENT THE DAY ORGANIZING HER WORK area, setting up the control units. When the sun set, she went outside and put the bomb mechs to work clearing the artillery shells from the wreckage around them. Each shell had to be carried into the desert a mile away and quietly rendered inert. Which was a bit of a bummer— all those explosives would have made a good-sized boom.

It took longer than she expected. She had to call it quits at sunrise with about half the job still undone.

"Half day, huh?" joked Johnny as she closed down the units.

"Yeah, I'm a slacker," she told him. "Calling it quits at twenty hours. What are you doing?"

"Patrol."

"Good luck."

He looked pretty good in his long Arab shirt and baggy pants, Chelsea thought as she went downstairs. Very movie-star-like. It was hard to believe that just a few months ago, he was on respirators and in a drug-induced coma, legs gone, chest full of blood.

A HALF HOUR LATER, JOHNNY JOINED TURK AND Christian and set out south in a pickup, aiming to launch a UAV over their target area. Turk—a former SEAL who looked like an Arab, though he was born in Indiana—was at the wheel; Christian, who despite his name was a first-generation Muslim immigrant from Kurdistan, rode shotgun in the back. Johnny handled coms, in contact with the base via supplied video feeds and old-fashioned radio. While they had brought helmets that could do the same, to a man the team considered the helmets too cumbersome to use except in an actual assault. Wearing them now would make it obvious that they weren't a patrol of Daesh soldiers—which was what they hoped to pass for, at least from a distance.

After they had driven for about a half hour, they stopped to launch a Hum. With the two battery-powered engines running full-out, Johnny ran with the aircraft across a flat stretch of sand until he felt it trying to lift from his grip. Putting his head down, he increased his speed, then threw it like a javelin. The UAV tucked right, then swooped back level and began soaring, climbing slowing into the night. The sound from its electric motors faded quickly; by the time it reached 1,200 feet, it was both impossible to see or hear in the night sky.

Johnny hopped back into the pickup. He had preprogrammed the little bird to fly a figure-eight pattern above the truck, acting as a scout.

"There's a checkpoint near the road to our

east," Johnny told Turk, showing him the screen. "Five miles."

They tucked east, then south, skirting a small settlement to reach a ridge two miles due northeast of Palmyra where they could survey the city and surrounding area easily.

A pair of highways intersected near the tip of the city, making it an important crossroads. The highways themselves were barely that: they accommodated a single lane of traffic in each direction, and though paved, it was hard to tell in places because of the sand that typically covered the pavement. An airport once used by the Syrian air force sat like a dog's tail at the southeast corner of the city. The runways were too cratered for use by planes, but the Daesh forces had about two platoons' worth of men stationed in barracks there. A brackish, seasonal marsh folded against the edge of an ancient lake bed at the opposite end of the city; a smaller, similarly dead lake sat nearby.

Daesh troops were scattered at intervals around Palmyra's boundaries. Turk mapped out a path between them and set off on foot, leaving Johnny and Christian with the truck. He walked around the back of the hill to a dried creek bed, using that to get within fifty yards of a building on the city boundary. He was just about to climb over a wall into the backyard when Johnny spotted movement on a nearby rooftop.

"Seventy meters to your left, two guys on that house," he told Turk.

Turk dropped behind the wall. Johnny watched

the two figures kneel near the bricks that marked the edge of the roof. They were looking in Turk's direction, but didn't seem to be able to pick him out of the shadows.

"They see me?" asked Turk.

"Hard to tell." A moment later, one of the men began spraying his AK-47 in Turk's general direction. He ran through the entire magazine before stopping. The firing was erratic, but near enough to Turk to make it clear he'd heard or seen something.

"Shit," muttered Turk.

"Yeah. We got lights."

"Patrol?"

"Maybe—pickup coming from the center of town. One of our guys is on the phone."

"I'm gonna back out."

"Stay low." Johnny turned to Christian, who was watching the feed over his shoulder. "Maybe we should do a diversion."

"Nah. He gets out without being seen, Daesh writes this off as two guys with overactive imaginations."

Turk crawled three hundred yards to a dirt road, changed direction slightly, and then half crawled, half ran, back in their direction. By that time a patrol had arrived. They did a perfunctory search, barely looking over the wall before heading back and returning to their post in a building near the city center.

A half hour later, sure that they hadn't been detected, Johnny recovered the UAV and the three Americans headed back to their base.

40

**Southeast of Dar al'Abid as Sud, Syria—
around the same time**

IT BEGAN WITH A CAR BOMB IN THE MARKET AREA AN
hour and a half after sunrise. The brothers
used too many explosives, but that was hardly
a drawback: Ghadab grinned as he watched a
woman a block away pitched into the air by the
explosion.

She wasn't wearing a head covering when the
bomb exploded. Clearly, God had seen her and
directed her demise.

The explosion set off an alarm at police headquarters. Three of the four officers on duty were
cut down as they rushed from the building. The
fourth came out with his hands up.

He was taken to Ghadab, who was supervis-
ing the raid from a roof across the street. Without bothering to question him, Ghadab slit the
man's throat. Blood fanned the air purple-red
before he even pulled the knife away.

The ravages of war had reduced the population
to barely over two hundred, the majority women

and children. Shouting and firing their Kalashnikovs as they went door to door, Ghadab's men rousted thirty-three males, all but two or three over the age of fifty or under the age of fifteen, to an empty lot in the shadow of the old storage tanks near the center of town.

"What a pathetic collection," Ghadab told Yuge the Iraqi. "Not one of them could fight for the Caliphate."

"That one there, the fat one," said Yuge, who'd begun interrogating the captives as they were brought over. "He claims to have fought for us."

"What is he doing in the city, then?"

"He says he is a spy, with information for the Commander."

"Bring him to me."

Yuge grabbed the man by the shirt and dragged him to Ghadab. His white shirt and pants had been soaked with sweat; dirt caked on them like mud. A coil of fat above his sagging shoulders supported his head.

"Who are you?" demanded Ghadab.

"Ari, son of Rhaddad," said the man, as if he expected Ghadab to have heard of him.

"What are you doing in this village?"

"I am preparing for the brothers," claimed the man. "The infidels are all around. They are planning to strike Palmyra."

"When?"

"Soon. Very soon."

Ghadab took hold of the man's arm and dragged him toward the others, who were watching to see what would happen.

"Tell me," Ghadab shouted. "Is this man a true believer?"

No one answered. Ghadab took his knife from his belt.

"Tell me," Ghadab shouted, pointing his knife at a gray-haired prisoner. "Is this man a true believer?"

The man began to shake, but didn't speak.

"I've seen him drink," said another man.

Ghadab let go of Ari and walked to the man who'd spoken. He pointed his khanjar at his face.

"When?" demanded Ghadab.

"After the Daesh were driven out."

"You swear this?"

"May God strike me down."

Ghadab walked back to the fat man.

"The man there says you are a liar," Ghadab told him.

"With God as my witness, I swear on my children and all that is right—"

His sentence ended in a sputter and cough, his windpipe and throat slit by the fat part of Ghadab's knife.

"To lie before God is a sin punishable by death," bellowed Ghadab, turning back to the others. "Who will join the Caliphate?"

It was foolish to resist, and yet the crowd was not unanimous. Only half volunteered, all but two arguably too young to be accepted.

"Put them in the truck," Ghadab told Yuge.

Yuge and two other men herded them to a pickup they had commandeered. It wasn't hard; the men went eagerly, thankful to be spared.

Ghadab looked over the others.

"None of you will fight?" he asked.

"Please," said one of the men. "We have been in our share of battles. We are worn from the fighting. All of us." He gathered up his long shirt and held it up to reveal a scar on his belly. "The dictator's troops gave me this scar."

Ghadab leaned over and with his knife touched the top of the jagged purple gouge on the man's pelvis.

"You fought on the government's side?" asked Ghadab.

"I fought *against* the corrupt dictator," answered the man.

"I have worse scars," said Ghadab.

He pushed the knife tip against the wound. To his surprise, the old man remained stoic even as the tip liberated a trickle of blood the pure color of a poppy whose leaves had just burst open.

"Enough," said Ghadab. And with that he slashed the knife horizontally against the man's midsection, so hard that the old man folded to the ground. Ghadab knelt and slit the man's throat, bringing him a quick death—a mercy. The smell of blood intoxicated him and he lingered for a moment, absorbing it.

By the time he rose, the rest of the captives lay on the ground, shot by his men. In the distance, he heard gunfire—the "volunteers" in the truck had all been killed.

"Burn the buildings," he said. "You can take what women are suitable as slaves. Kill the rest."

41

Boston—a few hours later

With Chelsea gone, Borya had little to do. No one would tell her where her boss and mentor had gone—very likely no one knew—but gossip pointed toward a project that would avenge the Boston attacks. Naturally, Borya wanted in. But no one was going to let a teenage intern get involved in such a thing.

Barely a barrier for her.

Smart Metal's work computers were tied to a "sterile system"—there was no access to the outside world, one of the more basic precautions that the company used to protect against viruses and espionage. They did, however, have computers that could access the internet without access to the company's internal system. One day, soon after Chelsea left, Borya decided to use one to find out all she could about the terrorists who had attacked her city. Her first sessions were Google searches primarily, and a lot of reading. From there, she began trolling chat rooms where ISIS supporters hung out, then explored so-called "dark sites" hidden from normal web searches and used for transferring propaganda and untraceable communications.

She found some pretty disgusting stuff. It was fascinating to see how the perverts thought.

This wasn't what the external links were supposed to be used for, and when she reported to work after school one day and found Bozzone waiting for her in the lab, she knew she was in trouble.

Not that she let on.

"Hey, Beef," she said, greeting the security chief like an old friend. "How's it hangin'?"

"Mr. Massina wants to see you."

"Awesome."

Borya was an old hand at getting in trouble; she visited the principal's office at her Catholic school so often the receptionist had nicknamed a chair "Borya's throne." But this was different. She loved working at Smart Metal, and the tone in Bozzone's voice made it clear that she wasn't being summoned to see Mr. Massina because he had a birthday present for her. But she feigned indifference, slinging her backpack over a shoulder and following Bozzone to the elevator.

"Think the rain will stop in time for the Red Sox game?" Borya asked.

Bozzone turned his head, raised his eyebrow slightly, but said nothing. Deposited in Massina's outer office, Borya had no time to settle on a strategy as the secretary waved her right in.

Massina was at his desk, staring at his computer, chin in one hand, pen in the other.

Was it the right or the left that was fake? She couldn't remember.

"Ahhhh, Ms. Tolevi." Massina frowned. "Have a seat."

"Hey, boss." Her voice squeaked. She tried clearing her throat, but suddenly her mouth and everything in it felt drier than sandpaper.

"I see that you've been doing some extracurricular work on my time," he said.

Extracurricular?

That's it! I can claim it's for a school assignment.

"I notice that you've been doing some research on Daesh," continued Massina. "ISIS."

"I want to kill those bastards," she blurted.

"As do we all," said Massina grimly. "Who told you to do it?"

"No one."

"No one?"

It was a way out: offer up the name of someone who'd said it was OK. But that was ratting out someone, which would be against her code.

More important, there was no one to rat out.

"I did it myself."

"And you found something interesting?"

"Not yet."

"What did you find?" Massina asked.

"They use anonymous servers and some repeaters, like routing things through Ukraine and the Checkers Republic."

"Czech."

"That's what I meant." Borya felt her face flush. That was a *stupid* mistake—she knew what the damn country's name was.

Checkers. Duh!

"There are chat rooms, and they encrypt stuff," she said quickly. "Like there are a couple of personalities on there that might be interesting to follow through and see."

"You're just free-forming?" asked Massina.

"What does that mean?"

"You're doing all this on your own, without an agenda. Just talking."

"I want to find out what I can."

"That's a good attitude."

Maybe I'm not going to get fired.

"Smart Metal computers are for work projects only," said Massina, once again stern. "For various reasons. Including your safety. Even if that weren't the case, provoking these people, even getting your identity known to them—it's very, very dangerous. These people are killers."

"I know that. B-but—"

"There really can be no buts. Is that clear?"

She nodded reluctantly.

"Does your father know about this?"

"No."

"You're to explain everything you've done in detail to Mr. Bozzone. And that's it. Understood?"

"I guess."

"That is *not* the right answer." Massina rose from his desk, angry. "Do not engage these people," he added. "Understood?"

"OK," she said meekly.

Massina sensed that he had scared her, but he also realized she wouldn't stay scared for very long. She was too curious, too adventurous, and she had grown up with a father who was both a spy and a borderline mobster. So when Bozzone came to ask how things went, Massina simply shrugged.

"She'll stay off for a few days, maybe."

"As long as she doesn't use our computers," said Bozzone.

"I'm not worried about the computers."

"Neither group that tried tracking her was ISIS."

"Not yet."

Two different hacker outfits had tried to trace Borya and the system she was using, launching crude probes on the off-site servers used for the "public" internet computers. Bozzone's people had, in turn, tracked them to Asian operations, where ISIS had no known connections.

"I'll watch her," said Bozzone, with the tone of an older brother being assigned to babysit a younger sibling. "We've locked out the sites and her chat functions."

"I'm sure she'll look for a way around them," said Massina. "Keep her safe."

"I'll do my best. But—"

"No buts on this," said Massina. "Make sure it happens."

42

T'aq Ur, northern Syria—a few hours later

Cʜᴇʟsᴇᴀ sᴛᴜᴅɪᴇᴅ ᴛʜᴇ ɪᴍᴀɢᴇ ꜰʀᴏᴍ ᴛʜᴇ Nɪɢʜᴛʙɪʀᴅ UAV circling above Palmyra. Flying at 15,000 feet, the aircraft was mapping every magnetic field in the ISIS-held city. Every motor, every current, was measured and recorded by the aircraft's powerful sensors. Once the data was gathered, simple filters would identify different motor types, showing the likely locations of computers, for example, or air conditioners—both likely markers of high-ranking Daesh commanders.

"Which one of these is the prison?" asked Johansen, standing over her and trying to make sense of the splotch-covered map.

Chelsea zoomed out and overlaid the display on the afternoon's satellite image.

"Here," she said, pointing to a square at the lower right-hand corner of the screen.

"Nothing there?"

"One computer," she told him, checking the data quickly.

"They're not using it as a headquarters?"

"Doesn't look like it."

The regime had emptied the prison some months before, then blown up most of the buildings with crude barrel bombs. But two buildings remained intact, and Johansen's original intelligence had indicated it was being used as a headquarters.

"Doesn't match what you're looking for," said Chelsea. "Unless Ghadab doesn't use computers."

"They all use computers," insisted Johansen. "They're pretty modern for people who want to send the world back to the Stone Ages. What about the school?"

Chelsea recentered the image, focusing on a two-story building on the western side of town now used as the operational headquarters of the local ISIS commander.

"Lots," said Chelsea. "Twelve in the scan, and the bird isn't done."

"Good."

They could blow up the school with the touch of a button—the Destiny drone was orbiting a short distance away. But it was at best a secondary target—unless Ghadab was inside.

"Here's a site that wasn't mapped," said Chelsea, moving the image farther south. "It's a house. There are at least twenty computers there, and three good-sized air conditioners. Look."

"Is there an internet connection?"

"Can't tell. But there's a cable line. You can see where it goes underground."

"Put it on the list to watch."

"Already have."

The UAV had found clusters of six or seven computers in three other buildings that had not been ID'd for surveillance by the CIA. Two were at small businesses on the western end of the city, closest to the ancient ruins. The last was within a hundred yards of the wall where Turk had been when he spooked the guards.

"There's a bunker up here that you had marked as abandoned," Chelsea added, showing him a location several miles north of the city. "Six computers there, printers. Everything on standby, though. The power profiles are low coming in, so I'm extrapolating."

"Not being used?"

"No."

"Put it on the list anyway."

"Already did."

"The list is getting pretty long," said Johansen. "Sometimes I think we'd be better off leveling the whole city."

WHILE CHELSEA WAS FERRETING OUT POTENTIAL targets, five three-man teams were crossing the desert south, preparing to plant a web of video and ELINT bugs around the city.

Two teams would enter the city on the western highway with commercial traffic after morning prayers; there were generally a half-dozen trucks entering at that time, and the guards tended to be blasé. The infiltrators were the best Arabic speakers in the group, and to a man, looked as if they'd been born in Syria. Their targets were buildings near the city boundary.

Two other teams would enter from the fields to the south, disguised as farmworkers going home for a noonday meal. Their targets were outside the main area of the city, less heavily traveled; they, too, were competent Arabic speakers, though two had papers identifying them as foreign workers as a cover for their looks.

The fifth team, which included Johnny Givens, would plant bugs in the most heavily trafficked and dangerous part of the city. Their mission was not only the riskiest, but it also had to be completed before the others: besides the bugs, they were planting boosters that were needed to transmit data from the other sensors. Without the boosters in place, the other bugs couldn't be turned on. The mission was so risky it would be done by bots under cover of darkness.

They chose an abandoned archaeological dig at the city outskirts as their command post. Sitting on the lee side of a hill, the digs were seventy-five yards from a former Syrian army compound. That, too, was abandoned, except for a Daesh military commander and his family. En route to the main objectives, one of the bots would plant a bug to cover the home as well. Black-shirt patrols ran at roughly two-hour intervals around the city each night; the bots' incursion and route was planned accordingly.

At some point in the war, a flight of Russian aircraft had launched a bombing raid against the city with spectacular results: they had managed to miss every one of their half-dozen targets. Most of their bombs had landed on vacant land near the excavations. Johnny and the others parked their truck in one of the craters, lugging their gear to a knoll at the edge of the archaeological site.

They launched a Hum. Christian trotted to a second hill on their eastern flank, commanding the roadway from the city; Turk and Johnny got the robots ready for their mission.

Nicknamed "koalas," the bots had been pre-programmed with GPS and satellite data. About a fifth of the size of their namesakes, each unit had twelve legs, six on top and six on the bottom. The legs had three small toes with claws that could grip and enable them to climb—like actual koalas.

"How do you know if they're right side up?" asked Turk.

"I don't," answered Johnny.

They had to wait through a lengthy startup routine. One of the units did not respond to the test. Johnny replaced it—he had two backups—then launched each unit individually with verbal commands. One after the other they marched off, kicking up a trail of dust.

"Out little army," said Turk as Johnny sat down in front of the control unit. His tone was somewhere between a sneer and admiration.

Their small size and legs made the bots hard to see, but it also limited how fast they could go; 2.5 mph was their top speed. To reach the city where their targets were, they needed to first cross about a thousand yards' worth of open terrain, enter and traverse the empty compound, turn into an alley, and cross the back of another yard before reaching the streets. Stopping periodically to consider data from the Hum and a Nightbird controlled by Chelsea back at the base, it took nearly twenty minutes for the lead bot to reach the compound. The units seemed overly cautious to Johnny, but short of taking over each one individually, there was nothing he could do.

The bots split up as they approached a row of houses on the other side of the empty compound, beginning to scatter as they sought out their targets. The houses were occupied; several had people sleeping on the roofs, common in the warm Syrian nights. The bots slowed precipitously as they neared the houses, stopping whenever any of the sleeping bodies moved.

"We're way behind schedule," said Turk. "At this rate we ain't gonna make it. By a lot. You gotta speed us up."

"The only thing I can do is remove the safety protocol," said Johnny.

"What'll that do?"

"They won't stop and update their data."

"Do it."

"Yeah."

No longer pausing or worrying about being seen, the koalas moved ahead on the last routes they had programmed. They still weren't very fast, but at least they were no longer stopping every few seconds.

"I'm hearing a truck," said Christian a few minutes later. "Coming out of the traffic circle in our direction."

"Yeah, OK, I'm looking at it," said Johnny, staring at the Hum's video screen. "Couple of pickups."

"Patrol?" asked Christian.

"Early for that," said Turk.

Johnny watched the vehicles continue toward the traffic circle near the ruins where Christian was perched. The intersection was in an odd place, a remnant of an earlier traffic pattern now shunted by the decision two decades before to route the highway farther east.

"The trucks are going south," said Johnny.

"Three guys in the back of the lead," said Christian, watching through the nightscope of his rifle. "All awake."

"Something new," sneered Turk.

The lead truck drove south toward the center of town—and their target buildings. Johnny started to relax—then saw that instead of following, the second vehicle turned right, then took a quick left directly in the path of four koalas. Before he could order the bots to retreat, the truck was on them. It missed the two bots closest to the corner, but caught the other two midway across the road.

You gotta be kidding me! Murphy's Law, right?

No, my dumb decision.

Stunned, Johnny stared at the overhead image for a few seconds before switching to manual control on K4, one of the koalas that had been hit. The bot responded with a diagnostic signal indicating that it had lost mobility. K6 gave him the same code.

All of the other bots were still active. Cursing himself, Johnny put them back into cautious mode. Each immediately stopped and reassessed their surroundings and path.

"We lost two bots," he told Turk.

"Shit. What do we do?"

"We can have units pick them up on the way back," said Johnny. "The question is how to get video bugs into the two spots they're going to miss."

There was only one backup, and it couldn't carry all the bugs they had to place. And there wouldn't be enough time to recharge one of the bots when it returned—that took an hour and a half, which would surely take them past dawn.

Johnny dialed into the secure com link to confer with Chelsea about possibly moving some of the bugs so they wouldn't need to place as many. She suggested a couple of changes, but the most they could lose were two bugs.

While they were talking, one of the pickups circled back toward the koalas. This time, with their protocols back in place, the units scurried for safety.

Scurry being a relative term.

The vehicle zoomed past the buildings, continuing north toward the traffic circle. It drove north through a large residential area, then headed past a mostly abandoned slum of shacks and refugee housing, speeding to a pair of ruined buildings just short of the hills north of town, a good two and a half miles from the highway. Two figures got out, then disappeared in the rubble. The truck immediately backed out and started for Palmyra.

"Chelsea, you see that?" Johnny asked over the radio. "There's a bunker there."

"We're working on it. We spotted it earlier."

"That's near the road we were taking out."

"We'll give you a new route."

"Roger that."

JOHNNY DECIDED TO SEND HIS LONE RESERVE KOALA— K10—to the farthest video spot, then use the first returning unit to plant the last bug by swapping out the battery from the disabled unit. That was harder than he thought—after struggling with the connectors, he had to reboot and reprogram the unit by putting it into "base memory," feed the GPS target coordinates one at a time, and then go through a series of diagnostic checks with Chelsea's help. They'd just finished when she told him that Johansen wanted to talk.

"If you have a moment," she added, joking.

The light note reminded him of home. It was jarring.

"That bunker in the desert," said Johansen. "You think you can plant a video bug on the roof?"

"Maybe."

"Good."

The line snapped off before Johnny could discuss the logistics. There was a clear view of the road from the ruins; no way they could get in there. A hill to the west would give them cover, but even so, the last quarter mile was wide-open; anyone outside could easily see them, and have an even easier shot.

"We'll be spotted easily," said Turk. "Look—there's a video camera. I'm guessing there are others. Can we scavenge the batteries from the dead units?"

"They're pretty crushed," said Johnny. "We can't count on them."

"No way we get across to the bunker without being seen. I'll talk to Johansen."

"No, I have an idea," said Johnny. "We'll hold back K3 with the battery from the malfunctioning bot. We'll use that."

"So how do we get the other bugs in place here?"

"I say we put it there ourselves." He held up the screen. "Clear run if we go now."

43

North of Palmyra—around the same time

GHADAB WAS TOO ENERGIZED TO SLEEP AFTER THE operation at Hum, and so after dropping off most of his men, he returned to the bunker. Success would breed success—his people had tasted blood, and would plan and recruit with new vigor.

There were three possibilities of targets, all stupendous. He would cripple a city, do so much damage that the infidels would have to come, and Armageddon would begin.

Which city? Rome, the most impressive.

Boston kept intruding in his thoughts, egotistical, boasting Boston. The mayor, the policeman who claimed to have sent ten martyrs to their reward.

The rich man, Massina.

Ghadab paced up and down the bunker's center hall. There were many things to do, things that only he should handle: travel arrangements for his scouts, weapons, money. But he couldn't focus on any of them.

The woman slipped into his thoughts surreptitiously.

He had not had sex with her. Shadaa's body was pleasing, and it was within his right as a fighter to take her—God's just reward. But something held him back, something beyond his religious beliefs.

He was pure. But so was she—something in the way she presented herself to him, how she bowed her head in submission.

"Enough," he said aloud, urging himself back to work. He went to his office and began jotting down his orders to send his scouts to their various assignments.

But even as wrote, his thoughts drifted.

Maybe I'll go back to the restaurant when I'm done. I should check on the girl to make sure no harm has come to her.

44

Palmyra—around the same time

JOHNNY AND TURK HAD JUST REACHED THE WALL OF the abandoned compound when Johansen hailed them on the radio with a string of expletives.

"What the hell are you doing?"

"Planting the last bugs," said Turk.

"It's too risky. Send the bot and forget the bunker."

"We'll be in and out in ten minutes," said Johnny. "Relax."

They scrambled over the wall and dropped into an alley between the compound buildings. Viewed from the koalas' cameras, the alley had looked as wide as a highway. But Johnny scraped his shoulders as he followed Turk to the central courtyard. They stopped, checking with Christian to make sure it was clear, then sprinted across to the west wall. Johnny vaulted over like a gymnast. He ran up the street, waiting for Turk in the shadows near the corner.

Turk was huffing when he caught up. "Got the rope?" he managed.

"Yeah. Give me sixty seconds, then come."

Johnny crossed the street, bolting to the side of a two-story building. He leaped, arms up, and grabbed the metal edge of the roof. But the edging was too thin—he couldn't get a grip.

His legs took the shock easily but the stumps above them reverberated with the impact, sending it through his body. He took a breath, stepped back, and sprang upward again. This time he willed himself higher and managed to get his right elbow on the roof. Then he levered himself over the edge.

Johnny pulled the rope out of his ruck and tossed it down, anchoring Turk as he climbed up. Turk was halfway up when Christian warned that the patrol was approaching their street.

"Next building," said Johnny when he got up. They jumped over and ran to the lip, a low wall just high enough to keep them from being seen from the ground. Once the patrol passed, they could plant the bugs on the corners and leave.

"Damn," muttered Christian over the radio.

That's not good, thought Johnny.

IN THE COMMAND BUNKER NEARLY ONE HUNDRED miles away, Chelsea watched the Daesh patrol stop near the building where Johnny and Turk were hiding.

What had they seen?

She zoomed on Johnny, flat on the roof. There was no way the patrol could have seen him, and yet, there they were, all three men getting out of the truck.

Oh, God, she thought. *Don't let them spot him.*

Johnny heard voices over the rumble of the truck engine below. Reaching into his pocket, he took out the video bug, slid the tiny switch to activate it, then slowly edged to the corner.

"What are you doing?" whispered Turk.

"Planting the bug."

"Wait—"

"If we have to take them down—"

"No, listen. They don't know we're here," added Turk.

Johnny held his breath. The men were talking. He hadn't turned his translator on, but he could tell Turk was right—the voices were relaxed.

"They're saying how much they hate their commander," explained Turk. "They're peeing on the steps where he'll have to walk tomorrow."

There was laughter below. A few minutes later, the men were gone.

45

Boston—around the same time

"THIS IS THE BEST GAMING LAPTOP, PERIOD," DEclared the salesman.

Massina couldn't hold back a smile as the kid, barely into his twenties, waxed poetic about the laptop. "Better than Alienware?"

"Another awesome machine. But this is better."

"It's the one you own?"

"My laptop is a couple of years old," confessed the clerk. "And, uh, I couldn't afford either of these."

"You get a commission on sales?"

"Yes, well—"

"I'll take it. And that coupon for *Battlefield*."

The salesman's face lit up. "Your grandson will be very pleased."

"Grandson? It's for me."

AN HOUR AND A HALF LATER, MASSINA HAD THREE new laptops, each from a different store. He went to a Starbucks, bought a coffee, and set about creating a series of phony identities. He spread them liberally over the web, opening social media accounts and visiting chat rooms, establishing a different background for each. Then he accessed one of the chat rooms Borya had discovered.

He'd told Johansen that Smart Metal would no longer probe Daesh. But he'd said nothing about doing it himself.

"God, what a lot of rubbish," he muttered, scrolling through one of the conversations. He was looking for a user named GigaMan who accessed the site through a Kosovo provider who, among other things, supplied email addresses to Daesh gunrunners ID'd by Chiang.

GigaMan wasn't active. Massina posted a few comments, cursing the others as dupes and idiots. This got him a handful of negative responses, but for the most part, he was simply ignored. He tried calling out GigaMan, mentioning him in one of the posts. But he got no response. After about a half hour, he signed out under the name he'd used, then went back in, using an anonymous server service and a different identity.

Nothing.

By then it was past midnight, and the store was about to close. Massina was the last one left.

"Tomorrow," he said, closing down his computer. "We'll find you tomorrow."

46

Palmyra—around the same time

Bugs planted, Johnny and Turk headed to the Daesh commander's compound. In less than five minutes, Johnny had shimmied up the telephone pole at the side of the compound, pointed the bugs at the nearest window, and climbed down. Ten minutes later, they were heading north toward the bunker.

"Truck on the road ahead," warned Chelsea. "There's a turnoff on your right about a quarter mile. Take that and you can go north without being seen."

Johnny checked the route. It was longer and rougher, if safer.

"They're getting paranoid," Christian said. "Worrying too much. And we're only just starting."

They followed directions anyway, treading along shallow ruts to a wavy line at the base of a ridge. There was no moon, and in the dim starlight the terrain looked unearthly; Johnny felt as if he were on another planet, far out in the solar system.

He fought against a wave of fatigue. They still had work to do; he couldn't afford to relax. He shook himself, stretched, tried to find his concentration as he surveyed the landscape ahead.

The hills seemed to separate as they got closer, and Christian was able to find a pass east without consulting the satellite image. A thick layer of dirt slowed them as they got through, but beyond that they had firm ground and the outlines of a road. Christian drove with a lead foot; Johnny couldn't see the speedometer but he guessed they were hitting close to a hundred miles an hour.

"We need to stop a mile ahead," he told Christian, checking their position on the GPS grid. "We'll be a half mile east of the target."

"Done deal. Tell me when we're close."

47

North of Palmyra—around the same time

GHADAB MANAGED TO COMPLETE THE ITINERARIES before his concentration finally gave way. He locked down his computer and left the bunker, nodding to the lone guard as he walked out to wait for his car.

The vehicle was a concession to the African, who was right about the distance to the city—it was too far to walk on any but the most leisurely days. But he insisted it stay back in Palmyra: it would be easily spotted from above, drawing attention to the bunker.

The night was warm but not unpleasant; Ghadab examined the landscape, admiring how far it stretched, knowing that the vastness could only have been created by the one true God, whose word had been revealed by the Prophet, blessed be his name.

Shadaa snuck into his thoughts. She would be waiting for him at the door. She would help him undress, and then he would have her undress herself.

She was beautiful, and she was his, his entirely. His body ached for the gentleness of a woman's hand.

The sound of an engine rose over the desert. The car coming for him traveled without lights, and it took a moment to pick out its shadow against the terrain.

Soon I will rest, he thought, waiting for it to arrive.

48

CHELSEA WATCHED THE SCREEN AS THE VEHICLE LEFT.

"There's still at least one person inside the bunker," she told Johnny.

"Understood."

"Don't take unnecessary risks."

A foolish thing to say, she realized: the entire mission was a risk, and there was no way to know where the dividing line was between necessary and unnecessary.

Krista, sitting next to her, waved Johansen over. She was monitoring communication as well as liaising with the Air Force pilots supplying the Global Hawk feeds.

"Russian planes flying toward Palmyra," she said. "Su-27s. Air Force AWACS tracking them."

"Where's the Destiny drone?" Johansen asked. Even though they were outfitted for ground strikes, the Russian planes were potent air combat fighters and would have no trouble destroying a UAV.

"Grid Two."

"Bring it farther north, away from them."

"Nightbird?" asked Johansen.

"Two klicks north of the bunker."

"Take it low so the Russians miss it," Johansen told Chelsea.

"Right."

Chelsea put the aircraft into a sharp descent, finally leveling into a figure eight at ninety feet above ground level.

"Are those Su-27s still coming?" she asked Krista.

"No change. Ten miles."

Chelsea brought the UAV down to fifty feet.

"Russians are turning," said Krista. "Stand by."

The aircraft headed in the direction of an arms depot southwest of the city: a depot U.S. intelligence said had been emptied two days before.

Not that they were going to tell the Russians now.

"Clear," said Krista.

Chelsea waited two more minutes, making sure that the planes were gone, then pushed the UAV into a rapid climb.

"Johnny, can we get a sitrep?" she asked.

"Bug is placed. We're leaving."

Thank God!

"Good, copy," she said, suppressing her relief. "See you at home."

49

Palmyra—later

SHADAA WAS WAITING FOR GHADAB WHEN HE RE-
turned. It was exactly as he had foreseen. She
eased his shirt off and undid his pants. She
stepped back and at his gesture removed her own
clothes. She looked at the floor, ashamed of her
own beauty.

"Here," he told her. And he took her to bed.

GHADAB SLEPT AS HE HAD NEVER SLEPT BEFORE,
through the rest of the night, well into the next
day. He missed his prayers. When he woke, he
found Shadaa by the door, standing where she
always stood, watching him.

God's Wrath sat up slowly, unsure what to say.

There was a knock on the door.

"Who is it?" he snapped.

"Brother, we must talk," said the African.
"Downstairs."

Ghadab started to get out of bed, then realized

he was naked. He looked over at Shadaa, who was watching him expectantly.

"Turn," he said, signaling with his finger.

She turned toward the wall. He got out of bed and pulled on his clothes.

"Have you eaten?"

She shook her head.

"Wait for me. I will be up presently."

THE RESTAURANT WAS EMPTY, SAVE FOR THE AFRICAN and a waiter. Two cups of sweet Turkish coffee waited at the table.

"Take your coffee," the African said, rising. "We will be more comfortable outside."

Ghadab followed, understanding that the African's real purpose was to avoid the waiter's ears.

"You carried out an exercise," said the African, leaning against the wall. Songbirds with a nest nearby warbled at each other, marking their territory in song.

"My crew needed a reminder of why they were fighting," said Ghadab.

"Our situation here is complicated. That makes your situation complicated as well."

"I don't understand."

"You are a hero to some and a threat to others." The African sipped his coffee. "Everything you do is watched."

Neither spoke for a few moments.

"Thank you for your warning," Ghadab said finally. He started to rise.

"The Caliph wishes to see you in Raqqa, the

day after tomorrow," said the African. "You have no option. You must go."

"Of course I would go."

"By yourself."

"I would not think otherwise."

"Enjoy the day."

"As God has given it to us," said Ghadab.

50

Northern Syria—that evening

"THIS BUNKER WAS ABANDONED BEFORE THE WAR," said Johansen, his laser pointer circling it on the map. "Now there are computers there. Men come in and out, taken up from Palmyra by drivers."

The slide advanced to a diagram. "We're getting a U2 with side-penetrating radar to do an overflight. This is a schematic from a bunker with a similar profile. It's not huge, but it would be perfect for a planning cell, if that's where Ghadab is holed up."

"When do we go in?" asked Turk.

"When we know he's there." He looked over at Chelsea.

"If he goes in," she said, "the video will catch him. It has a good view."

"In the meantime, we have some possible sightings in the city," continued Johansen. "This may or may not be Ghadab."

He clicked through a sequence of shots taken by the sensors and the UAVs. There were only two partial images of a face. The recognition system believed it was him—but with only a 40 percent level of surety, not enough to order an attack.

"He's gone in and out of this building," said Johansen, showing an overhead of a restaurant surrounded by a park. "The Arab name is 'the inn in the park.' Which as you can see, pretty much describes what it is."

Johansen's orders did not specifically direct him to kill Ghadab. In fact, even in conversation, no one had actually *told* him to assassinate the man. It was just understood.

But the more he studied the situation, the more he fantasized about taking Ghadab alive: bring the prick back and make him stand trial. Make a real example out of him. Show the world what the face of terror really looked like.

Revenge was simpler, but this wasn't about revenge. This was about war, and a difficult one at that.

War required moments of moral clarity and public demonstration of those morals. Killing Ghadab in secrecy—as the U.S. had done with a number of other terrorists—would do neither. The nihilist cancer had to be exposed, and not just to Americans. Too many people saw the conflict as just a reaction by medievalists against modernity, or a civil war in Islam. But ISIS aimed at the complete annihilation of mankind. The Daesh leadership aimed to establish a "caliphate" not because they wanted to dominate the Middle East, but because they saw it as the necessary step to the end days.

That had to be exposed. Because sooner or later, the cancer would spread far enough to infect someone with access to nuclear weapons.

The cancer had to be attacked very violently, and the world needed to understand why. It needed to see what it was up against.

People didn't want to know, Johansen realized. They didn't want to face it. But if he brought Ghadab back, put him on trial, got him to spit out his vile wishes: at that point, there would be no avoiding the truth.

Taking Ghadab alive was a long shot. Johansen hadn't decided he would even try. But maybe he would. Maybe.

WHEN THE BRIEFING ENDED, CHELSEA WENT OUTSIDE to get some air. Johnny surprised her, calling to her from below just as she reached the top of the steps. "Where you going?"

"Just walking."

"Want company?"

"Sure."

The temperature had dropped more than twenty degrees from the middle of the day, and while that still left it well over seventy, Chelsea felt a little cold. She folded her arms across her chest, stretching as she walked.

The darkness around the bunker was complete; rubble and bomb craters notwithstanding, there was no way of knowing there was a war on.

"Think that's him?" asked Johnny. "The guy at that inn."

"Absolutely. Forty percent is very conservative."

"He didn't go to the bunker."

"Not yet. Or maybe that's not where it is."

"The inn?"

"No computers."

"How are you holding up?" Johnny asked.

Surprised by the question, Chelsea examined Johnny's face. Did he think she was falling apart?

I'm not scared.

I don't even think about what happened to me in Boston now.

"I'm good. My job's easy," she said. "How about you? How are your legs?"

"Bionic."

Chelsea sensed that Johnny wanted to talk, but she wasn't sure how to prompt him. Maybe he was having trouble with the mission.

Just because they're men, doesn't mean they have no emotions. Johnny lost his legs—talk about a traumatic event. How is he dealing with it?

Can he deal with it?

"I saw you jump up on that roof the other day," she said.

"Yeah. I'm pretty good at jumping."

The back of her hand brushed his.

I know you've been through a lot . . .

Do you dream of having your legs?

Is this all too much some days?

Do you have hope for the future?

Do you miss your legs?

Before Chelsea could think of a way to ask Johnny how he *really* was, they were interrupted by Krista Weather.

"Chelsea, Johansen wants to see you," she called, walking toward them. "Some sort of com problem they hope you can fix."

"And on my day off," joked Chelsea.

For a moment she thought Johnny might grab her hand—she hoped he would—but he just stood perfectly still as she pivoted and began to trot back to the bunker.

51

Palmyra—the next day

"WHY ARE THEY PERSECUTING ME? HAVE THEY become concerned with worldly power? It's the only explanation. The operatives we need are ready to strike—they have been there for years, recruited, bred, raised, trained. If we don't use them, why are they there? The council—they're blind. No. No, they've fallen away from the true belief. They have been seduced by power. They've forgotten prophecy. They're apostates. Very close. Very, very close."

Ghadab continued to rant. Nominally, he was talking to Shadaa, who was walking a few feet behind him, but in reality his only audience was himself and the sand around him. He'd driven out to the barbarians' ruins to be alone with his thoughts—to rant, really, to rail against the idiocy and venality of the council.

They had turned against him. Not all of them, but several. He didn't know exactly who, though he had theories.

Even the African was wavering. No one could be trusted.

Upon taking control of Palmyra, the Islamic State had destroyed many of the ancient buildings outside the modern city, toppling monuments that blasphemed against the one true God. Piles of rubble and swatches of a few structures remained, a reminder of how slowly history crawled, even toward the inevitable.

Ghadab walked to the columns of the tetrapylon. The sun was low on the horizon, sinking toward night; its rays burned red in the frames of bleached columns.

A sign: the apocalypse was close.

Ghadab glanced at Shadaa, struggling amid the huge stones to climb near him. As the sun highlighted the curves of her body, he realized how great her beauty was.

A revelation from God, surely, a hint of the glory that awaited him in Paradise.

"Come," he told her, turning back. "It is time to return."

Up in his room, Ghadab brooded. If the council was against him, there was little he could do besides appealing to the Caliph.

Allow me to carry out an attack against one of the plants, destroy one of their cities, and grant me the honor of martyrdom.

Surely the Caliph could not refuse.

The jealousy of the council was detestable, and surely fueled by an informer.

The African?

No. They went back too far.

Ghadab took the khanjar from the dresser. It felt solid in his hand, an extension of his arm.

What should he do with the woman?

She stared at him, unmoving.

"Are you a spy?" he asked.

She said nothing.

He stepped toward her, knife first. "Why have you spied on me?"

"I am not a spy. I am yours."

He put the blade to her neck. A trickle of blood appeared.

"Beg for your life!" he demanded.

"My life is your life," she said, her voice soft but her tone firm. "It is yours to do with as you please. This is written. This is what must be done. My fate."

"Your fate!"

But even as he screamed the words, Ghadab pulled back his knife. He knew she was not capable of betraying him. And he was not capable of killing her.

HOURS LATER, AFTER HE HAD LAIN WITH HER, GHADAB rose and swiftly dressed. He was ready to go to Raqqa and restore the Caliph's favor.

"Good night," he whispered at the door. "Do not despair. I will return."

Shadaa stirred but did not wake. Ghadab paused, tempted to linger, but duty won out.

"I will be back," he whispered, closing the door.

52

Northern Syria—twelve hours later

THE BUNKER WAS EASY TO WATCH AND RELATIVELY easy to hit; Johansen had no trouble mapping out a plan. The only problem: Ghadab wasn't there.

The video bug covering the bunker entrance gave them an excellent view of everyone coming and going; Ghadab wasn't among them. The man they *thought* was Ghadab—the computer had now increased its confidence level to 58 percent—had left the hotel a few hours before but not shown up there. Or anywhere.

"You're positive he left?" Johansen asked Chelsea as she worked the monitors.

"That's him."

"Did he go to the council buildings?" asked Rosen, watching with them.

"No," said Chelsea, "we have good views."

"Maybe he's back in the hotel," suggested Johansen. "Went in through the park." They had limited coverage of the rear.

"Go back to that bunker sequence around seventeen hundred," said Rosen. "Maybe he's one of them."

Chelsea clicked up the two shadowy images of men entering the bunker around 1700. Their faces were obscured by dark hoods. The system could not ID them.

"I don't think so," said Chelsea. "Their bio identifiers don't match. They're heavier."

"Not by much."

Chelsea pulled up Ghadab's profile data and laid it out in the biometric grid against the other two men. All three were about the same height, but the computer estimated that Ghadab weighed five and eight pounds less than the other subjects.

"That's nothing," said Rosen. "Five pounds? And it's guessing from the clothes."

"The computer is good at this. It assesses a lot more than just the weight. How he walks, how he moves—look, it's not a match."

"It doesn't say they're not him," interrupted Johansen. "It just says it can't make a definite match."

"That means it's not a match," said Chelsea. "It's just being scientific."

"But it doesn't say that."

Chelsea leaned back in exasperation. It was difficult to explain to a nonscientist the way the algorithms worked. Technically, he was correct—the computer *was* saying that it couldn't be sure. But the bar was set extremely high—way higher than a person would set it.

"He never wears a hood like that," Chelsea told Johansen. "He doesn't dress like that. The clothes don't match."

"Maybe he's disguised," said Rosen.

"You can't disguise the way you walk."

"Maybe we have the wrong guy," said Rosen. "Maybe we've misidentified one of the people inside already."

"No." Chelsea bent over her keyboard. The surveillance system used the inputs from the video bugs planted around town as well as over-head images and electronic intel to keep track of designated individuals. The bugs did not cover the entire city, so people could slip off their net, as Ghadab had. "I have another idea," she said. "What if we concentrate on the woman? The one who was with him in the ruins?"

"OK," said Johansen. "Where is she?"

"She went out to the market," said Chelsea. "She came back a little while ago."

"Maybe we should grab her," suggested Rosen.

"I doubt he tells her anything," said Johansen. "She's just his whore."

"You never know," said Rosen.

"Show me the hotel, would you?" asked Johansen.

Chelsea put the image on the far-right monitor. Johansen leaned so close she thought he was going to put his nose on the panel.

"Can I see the map?" he asked. "Where it is?"

Johansen studied the map. "We don't have the back?"

"This is the only view." Chelsea selected an image from a bug planted several blocks away. The rear was obscured by trees and vegetation. "The hotel wasn't a target."

"We can go in there and look for him," suggested Rosen.

"Too risky unless we know he's there," said Johansen. "An operation will tip everyone off. Keep tabs on her. He'll come back eventually. If he's not already inside."

"What if he doesn't come back?" asked Rosen. "We have only forty-eight hours before the batteries in the bugs start to fail."

"The hotel's risky," said Johansen. "There are guards at the entrance. We have to assume they're inside as well. We'd have to hit it pretty loud. Once we do that, the operation's over. They'll know we're here. So we really only have one shot."

"We need to bug the hotel," said Rosen.

"That's too risky."

"We can bug her," suggested Chelsea. "Or put a tracker on her."

"That'll be even harder than bugging her room," said Johansen.

"We could do it in the market. Have a UAV follow the tracker. We can watch her wherever she goes."

"Yeah," said Rosen. "Easier than grabbing her. We track her in the city. Odds are she takes us right to him."

"Hmmm," said Johansen.

Gps TRACKERS HAD A VARIETY OF APPLICATIONS; IN their simplest forms, they helped trucking companies keep track of their vehicles, and phone owners find their phones. In most cases, the trackers were relatively large and sent out a signal that could be detected.

The CIA, working with a private company (not Smart Metal), had constructed a tracker that had all of the advantages of the standard units, without most of the drawbacks. First of all, they were tiny, barely the size of a jewelry bead. They emitted no signal; instead, they were tracked by a series of transponders—think of the antitheft devices that would set off an alarm in an electronics store.

Plant one of those on the woman, and she would take them to Ghadab.

Maybe. Or maybe she'd just stay in the hotel.

Going inside the hotel was risky as hell. The market was easier.

Still risky, though.

Which chance to take?

"All right," Johansen told them. "I'll work something up."

53

Northern Syria—midnight

JOHANSEN'S PLAN WAS SIMPLE IN OUTLINE:

A team would enter the city from the south and wait as Krista Weather joined the women coming from the north to work just before dawn. She would make her way to the marketplace, wait for Ghadab's woman, then put a tracking device on her burka.

It was an easy plan—until Krista tumbled down a ravine at the side of the road moments after arriving at her hiding place north of the city.

Chelsea watched the accident unfold on a feed from a Nightbird they'd launched to shadow the operation. She ran and got Johansen, who'd gone to grab some rest.

"That's what I get for taking a nap." He sat at the console, shaking his head. "Scrub," he said over the radio. "Bring her back. Everybody back."

Turk argued that one of the men could take her place.

"The market is segregated. You can't risk getting close to a woman with the Daesh enforcers," said Johansen. "Just come home."

"I can go," said Chelsea.

Johansen shook his head. "Your Arabic's not that good."

"It's better than half their slaves'."

"Too great a risk."

"It's no more of a risk for me than it was for Krista," said Chelsea. "In and out."

"In and out."

"This whole mission was dangerous," said Chelsea. "We want to get this bastard, and this is our best chance to do it. Otherwise, you're just going to bomb the bunker and be done with it."

JOHANSEN MADE UP HIS MIND AND CHANGED IT AT least a hundred times in the next thirty seconds.

He'd promised Chelsea would stay behind the lines, and so far he'd kept that promise. But that was a personal thing and shouldn't, couldn't, override the mission.

And it wasn't necessarily that dangerous. As long as they got her to the outskirts of the city before daybreak, she would have no trouble getting in.

They could post teams to watch over her, just as with Krista.

In and out.

In, yes. But she'd have to wait until Ghadab's woman appeared.

The marker was encased in an artificial seed-pod designed to look like a seed from *Uncarina grandidieri*—a hitchhiker seed with thin spikes that was considered among the most annoying to remove in the world. Dropped on the back of her dress toward the hem, it would be almost unnoticeable.

Did they really need to track her to find Ghadab?

"You have to let me go," said Chelsea. "I came to get the bastard who hurt my city. I'm the only one here who these guys attacked personally. I deserve this chance."

"You don't deserve to die."

"I'm not going to."

Yes or no?

Yes or no?

"Get dressed," Johansen said finally. "Stay in radio contact the whole time. I give the OK to move into town; I give the OK to go to the market. You don't do anything without my say-so."

"Agreed."

54

Boston—around the same time

An hour after he started his nightly session—this time at a Starbucks in Acton—Massina's laptop was infected with several dozen new viruses.

Decent start.

Clicking on every possible link and accepting every possible download, Massina hoped one of his invented personalities would "catch" something that could be linked to Ghadab's organization by tracking back through the servers they used to get to him. But while four of the viruses were advanced enough that Norton couldn't detect them, they turned out to be linked to Russian gangs, not Daesh.

So he went back to trying to call GigaMan out by name in the chat rooms.

No luck.

Massina turned to card shops, poking around to see if he could find a customer list or anything that might overlap with Daesh's financial network. The terrorists used stolen credit cards to fund some of their operations; Massina hoped he might find a link back to a legitimate Bitcoin account, which he could then trace. He bought a few thousand cards stolen in batches from Americans and western Europeans, then used a homemade tool to track the sellers to a server in Kosovo. Armed with that information, he used different credentials to purchase a "confidential" site from the server's owners. But he made a rookie mistake: he used one of the credit cards he'd just bought.

A skull-and-crossbones symbol flashed onto his screen, declaring him a fraudster and saying the sale did not go through.

Takes one to know one, he thought. It was his bad: he should have suspected a close relationship between the server owners and the card shop.

Massina backed out. He'd have to try again, this time using Bitcoin to pay.

He was debating whether to try again that night or not when a message popped on the screen from the tracking app. Among those who had visited one of his phony Facebook pages was a user allegedly from Romania—a user whose trail included servers Borya had associated with GigaMan.

Too many for sheer coincidence.

Massina went up to the counter and ordered a venti cappuccino—this was going to take a lot of caffeine.

55

Nearing Palmyra—an hour before daybreak

SOMEWHERE ALONG THE DARK, WINDING ROAD NORTH of the city, doubt tiptoed into Chelsea's mind, shaking her resolve. Emotion gave way to logic, and logic was freighted with reasons it wouldn't work. Logic suggested things that would go wrong.

She wouldn't find the woman, she wouldn't get the tracker to stick, she'd be caught.

Try as she might to tamp it down, her fear grew with every mile. Sitting in the back of the pickup truck with Johnny, Chelsea stared out the window, hoping he wouldn't notice her anxiety.

"Pretty night, huh?" he asked.

"Yup."

"We're almost there."

"Uh-huh."

"It's funny. This is Daesh territory but there are no fences, no front like in a war."

"It is a war."

"Yeah, but without real boundaries," he insisted. "Civilians move back and forth all the time."

"Unless we're caught."

"You worried?"

"I'm fine. I didn't mean it the way it sounded."

He patted her on the shoulder. It wasn't sexual, but there was electricity nonetheless.

"Gonna be a piece of cake," said Johnny.

"I know." She patted his leg. "I got it."

Chelsea left her hand on his knee. It was the most mundane thing, but it calmed her.

The truck slowed abruptly. She pulled her scarf up, adjusting it so the earpiece that was attached to the fabric sat perfectly over her ear. Her translator was off, but she would turn it on when they started into town.

"Everyone out of the truck," said Rosen from the front. "Quick!"

Chelsea grabbed the door handle and pushed out, following the others as they ran toward a nearby hill. She heard a sound behind her from above—a jet in the distance. Two.

"What the hell's going on?" she asked, dropping next to the others next to the base of a pygmy tree about twenty yards from the truck.

"Russian fighters," explained Rosen. He'd been on the radio with Krista and had gotten a warning. "They're coming south."

Chelsea stared at the sky, looking for a shadow or a streak. Lightning flashed to the south and the ground shook; the jets had dropped their bombs.

Chelsea expected more flashes, a fireball, but there was nothing. According to Krista, who'd taken her place, broken leg and all, at the monitors, the Russians had dropped bombs in the southwest quadrant of the city, hitting exactly nothing.

"Why didn't they bomb the airport where most of the ISIS troops are?" asked Chelsea.

"Because they're Russian," said Krista.

A HALF HOUR LATER, CHELSEA JOINED A PROCESSION of women trudging toward the city center from the slums in the northwest corner of Palmyra. Turk and Christian had come up north, joining Johnny as a close-in surveillance team. Johnny and Turk were about fifty yards behind her, walking with a small group of men; Christian was back with the truck, watching what was going on with the help of a Hum UAV.

Most of the walkers were day laborers, a mix of refugees who had wandered into the area and lost the energy to go elsewhere. They lived in a potpourri of shacks and lean-tos constructed around the ruins of residential buildings destroyed during the government's first siege. They wore stoic expressions, masks of resignation against the day's coming insults and depravity.

Work was scarce, and payment was in scrip worthless outside of town, and not particularly valuable inside. Most of the women would go home worse off than they had come, exhausted, worn down a little further. The men, though, were in even rougher shape: all were old or maimed or both, as anyone near fighting age was expected to join Daesh. Johnny's arm was in a sling and his jaw bandaged—conveniently making it hard to talk—as if he had been battered in a recent battle. Turk's hair and beard were dyed gray, his leg wrapped and braced; he walked with the aid of a cane. Yet even if their ailments had been real, they would have been the fittest of the group.

The path to town flanked what had once been a fancy soccer field. Sports were officially banned, but there were youths on the fake grass of the pitch, kicking balls back and forth. A few old cars, missing various parts scavenged for others in working order, were parked in a neat row where the grandstand had once stood. One or two men stood at the edge of the field, smoking cigarettes. Given the Caliphate's prohibitions against smoking, this most likely meant that they were not Daesh, though it was never safe to guess.

A checkpoint manned by a solitary Daesh soldier in his early teens blocked the path at the far end. The youth leaned against a Toyota pickup, one hand on the AK-47 slung from his shoulder. He wore a black uniform two or three sizes too big; they looked like pajamas on him. The boy frowned at the women, but did nothing; they were too old and too worn for him to bother with.

Chelsea drifted into the half of the crowd

turning toward the market area. Vans and small trucks were parked haphazardly on the sidewalk; a few were delivering goods; others were selling or setting up to do so. In most cases their wares were pathetically small—the best-stocked merchant could offer only a half box of vegetables. Prices were set by a local Daesh council, which, in theory, kept them within reach, but added to the scarcity by making it not worth the risk for many merchants to brave government forces west and south to bring goods in.

Chelsea walked around the market area. While she'd studied the overhead images and the view from the bugs, it was far different in person. After a few turns, she walked down the street to an open grove at the edge of the bazaar. She was not alone; in fact, the grove was crowded with women gossiping and watching children, waiting for a favorite store to open or a specific merchant to arrive, or just hoping to pass the time. Children played in the dirt between the trees. Others squatted in the shade, staring at the world with eyes made blank by the fear that what they had seen in the past would soon be done to them.

"You're looking good," said Christian over the radio. "Our girl just left the hotel."

"Mmmm," said Chelsea, clamping her teeth tight against the fear-induced bile rising in her throat.

"Just stay where you are," added Christian. "I'll let you know when she's close."

56

Northern Syria—around the same time

THE BOMBING ATTACK BY THE RUSSIANS WORRIED JO-
hansen not because the aircraft presented an immediate danger to his operation, but because it
portended a change in strategy that might force
him to pull the plug.

Over the past few months, the Russian air force
had stopped attacking Daesh sites, concentrating
on rebels closer to Damascus, where the puppet
dictator was holed up. An attack here might just be
a random "hey, we're still here" thing. Or maybe
it heralded a new push by the Syrian army, and its
Iranian and Lebanese mercenaries.

The latest briefings noted some troop movements in the area, but he wasn't concerned until
he saw a set of IR images that showed a half-
dozen Land Rovers had moved overnight into
positions fifteen to twenty miles south of the
city. Though not identified, Johansen knew from
experience the trucks would belong to Hezbol-
lah commandos, scouting for positions the Syrians could use for their heavy artillery.

The Syrians always used artillery at the start of an assault; they had been known to bombard a city for weeks on end before moving in. Their big guns were currently parked in depots only two hours from Palmyra.

Johansen dialed into the intel net to get the latest assessment of Russian bombing targets. The assessment was a CIA "product"; the Russians refused to share their target list ahead of time with the U.S. Palmyra did not appear on the list. But a note added that the Russians had flown new refueling and UAV assets into the southern quadrant—something they would do if they were planning a major assault.

Johansen could call the Russian staff liaison and ask if activity was planned in the sector. He *might* even get a truthful answer. But doing so would tell the Russians he was planning an operation.

Tell the Russians, and you told the Syrians. Tell the Syrians, and Daesh would know within the hour.

"The girl's about a block from the market," said Krista, sitting at the console on the other end of the command room. Johansen heard the wince in her voice: they'd taped her ankle and given her crutches but no painkillers; she needed a clear head to work the com gear. "Chelsea's ready."

57

Palmyra—a few minutes later

CHELSEA DUCKED HER HEAD AS SHE SLIPPED OUT OF the shade, eyes blinded by the sun. A hum rose from the street as she walked past the buildings: cars and trucks rode up and down the road, one of two major highways that ran through town. Women milled around the storefronts and tables, even those that were bare or closed.

Her language translator whispered in her ear as it picked up snippets of nearby conversation:

"... two houses destroyed, all dead ..."
"... chickens at Ahmed's but so expensive ..."
"... he raped her, then left her for dead ..."
"... my brother called. They are safe but ..."

This must be what LSD is like, she thought. *A babble of voices in your head, scattering your own thoughts and simply adding to your confusion if you try to focus on any one of them.*

A man lurched in front of her.

"*Ladayna alkhudar alkhus,*" he said.

"We have greens," whispered the translator.

"*Yawm ghad*," she answered. "Tomorrow."

She spoke the phrase perfectly, but the man gave her a confused look.

"We have lettuce greens you will want to buy," he insisted. "Very rare. Gone tomorrow."

Chelsea turned, looking in the direction the man was pointing. The storefront was empty.

"No," she told him.

He raised his hand, moving it toward hers. Fearing he was going to pull her inside but not wanting to draw too much attention to herself, she took a step back and raised her hand.

"*Leave me, brother*," she said sternly in Arabic. "*God be with you*."

The man froze, then put up his hands, waving them and stepping back. She hurried on.

"What was that?" asked Christian, who'd heard the exchange.

"Nothing," she said under her breath, not sure herself.

JOHNNY FELT HIS HEART BEGIN TO RACE. HE PICKED up his pace, walking quickly in case the man went after her. But instead, the merchant ducked back into the doorway.

"I'm trying to sell greens," said the man, speaking to no one and everyone. "I have a good deal. They are rare."

Johnny crossed the street, closing to within a few yards of Chelsea. Men were only allowed here during the morning if they had some business, but his fake wounds would make it appear as if he were a Daesh soldier, and it was therefore unlikely he'd be questioned by anyone other than an ISIS soldier.

Daesh troops came through the district at least every half hour during the day, ostensibly enforcing the laws of dress and conduct; more often they were simply shaking down the locals for whatever contraband they could take. Christian was watching for them on the UAV.

A man leaning against a doorway held up a cigarette to Johnny. Though cigarettes were theoretically outlawed, many men smoked them openly on the street, and even the Daesh enforcers didn't go out of their way to reprimand people about them—unless they were confiscating them for their own use.

Johnny shook his head and pointed to the bandages, then gesturing with his hand as a thank-you.

He turned back to look for Chelsea. In the time it took to shake his head and look apologetic, she had disappeared.

CHELSEA TURNED THE CORNER AND QUICKENED HER pace, trying to put some distance between herself and two women who seemed to be following her. She could hear the clip-clop of their shoes as they turned down the alley behind her.

Women enforcers?

Chelsea had a pistol strapped to her leg beneath her dress. Closer was the knife in her pocket. She pushed her hand between the folds of her robe and took hold of the hilt.

"*Wawaqf,*" said one of the women. "Stop."

Chelsea kept walking.

"Sister, stop," repeated one of the women.

A man appeared at the other end of the little street she'd turned onto. The passage was narrow, little more than an alley: a good place for a trap.

"Sister!" yelled one of the women.

Chelsea spun. "*Madha?*" she said harshly. "What do you want?"

"That man, was he bothering you?" asked the woman who had been calling out to her. She was nearly a foot taller than Chelsea and at least twice as wide.

"Was he trying to attack you?" asked the other woman, pulling her veil away from her mouth. Her voice was gentle.

"No," she said. "He had vegetables."

The taller woman frowned. Chelsea glanced over her shoulder toward the man who'd come up the alley. She pulled her veil closer, as if worried about her modesty.

"Don't be ashamed, sister," said the younger woman. "There are perverts and sinners everywhere."

Act frightened, Chelsea told herself. *Not hard to do.*

The man passed them. Chelsea watched him and saw Johnny appear at the far end of the alley, walking swiftly in her direction.

"Thank you," Chelsea told the women. She wanted to say she was OK, but couldn't find the words and didn't trust the suggestions the translator was giving her for conversation.

"Are you certain you are OK?" asked the taller woman.

"Fine, yes," said Chelsea. "Thank you."

JOHNNY KEPT HIS PACE STEADY AS HE WALKED PAST the two women. When he came to the street, he crossed, then turned back on the sidewalk to make sure they hadn't followed.

Chelsea was walking down the block.

"What did they want?" he whispered as he passed.

"They're some sort of women's patrol or something. They asked about the guy who bothered me."

He kept walking. When he reached the corner, he turned and put his hand to his ear to use the radio. "They said something about your accent. They thought you were from Lebanon."

"Good."

"Target is just turning onto the block."

"I'm going."

GHADAB'S SLAVE WAS A FEW INCHES TALLER THAN Chelsea and a good forty pounds heavier, though that was hard to judge from the bulky clothes and long veil. She walked with her head down, arms close to her body, modest or timid; it was hard to tell.

"You're on her," said Christian as she fell in behind the woman.

Chelsea took the bead in her fingers, getting ready.

The woman paused at a cart where they were selling oranges and lemons. Chelsea sidled up next to her, picked up a lemon, and as she did, dropped the bug from her hand. It rolled down the side of the woman's dress, catching below her hip.

Done.

Chelsea was about to turn away when the woman abruptly moved back from the cart and blocked her way.

"Min 'ant?" asked Ghadab's woman. "Who are you?"

Chelsea put up her hand. "No."

The woman said something else but between the speed of her voice and its accent, the translator was baffled; it gave no translation. Chelsea started to leave, then noticed the two women who'd accosted her earlier staring a few feet away.

"I was a stolen one," said Chelsea, using the phrasing she'd memorized. It meant that she was a slave, now assigned to someone; it was dangerous to associate with her. "You must not speak to me."

Ghadab's woman nodded. "My name is Shadaa."

"Baidda," said Chelsea. She saw sympathy in the other woman's eyes—she was talking to a fellow slave, another woman who might be disposed of in a week or a day or an hour.

Until that moment, Chelsea had felt nothing for the woman. Now she felt a surge of pity.

"Goodbye," she said gently. She moved to the

next cart, pretending to look at the tomatoes. They were large and ripe, a rare find, but prohibitively expensive.

Chelsea looked over and saw the women talking to Shadaa. She shook her head and moved over to another stand.

"The bug's not moving," whispered Christian.

Shit, thought Chelsea. Realizing it must have fallen to the ground, she walked over to retrieve it. As she got closer, her way was blocked by a sudden gaggle of girls. By the time they passed, Shadaa was no longer in sight.

Chelsea scooped up the bug. Its spiky arms had been crushed by someone's feet.

"Bug fell off," whispered Chelsea. "Which way did she go?"

58

Northern Syria—around the same time

"WE HAVE A LOT OF TRAFFIC ON THE RUSSIAN commo lines," Krista told Johansen. "The air force AWACS just sent an alert that they have a full squadron of fighter bombers heading for the runway at Latakia. Su-35s."

The Su-35 was an updated attack version of the Su-27. As Russia's most advanced aircraft in the conflict, it had a starring role in the intervention: the Russians used it for the biggest battles. If the planes were coming this way, a full-on ground assault against Palmyra would surely follow.

Sure enough, there was a dust cloud near the Syrian artillery camp. They were on the move.

59

Palmyra—around the same time

CHELSEA MADE HER WAY THROUGH THE CROWD AS quickly as she could without running, aiming to cut Shadaa off as she walked home. Sweat rolled down her collar, soaking through the light underlayers. The heavy robe made her feel as if she was encased in a sauna.

"She's a block away, coming toward you," said Christian.

Chelsea stopped. She was alone on the street, save for a lone man at the other end.

Turk.

Johnny was nearby, too, a half block away, out of sight.

Guardian angels. But what good were angels in the bowels of hell?

Chelsea adjusted her scarf and then started walking again, back to Shadaa as she passed.

"Oh," she said loudly. "You."

The Arabic flowed from her mouth. Shadaa stopped and turned, confused.

"You," said the woman, echoing her thoughts. "Do you live near here?"

It took a few seconds for Chelsea to process the translation and the suggested phrase, "next block: *kutlat almuqbil.*" That wasn't a safe answer—what if she wanted to go with her there?—so Chelsea simply shrugged.

"You are a slave," said Shadaa.

Chelsea couldn't think of an appropriate answer quickly enough. But in this case confusion was just as appropriate.

"Come, we are sisters," said Shadaa, taking her arm.

"WHAT THE FUCK'S GOING ON?" ASKED TURK OVER the radio.

"She asked if she was a slave," said Christian.

"I'm about fifty yards behind them," said Johnny. "I'm going to get closer."

Johnny leaned forward as he walked. He saw the women cross the street. Shadaa, taller than Chelsea, had clamped her arms around Chelsea's and bulled ahead. She was talking: Johnny could hear her through Chelsea's open mic, but he couldn't understand the Arabic without turning his translator on.

"Johnny, ease up," said Christian. "Ghadab's girl is telling her they're sisters and that she's going to help her. But you're spooking her. She thinks you're going to molest them because they're slaves. That's why she clamped on to

Chelsea. She just told her to run when she gives the signal."

"Let's just take her down," said Johnny.

"*Chill.* Chelsea's fine."

"I'm two blocks away," said Turk.

Johnny stopped and turned toward the street. There were no cars; he crossed.

"It might be a ruse," Johnny told Turk. "I don't trust this."

"No, she's talking about being a slave. Dump your jacket for a different look."

"All right," he said, still reluctant.

A DAESH PICKUP TRUCK WITH A TEENAGER HANGING on to the machine gun mounted in the back roared past Chelsea and Shadaa as they turned onto the street with the hotel. The kid bounced up and down, swinging the gun and grinning like a three-year-old on a merry-go-round. Dust billowed behind the truck as it flew down the street and turned.

"What's going on?" Chelsea asked.

It was an Arabic phrase she had practiced quite a bit, but Shadaa seemed confused.

"Where are you from?" Shadaa asked.

"Somalia." Chelsea lowered her eyes, as if admitting this was an act of shame.

"You're Christian?"

The translation was slow, and the device offered no possible responses.

Chelsea shook her head.

"Does he beat you?" asked Shadaa.

Chelsea froze.

Shadaa interpreted that as a yes. "Come with me and I will get you some food."

JOHNNY CAME UP THE BLOCK JUST IN TIME TO SEE Chelsea going into the hotel.

"She's going in," said Christian over the radio. "Hot damn."

Johnny continued up the street. He was about ten yards from the entrance when one of the two guards stepped out and, with his submachine gun, motioned him away.

Johnny crossed the street. The guards were well equipped: rather than the ubiquitous AKs, they wielded MP5 submachine guns. The weapons suggested a higher degree of competence, or at least investment.

Johnny walked about twenty yards past the restaurant entrance before crossing back. They were still watching.

Turk was waiting around the corner.

"Get a look at those goons?" he asked Johnny.

"I saw them." Johnny frowned. "You have a fix on where Chelsea is in the building?" he asked Christian.

"She said something about tables—must be a dining room. Stand by; I gotta talk to Yuri."

Johnny folded his arms. Before the war, this had been a fashionable block. It was still something of an oasis—if you ignored the shrapnel marks on the low walls and the crater at the side of the street.

"Johansen says the Syrians are gearing up for an attack," said Christian. "Russian planes are on the way."

"Tell Chelsea to plant the damn bug and get out of there," said Johnny.

"Relax," said Christian. "She's doing fine. I moved our pickups into the city," he added, referring to the trucks with backup team members in case anything went wrong. "Destiny is above; we can get out anytime we want. Let her do her thing. I'm listening and she's doing fine." He paused, then added, "Russian planes are about zero-five away."

CHELSEA TRIED TO THINK OF HOW TO GET TO GHA-dab's room. She needed strategy, words.

Go to the restroom, use the translator.

"You don't speak very good Arabic," said Shadaa. They were alone at the edge of the dining area's patio—distant from help.

"I don't," admitted Chelsea.

"What do you speak?"

"Somali," said Chelsea.

Shadaa reached to Chelsea's face. She brushed her cheek gently, then lifted her scarf back. Chelsea reached to stop her, but it was too late; the cloth fell back, taking its earpiece with it. The piece would automatically shut off when the veil was back, so there was no chance of it being detected, but now Chelsea didn't even have the rudimentary translator to help.

"I don't know Somali," said Shadaa. *"Français?"*

Chelsea shook her head.

"English?" asked Shadaa.

"A some," said Chelsea haltingly. "A some I can talk."

"You mean, 'I can speak a little.'"

"This."

A shriek from the street interrupted them. It was an odd, unexpected sound that morphed and changed, beginning like the whistle from an old tin toy. It lengthened, becoming a woman's scream.

In the next moment, there was a loud *crack* and the ground rumbled from an explosion.

"Bombs!" said Shadaa, speaking once more in Arabic. "Come with me. Quickly."

The ground rumbled again, this time violently enough to fell several chairs. Chelsea had a hard time staying on her feet as she followed Shadaa into the hotel's dining room.

The room went dark before they were midway across. Another explosion, this one so close that it shook the ground sideways, sent Chelsea to the ground face-first. She struggled to her knees, then her feet, wincing and then coughing with the plaster dust shaken from the ceiling.

Shadaa lay a few feet away.

"Ayn?" asked Chelsea, helping her up. "Where?"

Shadaa blinked, dazed.

"Room?" said Chelsea in Arabic, then English. "Your room? To go? Safe?"

The ground shook again. Shadaa took Chelsea's hand and led her from the dining room to the basement stairwell. There were sirens in the distance, and the heavy *ra-thump* of antiaircraft fire.

With the electricity off, the stairs were dark, the basement impossibly so. Shadaa walked with her hands out, feeling her way until she came to a wall. She collapsed against it, sinking to the dirt floor. Chelsea did the same.

The bombing continued for another minute and a half, the explosions moving away. As they waited, Chelsea reached into her pocket and took out the bug, slipping it onto the hem of Shadaa's dress.

It was time to leave; she'd pressed her luck too far already.

"*Yjb 'an 'adhhab*," she said, rising. She slurred her words to hide the flaws in her pronunciation. "Must go."

Shadaa surprised her by jumping to her feet. "With me," she told Chelsea, grabbing Chelsea's hand and starting for the stairs.

They stopped at the top of the stairs. Chelsea glanced toward the door.

Run?

Run!

"This way," said Shadaa, pointing down the hall.

Is that where Ghadab is?

She should leave; she knew she should leave. But this was too good an opportunity.

"Yes," she told Shadaa. "With you I am."

60

Boston—about the same time

GigaMan was not, Massina learned to his surprise, a single person. Instead, the identity belonged to three different users, the most prominent of whom had a home base—if you could call it that—in southern Turkey. The other users were based in Germany and Albania. They all shared the same botnet and servers based in Morocco and Ankara, and occasionally were online at the same time.

Their credentials proved remarkably easy to steal, thanks to a photo Massina had surreptitiously included in the root directory of one of his computers: inspected by their botnet's virus, it back-infected its attacker; within an hour Massina made the botnet his own.

"Prime GigaMan" had contacts throughout the Middle East. The one that interested Massina was in Fallujah, an Iraqi city under Daesh control. The contact used a web provider in Croatia to post comments on a website devoted to a youth football league—soccer to an

American—in England. The posts appeared to be innocuous, mostly scores and credits to players for goals and assists.

But why would someone from Croatia with a difficult-to-track pedigree do that?

It took a little bit of experimenting, but Massina eventually realized that the numbers, when strung together, yielded web addresses. These pages were filled with seemingly meaningless gibberish—encryptions, he was sure. But to decipher them required more firepower than he had in a laptop.

HE DECIDED, IN THE END, TO TELL THE CIA WHAT HE had. That meant talking to Demi Ascoldi, who was filling in for Johansen.

He asked if she could meet him in the Box; she countered with a restaurant.

A sure sign that she wasn't taking him seriously. But he acquiesced. She was on time, at least.

"You'll find this useful," he told her, pushing a flash drive across the table as she sat down. "It lists contacts of your subject and some of the people who work with him. They use state-level encryption stolen from Turkey. We've left it intact."

Ascoldi frowned. "Is this why you called?"

"I get conflicting signals from your agency," said Massina. He hadn't expected her to do jumping jacks in gratitude, but neither had he expected an antagonistic response. "You want my help, you use my people, but when I do help—"

"Some things are better left to the professionals, Mr. Massina." She rose. "Thank you for lunch."

He didn't bother pointing out that they hadn't eaten.

Bozzone met Massina outside on the sidewalk.

"Go well?" asked Bozzone.

"Better than I expected," replied Massina sarcastically.

61

Palmyra—around the same time

JOHNNY AND TURK RAN TOWARD THE HOTEL EN-
trance, hoping that the guards would be inside.
But they remained at their posts, crouched under
the awning.

"Can we take shelter?" asked Turk.

The answer was a burst from one of the guard's
weapons—fortunately, into the air.

Turk and Johnny retreated back down the
block.

"Let's go in through the park," yelled Turk.

The bombs and missiles were aimed at the
southern end of town a mile away, close enough to
break windows and unsettle the ground. Johnny
barely kept his balance as he ran behind Turk.

Someone with a machine gun began firing
from a nearby roof.

"That's a waste of bullets," said Turk, stopping
at the gate to the park.

The gate was chained, but there was plenty of
slack. Johnny slipped through easily; Turk had
to squeeze.

"Gotta lay off the beer."

They walked a few yards along the perimeter wall, stopping when they saw the low wall at the rear of the patio.

"Christian, any guards back here?" asked Turk.

"Not in view."

"Where's Chelsea?" asked Johnny.

There was no answer.

"Christian, you there?" asked Turk. He waited a moment, then asked again.

When there was still no answer, Turk switched frequencies to call the command bunker directly. There was no acknowledgment.

"Probably our relay unit got hit," suggested Johnny.

"Yeah."

"Let's get Chelsea out," said Johnny.

He started toward the rear of the hotel.

"Whoa, go slow," said Turk.

"We gotta get her out."

"She's not in trouble right now. We don't want to blow it."

"Who says she's not in trouble?"

"Relax. Let's take this one step at a time."

"I'm not a relaxing kind of person," said Johnny. But he knelt back down, waiting to see what plan Turk came up with.

62

Northern Syria—around the same time

KRISTA POUNDED THE CONSOLE.

"That's not going to get the coms back," said Johansen.

"Why do the Russians always screw everything up?"

"That's what they do," said Johansen. "Keep the drones out of the way if they come back."

"Yup."

Outside, Kevin Banks had almost finished prepping the UAV that would take the place of the ground dish knocked out by the Russian bombing. Using the UAV had two major disadvantages: it had a smaller bandwidth, which meant less information in real time, and it was easy to detect, as it had to fly over the city.

Johansen stared at the control handset.

"Problem?" asked Banks.

"Forgot the password," Johansen confessed.

Banks took a step, but Johansen's fingers took over, remembering the sequence by rote. The plane beeped with an acknowledgment. From there it was easy—a voice command told it to preflight according to its standard checklist; another got it in the air.

They watched the aircraft flutter away, unsteady in the wind.

"The way things are going, I thought it would crash," said Banks as it finally straightened out.

"Bite your tongue," Johansen told him.

63

Palmyra—around the same time

THE MUSCLES IN CHELSEA'S NECK TIGHTENED AS SHE walked up the stairs behind Shadaa.

Now I'm scared. I can admit it.

Worse than Ukraine.

I should have been more scared in Ukraine. That's the advantage of being naive.

She gave herself a silent pep talk, not with words but with feints of emotion, a push to be brave without spelling it out:

Johnny and Turk . . . out there . . . ready . . .

The knife beneath my pocket if I need it . . .

If he is here . . .

Hope he is here . . .

She wanted Ghadab to be there. She wanted to be the one to shoot him.

Which she could do, would do, even though they hadn't even discussed the possibility.

Take the chance!

Shadaa slowed her pace at the landing, then turned to walk down the hall.

Almost there.

Walk. Push everything out of your mind.

Shadaa stopped in front of a door.

His room?

Chelsea involuntarily blinked as Shadaa opened the door.

I should have my gun in my hand.

"My master is very important," said Shadaa, using English as she stepped into the room.

Empty.

Not here!

Damn!

Chelsea fought against the disappointment.

Time to leave.

"I go," she said.

"I don't think so." Shadaa turned around to face her, a pistol in her hand.

THE RUSSIAN BOMBARDMENT HAD ENDED; A THICK cloud of black smoke rose from the southern side of the city. There were sirens in the distance; here, everything was quiet.

"We go in and have a peek," said Turk. "Someone comes, we say we're looking for volunteers to fight the fires."

It was thin cover, but Johnny didn't argue.

Before they could start for the wall, a man appeared on the rear patio from the building. He had an MP5. Another came out behind him.

"Wait?" asked Turk.

"No. We need to get her out."

Turk rose. "Guy on the right's mine."

"**I** KNOW YOU ARE A SPY," SHADAA TOLD CHELSEA IN English. "Get inside."

"No spy."

"Who do you work for? The council? I doubt it. The Americans? Turkey?"

"No spy. Somalia."

"Stand against the wall."

Chelsea moved slowly, trying to relax her muscles, trying to remember the exercises—they had done this in training, this exact scenario, an attacker coming behind you with a gun. The Krav Maga instructor was bigger, stronger, ready to fire.

Toooch . . . toocch.

Gunshots, below, not here.

Chelsea saw Shadaa jerking around, looking toward the door at the sound of the bullets.

What happened next was reflex, hammered into her by weeks of training with the team.

Pivoting on her left foot, she swung her elbow with all her might into her captor's side, then punched up with her right fist, aiming for Shadaa's chin. Shadaa, taken off guard, fell back; Chelsea's fist hit her neck instead.

Then it was about anger and fear, but mostly anger.

Chelsea threw herself at the other woman, crashing her against the wall. She wanted to knock the gun from Shadaa's hand but couldn't see it. Instead she pushed her against the wall, grinding her shoulder and wedging her legs, springing into her.

A sharp elbow to her rib caught Chelsea by

surprise. As she started to fall, she grabbed the other woman by the throat with her left hand and together they tumbled over, spinning onto the floor. Chelsea went down on her back, pinned by the larger woman's weight.

Shadaa had lost the pistol, but instead of trying to retrieve it, she squirmed around, punching Chelsea in the face. Chelsea twisted and the next blow missed.

Knife! Knife!

Chelsea struggled to get up but her feet tangled in the long dress. Shadaa grabbed her right shoulder and pulled her down, trying to twist her over so she could strike her face. Chelsea's fingers groped in her pocket, searching for the hilt of her weapon. Shadaa, knee on the floor for leverage, jerked Chelsea backwards, lifting her slightly, angling into a body slam the way a wrestler would.

The blow nearly knocked Chelsea out. She flailed with the knife, jabbing through her dress. Shadaa lifted her again, aiming to smash her hard against the floor, but instead she collapsed, stung by the slashing pain that tore up her side.

Chelsea looked into her face. Shadaa's eyes crossed.

Chelsea plunged the knife into her enemy's stomach.

Harder! Harder!

JOHNNY BEAT TURK TO THE PATIO, PIVOTING OVER THE short wall with a quick jump. He grabbed the

MP5 from the man he'd slain, pulling the strap off the dead body with a sharp yank. Blood burbled from the man's forehead, spreading across the stones like spilled ink, more purple than red.

"Inside," said Turk, coming up behind him.

They left the bodies there, rushing through the large, empty dining room.

Johnny halted, swiveling his head right and left to make sure she wasn't there. He fought the urge to call her name—it would only put her in more danger.

"Stairs are back this way," prompted Turk. "Come on."

IT WAS ONLY WITH THE LAST BLOW THAT CHELSEA REmembered she was plunging her knife into a human being. By then, Shadaa was long dead, her blood everywhere, spurting and oozing and leaking, soaking into the carpet and floorboards.

Fifty blows with the knife. So much anger.

Was it gone now?

Chelsea got up. Blood covered the knife and her hand, already sticky. The smell was pungent, similar to the smell of a field-gutted deer in the hot sun, if you'd smeared yourself with the blood and gizzards.

The door sprung open. Chelsea whirled, knife out.

"You OK?" Johnny Givens filled the doorway, one of the guard's MP5 in his hands. "You OK?"

64

Northern Syria—a few minutes later

"Coms coming back online," Krista told Johansen. "But it looks like we've lost a few of the video bugs."

"Government center?" asked Johansen.

"Still working. No damage to the buildings. Leave it to the Russians to miss anything important."

Johansen looked at the screen showing a live feed from an Air Force Global Hawk coming south to get a better view of the attack. A Russian fighter to the west challenged the UAV by turning on its target radar. The American pilot ignored it: what was a little petty harassment between hostile almost-allies?

The Russians had hit the south side of Palmyra—an indication of where the Syrians and their allies were planning their assault. They had also bombed the airport—a first. But aside from putting two good-sized craters in the already unusable runway, the Russians had done little damage.

"Air Force says Syrian helicopters taking off

from Damascus," said Krista. "The attack's coming soon."

"You have coms with Christian yet?"

"Negative."

"Keep trying. It's time to get everyone the hell out of there, and us, too."

65

Raqqa—about the same time

GHADAB HAD NO PATIENCE FOR WAITING, AND DE-
spite the great respect he owed the Caliph, he
could not keep himself from pacing back and
forth inside the mosque. An aide had been assigned to him, ostensibly to see to his needs; the
young man was more a guard assigned to monitor him. He was too skinny to do much more
than that, though the radio he held in his hand
would undoubtedly bring a phalanx of guards if
Ghadab tried to do something so unworthy as
to burst into the consultation chamber at the far
end of the prayer hall.

All morning long, different delegations, advisers, commanders, messengers had come and
gone. The hall was filled with them, and many
others roamed outside, awaiting an audience.
The crowd included a few old acquaintances, but
to a man they had greeted Ghadab with barely a
nod. It seemed word of the council's displeasure
had spread.

Unable to focus, his thoughts flew in different

directions: plans for different attacks, the idiocy of the Americans, the coming apocalypse, Shadaa.

She kept intruding.

He remembered the weight of her body against him, the curve of her side, the way she felt beneath him . . .

He forced himself to think of his mission. Nearly everything was in place; the students had been infiltrated two years before and needed only to be activated. All that waited was settling on a target. Rome, Amsterdam, America again . . . Boston . . .

Ghadab walked the length of the hall, then back. His minder stayed at his elbow.

"Ask your radio how much time," he said to the young man. "Find me when you have an answer. I will be outside."

The young man's brow knitted, but Ghadab didn't wait to hear his protests.

The mosque was constructed on a stone platform; a gentle slope ran to the walls, which separated the holy grounds from the street. Men clustered in groups all across the yard. The only thing they all had in common were the AK-47s dangling haphazardly from their shoulder straps. There were young and old, traditionally dressed, combat clothes, and a few in Western-style suits.

A man in a black military uniform ran up from the street and went straight into the mosque. Ghadab thought nothing of it until another followed a minute later.

"What's going on?" Ghadab asked his minder.

"You are on the schedule. Soon—"

"No. The messengers?" He gestured toward a third, just running up from the street.

A few feet away, one of the brothers was listening intently to his mobile. Ghadab turned from him and saw that several others were doing the same.

"Something *is* going on," he told the minder. "Find out."

Ghadab walked over to a man in a camo uniform whose phone was pressed to his ear. He was an older man, his beard mostly gray; he bloused his uniform pants at the top of his high, paratrooper-style boots.

"Commander," said Ghadab, "what is going on?"

The man frowned at him.

"I am Ghadab min Allah."

"I know who you are. The apostates have launched an attack on Palmyra."

"Palmyra?"

Without another word, Ghadab started for the main gate. He needed to get back to the city.

"Brother, where are you going?" asked his minder, struggling to keep up as he cut through the crowd.

"Palmyra," said Ghadab. "They are under attack."

"You have business here."

Ghadab halted abruptly. "Is the Caliph ready for me?"

"He has much business at the moment," said the minder. "Later—"

"Tell the Caliph I will return when I am sure his city has been adequately defended," said Ghadab, setting off for his jeep.

66

Palmyra—about the same time

CHELSEA STARED AT THE BLOOD POOLING AROUND Shadaa's body. She felt no guilt or remorse, nor elation or even relief.

She felt nothing, emotion a null set.

"You all right?" asked Johnny, gripping her biceps.

Johnny?

"Come on. The city's under attack. We gotta go."

Across the room, Turk ransacked the dresser.

"Time to go!" repeated Johnny.

Chelsea moved in a gray-tinted daze. It was like Boston, after the attack. She'd gone home and sat in the shower for an hour until her skin felt as it had when she was a child and spent the entire day in salt water.

Someone shouted below. Chelsea dropped to her knee in the middle of the doorway and took the pistol from her calf holster. A Daesh guard rounded the corner from the stairs in the hall. She fired, aiming for the face in case he wore a vest.

Her first bullet went through his mouth, the second above his nose.

Another man came up behind him. Something exploded in her ear.

Johnny was behind her, firing an MP5. The second guard went down.

"We are out of here, now!" shouted Johnny.

"I have coms," said Turk, touching his ear. "The extract team is outside."

A SECOND WAVE OF RUSSIAN PLANES APPROACHED the city, once more aiming at the southeastern quarters. The Daesh commanders realized this was a prelude to an assault and scrambled men into their positions.

A stream of vehicles passed the building as Chelsea, Johnny, and Turk ran to the hotel's front entrance. Chelsea, head still foggy, ran between the two men, sure that if she stopped even for a moment she would fall into a hole she could not see.

"Here we go!" yelled Johnny, swerving into the street.

A pickup truck stopped a few yards away. Another veered close.

"In, in, in!"

Chelsea felt herself being lifted up into the truck bed.

"Mind the gun," said Turk.

"Out of here, let's go." Johnny leaped in behind her. "Keep your head down," he added, putting his hand on her head.

Her head bounced against the hard metal floor as the vehicle sped down the road. There was gunfire in the distance, the explosions, most muffled, a few loud enough to make her tremble.

She smelled blood, the girl's blood.

They drove for ten minutes. Someone in the truck fired off a few rounds from an AK, but Chelsea didn't look to see who it was. Only when they were outside of the city, heading back toward the staging point where they'd originally left the truck, did Johnny tell her it was OK to get up.

"The Syrians are launching an assault," he told her. "Their artillery will be in range within the hour. They have troops behind that."

"Ghadab," said Chelsea. "He wasn't in the hotel."

"He has to be at the bunker," said Johnny. "They'll get him when they attack. They're setting up now."

"We should help them."

"That's what we're doing," said Johnny. "We'll be there in a few minutes."

67

Northern Iraq—twenty minutes later

From a long-term strategic view, the Syrian assault on Daesh at Palmyra was excellent news. Whether the government took the city or not, the attacks would drain terrorist resources, tax their infrastructure, and damage their ability to conduct operations outside of the area.

Johansen wasn't particularly interested in the long view at the moment. The attacks were screwing up his operation. He'd lost about half of his surveillance net, and between that and the attacks, operating inside the city was no longer viable.

None of this would matter if Ghadab was in the bunker. But that seemed unlikely. There were six men there, none of whom bore any resemblance.

Still, they'd hit it for the intel: maybe something inside would tell them where he was.

Then they'd wipe it out with Option B: an Air Force F-15E Strike Eagle, or more specifically, the BLU-116 2,000-pound penetration bomb it carried. The so-called "bunker buster" would be guided into the bunker by a laser designator wielded by Johansen's team. Nothing inside would survive the blast.

He could go to Option B now if he chose.

"Bunker team wants to know if they have the go-ahead to attack," Krista told him.

"I want them to wait for the teams coming up from Palmyra," he told her. "The bunker will be on alert."

"Christian just radioed that they're ten minutes away."

"Good." Johansen studied Krista. She looked extremely tired, worn by pain as well as fatigue.

Their only casualty so far.

He could just go with the bunker buster. Everyone would be safe.

But the mission would be a bust. No one would blame him—the Russians had screwed everything up—but he would know they'd failed.

They might fail yet. And lose people. What would he say at their funerals?

"Tell them they're clear once the rest of the teams are in place for backup," Johansen said. "Tell them Godspeed and we're with them all the way."

68

North of Palmyra—the same time

Chelsea's head cleared by the time they joined the team at the bunker. She followed Johnny and the others as they reported to Rosen, who was in charge of the attack.

"What do you want me to do?" she asked him.

"Nothing. You've done a lot." He stared at the side of her dress, covered with blood. "That yours?"

"No, I'm fine. I'll work the bots."

"It's all right. Bobby's on that. The bomb mechs go in after the TOW missiles."

"You know they won't see through the dust, right?"

"It'll clear."

"I thought of something quicker."

Rosen frowned. "When?"

"Just now."

"You gonna share?"

"I will. But I doubt anybody but me can fix it so it works."

This time he shook his head. But instead of

telling her to get back in the truck, he called over to Bobby.

"Get with Taylor on the second team," he told him. "Chelsea's gonna take over for you. No sense giving a genius only half a day's work."

THEY CALLED THE MAN WITH THE TOW MISSILE "Swift," either as a tribute to his intelligence or a cut on his slow-running times. Whichever it was, he was just as impatient as anyone else.

"We going in today, or tomorrow?" he asked Johnny, who was standing next to him and monitoring the radio.

Johnny shrugged. He'd launched two Hums, and the Nighthawk was now overhead; they had plenty of visual on the bunker, and plenty of firepower, between their own weapons and the Destiny UAV.

"Sixty seconds," said Johnny, relaying Rosen's call. He glanced over his shoulder at Chelsea. Cross-legged on the ground between the rocks, she had a laptop on either leg.

She raised her thumb.

Nothing stops that girl.

Two mechs crept out from behind the nearby rocks. They were going in after the TOW missile to detect any booby traps. Peter, their multipurpose bot, sprung up on its legs nearby. He would go in ahead of the assault team, providing real-time video and audio.

"Do it!" said Rosen. "Showtime!"

On Chelsea's monitor, it looked like a Wile E. Coyote cartoon with the Road Runner bursting through the painted hole on the canyon wall.

The first TOW missile hit the outer door. A second, fired from a position to Chelsea's right, hit a few seconds later.

She ignored the temptation to look up from the screen. The mechs, held back to escape the blast, scurried toward the bunker entrance.

"Did we make it?" asked Johnny.

"Stand by." Chelsea moved her finger on the control board, clicking the button that allowed her to speak directly to Peter. "Move into position."

Chelsea had reprogrammed the sensor array Peter ordinarily used to check the depth of ravines or other depressions before trying to cross, turning it into a kind of forward radar.

It wasn't perfect, but it told her what she needed to know.

"The inside barrier is still intact," said Chelsea. "We need another hit."

The missile took off a fraction of a second later, bursting from the launcher with the sound of a very large can of shaken soda being opened. This was followed by a noise resembling the ignition of a thousand bottle rockets. The winglets extended and the rocket's main engines flared.

Then there was the explosion, barely muffled by the surrounding rock.

"We're through!" said Chelsea as Peter's distance marker jumped.

"People?" asked Rosen.

"Not that I see."

"Gas the place," said the commander, ordering the launch of CS grenades.

Chelsea switched her command line to the mechs, sending them in to check for explosives. Neither of them could see through the smoke, so she had them crawl against the walls. The sniffer didn't need to see to detect intact explosives.

They had expected the soldiers to come out of the entrance and put up a fight, but so far that hadn't happened. Nor had they discovered a back door—the Nightbird had a clear view of the ground for several miles, and the computer would alert her if it detected a human heat signature suddenly popping up.

"OK, Peter, it's all you," said Chelsea, tapping the button on the bot's control screen. "Go find out what's happening inside."

The little bot walked into the billowing smoke. One of its arms had been replaced with a stun gun; two of the others had CS gas canisters. Two more bomb-disposal mechs followed. These had been modified to carry CS gas in large, tool-case-sized boxes; if Peter encountered any resistance, they would move forward and detonate the gas.

Peter was the one making the decision because they couldn't count on communicating with it once it went inside the bunker; a pair of L turns formed a baffle that could hinder full communication. To get around this, Chelsea had prepared their last bomb mech to act as a relay station. She sent it off now, aiming to park itself at the end of the first turn.

Peter's video feed was all smoke. Something loomed in the middle.

A man. He quickly fell to the ground; Peter had downed him with a zap of his Taser.

"One down. Not Ghadab," said Chelsea, studying a freeze-frame of the terrorist.

"Just for your information we have a new flight of Russian jets inbound," said Krista over the radio. "It's flying a more northern vector than the others."

"Is it targeting the bunker?" asked Chelsea.

"No way of knowing. But it is flying in your general direction."

"We're going in," said Rosen.

"Give the bot a chance," replied Chelsea. "The gas still has to clear through their ventilation system."

"No time. Set off whatever CS you've got left."

Chelsea picked up the control unit for Peter and hit the preset to take over manual control.

The unit didn't acknowledge. Instead, a message popped up on the screen:

Out of control range

"Shit." Chelsea hit the key again. "If I'm close enough for video I should be close enough—"

The video screen blanked. The unit was out of range for all communications, its transmissions blocked by the zigzag of the bunker layout and the thick walls. It was completely on its own.

JOHNNY PULLED THE HELMET DOWN OVER HIS EARS, then snapped the collar in place so that he would be hermetically sealed from the gas-filled interior of the Daesh bunker. His breathing was loud in his ears, nearly drowning out the radio.

"I'm out of communication with Peter," said Chelsea, broadcasting to the entire team. "We won't have a link until I can get the com mech inside. It'll take another minute at least."

Johnny switched on the display in the lower-right corner, which he'd preset to get the feed from Peter. It was blank.

"Be careful," she added.

Her voice wobbled, her worry exposed.

"Yeah, yeah, we're good," said Johnny, rushing to join the others.

Shorty, their best door buster, was in the lead, followed by Spider. Turk, now the senior man on the team, had been slotted in as the third man in the assault team. Johnny was right behind him. Christian was tail gunner on Team One, designated to stay at the entrance. They had another team in reserve, not only to back them up but also to run down "squirters" if there turned out to be a rear entrance they hadn't detected.

They ran from the hill toward the entrance, passing the small bomb mech that was to enter as a com link.

"Do it, Shorty," said Turk as they reached the entrance.

Johnny took a deep breath and held it as he plunged inside. There was a flash of light, then an explosive glow in the fog accompanied by a boom—Shorty had passed through the double L and tossed a flash-bang grenade down the long corridor that ran through the main part of the enemy bunker.

"Go! Go! Go!"

Everyone was yelling; everyone was saying the same thing:

Go! Go! Go!

Johnny moved to cover the hall as the assaulter in front of him entered the room nearest the entrance. Even with the enhanced optics embedded in the helmet, it was difficult to see because of the gas and dust in the hallway. He switched to infrared, which was little better.

Someone started firing a gun.

"Who's shooting?" asked Turk. "Who's firing?"

The gunfire stopped. Johnny's preset screen flashed on—Peter was ahead, standing at the end of the hall.

A body lay in front of it, a gun nearby.

"Tango down near the bot at the far end of the hall," said Johnny. He moved up to the next doorway, pausing to wait for the next pair of paras to take the room.

"Ghadab?" asked Turk.

"Too far to see."

"He's down?"

"Yeah. Gun's on the ground, a few feet away. The bot Tasered him."

"Get the room."

Another flash-bang announced that Shorty and

Spider were going in. Johnny moved up again, sliding to a knee as he saw a blur near the bot. This time there was a flash as Peter's Taser charge went off. The man went down.

"Another down," said Johnny. "They're in a room at the back."

"Stick to the plan," said Turk. "Johnny, hold position."

"Yeah, yeah."

Flash—bam.

"We got two prisoners. Incapacitated," said Shorty, working through the third room. "They're having trouble breathing. No threat. No weapons. Tying them."

OUTSIDE THE BUNKER, CHELSEA CRINGED EVERY time a flash-bang exploded. Hearing the explosions through the radio and in person gave them an odd, surreal tone, extending them into a strange, overlapping echo.

The mech with the com link finally got far enough into the bunker to pick up and relay Peter's feed. Peter was standing near the last room of the bunker.

Two team members ran up past the bot and entered the room. There was another prolonged bang and a flash on the screen.

"Moving ahead," she heard Johnny say. Then a shadow loomed in front of him at the end of the hall. He started falling back; a split second later she heard a loud bang—he'd been shot.

By THE TIME JOHNNY REALIZED THE BLUR IN THE hallway had a gun, he was already falling backward, knocked off his feet by a slug fired at close range. The bullet didn't penetrate his armor, but the impact hurt like hell, and for a moment he couldn't breathe.

Bullets sailed a few inches from his body, ricocheting off the walls. He tried to curl up and turn over to protect himself, but his limbs wouldn't move. Something dinged his right leg, then his left, twice.

A team member ran past, above him, shouting something. There was a flash and a bang—they entered the last room. Gunfire, and then nothing but a hollow echo in his ears.

Turk knelt over him. "You OK, bud?"

"Yeah."

"You got hit in the chest, point-blank. And the legs," Turk added, looking at his torn-up pants. "Ripped up."

"As long as they're still there," said Johnny. "Help me up."

"Let's get you outside to Docky."

Docky—aka David "Doc" Martin—was the team medic.

"It's just gonna be a really bad bruise," said Johnny.

"Not your legs."

"I'll trade them in."

Johnny pulled off his helmet as soon as he cleared the door. The fresh air was like an adrenaline shot.

Chelsea ran to him and began pulling him back.

"Get behind the rocks," she said.

"The bots."

"Peter can take care of himself."

"Me, too," insisted Johnny. But she wouldn't let go until they were behind the rocks. He sat down and pulled off his vest to inspect the damage.

Skin intact. Purple, but intact.

The others started dragging out the captured terrorists. They'd taken three alive; each had been given a strong dose of sodium pentothal inside the bunker, rendering them more or less inert.

Four others were dead, including the man who had shot Johnny.

"I have to get the bots packed up," Chelsea told Johnny, "then help retrieve the computers and such. You all right?"

"Yeah, I'm good," he said. "Real good."

"Pretty bruise you got," she said.

"Naw, just a birthmark," he said.

It hurt to laugh, but he did so anyway.

69

Northern Iraq—a few minutes later

THE RUSSIANS WERE GOING AFTER PALMYRA HARD. They had two more flights of fighter bombers heading in the general direction. Meanwhile, the Syrians were almost ready with their artillery.

So, the $64,000 question: Would they attack Johansen's people at the bunker? Or when they were on the way home?

He couldn't take the chance.

Johansen picked up the satellite phone he'd set aside to use only for contacting the Russians. He hesitated, then hit the quick-dial combination.

A voice in Russian told him to leave a message.

"We have an operation north of Palmyra," he said in English. "We're evacuating the area now. We need to exchange clearance IDs. Use the red circuit."

Useless. They aren't going to call, ever.

He hung up and looked over at Krista. "Tell the Air Force to scramble Option B. Fuckers."

70

North of Palmyra—the same time

JOHNNY WHEEZED WITH EVERY BREATH.

"Nothing broken," said Docky. "But it will hurt like shit. You want morphine?"

"Don't need it," insisted Johnny. He wanted to keep his head as clear as possible.

Rosen bent down to check on him. "You OK?"

"Yeah. Just bruised."

"Handle the phones?"

"I can do coms, sure."

Still a little woozy, Johnny followed the team leader to the trucks. With the bunker secured, the team was carting out everything they could. Rosen wanted to supervise, but with Chelsea inside examining the terrorists' computers, someone had to handle the communications and keep watch on the UAV screens.

"Ghadab?" asked Johnny.

Rosen shook his head.

Johnny put on the headset. He stared at the video from the Hum overhead, orienting himself—his brain felt as if it were still working in slow motion, and it took him several seconds to sort out where he was on the ground. The terrain around them was clear; the terrorists had not alerted anyone to the attack, or if they had, no help was on the way.

Johnny switched over to the Nightbird screen, which showed a wider view. Palmyra was at the bottom of the screen, a collection of shadows and flares as night came on—the Syrians had begun to shell it.

"Alpha Seven?" said Krista over the control frequency.

"This is Johnny," he answered. "Rosen is in the bunker. What's up?"

"We want you to take shelter," she told him.

"Shelter where?"

Johansen broke in. "There's a wave of Russian attack aircraft, Su-24s, about to hit Palmyra," said Johansen. "That's the second wave—the first came north after dropping their bombs. They just shot up a truck on the road. They must be looking for targets of opportunity—and you're all they'll see."

"What do you want us to do?" asked Johnny.

"Get in the bunker. All of you."

"What if they bomb that?"

"Better to be in the bunker than in the open. You have two minutes."

INSIDE THE BUNKER, CHELSEA FINISHED INVENTORYING the terrorists' computer equipment. None of it was special; the CPUs could have been purchased at any Walmart. The modems had boxes next to them, which Chelsea assumed were used for encryption, but otherwise there was nothing here that would look particularly out of place in a home office. After having the mechs check for explosives, they cut the power cords, severing the connections with the backup power supplies, and began carting the gear out. It was possible, maybe even likely, that they had already erased the hard drives, but Chelsea was fairly confident that data could be recovered as long as the drives remained physically intact.

Peter had been hit by several bullets; one had wiped out his radio connection. There was also damage to his IR sensor. None of the damage, though, explained why the bot had failed to neutralize the terrorist who shot Johnny. Its autonomous programming should have done that.

"Peter, give me a quick diagnostic read on AI section memory and logic circuits," she told it.

"Memory optimum. Logic . . . no problem detected."

"Let's go outside," she told it.

The bot turned and began walking down the hall. Chelsea followed it out, walking with it in the direction of the truck.

Johnny met her a few yards from the entrance.

"Where's your headset?" he asked.

"I took it off while I was working with Peter. There's something wrong with his AI. He should have protected you but—"

"Come on! Back inside," he told her.

"What's going on?"

"Russian planes. They're shooting up everything. They're close—hear them?"

"But—"

"Inside!" yelled Rosen, running up.

"I need to get Peter."

"Inside!" he yelled, grabbing her.

"Peter!"

Chelsea's shout was drowned out by the sound of gunfire as one of the Su-24s began shooting at the ground.

FAILURE TO CLOSE

———

Flash forward

Approaching the Syrian-Turkey border— two weeks after the fall of Palmyra

GHADAB HUNKERED DOWN AGAINST THE STACK OF *empty sacks, pretending to be sleeping. He was in the back of an empty vegetable truck, being ferried out of Syria with a half-dozen other men. They didn't know who he was, a precaution against being betrayed. His fellow travelers were likewise guarded about their identities; he assumed most were Caliphate deserters, though they presented themselves as simple refugees.*

They were a ragged, depressed bunch. They'd spent most of the past half hour complaining. But that was a typical pastime of men no matter what their condition.

"The war is lost," said one of the men. "The dictator will never be overthrown."

"The Iranians are to blame. Them and the Russians."

"I blame the Americans. They could have ended it."

Another man spit loudly at this. "The Americans

cannot finish a meal, let alone a war. They leave and expect others to pay the bill."

"As we have."

"I wish someone would serve them justice. Kill them with their drones."

"Explode them into space. That is what the Caliphate wished."

"What will happen now that they are defeated?"

"The Islamic State will not be defeated."

"They have been. All of their cities fall. Aleppo is next."

Ghadab resisted the temptation to argue. It was difficult, though.

But there was truth in what they said. The immediate strategic position would not hold. The dream of creating a state on earth before the end days was impossible to fulfill.

Surely, he had felt that. He had never had that ambition.

The men in the truck continued to talk. Maybe they weren't deserters after all—they seemed too critical of the Islamic State. It was harder and harder to pretend not to hear.

The truck came to a sudden stop. Ghadab felt someone kick him in the shoe.

"Up, up," said a voice in a half whisper. "The border is a half mile away. There are guards. Walk with the others to the east, and you will be safe enough."

Ghadab rubbed his eyes and slowly unfolded himself from the truck bed.

"Go with God," the driver told him after he jumped down. "But go. I don't need any trouble tonight."

"God be with you," Ghadab told him. "And don't despair. Great things will happen for all of us. There will be salvation."

"Not in my lifetime," said the driver, walking away.

71

North of Palmyra—two weeks before

CHELSEA SCREAMED FOR PETER TO FOLLOW, BUT her shouts were drowned out by the exploding bombs. Aiming for the entrance to the bunker, the Russian aircraft dropped two large unguided or "dumb" bombs; both missed, but not by much— the first hit the roof above the second barrier, and the second struck a few yards away. Already weakened by the TOW missiles, the roof there collapsed; a hurricane of dust and debris knocked everyone nearby back through the hall.

Chelsea flew against Rosen, who himself hit the wall. Cushioned, she rolled over, coughing and blinded. All but two of the battery-powered LED lamps they'd placed in the hall were smashed; the light from the others was not enough to penetrate the dust-filled dimness.

"You OK?" It was Johnny.

"I'm OK," she said. "Where are you?"

"Here." He patted her leg. "Rosen?"

The team leader grunted. A flashlight pierced the darkness. "Johnny?"

"Here."

"Rosen?" asked Turk.

"Uh."

The beam of light found Rosen's face, a dark grimace of pain. Christian came out of the room behind Turk. He pulled a small med pack from Rosen's leg.

"No morphine," managed Rosen.

"You got two compound fractures," said Christian. "You're gettin' stuck."

He jabbed the needle home.

The rest of the team had taken shelter in the rooms before the bombs hit and, except for minor bruises and a few cuts, were all right. Johnny, rising slowly, took out his own flashlight to lead the way out. Chelsea followed.

They got only to the first bend. The bombs had knocked down the weakened structure, trapping them inside.

"Son of a bitch," he muttered.

Those were the last words anyone said for a few minutes. Without orders, the team silently formed a chain and began removing pieces of debris from the pile now blocking their way. The narrow hall felt claustrophobic, the dust still thick in the air.

Suddenly Chelsea threw herself on the pile.

"Help!" she screamed. "Help!"

"Calm down," said Johnny, trying to pull her back. "It's OK. We'll get out."

"You don't understand," she insisted. "Help! Peter, get us out."

She was talking to the robot outside. Many of

its trials were aimed at rescuing people from collapsed buildings and earthquakes.

Within seconds, they heard scraping from the other side of the wall.

Even with Peter's help, it took two hours to get a hole big enough cleared for Chelsea to crawl through; another half hour of work was needed to make the passage big enough to slide Rosen out. By then, Johansen had arrived with two more vehicles and the rest of the team, except for Krista and Thomas Yellen, back at the base.

The Russian fighters had torn up the trucks and most of the gear pretty well; they'd also inadvertently killed the terrorists the team had taken from the bunker, who'd been handcuffed in the backs of the trucks.

A shame, thought Johansen—not because of the loss of life, but the intelligence they might have provided.

With the attack on Palmyra proceeding to the south, Johansen didn't want to take the time to sort the debris into usable and nonusable; they piled everything they could into the backs of the two trucks they'd come down with, then blew the others up.

By the time they got back to their temporary base in Kurdistan, Krista and Yellen had secured the gear they were taking in a large mobile cubicle. Two Ospreys were already en route, tasked to bring them across the border to Turkey, where a C-17 was waiting.

Johnny and Chelsea sat next to each other on the fabric bench at the side of their Osprey as they took off.

"Hell of a day," said Chelsea.

"Yeah," said Johnny.

"Do it again?" she asked.

"Not in a million years."

72

**The desert near Palmyra—
around the same time**

GHADAB SMELLED THE DESTRUCTION BEFORE HE could see it. It was the scent of sand pulverized and burned in a pit of old, dry wood soaked with kerosene.

The sun had gone down, but the sky beyond seemed even darker than normal as they crested the last hill above the plain where the city sat. A jumble of black lumps pockmarked with red flares and ribbons of yellow lay across the horizon.

"Take the west highway," Ghadab told the driver.

"That way may not be safe," said the man. "The apostates' attack—"

"It's faster."

The driver complied, his foot pressing the gas pedal to the floor nearly the entire way. Yet even as they neared the city, Ghadab knew in his heart that the worst had occurred. He could feel the loss already, even as he fought against acknowledging it.

He also knew the outcome of the battle had been decided, though for now the city remained in the hands of the faithful. Caliphate fighters trudged north along the barren fields at the north end of the city, heads hung low, weapons gone.

"Traitors!" he yelled.

He took out his pistol and rolled down the window of the car, shooting at several as they passed. Two fell.

The driver hurried on. A row of houses in the northern residential area had caught fire after one of the bombing attacks. Now out of control, the inferno blocked off part of the road, flames shooting sideways, scorching two abandoned trucks. A small crowd milled around the edges of the flames, watching their homes being incinerated. The reddish-yellow hue of the fire made them look like aliens, marooned on a planet unfit for life.

They took a shortcut, picking a way around debris and burned-out cars before getting back to the highway. A few minutes later, they came across a pickup truck parked across the road. As they stopped, a dozen men surrounded their vehicle.

Ghadab jumped from the car and started yelling, demanding to know who their leader was. A slim youth parted the crowd. He was a brash sort, displaying the anxious but cocksure bravado of someone who'd never actually tasted battle.

Ghadab did his best not to sneer in the boy's face.

"I am Ghadab min Allah," he said. "I have business at the town center."

"Prove you are the Prophet's favored son," said the young man.

Ghadab glanced at the others. They were even younger.

"And what proof would you accept?" demanded Ghadab.

The kid held his ground. "Where was your last target?"

"Anyone could answer that," snapped Ghadab. "What is your name?"

"Saed. From Tunisia." Finally, there was a note of humility in his voice.

"We attacked Boston," said Ghadab. "Before that, Paris, Belgium—I was fighting when you were in shorts."

"I recognize you now, Commander. Forgive me."

"Have the apostates reached the city yet?" Ghadab asked, softening his tone.

"No, Commander," said Saed. "They're not yet at the ruins. We are planning a counterattack."

"Good."

Ghadab got back in the car.

"Do you need an escort?" asked the man, following him.

"We know the way."

"God is great," replied Saed.

His heart is in the right place, thought Ghadab, deciding not to hold the young man's youth against him. *If we had a thousand more like him, things would be different.*

No one stopped them the rest of the way. In the meantime, the government shelling increased, until at last a fresh shell shook the city every ninety seconds. Ghadab could not see where the shells were landing, but if experience was any guide, the Syrian army would systematically destroy the residential areas, aiming to weaken the resolve of the fighters as well as produce as many casualties as they possibly could. That meant the attack would be aimed first at the south and the west, gradually moving east.

Ghadab agreed with the strategy. The only way to defeat an enemy was to wipe him off the face of the earth; extinguish him and remove all trace, so that others would not follow his apostasy. This was a thing Westerners didn't understand. Wars didn't end until the last enemy was vanquished. Generations might die in the meantime.

A bomb had landed near the entrance to the hotel, cratering much of the road. Ghadab's driver saw it only at the last minute, stopping so close that the front-right tire was poised over the edge.

"Be careful, Commander, when you get out," he told Ghadab.

Ghadab grabbed his AK-47. "Find a better place to sit and wait for me."

The guards who normally manned the front door were not here. Ghadab strode inside, steeling himself against what he might find. Night was falling and the power had been cut in much of Palmyra, but here a backup generator powered enough lights that the interior, though a gloomy yellow, could be easily navigated.

Ghadab walked through the lobby, holding the gun by the grip as if he were planning to fire, his finger against the trigger. The khanjar was sheathed in his belt below his shirt. He felt for it as he approached the stairs. He stopped, shouldered the rifle on its strap against his back, and took out the knife. He held it in his right hand as he started upward. It felt heavy and strong, warm.

A body lay folded across the rail at the top of the stairs. Ghadab pulled up the face and recognized the man as one of the guards from the front. His clothes were soaked with blood, his eyes the vacant orbs of a man whose soul had fled to heaven.

Another body lay a few feet away. Ghadab stepped over this one and continued to his room.

The door was open. He stopped and closed his eyes.

Later, he wished he had said a prayer before opening them. But that would not have changed what he saw, what he knew he would see: Shadaa, lying in a pool of blood, dead.

His love's destiny, dead.

GHADAB STOOD IN THE ROOM, SHOES IN HIS LOVER'S blood, for several minutes. Finally, he backed out, walking like a robot down the hall and down the stairs. As he reached the landing, he heard something moving behind him. He spun and came face-to-face with one of the waiters who had served him.

"Who did this?" Ghadab demanded. "Who killed the woman?"

The man shook his head.

"Who were they?!"

"Intruders—"

Ghadab sprung at him, pinning him against the wall. He put his knife to the man's throat. "Who?"

"I hid in the closet," stuttered the waiter. "They spoke English."

"Americans?"

The waiter didn't know.

"Where is the video?" demanded Ghadab. "To record." He pointed to the camera at the far end of the hall. "Where is it? Show me."

The man didn't move. Ghadab withdrew the knife, then grabbed his arm and pulled him away from the wall. The waiter looked toward the stairs.

"Is it upstairs?" demanded Ghadab.

"Y-yes."

Ghadab threw the man toward the steps. The waiter was not small, but Ghadab felt as if he had gained the strength of a dozen men; he could have hoisted him with one hand.

"Don't stop! Go!" yelled Ghadab.

Still tentative, the waiter moved up the stairs slowly, delicately stepping around the dead man and pulling a frame of a decorative textile off the wall, revealing a tape machine. The vacant eyes of the guard stared at them both.

The waiter started to leave. Ghadab grabbed him before he took a second step.

"I have to go to my family," said the waiter.

"Go to them all," said Ghadab as he slit the man's throat.

73

Louis Massina clenched his fists as the airplane touched down on the long runway, trying unsuccessfully to tamp down his excitement. He was happy his people were home, and proud of the work they'd done, and that he'd done, at least by extension.

It seemed to take an eternity for the leased 757 to come around to the hangar, where Massina was waiting with a group of CIA and Air Force officials. No brass band, no flag ceremony greeted the plane as it came to a stop. No one rolled out a red carpet.

The families of the men and women aboard hadn't even been invited. In fact, as far as most of the families knew, their loved ones were still in Arizona somewhere, training for some athletic competition. Most would never know anything about the mission.

The plane's rear ramp settled to the tarmac.

Johnny was the third man off the plane.

Chelsea followed, joking with Johansen as they came off.

"How are you feeling?" Massina asked Johnny.

"Good. Thank you for the vest."

"I'm sure you would have been all right without it."

"Lou!" Chelsea practically knocked him over, hugging him hard.

Massina patted her back awkwardly, surprised and touched by her greeting.

"I'm so glad you're safe," he told her. "I'm very glad."

WAITING TO BE FULLY DEBRIEFED BEFORE HEADING home, the team stayed in a guarded barracks on the base. Massina, meanwhile, headed for a nearby hotel. He had arranged to take Johnny and Chelsea back on the plane he'd leased—a concession to convenience he felt they both deserved.

He'd just gotten to his suite when Johansen called.

"I wonder if we could have a drink," asked the CIA officer.

"Sure," said Massina. "Pick your spot."

An hour later they met at a club near the San Antonio Museum of Art. Massina, surprised to find that he had gotten there first, ordered a bottle of San Pellegrino.

"That's as strong as you drink?" asked Johansen, sitting down just as the sparkling water arrived.

"I have a few calls to make later."

Johansen ordered a double Scotch.

"To your continued success," offered Massina when the drink came. Johansen raised his glass, but he had a frown on his face.

"We didn't get him," he said. "We came up short."

"I'm sorry," said Massina. He already knew that. "But you got his headquarters."

"Yeah. We'll see what value that is." Johansen took a slug from the Scotch—it was Dewar's—took another, then finished it. He pointed to a waiter, signaling for a refill. "The Russians complicated things. And the Syrians. They're still fighting there."

Johansen continued for a few minutes, forecasting the fate of ISIS—it would be chased from Syria and much of Iraq; the so-called Caliphate would collapse. But it would continue to export terrorism around the world. Its violence would live on.

And Ghadab?

It was possible, Johansen thought, that he had died in the attack on the city. "We'll know eventually. Hopefully before another attack."

"I still want to help get him."

"I appreciate that." Johansen's refill arrived.

"While you were gone, I gave your liaison information that we had tracked down on our friend," said Massina. "She didn't seem all that . . . enthusiastic."

"Probably not."

"Why?"

"Some people in the Agency think we're using you to get around the law," said Johansen bluntly.

"Are you?"

Johansen didn't answer at first. He was clearly tired, his eyelids hanging heavy. "My feeling is that we have to get things done, by whatever steps are possible. Nothing that you, or your people, did was illegal. But if it came to that, and it meant saving lives, I'd be all for it."

"So would I," said Massina.

The two sat in silence for a few moments. Massina sipped his water and looked around at the mostly empty club. Two women were gossiping in the corner, stealing glances at a young man at the bar.

"They were looking at cities around the world," said Massina. "Data requests. Boston was one."

"They've hit Boston already."

"True. And there were résumés, student résumés. Physics Ph.D.s."

"Interesting."

"She told you none of this?"

"I haven't been back."

Massina nodded.

"Director Colby truly appreciates your help," said Johansen. "And continued help. Your assets were extremely valuable in the field."

"My people or my machines?"

"Both." Johansen flagged down the waiter.

"That's a lot of Scotch," suggested Massina.

"I have to make up for lost time."

74

En route to Boston—the next day

AFTER THE C-17, EVEN THE MIDDLE SEAT IN THE LAST row of a 787 would have seemed luxurious to Chelsea.

The thickly cushioned leather seat in the Citation X was a long way from that.

"Champagne?" asked the attendant, giving her a big smile as he leaned down. He had a half-filled glass in one hand and a bottle in the other.

"Why not?"

He handed her the glass. "Should I leave the bottle?"

It was tempting, but she passed.

"For dinner, salmon or steak?" he asked. "Or both?"

"Salmon," she told him.

He nodded and moved on.

Good-looking guy, thought Chelsea. *He could be a movie star.*

Not as good-looking as Johnny, nor as tall, or as brave.

No one could be as brave as he is. To come back after the accident? To be a hero?

Johnny was sleeping in his seat across the aisle. She looked over at him, studying his baby face. So peaceful.

I wish I could sleep like that.

Chelsea dug into her bag for one of her sudoku magazines. She'd barely looked at any of them while she was gone.

Flipping to the middle of the magazine, she picked out a medium-hard puzzle and began working it, only to lose interest less than halfway through. Leaning back in her seat, she thought about what she'd been through over the past few weeks—not just in Syria, but at home in Boston.

I'm not that scared anymore.

Was I even scared in that room? I knew I'd survive it somehow.

"Excuse me, sir," said the attendant, tapping Johnny on the leg. "We're going to be landing in five minutes."

Johnny opened one eye.

"Thanks."

"You, uh, the leg's all bandaged?"

"Yeah, it's got a couple of holes in it," said Johnny. "I'll have to wait until I get back to get some new skin."

The attendant went away flustered. Amused, Johnny got up to stretch.

"What are you watching?" he asked Chelsea.

She'd turned on the TV that was in front of her seat.

"Soccer."

"Not baseball?" He glanced at his watch. "I think the Sox are playing."

"Not for another hour," she told him. "I checked."

"You like baseball?"

"Sometimes."

"Maybe we could catch some of the game," he suggested. "After we land."

"At Fenway?"

"Too late for that. It'll be sold out. But at a bar or something."

"You're not tired?"

"A little. But I don't feel like going home."

"Please, sir," said the attendant from the front of the plane. "We're about to land."

"I wouldn't mind it," said Chelsea. "It might be fun."

JOHNNY TOOK HER TO HALLIGAN'S, A SMALL PUB A few blocks from his house. Like just about every bar in Boston, it was Irish and it was red—Red Sox, that was.

But unlike many, it had a section of quiet booths where you could sit and watch the game in relative quiet. Given that the Sox were playing the Rangers, who were mired in a two-for-fourteen stretch, the place was only about half-full.

The only problem for Johnny was that Chelsea had mentioned the game to Massina, and then to Bozzone, who'd driven to the airport to pick them up. She'd invited both to come along, and to Johnny's great surprise, they accepted.

So it was the four of them. At least the Red Sox were winning.

No one seemed in a particularly talkative mood until the fifth inning, when, with the Sox up by five, Juan Fernandez was called out on a pitch way out of the strike zone. Fernandez argued and was immediately tossed from the game.

"The umpire was dead wrong," said Massina. "Look at the replay. The ball was almost a foot off the plate."

"Why don't they call balls and strikes electronically?" asked Chelsea.

Massina stiffened. "No. You can't do that."

"It's easy."

"Doesn't matter. You can't do that."

"Why not? Then there would be no arguments."

"It's a human game. Some things computers shouldn't do."

Johnny actually agreed with Massina—he wasn't even a fan of review—but he found himself arguing on Chelsea's side.

"The strike zone changes with every ump," Johnny pointed out. "It's so inconsistent it's ridiculous."

"You need space for the human element," insisted Massina. "It's a *game*."

"A precise strike zone is still human," said Johnny.

"You need a little leeway," said Massina.

"Otherwise, there's nothing to argue about,

right?" said Bozzone. "And that's half the fun of baseball."

They stayed until the seventh inning. Johnny declined the offer of a ride home—he only lived a few blocks away.

He was disappointed, though, that Chelsea didn't agree to walk as well. Admittedly, she'd have had a good hike if she did.

He would have carried her on his back.

"What do we do with your bag?" asked Bozzone. It was a large suitcase, though only about half-filled by his dirty clothes and two books he'd brought to read during training but never got around to.

"I can take it," Johnny said. "Or if you want, if you could, you could leave it at my door."

"Are you sure?" asked Massina.

"Yeah."

"You sure you want to walk?" asked Chelsea.

"Yup." There was no sense backing down.

"We'll see you next Monday," said Massina.

Johnny watched them drive off.

I need to ask her on a real date, he told himself. *I need a real plan. If I'm serious about dating her.*

Gotta give it a shot.

Johnny got a half a block before deciding he didn't really feel like going home. He turned around and went back to the pub, standing at the bar to watch the rest of the game.

75

Central Syria—a few hours later

GHADAB HAD NEVER BEEN A FOOT SOLDIER, BUT HE recognized a losing battle when he saw one. The brothers manning the positions on the southern side of the city moved with the slackness of men half-dead. They dragged themselves back and forth, stopping occasionally to see if they could find a target, but never shooting, as the barbarian government troops stayed far outside of their range. The Syrian army let the artillery do its work, shelling the city with various intensity during the day, easing off at night, though never letting more than a half hour go by without a shot.

The target wasn't the defenses but rather the residential areas behind them. The government aimed to wear down resistance, terrify the inhabitants, and unsettle whatever patterns of daily life remained. They had done this in Homs when Ghadab was there, spending weeks bombarding the city. That was one thing they got right: they knew war was a corrosive that must be applied endlessly.

Ghadab knew this, too. And for the first time in his life, he knew how desolate it felt.

Shadaa.

Such pain over a woman seemed completely unimaginable—not unlikely but rather impossible. The fact that she had been a slave, an insignificant piece of driftwood tossed to him by the hierarchy, made it even more unseemly. Yet her death wrenched him.

She was a diversion from his path. Ghadab told himself that God had taken her because she was a threat to his destiny. But it was hard to convince himself of this.

For the first time in his life he had felt love. Now he felt pain, true pain.

And something else: doubt.

Doubt in the prophecy. Doubt in the inevitability of Armageddon. Doubt in his role in bringing it to pass.

And what did that doubt mean but the ultimate heresy: doubt in God.

The bunker had been ransacked, all of his men killed. Much of his gear had been taken. There had been a battle; the place when he arrived still smelled of a putrid gas and gunpowder. He had no definitive way of knowing who had attacked, but he thought it must have been the Americans, seizing on the raid for cover to hit him.

They had missed him, but gotten everyone else close. Perhaps even the African, as Ghadab hadn't seen him since he had gone to see the Caliph.

Walking among the men who manned the city's defenses, Ghadab considered the idea of staying among them and becoming a martyr with the first assault. It would be an easy thing: stand up and fire as the heretics came on. Stand until a bullet found him.

Would she have wanted that?

More important, did God want that?

The commanders whom Ghadab met gazed at him with the same confused expressions of the soldiers on the front line: dazed, they were so shaken as to be incapable of logical thought. But the most unsettling thing was seeing that same gaze in the mirror when he returned to the apartment he had commandeered.

It was only by the strangest coincidence that Ghadab found the African. He was in the middle of his thoughts, sitting cross-legged on the floor, when two men with rifles barged in. Ghadab, his own AK next to him, looked up at them.

A man walked in behind them. It was dark, and his complexion was dark, and at first Ghadab did not realize who it was. Only when the African spoke did he know that God had sent him.

"You! I thought you were dead!" The African's shout filled the room.

"I am not dead," said Ghadab, rising.

He absorbed the African's embrace, enduring it, but not returning it.

"Are you all right?" asked the African. "You have blood on you?"

"I'm all right."

"Have you been to the bunker? How did you escape?"

"I was waiting for the Caliph when they attacked."

"They think you are dead. Your name was added to the scroll of the martyrs."

"It will belong there soon."

"No. You must go to the Caliph. He will have something for you."

Ghadab said nothing.

"You must use your talents to strike back," urged the African. "You must carry on the battle. Take it to their homes."

"I'm tired," said Ghadab.

He meant only that he wanted to sleep, but the African interpreted it to mean that he wanted to leave the fight.

"You mustn't give up. You have to avenge our brothers. You have to bring about the prophecy."

"Yes."

"Are there others here? We'd like to get rest."

"There's no one here but me," said Ghadab.

"Do you mind?"

He gestured that they should go right ahead. Each man took a separate room. Ghadab went back to sitting, thinking. It was not logical thought—no plan entered into his mind, no list, no theme. He saw the walls in front of him, lit by the afternoon sun.

Eventually he heard snores coming from the rooms. Only then did he know what he must do.

He slit the first guard's throat through his

beard, plunging the khanjar in an awkward slashing jab just as the man seemed to stir. He was more thoughtful taking the second—he carried a pillow with him to muffle any noise. Propping it near his head, he delicately lifted the man's beard with his left hand and sliced deep, hard, and fast with his right. Immediately his victim began to choke, blood gurgling; Ghadab pressed down with the pillow over his face until the convulsions stopped.

The African lay on his stomach. Ghadab raised the knife, then realized he wanted the man awake, to see his fate.

He was heavy.

"Turn, you bastard," Ghadab growled, pushing him over. "Turn over and wake up."

One eye opened. Then the other. The African started to raise his head, his neck meeting the knife.

"You didn't protect her. It was your duty." Ghadab plunged the khanjar so hard it broke through the African's windpipe, nearly severing his head. Blood spurted and flooded and rushed. "You didn't protect her. And for that, you die."

76

JOHANSEN STOPPED AT THE STARBUCKS ON THE MAIN floor of the building before going up to see the Director. He'd already drunk the equivalent of a pot and a half that morning, but needed the caffeine—he hadn't slept more than four hours total since coming off the plane from Turkey.

"Venti latte with eight shots."

The barista didn't bat an eye. A latte with the equivalent of eight espressos mixed in was not out of the ordinary here.

The coffee smell filled the elevator as he rode up to the top floor. He went straight to the Director's office; for once, he didn't have to wait before being shown in.

Which was a shame, because he'd have preferred to finish the coffee.

"Good to see you back in one piece," said James Colby. Though there was no doubt he meant it, the Director said this without enthusiasm. He came out from behind his desk and shook Johansen's hand. Then he pulled over a chair so they could sit opposite each other without the desk in between.

Johansen told him what had happened, repeating a brief he'd given no less than eight times in the past two days. He ended by mentioning his disappointment at the failure.

"I don't see it as a failure," said the Director. "The girl—she was a Russian spy?"

"We think so. We think we've correlated her with a Chechen woman agent that we saw being trained two years ago. It's hard to tell—there's been no intercepts regarding her."

"Did the Russians plant her on purpose, or was it a coincidence?"

"No way of knowing at this point."

"Is he dead?"

"I don't think so. Our friend Louis Massina gave us some leads on his network. That led us to a credit card that's been dormant, had been dormant until yesterday. We also have a source who claimed to have seen him in Raqqa the day before."

"So he's still alive?"

"It would appear so."

"Our friend Mr. Massina—he's been very useful," said Colby.

"He has. He's interested in doing more."

"He's done a lot already." The Director rose. "I have to go before the Intelligence Committee this afternoon. You know, there have been rumors about the operation."

"Really? That's impossible."

"They come from Massina?"

"No way."

"You could swear to that?"

Johansen studied his coffee. No, maybe he couldn't swear, but he thought it highly unlikely.

"I don't think he'd tell anyone. We used his people for support and they got involved more than we'd planned, but I don't think either one of them would have said anything to anyone. No one on the team would."

"Hmm."

That's all we need, thought Johansen, *a witch hunt for leaks.*

"I want to keep looking for Ghadab," said Johansen. His assignment had been temporary, and as a general rule he would be given a good hunk of time off and rotated to a new assignment when he reported back.

"Turner was going to take over the team."

"I don't think he should. For one thing, he doesn't play well with others, especially outside of the Agency."

"I think that's a matter of opinion."

"I want to stay on. I want to get this guy. I'm pretty close. There's no learning curve. We can't afford an interruption now. And with Massina—I don't see Turner getting his help."

"You said he's already helping."

"More help."

"What about Demi?" Demi Ascoldi was second-in-command of the team. "She could take over."

"She's worse than Turner."

Colby laughed. "Yuri Johansen, the indispensable man."

"No."

"All right, stay with it. Your show for now. But, Yuri—keep our friend Massina under control."

"I was told he was very laid-back."

"That's not Ascoldi's view. And yes, he would be a convenient scapegoat if it came to that. But I'd prefer not to throw him under the bus."

The Director returned to his desk, signaling the meeting had come to an end. But then, as Johansen was leaving, he asked if he had seen the morning reports from the NSA.

"I haven't had a chance," confessed Johansen.

"Chatter level is way up. Not a good sign."

"No," admitted Johansen. "Not a good sign."

77

"Now we come to RBT PJT 23-A . . . aka Peter."

Johnny watched Chelsea as she began flipping through some brief video captures from the drone as it had ventured down the center hall of the bunker in Syria. Her tone remained scientific, but there was a frown on her face. The drone had not performed as expected.

Which of course he knew, given that he had been the one shot.

"It saw the terrorist," continued Chelsea, freezing the frame that showed the shadows in the dark room at the end of the bunker, "but it did not perceive him as a threat. Why not?"

Her laser point circled the shadow at the corner. That was the son of a bitch who'd shot him.

Prick. But he'd paid the ultimate price.

Chelsea flipped to a screen filled with computer code and began discussing what the letters and numbers meant. The engineers in the small auditorium—there were nearly fifty, with every seat taken and a few people standing on the side—seemed to lean forward en masse, and more than a couple had their lips moving as they followed along, parsing the lines.

Johnny was lost in the weeds, but he didn't care; he was focused on Chelsea, watching how she moved, how intense she seemed.

How pretty she was.

This was the first time he'd seen her since getting back to Boston. He'd spent his downtime sleeping at first, then in New York with some friends to see the Sox sweep the Mets—not as sweet as beating the Yankees, but up there. When he came back, Bozzone asked him to prepare a proposal for increasing the company's security division, integrating more bots and technology into an "action team" that could accomplish missions similar to what they'd done in Syria. It was a heady assignment, somewhat beyond his comfort level as it had to include budget and revenue projections . . . It was supposed to make a profit.

He had no idea what sort of revenue was possible until talking to some old acquaintances who were now working for international security firms.

Their answer: A lot. Maybe a lot a lot.

How much depended on specifics he couldn't give. So he mostly punted. Or would: he was still working on it.

"I wonder if it thought the terrorist was on your side," suggested Jin Chiang. "Because you have other guys in that environment who look similar. And you know its basic AI is working—it rescued you."

"It did," agreed Chelsea.

"It does register a threat after the fact," pointed out another software engineer. "Look at line 302. But I bet Johnny wishes it had recognized the threat sooner."

It took Johnny a moment to realize everyone was looking at him.

"What?" he asked. "Oh, right."

Massina interrupted the laughter that followed.

"I think we've gone as far with this as we can today," he said. "Right now, Ms. Goodman and Mr. Givens have appointments at city hall. And the rest of us are invited to witness it."

This was the first Johnny had heard of that, and judging from the look on Chelsea's face, it was a surprise to her as well.

"But before we wrap up," added Massina, "I think we can all show our appreciation for our two people who risked their lives helping give a little payback to the bastards who did so much damage to our city. For Boston!"

Massina sounded more like a football coach than an intense but pragmatic scientist.

The engineers cheered. A few behind Johnny tapped him on the back, nudging him to stand.

He felt his face warm with embarrassment.

"Just doing what I can," he mumbled.

He made his way up to Massina in time to hear Chelsea ask what was going on. He was glad of that: it saved him the trouble.

It also gave him an excuse to look at her.

"It's just a little thank-you the city has arranged," said Massina. "No big deal."

"Is this for Syria?" she asked.

"No. That's strictly confidential. This is for the attack. Bravery under extreme circumstances."

"The city arranged this?" asked Chelsea. "Or you?"

"The city," insisted Massina, but he had the slight impish look he got when he was foisting a surprise on someone.

A good surprise.

"Are you in on this?" Chelsea asked Johnny as he walked up to the front.

"No. Not a clue."

"Downstairs, both of you," said Massina. "We're running late."

Chelsea grabbed her laptop and briefcase.

"You'll want to leave that upstairs," added Massina. "You'll be gone all night."

Johnny and Massina were waiting when Chelsea came down. There were three black Yukon SUVs parked in front of the entrance.

"We're in the middle," said Massina.

"The hotel is three blocks away," said Chelsea. "Can't we just walk?"

"Easier this way," said Massina.

"I doubt it," said Chelsea.

"You're in a grouchy mood," said Massina mildly. "Not enough coffee today?"

"You should have told us."

"I did."

Ten minutes later—traffic was relatively light— they arrived at the hotel and pulled into the downstairs garage. Johnny unfolded himself from the back, following along behind the others. Standing next to Chelsea as they went up, he made it a point to look away from her.

They stopped on the third floor. Johnny was surprised to see a throng of people in the atrium lobby as they turned the corner from the elevators. They were all very well dressed, the men in suits and ties.

"This is a fancy thing," said Chelsea.

"Black-tie," said Massina.

"Crap—all I have on are jeans."

"I'm a little out of place, too," said Johnny. Though he had a sport coat, he was wearing jeans and sneakers.

"There's a solution for that," said Massina. "For both of you, actually. Come on."

He led them down the hall to a suite. Two racks of clothes stood in front of the couches in the living room. One contained dresses; the other had a tuxedo and white shirt. Two women were standing nearby.

"Take your pick," Massina told Chelsea. "These ladies will help with any alterations you need." He turned to Johnny. "I'm afraid you're on your own, but we did use your measurements that you had for the gear in Syria."

IT WAS AN EXCEPTIONAL NIGHT, ONE THAT PLEASED even Massina, who was ordinarily deeply bored by these sorts of things. Not only did he sit patiently through the speeches, but he gave one of his own.

"Boston is too strong to be hurt by terror,"

he said. "We kicked out the Red Coats, and we haven't stopped since. Do your worst; we'll kick you in the teeth."

He wished he could tell the audience about the recent actions in Syria, but he knew that would only hurt the country. The best he could do was say he "hoped" the perpetrators of violence would be brought to justice.

But all in all, he thought it was an exceptional night.

THE SPEECHES WERE BAD ENOUGH; THE REPORTERS' interviews were even worse.

Chelsea didn't realize that saying she would talk to one journalist meant that every other one in the building would queue up behind him, subjecting her to a marathon of squinting into a camera while repeating the words "overwhelmed," "humbled," "very happy" over and over again. At least a dozen other people who had been held hostage at the hotel were honored as well, but the reporters seemed to zero in on her. She kept glancing over at Johnny, who somehow managed to avoid the reporters while milling around with Bozzone and some of the other Smart Metal people.

"He's the real hero, you know," she said finally, pointing to him as he went to the bar nearby. "He broke in and rescued me."

Johnny rolled his eyes and shook his head, continuing in a beeline to the bar.

Finally, the reporters were done. Chelsea got up, only to find that the bar had been shut down.

"Hey," said Johnny.

She punched him in the shoulder. "You suck."

"What?"

"I had to talk to all of them. You should have been the one. You saved me."

"Eh. You saved yourself. I got there after the fact."

He's right, isn't he? Maybe I did save myself.

"Thirsty?" Johnny asked.

"Dying."

"Let's try downstairs."

They went down to the bar on the first floor, but it was so crowded they couldn't see the actual bar.

"I think we should go somewhere else," suggested Johnny.

"How about that cute place you took us to when we got back?"

"Sure."

Johnny started to lead her out of the lobby.

"Wait," she said, grabbing his arm. "Don't you think we're a little overdressed?"

Johnny looked down at his tux, then over at her. "You're not," he said.

Chelsea laughed. "I think we better change."

78

Agadir, Morocco—about the same time

"HOW LONG WILL YOU BE STAYING WITH US?" ASKED the hotel clerk.

"Three days," said Ghadab.

The man reached for the passport Ghadab had placed on the marble counter. "I need to make a copy."

Ghadab nodded. The clerk went into a closet-sized room directly behind the registration desk; in the dim light of the lobby, the flash of the copy machine as it moved its platen seemed like the spark of an explosion.

About midway down the Moroccan west coast, Agadir was something of a budget beach destination for young European tourists during the winter. During the summer, however, it was relatively quiet, an easy place to strategize.

The hotel clerk returned, handing him the passport as well as a key.

"Free internet," said the man. His Moroccan-flavored Arabic was hard for Ghadab to decipher. "Type *Guest* as the password."

Ghadab thanked the man politely. Even if he'd had a computer or other device with him, he wasn't so foolish as to use a hotel's internet for anything beyond looking up the weather.

Upstairs, he checked the room for bugs. His search was crude—he looked for alterations, wires even, knowing that he would miss anything sophisticated. But the discipline was what was necessary; to rebound, one had to return to basics. And at least a search would detect anything the locals could manage.

Satisfied, Ghadab washed up. The porcelain in the sink was cracked and the water warm rather than cold; neither was unexpected. Refreshed if not restored after his long trip, he went out for a walk. The hotel was far uphill from the beaches and the large, ultramodern resorts that hugged the water, but even here the buildings were not very old; an earthquake in the 1960s had eradicated much of the town, and for the most part the cement-faced structures he passed were less than thirty years old.

It helped, too, that war had not visited the city for many years. The creases in the faces of the people he passed came from age, not constant fear; if there were marks in the facades of the buildings, they were from shoddy workmanship rather than gun battles.

Ghadab had shorn his head and beard before leaving Syria, and he doubted even his own mother, God rest her soul, could have recognized him. He wore Western clothes—black jeans and a soccer jersey with the number of

Lionel Messi, the Argentine player so famous even here that the shirt was as anonymous as a paper bag. Ghadab had left all of his belongings at the border with Turkey when he fled.

The only item he regretted leaving was the knife. But he couldn't have taken it on the airplane, and in any event the symbolism of the sacrifice was important; to continue he needed to strip himself of all.

Making his way through the crowded streets, Ghadab recognized many of the small shops. It had been two years since he'd been here, and his memory of the place had faded, dimmed by hundreds of other cities and towns, large and small, which to varying degrees had similar qualities. Finally, he found what he was looking for—a secondhand computer store. Halfway between a pawnshop and a discount retailer, it featured everything from point-and-shoot cameras to the latest Macintosh computers, insisting in semiliterate Arabic that all were "new out of box" while at the same time noting that "all sale final no warrants."

After a bit of haggling, Ghadab bought an old tablet computer for fifty euros; down the street, at a coffee shop that offered Wi-Fi, he created an account and began surfing the web, randomly moving from page to page, watching a few YouTube videos of car races, then checking the news, then a travel site for flights to Athens.

He'd landed on Google News when a headline caught his eye: *Les victimes du terrorisme honorés à Boston.*

Terror victims honored in Boston.

It was about his Boston triumph. Apparently there had been a ceremony in the city.

His French was too rusty to read the entire story reliably, so he had it translated to English; when the page came into focus, he realized the woman in the photo that accompanied it looked familiar.

He couldn't place her at first. There was a video with the story. He clicked it and watched as an older man talked about how his city couldn't be defeated.

"Louis Massina," declared the caption.

Oh, yes, he knew who he was. But the woman . . .

Ghadab stopped and replayed the video. The announcer said two employees had been honored. A photo showed the woman and a man, and Massina. He was their boss, a business owner in Boston.

The woman . . . the same one on the video from the hotel, the one who'd gone up to the room with Shadaa.

Was it?

It seemed far-fetched and yet . . .

No, of course. It made complete sense. This Massina had sought revenge for his city. That was what he wanted.

And he had achieved it.

More.

Boston.

Boston.

That would have to be the final target. Honor demanded it.

79

Boston—about the same time

JOHNNY FELT A LITTLE LIGHT-HEADED AS HE CLOSED the door to change. He'd had only two drinks, so it wasn't the booze. And though the doctors had changed his medicine as soon as he got back to accelerate his healing after the bangs and bruises, he couldn't blame that either—they'd made it clear that the drugs didn't interact with alcohol.

So it had to be Chelsea, who was changing a few feet away, slipping out of the formfitting gown she'd been wearing.

There was a wall between them, so he couldn't see her. But he certainly could imagine. He'd thought she was beautiful before tonight, but in the gown she was stunning.

Beyond stunning.

Maybe that was an exaggeration. Maybe she didn't quite look like a model. Probably she wasn't the perfect woman, every young man's wet dream.

But she was close. Certainly to him.

There was a knock on the door.

"Ready?" Chelsea asked.

"Just a minute," he said.

"And they say women are slow." Chelsea laughed. "Meet you downstairs in the lobby."

HALLIGAN'S WAS FARTHER THAN CHELSEA THOUGHT, but the night was warm without being hot, and walking with Johnny felt incredibly right. They talked about the ceremony, how goofy it had been; they talked about the reporters, how little they knew; they talked about the interviews, how little they could say.

Finally, they talked about Syria itself.

"Were you scared in town?" Johnny asked.

"Very. Were you?"

"The first time we went in, I was a little nervous at different points. But we trained so much, I was kind of confident. Except for the language."

"I know what you mean. Using the translator was kind of weird. I have a couple of ideas for fixing it."

"I'll bet you do."

They walked a half block without saying anything. Johnny broke the silence.

"I was worried about you. That last mission. I wasn't scared for myself at all, but I was worried that something would happen to you. Maybe focusing on that makes you forget to be scared about yourself."

"Ukraine was like that for me," said Chelsea. "I was too dumb to know to be scared."

"That's a funny word to use."

"What?"

"Dumb. You're the opposite of dumb. Like, a genius."

"I'm not a genius. I know some geniuses."

"There are people smarter than you?"

She smacked him on the arm.

"Hey, that was a serious question. I wasn't making fun."

"I'll bet."

"Really."

Johnny suddenly stopped. "I feel like a robot."

"What?"

"Like I'm not human. Because of my legs."

"Jesus—they're better than your real ones. And they keep improving them and with the drugs—"

"That's just it," said Johnny. "I don't—it's not totally me."

"I think you're still you," insisted Chelsea. "Your legs are just part of you, not the entire thing of who you are."

"If you lost your legs, would you feel whole?"

"I don't know," she admitted.

The bar was full with the post-happy-hour crowd, and there were no open booths or tables.

"Don't you live near here?" Chelsea asked Johnny after surveying the crowd.

"Couple of blocks."

"Why don't we go there?"

JOHNNY'S HANDS TREMBLED AS HE AIMED HIS KEY FOR the lock. He felt as nervous as a teenager on his first date—more nervous, really.

Chelsea stroking his arm didn't help.

Not that he wanted her to stop.

He got the key into the lock and opened the door.

"It's not much," he said. "The main attraction is the location."

"Oh, it's nice." Chelsea walked in behind him, taking in the front room, which was decorated in what might be called contemporary mishmash—a largish sofa and a wooden rocker sat opposite a sixty-inch flat screen flanked by an orphaned dining room chair and an end table he'd assembled himself. The main function of the last two pieces was to hold the large JBL monitors that formed the heart of his sound system. There was a bookcase on the far wall, along with two baskets of dirty sheets and clothes.

"So, wine?" he asked, heading for the kitchen.

"Sure."

As Johnny stepped into the kitchen, he realized he wasn't sure if he even had any wine.

"Or beer?" he asked, turning quickly.

He was surprised to find Chelsea right behind him, a foot away.

Inches, actually.

Her eyes were wide and round, her face the color of a rose in twilight.

"Whatever you have will be fine."

She stretched her neck, lifting her face toward his. He leaned closer, and they kissed.

PUPPET MASTER

—

Flash forward

Boston—two months later

*T*HE LAUGH WAS DEEP AND DARK, THE SORT THE DEVIL
himself would make if he came to life.

*"You control these people," said the terrorist. "You
put them on the stage like puppets."*

"I control no one," replied Massina.

*"It's your time to die, Puppet Master. You and your
city. Time for the apocalypse and God's final glory."*

80

Boston—eleven days before

Chelsea turned over and opened her eyes, struggling to focus on the alarm clock's small blue numbers. She saw a 5, but couldn't make out what followed.

4.

8.

5:48 A.M.

Shit!

She needed to be at work at six for a test run of a new bot series. She swung her feet over the side and slipped out of bed, heading quickly for the bathroom.

Johnny stirred under the covers.

In the two months since they had first kissed, Chelsea had spent many nights with Johnny. It was a unique experience, first because he lacked "real" legs and generally, though not always, took them off to sleep.

But there were other things that made it unique, special. Most of the men she had dated were computer or science geeks, whizzes who fed that part of her. Johnny was the first man who fed something else, a part more physical, more emotional.

They had things in common. First and foremost, they'd had similar life-and-death experiences, and in the same places at the same time—she'd been there when he'd lost his legs; he'd been there when she was nearly raped and killed.

More: They were both Red Sox fans. They liked to take long walks and bike rides, especially by the water. They both liked to listen to indie music. They liked to share interests. Chelsea was starting to like alt-country, thanks to Johnny. Johnny was starting to appreciate fusion cooking, thanks to Chelsea.

But there was no denying basic differences: He didn't spend his days thinking about computer code or how to best train a piece of software to be self-cognizant. And she didn't spend her days thinking of how to preserve situational awareness while escaping a kidnapping attempt or consider the pros and cons of nonlethal shotgun charges.

They came at life from different directions, with just enough in common to meet at many different intersections. And that seemed to be what both of them needed.

And the sex.

Awkward and nervous at first—*how do you make love to a legless man?*—it was now comfortable and gentle, yet reassuring and fulfilling and all those other words teenage magazines promised and adult magazines said were difficult to achieve.

The fact that Johnny didn't have his legs was always a fact, always something they were both aware of—how could they not be? And yet it wasn't the *only* fact.

Caffeine. I need serious amounts of caffeine.

"See you later, Sleeping Beauty," she said, grabbing her Nikes and tiptoeing for the door.

CHELSEA MADE IT TO THE LAB WITH ABOUT THIRTY seconds to spare. She walked directly to the test board, where the test coordinator and a half-dozen other engineers were waiting. They'd already run through all of the pretest workups; the systems were green and recording.

Also waiting were eleven Smart Metal employees who'd volunteered to participate in the exercise. And it *was* an exercise: they were going to play soccer with Peter, who was sitting beyond the cones and taped field boundaries in the cavernous interior of Subbasement Level 3. Peter had not been programmed to play and had never even watched a game. Once the session began, Chelsea would give him a verbal command to join one of the squads. What happened next was up to him.

"Ready?" asked the test director.

Chelsea donned a headset and walked over to the robot. "Peter?" she said.

RBT PJT 23-A acknowledged by turning one of its claws. Chelsea looked back at the director and gave a thumbs-up.

A whistle sounded, and the game began, "red" with the ball and moving into "blue" territory. Blue was down a man but otherwise the teams were evenly matched.

"Peter," said Chelsea as the whistle blew. "Observe game. Join on blue's side."

Peter reoriented his "body," directing all of his visual sensors toward the field.

By the time Chelsea had returned to the bank of monitors, Peter had walked onto the pitch. He appeared to be observing, taking a spot near blue's penalty area.

Eight different screens at the main test bench recorded the bot's thought processes as it worked, with different analytic tools analyzing the data. Chelsea focused her attention on a tool that selected out open questions—queries by the AI engine as it proceeded.

Peter had tried to access Smart Metal's information system to gather information about the game, but the system had been closed to it. So it turned its attention to the game.

Most of its attention. It devoted about 20 percent of its resources to trying to break through the security system barring it access.

An interesting decision, thought Chelsea.

One of the red players took a pass and began dribbling in Peter's direction. Peter took a step forward—then promptly sat down. Play continued around it, but the bot remained frozen on the ground, not even watching the action.

Expecting a malfunction, Chelsea looked at the

monitors. Peter's "brain" was still operating normally, according to the data; it just wasn't moving.

And it was still using twenty percent of its processing power to try to get into the Smart Metal system.

"So is Cristiano Ronaldo in trouble or what?"

Chelsea jerked around. Louis Massina had snuck in to watch the demonstration.

"I'm impressed that you know a soccer player," said Chelsea. "But Peter's on defense, and Ronaldo plays forward."

"He doesn't seem to be playing at all."

"I know. I'm not sure why."

"What's he doing?"

"Analyzing every play he's seen," said Chelsea, freezing the screen that displayed data on the processors. "It accesses recent memory, but it's also looking to compare it to its stored history."

"Why?" Massina bent over her shoulder to examine the data.

"I don't know. I could arbitrarily put a limit on the processing loops or time—"

"No, I don't think so," said Massina. "It has to learn. It should be able to set those limits itself. But it is similar to Syria. He adopts a base position when confused."

"But he's not in base position." Chelsea suddenly felt as if she had to defend the bot. "He's thinking."

"He should react."

"He usually does."

Massina smirked, and Chelsea knew why—

usually wasn't good enough. And a human being in either situation would not have hesitated.

"The interesting thing is that this is new," noted Massina. "Peter has learned to hesitate."

Chelsea furled her arms in front of her chest and leaned back in the chair. She hadn't thought of the situation that way before, but Massina was right—the bot had performed without hesitation in hundreds if not thousands of roughly analogous situations before.

Was this good or bad?

She glanced at him for an answer, but instead he looked at his watch and changed the subject. "I need to show you something."

"OK. When?"

"Now."

"I'm supposed to supervise the rest of the experiment," she said.

Massina nodded at Peter, frozen on the field as the players moved around him. "I think he's gone as far as he's going today."

"But Peter—"

"They can continue the tests and diagnostics without you. He's grounded until we figure it out anyway."

"But—"

"This is more important," said Massina, starting away.

TEN MINUTES LATER, CHELSEA GOT INTO THE BACK of one of the company's black SUVs, joining

Massina. The truck had no driver; or rather, no human driver—it was guided by Smart Metal software, still being tested for commercial use, but more than adequate according to Massina.

"Where are we going?" she asked.

"Across the river."

"Is this one of our projects?"

"It is, and it isn't," he said.

"Shouldn't one of us sit in the driver's seat?" she asked.

"You're welcome to if you want."

"Will you tell me where we're going then?"

"The car knows. That's enough."

Chelsea stayed in the back. Massina spent the ride going through emails, checking in with his assistants—both real and virtual—and in general clearing away as much of his normal routine as he could.

Thirty minutes later, the SUV pulled into the parking lot of an abandoned shopping center. Built in the late 1960s, the place had succumbed to the competitive pressure of Amazon.com and Walmart a few years before. Its metal facade, virtually untouched since its opening, was streaked with rust. The sun-faded outlines of letters from old store logos lined the roof, a ghost alphabet of now-dead retail.

"Are we going shopping?" asked Chelsea.

"Not quite. Come on."

Massina got out of the truck and guided her to a door that had once led to a restaurant at the side of the complex. Two armed guards were standing just inside the door. They nodded at Massina as he passed.

He walked through the former restaurant, now empty of furniture. A single light lit the interior until he reached the mall proper, where the light from the skylight was augmented by an array of LEDs whose color and output changed depending on the time of day.

"The escalator doesn't work," he told Chelsea. "So watch your step."

Another pair of guards waited downstairs. The security station was augmented by a sniffer and a metal detector; a pair of combat mechs stood nearby. Each was a miniature gun chassis, with four 9mm machine guns. An elevator door stood about fifty feet away; Massina walked to it.

"Put your hand on the plate," Massina told Chelsea after demonstrating. "We can't go anywhere until it decides you are approved."

"Am I?"

"Up to them." Massina smirked.

Chelsea did as she was told, putting her hand on the plate. A light at the bottom glowed green, and the doors closed.

The elevator took them down to a mechanical level. Well lit, it was filled with large pipes and conduits, as well as stacks of furniture and other items taken from the stores above. Massina led Chelsea past them to a solid steel door, remarkable only because it was brand-new. He put his hand against another glass panel, then motioned for Chelsea to do the same.

The door opened with a pneumatic hiss. Behind it was a computing center. Six men sat at terminals. Two typed furiously; the others were scrolling and reading.

"What's going on?" Chelsea asked.

"We've broken into Daesh's communications network," said Massina. "We're monitoring what they're up to."

81

Pierre Trudeau International Airport, Montreal—around the same time

ISHMAEL PETERSON—OTHERWISE KNOWN AS GHADAB min Allah, aka Samir Abdubin, aka the Butcher of Boston—squeezed his fist as the airplane rolled toward the gate.

It had taken him nearly forty-eight hours to arrive in North America. He still had a long way to go, but he'd calculated that the airport would be the most difficult hurdle, the one time when he had to stand face-to-face with the authorities.

He would show no fear, but that was hardly enough.

The door to the cabin opened. He rose from his seat in first class and joined the parade of passengers leaving the plane.

"Have a pleasant visit," said the steward at the door.

He smiled, unwilling to test his accent even with a single word. His English itself was fine, but he wasn't positive about the accent. He'd practiced by listening to podcasts for several hours each night over the past several weeks, but there had been no way of testing himself adequately.

Ghadab's Canadian eTA—an electronic travel authorization—showed that he was an Israeli citizen. This matched his passport and driver's license, as well as his credit cards and two receipts tucked in amid the bills. He also had a letter from his "cousin" in his pocket and pictures of his "family." He'd memorized the details, of course, as well as his explanation for why he was visiting—sightseeing and vacation—as well as an extensive backstory.

But one little mispronunciation—a long vowel where a short was expected—could upend everything.

The bags took a while to arrive. Two men in uniform walked dogs around the crowd. Ghadab smiled at the dogs—more for practice than anything else. They took no notice of him.

Reunited with their luggage, Canadians headed for a lineup of machines that allowed for automated processing. Ghadab went with the other foreigners, joining a queue that looked almost exactly like the ones he had studied before starting his journey.

He clenched his fist again as he joined the line. The hardest thing was to smile.

Smile.

Who could smile after such a long flight? The passengers behind him looked worn and tired. A few were annoyed.

He'd fit right in.

Something banged up against his leg—a four- or five-year-old tot had escaped its parent.

Before Ghadab could find something to say, a woman appeared with another child in tow. She grabbed the youngster who had bumped against his leg, scolding him in French.

"I am sorry," she told Ghadab in English.

"Go ahead of me," he said.

"Are you sure?"

She reminded him of Shadaa. Not physically, but the way she spoke—tender, yet sturdy.

Now it was easy to smile, though it was leavened with sadness.

What I have lost!

"Go ahead. You have children. I have . . ." He shrugged. "Nothing."

The woman herded the two children and a large suitcase into the line. The queue suddenly spurted ahead, and Ghadab found himself facing a border-entry guard. He held out his passport.

"You're with them?" asked the man.

"No."

"It was nice of you to let her go. How long are you visiting?"

"A week. My flight—"

The guard's machine beeped, having already read the passport and matched it with its central records. "What do you have in the bag?"

"My clothes."

"Nothing to declare?"

Ghadab shook his head.

"Have a good visit," said the guard, waving him through.

82

Boston—an hour later

THE TERMINALS IN THE COMPUTER CENTER—NICKNAMED the "Annex" by Massina—were connected to a Cray XT5 system, whose Opteron quad-core processors were arrayed to produce almost 2.7 petaflops—roughly 2,700,000,000,000,000 floating-point operations per second. That was computing power of an extreme magnitude, beyond even what Smart Metal housed. As a point of comparison, the National Center for Computational Sciences at Oak Ridge National Laboratory was capable of 1.3 petaflops (or at least had been, when first delivered some eight years before; there had been modifications since). A personal computer might run 7,000,000 flops, assuming neither its processor or software had been optimized.

But what impressed Chelsea most was not the Cray, or even the fact that it could penetrate in real time the encryptions used by the Daesh terrorist network. It was the fact that Massina had erected the center without her knowing. The personnel—two hardware engineers and a soft-ware expert pulled from security projects, along with a human-language specialist—reported for work each day at the regular Smart Metal build-ing ("home base"), and were then surreptitiously transported here.

"A lot of the work is being done by automated scripts," said Massina, continuing his tour. "We collect, decrypt, analyze. We're spending a lot of time in their chat rooms." He gestured at an empty workstation, where lines of dialogue scrolled up the screen. "The translator gives us conversational Arabic, but it's not as necessary as I thought. Besides our own identities, we've managed to masquerade as other members of the network. Not everyone here is Daesh. Most aren't. But two of the personalities check out as commanders—we buffer them out after they come online, subbing for them."

"Does the CIA know you're doing this?" Chel-sea asked.

"Not to this extent," said Massina.

"Shouldn't you tell them?"

"They have not been the most cooperative," said Massina. "Frankly, I'm not sure whether to trust them. I think they originally got us in-volved so they'd have someone to blame if things went wrong."

"We were an important part of the operation."

"As it turned out. They play a lot of politics, Chelsea. I'm sure you've noticed."

Chelsea couldn't argue, but she did trust Johansen, as well as the others on the team. They were truly patriots and believed in what they were doing.

"Come over to this station." Massina led her to a computer at the far end of the room. Converted from space that had stored the mall's vehicles, it still smelled faintly of diesel. The interior had been lined with a double layer of copper to isolate communications. It had then been covered with insulation and Sheetrock, but never painted; the screws that held the walls in place looked like rivets in the plastic ribs that ran from floor to ceiling.

"This is Ghadab's last appearance online, an email." Massina tapped a few keys and an email appeared on the screen. It was from an AOL address to a Gmail address. "Unencrypted, and not a direct code as far as we know, but obviously a signal of some sort," he added.

I want to visit Notre-Dame on the 13th.

"The 13th is today," said Chelsea.

"Maybe."

"Notre Dame—Paris?"

"I don't know," said Massina.

"Notre Dame—that's a huge cathedral in Paris."

"Yes, but I doubt that's where it actually refers to. This was open—I'm sure they would call it one thing and mean another. But the French have been hit hard over the past year and a half," added Massina, "so just in case, I passed the information on. Security was increased there, especially at the Île-de-France. All of Paris is on high alert."

"That's good."

"We have tracked the email recipient, or at least where it was physically read."

"Where?"

"Montreal. They're on alert, too. Or so the CIA says."

"So—why are you telling me all this?"

"I want to adapt some of our AI programs to examine the communications and the points of contact they use. I need someone who can adapt the programs quickly, someone who's already familiar with them."

"You want a program that can learn how to hunt for terrorists without being instructed on every step," said Chelsea.

"Exactly. Something that could make up its own rules on procedures—that would be smart enough to invent new identities if that was necessary. And more."

"More like what?"

"If I knew what more I needed, then I wouldn't need the program."

83

Langley—around the same time

At almost that exact moment, Johansen was arguing that the Agency should form a formal partnership with Massina and share everything it knew about Ghadab and his operation. What he had turned over to the Agency—through Johansen—indicated he was already running a parallel intel operation, and getting good results.

"He's getting rumors," CIA Director Colby replied. They were sitting together with two members of the Daesh Terror Desk, the agency's unit coordinating efforts against ISIS, and the DDO, Deputy Director of Operations Michael Blitz. Blitz was here mostly as a courtesy; though he was Johansen's boss, the mission had been routed through the Daesh desk, specially established and answering directly to Colby. The secure basement room was shielded from eavesdropping by (among other things) a layer of copper foil.

"He's fleshing out Ghadab's network," said Johansen. "He's done more in two months than the NSA did in two years."

"That's not fair," said Colby. "The NSA gave us similar intercepts. A lot more. What's his motivation?"

"I don't understand."

"Why is he doing all this?"

"Revenge. He wants to get the bastard."

"He wasn't personally attacked."

"No, but he feels as if he was."

"I could see if there was a contract involved. Money. But just revenge?" The Director shook his head. "What if he's purposely misleading us?"

"Impossible. Let me share the data we found in the bunker," suggested Johansen.

"How's he going to use it?"

"I don't know. That's why I want to share it."

"If it gets back to Ghadab—"

"He already knows we have it, or at least suspects," said Johansen. "It makes sense to work with Massina. He's helped us a lot. We have to trust him."

"We don't have to trust anyone," said Colby flatly. "Go ahead. Talk to him. While you're at it, find out the extent of his operation. I want to understand exactly what he's capable of. And remember. He is not us."

I'm sure you won't let me forget, thought Johansen, standing to go.

84

Boston—later that night

For Johnny, love was like a constant, mild high punctuated by moments of wild joy and the occasional flip into a dark hole of pessimism. He'd been in love before, but that was back in high school and his first year of college, and most likely a simple crush, as those things were defined. The rest of college saw a series of extended hookups, satisfying at the same time but never particularly deep or long-lived. Joining the Bureau led to a long dry stretch, imposed by lack of opportunity as well as the rigors, first of his training and then his early assignments.

Then came the accident, his legs. Even after he was fitted and moving around, the drugs killed his libido, an unfortunate but common side effect. The next round of meds had the opposite effect, but meant mostly frustration: what woman, he thought, would want a legless lover?

And then came Chelsea.

Finding out that he could make love, that he

could enjoy it and that she could enjoy it—it was like he'd been allowed to live again.

Recuperating from the accident had been extremely difficult physically. But mentally—in some ways he'd used his physical rehabilitation as a crutch, a way to focus on something, anything, rather than what it meant to be a man without two legs.

If I want to get better, he told himself, *I have to build my muscles. I have to get my body to adjust to the meds. I need to push, keep pushing.*

Do it. Think about nothing else.

Pushing himself physically to his limits meant he didn't have to think about anything else. Pushing himself to take the job, to keep up with others, to surpass the others . . . he was too exhausted at the end of the day to give a lot of thought to what it would mean to make love to someone. Or not be able to do that.

The relationship wasn't just sex.

Talking to her, having dinner with her, sitting on the couch with her bunched up against him, walking along the river—he wanted to be saturated with her presence. He couldn't get enough.

Johnny realized this was all a phase. Part of him was on guard against it—because part of him believed that the attraction wouldn't last. Not for him: that was solid and unshakable. But Chelsea—she could do better than a man without legs.

They were very different people. She was smart

and he—he wasn't *dumb*, but few people were in her ballpark even.

And their backgrounds. Hers was very solid upper middle-class; his was working-class. In the good years.

He was white, she was black, or *part* black, to be precise. And on and on and on . . .

So, inevitably, given all their differences, Johnny knew, Johnny feared, that eventually they would split. But these moments of fear were far outweighed by the sheer joy of being near her, thinking about her, and making love to her. He thought about her constantly, at work, at home, in the gym.

"Smith machine today, huh?" asked one of the trainers, walking over.

"Nobody to spot," said Johnny, pushing the weighted bar up to complete his set.

"How much can you bench?"

Johnny shrugged. He had worked out the week before with 750 pounds—nearly four times as much as he was able to do before his accident. The drugs had done more than just help him recover; they'd made him better. Literally.

"I'll spot you," said the trainer.

A HALF HOUR LATER, WORKOUT DONE AND FRESHLY showered, Johnny tossed his gym bag over his shoulder and headed out the door, walking toward the restaurant where he'd arranged to meet Chelsea for dinner. The recent run of good weather held; a slight breeze off the ocean nudged the temperature just below seventy-five. Johnny detoured briefly to drop off his bag at his house, then continued to the restaurant, Zipper, a fifteen-minute walk away.

Zipper was an old-school neighborhood bar turned punk performance space transmogrified into a hip grill before reemerging as a quasi-neighborhood grill. It had more substantial fare than the average bar, but it lacked televisions, so there was no possibility of catching a game afterward. Chelsea loved its food, and with the Red Sox on the West Coast, there wasn't any good baseball on until later anyway.

As usual, he beat her there. The hostess gave him a table next to the window. He ordered a beer, then checked his email and Facebook account; fifteen minutes later, he was three-quarters of the way through the beer and Chelsea had yet to arrive. He texted, but got no reply.

She'll be here. Her phone is dead or she's on the T or somewhere something not to worry not worry. Don't.

Twenty more minutes and another beer passed before Chelsea rushed in, nearly out of breath.

"Hey," he called.

"I'm sorry I'm late," she said, leaning into the booth to kiss him.

"Didn't even notice," he lied.

"How was your day?"

"Easy." He shrugged. "After Syria, everything's easy. How about yours?"

"Mr. Massina offered me a new assignment."

"Oh, yeah? What?"

She shook her head.

"You're not going to tell me?" he asked.

"Can't."

"Not a little?"

Another head shake.

"Are you taking it?" Johnny asked.

"I'm thinking about it. Seriously."

The waitress came over. Chelsea ordered a white wine. Johnny asked for a refill.

"So, like robotics or AI?" asked Johnny.

"I can't say."

"Even to me? I'm in security, you know. I'll find out."

"I don't think you will." Chelsea put her hand on his. "I'm sorry I was late."

"Not a problem."

"I may be late a lot, on this new project."

"Hmmmm," he said, drawing a breath as a sharp twinge of fear hit. It was physical—his stomach tensed and he could feel himself wincing. Fortunately, the waitress had just returned with their drinks.

"I think you should take it," Johnny said, knowing it was the right thing, the only thing, to say. "I really think you should."

85

Northern Vermont—three days later, before sunrise

GHADAB SAT AT THE BOW OF THE SMALL BOAT, watching the quiet shore to his right as they moved slowly south across the small lake. The glow of an American customs and immigration station lit the top of the trees about a half mile from the water; his boat's electric engine was so quiet he could hear a truck pull up to the stop to be inspected.

The man at the tiller said nothing. He was in fact a very quiet man; since picking up Ghadab at the airport, he had spoken less than a dozen words.

There were many places to cross the Canadian-American border without being detected. Most were on land, but Ghadab had chosen a water route; he'd seen so much of deserts lately that the wet morning chill and rising fog were more than welcome.

Vermont stretched out in the distance, a gray hulk behind a grayer screen. Ghadab shivered beneath his heavy sweatshirt, watching for any unwelcome movement. The small skiff turned to port, angling to a spot a few hundred yards beyond the floating dock of an abandoned camp. The man steering the boat at the stern killed the power and they drifted to shore, riding the momentum and a slight push from the wind until the keel hit sand. He hopped out, pushing the boat farther onto the beach.

Ghadab tossed his knapsack onto the sand. He'd bought it in Montreal, the same day he replaced the clothes he'd carried in the suitcase.

Among his other purchases was a large combat knife.

He gripped the knife now in his left hand as he put his right on the gunwale. Pushing down, he jumped off. The sudden shift in his weight unsettled the boat; it flipped down and began taking water over the side.

"So sorry, brother," he said as the other man grabbed for the boat.

By the time the man thought to reply, his throat had already been slit. The blade was sharp, but not very long, and Ghadab had to push it back and forth, as if sawing a piece of wood.

The man fell back against him. Ghadab pushed him over and then with his foot held him in the water until he was sure he was dead.

"To have witnesses would not be acceptable," Ghadab whispered. "Go to God."

He tossed the knife far into the lake, then hiked ashore. There, he took off his pants and shirt, exchanging them for dry clothes from his pack. He put on a pair of sneakers, shouldered the rucksack, and began walking through the open field opposite the lake where he'd come in. Once used as a summer camp for overweight teens, the lot and surrounding property had been vacant for over a decade. A faded sign near the road proclaimed it the new home of a housing development that had gone under in the bust.

Ghadab walked south on the road for about fifteen minutes, until he saw a pair of headlights approaching. He checked his watch, then stopped and waited.

Revenge was almost at hand.

86

Boston—four days later

"COOPERATION IS SUPPOSED TO BE A TWO-WAY street." Massina folded his arms over his plate of now very cold spaghetti. "I give you information, and you give me information. We work together to develop leads, to solve problems. I help you, you help me. I can't help you if you don't tell us what you know."

"I've given you everything I'm authorized to give you," said Johansen. "And more."

They were sitting in the basement of an Italian restaurant in the North End. Massina knew the owner, who'd opened the room just for him and the CIA officer. It was one of the more private places to talk in the city, assuming you wanted a plate of pasta at the same time.

"I don't want to argue with you," said Massina. "But our results do depend on what we start with."

"The disk I gave you has all the data from Syria."

"I needed that two months ago," said Massina. "We could have decrypted it for you."

"We're on the same side here, Louis. You just need to bear with us."

"You know where our friend is?"

"South Africa, we believe."

"You're wrong," said Massina. "We think he bought a ticket to Argentina a few days ago."

"Argentina?"

"The problem is, I'm not sure whether to trust you or not. So I don't know if you said South Africa to throw me off."

"No. Of course not."

Hearing someone coming down the steps, Massina held his tongue. Johansen turned to see who it was.

"More wine?" asked the maître d', appearing with a bottle. He was the owner's son and had known Massina since his father opened the restaurant some eight years before.

"I think we'll just finish the water," said Massina. "Come back in a few minutes and ask us about dessert."

"Very good." The maître d' glanced around quickly, then headed back to the stairs.

"I'm trying, Louis," said Johansen. "We want to work with you. We do. The Director does, not just me."

"All right," said Massina. But it was a noncommittal "all right." He'd considered showing him the Annex as a gesture of goodwill, but had changed his mind.

"How good is your information on Argentina?"

"Solid. The question is where he went from there."

"No clues?"

"None."

Johansen nodded. "We'll look into some of the chat rooms, go from there."

"Fine." Another neutral comment.

"I'd love to say hi to Johnny and Chelsea," added Johansen. "Since I'm here."

"I think we can probably arrange that," Massina told him.

"I know it can be difficult dealing with us," said Johansen. "But believe me, we are doing everything we can to get this guy."

"You'll want to save a little room for a cannoli," answered Massina. "They're incredible."

87

North of Boston—about the same time

STRICTLY SPEAKING, CHELSEA HADN'T DONE ANY programming in the three and a half days since she'd started working at the Annex. Her task was more like that of a curator, or maybe a tutor employing a modified version of the Socratic method. She'd installed the latest version of an AI engine they used as the kernel for many of their bots, adding two extensions that made it easier for her to monitor its progress and to add information.

After loading the program, giving it access to a database provided by the CIA, and connecting it to the internet, she'd told it to locate Ghadab. Since then, the computer had built a lengthy profile on the terrorist that included a number of aliases not in the original files the CIA had provided, and two look-alikes whose facial features were close enough to fool most visual-recognition systems.

It had also traced a series of financial transactions involving stolen credit cards and two legitimate Daesh bank accounts, one of which had been used to pay for a credit card that purchased a ticket to Buenos Aires from South Africa. At the same time, it had prepared a psychological profile that would have surely wigged out a human profiler and provided a number of further clues, most especially his interest in knives, which inspired the program to check arrest records and crime reports in hopes of finding hard data.

It had also wandered around the world, turning up things that had little bearing on the situation. Socrates—the AI program didn't actually have a name, but since it operated largely by asking itself questions, Chelsea had tentatively dubbed it that—had decided to flesh out Ghadab's ancestry, trying to construct a family tree. This produced a small booklet-sized list of ancestors and possible ancestors—many more of the latter— which the program then examined in depth with no visible payoff. Ghadab's parents had come from Oman, and it was *possible* that some generation before the family on the father's side had been related to the sultan's family. But no present member of the extended clan, let alone anyone remotely close to the ruling family, had been in contact with him for over a decade. His parents had died when he was very young; he and a brother were raised in an orphanage. Accessible records were scant at best, but the brother did not appear anywhere, not even on the rolls of the local school Ghadab had attended; the program posited a 95 percent chance that he had died.

There were similar branches and dead ends, explorations of trivia and probes that seemed to lead nowhere.

The others had infiltrated the Daesh communications network, developing enough information to identify the key members of its recruiting team in Europe, along with a list of places where recruits would go. So far, however, they had failed to turn up the same sort of contacts in America. Did that mean there was no recruitment network in America? Chelsea doubted that could be true and had proposed using the AI program as part of the effort to investigate it. Her idea was a very contemporary take on the Turing test, first proposed by AI pioneer Alan Turing in 1950: a computer that could fool a human into thinking he or she was talking to another human would demonstrate independent intelligence.

Massina had vetoed the idea, not because he thought the computer would fail the test—on the contrary, he had every expectation it would pass—but because even he didn't have infinite resources to devote to the project. And as important as uncovering an American recruitment network might be for the country's security, they had no reason to believe that it would help them find Ghadab.

And Massina was all about finding Ghadab. He was obsessed with it.

Chelsea had known Massina for several years, since meeting him during a lecture at Stanford she'd been invited to as a high schooler. Though others found him somewhat standoffish and often irritatingly driven, she liked him and was easily the engineer who was closest to him. Massina was relentless when pursuing a technical problem or exploring some area of science that interested him. Now that same obsession had been turned on Daesh.

How far was he willing to go? He had given the government a host of equipment and the services of two employees in an effort to nab him. When that didn't work, he'd started this—an effort that must be costing him millions of dollars.

What if this didn't work? What would he do next?

What would satisfy the obsession?

Chelsea's workstation pinged a message from Massina:

> Can you come Home in an
> hour and discuss latest?

She typed back an answer saying she'd be there, then sent a message to the automated driver tasked with bringing everyone to and from the Annex.

In the meantime, the program had been busy exploring knives. It had taken a special interest in khanjars, curved daggers often used for ceremonial purposes.

"What's the connection to Ghadab?" she asked, scrolling through the list of databases and websites the program had consulted. It had gone into a museum, slipping past security protocols to find a list of artifacts available only to curators; it had looked up news stories and examined medical records.

Chelsea opened the inspection tool to see what the machine was finding. Among other things, the curve of the blade tended to make a deep but straight cut . . .

"Well, duh," she said.

The AI began searching through police records. There were many knife attacks in the country, but none used a curved blade.

It retooled, examining the wounds that led it to conclude a khanjar had been used, then trying to extrapolate the killing action—how the knife was wielded—against different blades.

There had been several deaths in New York City recently, but the string had started a month ago, when Ghadab was still in Africa.

Then it brought up a seemingly random crime— a Canadian found with a slit throat in northern Vermont.

And from there, an avalanche ensued.

88

Burlington, Vermont—about the same time

GHADAB KNEW ONLY ONE OF THE AMERICAN BROTHers: Amin Greene, whom he'd met at a Pakistan training camp as a young man. Greene, several years older than him, was an American citizen, and after working with the Taliban in Afghanistan under a false name and passport for a short time, he had returned to America to wait. Initially a member of a cell funded by al-Qaeda, he had become associated with the more enlightened branches of jihad and renewed his acquaintance with several important brothers, including Ghadab, through visits to Belgium over the past four years. He was an extremely careful man—he would never fly directly to Belgium, for example, rather entering the country by car or train with a false passport to make himself more difficult to track—but at the same time he was obsessed with explosives. The look on his face, even when lighting a firecracker, betrayed something akin to sexual ecstasy.

And he loved lighting firecrackers.

"You're going to draw attention to us," scolded Ghadab after Greene lit and tossed a small pack of firecrackers off his back deck.

Greene stared intently at the yellow speckles as the firecrackers popped and sizzled on the rear lawn. The smell of spent gunpowder tickled Ghadab's nose, reminding him of the fight he'd left behind some months ago. It was a sacrilegious tease.

"Aren't you worried about a fire?" asked Ghadab.

"Overrated." Greene's accent was very American, but then he'd spent his entire life here. He barely looked Arab at all, though his grandfather and mother had been Iraqi.

"The police may hear," suggested Ghadab.

"State police are twenty miles away, and they know me," said Greene. "We don't have town cops. Even if we did, I'm way out in the boonies. Relax."

"We have important work."

"Of course."

"I need to retrieve the diagrams. And to find the woman."

"I understand all of your requirements. It will happen. For now, relax. Have a beer."

Ghadab frowned. "You have a good life here. Perhaps it is too much of a distraction."

Greene smiled and lit another firecracker. He waited a moment, then tossed it so high it exploded in the air.

"I'm ready," he told Ghadab. "I'm more than ready."

89

Boston—a half hour later

UNDERSTANDING THE PROGRAM'S ANALYSIS REQUIRED a crash course in forensics and anatomy, and as smart as Chelsea was, there was no way after half an hour for her to be absolutely sure that Socrates had drawn a valid conclusion about the knife wound. And if it had stopped there, she might well have written it off. But while she was reading up on wound patterns and the location of blood vessels in the neck, Socrates was out making other connections, exploring boat rentals and gas station purchases.

Collecting a good portion of this work involved penetrating supposedly secure networks—problematic at best from a legal point of view, but that wasn't something Chelsea spent a lot of time thinking about until after she got the text from Massina saying that Johansen was in town and wanted to say hello. By then, she had already worked up a quick presentation for Massina on what she (or rather, Socrates) had found. She called over the car and ran for it as quickly as she could, eager to share what she had found.

It was an age-old question: in the race to save lives, did the ends justify the means?

Clearly, the CIA thought so—but they also wanted to cover their butts, which was why they had gotten Smart Metal involved in the first place. Any illegal, or even questionable, activity could be blamed on the company.

Massina was OK with that. Was she?

How far had she come in the past year, from creating bots that could rescue people from burning buildings to this?

I haven't done anything wrong. Not even illegal that I know. I'm helping save lives.

Chelsea told Massina she would meet Johansen in the Box; the two men were waiting when she arrived. Walking in, she waved her hand perfunctorily, freezing Johansen as he rose to greet her. She put her flash drive into the receptacle used by the presentation computer and immediately launched into a brief. A map flashed on the screen, flight data, a receipt, then an autopsy photo, a close-up, more close-ups.

"The cut pattern is exactly the same," Chelsea said. "That doesn't prove that these people were killed by the same person. But it's an interesting coincidence—especially given that the dead man was on the RCMP watch list."

"If the dead man was so dangerous," said Massina, "why didn't the Mounties pick him up?"

"You'd have to ask them," said Chelsea. Socrates

had data on him, but she hadn't bothered to bring it. "He traveled to Jordan two years ago, which I would guess got him on the list."

"Was he on ours?" Massina asked Johansen.

"I'd have to ask Homeland Security. Canadian citizen—I assume he probably wouldn't have been let into the country. Or if he was, would have been followed."

"The boat was rented," said Chelsea, bringing up the receipt.

"I'm not going to ask how you have all of this data," said Johansen. "Why kill him? Frankly, that argues that this wasn't Ghadab—he's going to need help."

"Not if he's coming to the U.S.," suggested Chelsea. "This guy is of no more use."

"You usually don't burn your bridges," said Johansen. "Not even Daesh."

"The parable of the scorpion and the tortoise," said Massina. "It's what he does."

WHILE IN JOHANSEN'S MIND THE CONNECTION WAS tentative, it was far too important to be dismissed. If Ghadab was in the U.S., an attack was imminent. And if he was involved, it was going to be huge. So instead of flying down to New York as planned, he rented a car and drove over to Hanscom Air Force Base in Bedford, where he could use a secure line to talk to Langley. His creds impressed the security detail at the gate, but inside was another matter, and it took nearly a half hour for him to get clearance to use the system.

He fretted in the meantime. The analysts had always predicted that there would be an upswing in terror attacks as ISIS lost ground. No longer able to contribute in the Levant, as Daesh called it, the sociopaths they attracted would kill in their homelands. The potential targets were limitless.

But Ghadab was a special case. He went big, and if he had concluded that the cause was lost, he'd want to go out in style. He'd want to make 9/11 look like a random IED attack compared to his finale.

Johansen quickly briefed the desk on what he had found. Still hoping to make his flight to New York, he was about to hang up when the Director himself came on the line. Colby had happened to be standing nearby when the call came in.

"I heard," he told Johansen. "How sure of this are you?"

"Reasonably. It's only circumstantial, as I explained."

"This is Massina's work?"

"His people."

"We're at arm's length?"

"I don't think that's an issue," said Johansen sharply. All this cover-my-ass shit was wearing on him.

"Get back right away," said Colby.

"I was going to New York. I have a commercial flight and I was going to meet Moorehead."

"Where are you?"

"Hanscom. It's an air base outside—"

"I'll arrange for a flight. Stand by."

90

North of Boston—five hours later

THEY WERE WORKING ON POWER PLANTS. THEY wanted to create another Chernobyl.

Or so Socrates thought.

It was a roundabout conclusion that began with an analysis of the data from the Syrian bunker—a chat-room handle that turned up as a user name on a Russian database. That was a weak link, admittedly, but the search trail was highly suggestive, and using time stamps, the program made a host of other connections.

Intuitive leaps, if a person were making them. Algorithmic inferences if you were talking about a computer.

"Algorithmic inference" had a bit of a negative connotation to Chelsea, since it implied that the machine's thinking was fatally limited by the construction of its programming. And while she had to be always aware of that possibility, in the brief time since developing the program's present incarnation, she believed Socrates was no more limited by its circuitry than humans were.

But that was all theory. Finding what Ghadab and his minions were up to was reality. Hard reality.

The team Ghadab had assembled in the bunker had accessed a great deal of information about the Soviet (now Ukrainian) Chernobyl power plant and its meltdown in 1986. They had examined schematics of the plant, along with a detailed timeline and even precise calculations of what would have been happening inside the nuclear pile from two months before. They had apparently taken great interest in the response of the people running the plant, as well as the evacuation of the town that followed.

The specific information regarding the accident wouldn't be of much use: the plant was essentially a one-off technology-wise, dissimilar to plants outside of the old Soviet Union, especially those in the U.S. The circumstances that led to the meltdown were also somewhat unique, with cascading failures and overrides that would be difficult to duplicate.

But the *idea* that Ghadab was interested in had universal application for most nuclear plants. And Socrates had traced further research—though here the computer's confidence level on its links dipped below 70 percent—to other types of plants. Ghadab's team appeared to have been doing research on Fukushima in Japan, among others. Another one-off, perhaps, given the circumstances, but highly suggestive.

Meanwhile, internet-based attacks had been made on nuclear power plants in Italy, France, and Germany. Such attacks were almost routine now, and in any event the ones Socrates recovered had all been turned back. But neither Socrates nor the respective authorities had pinned them on the usual suspects—China and Russia most prominently. The timing suggested they were "due diligence" attacks by Ghadab's people—probes designed to see if they could easily gather data.

In that case, they'd failed: the sort of detailed schematics of the buildings and security precautions Chelsea thought she would see in preparation for an attack had not been downloaded.

There were other things in the files that Socrates momentarily found interesting—Bitcoin accounts, chat-room records, and even house listings for Argentina. The AI program, however, concentrated most of its effort on the nukes.

Was this an inherent bias in the program? A nuclear meltdown was a very severe threat, and therefore deserving of the most resources? Or was the evidence there strongest?

Chelsea couldn't decide. And she worried that while Socrates had studied past terror events, it hadn't correctly concluded that these were all "black swan" events—rare and seemingly random. In short, she was concerned that the computer was making the same mistakes a human might. And there would be no way to tell until they caught Ghadab.

Energized by her meeting with Johansen, Chelsea threw herself into her work, examining Socrates's logic, working on new extensions that might help it streamline its thought process. She was so deep into her work that she missed several buzzes of her phone announcing incoming texts. It was only when she took a bathroom break to hit the john that she realized Johnny had sent her several over the past hour:

> So, we doin' dinner?
>
> 59 Minutes ago
>
> Dinner?
>
> 28 Minutes ago
>
> You around?
>
> 13 Minutes ago

She texted him back:

> Oh, God, I forgot. ☹ I am hungry but kinda late

He responded almost immediately.

> I am at Halligan's watching Sox— be there or be square.

(Texts didn't come through the regular network here; Massina had modified the phones of Annex employees to take calls through the cell tower nearest Smart Metal.)

SHE GOT THERE A HALF HOUR LATER, DROPPED OFF by the driverless car. Johnny had finished eating long ago and was sitting in a booth watching the Red Sox demolish the Nationals.

"I saw you this afternoon," he told her after she'd ordered a burger. "Where were you going in such a hurry?"

"Just back to work."

"Where?"

"Work."

"I know Massina set up something new off campus," said Johnny. "Why all the mystery?"

"You of all people should know I can't talk about things with anybody."

"Not even me?"

"Not even you."

The burger came. She regretted ordering it; she wasn't nearly hungry enough to finish it. She wasn't really hungry at all. She picked at the fries.

"I want to tell you," she said. "I really do. But . . ."

"Yeah?"

"It's awkward."

"What you're doing?"

"No. No. This."

"Yeah, those fries look a little burned."

"I mean, the situation," said Chelsea. "You can be such a wiseass at times. Inappropriate times."

Johnny grimaced.

Maybe I'm being too harsh, she thought.

"Want some fries?" she asked.

"No."

He just said they looked burned. Duh.

"What did you do today?" she asked.

"Usual. Trained some new guys. Worked out."

"No more personal security for Lou?"

"He doesn't think that's necessary anymore."

"What's Beefy think?"

Johnny shrugged. "Massina signs the checks. Or maybe he does—how does that work with direct deposit?"

"I don't know."

"That wasn't a real question," said Johnny. "I was joking."

"I knew that," she said, though in fact she hadn't.

How did that *work? It went through the clearing-house system, with tokens attached permanently to the account numbers . . .*

Why wasn't Socrates following the money trail?

It was discounting it for some reason.

Nice pun.

There must be something there. The Canadian who'd been killed—at some point he must have gotten money from Daesh, maybe years ago.

The algorithms were using an arbitrary time limit: the original program had a cutoff because its processing power and memory were limited. So the search would, by necessity, only go back so far.

The parameter was set by the initial assessment, which in this case probably went to the original attack, and whatever Socrates decided was a reasonable planning period. Or it could go back to Syria—yes, that would seem reasonable, since that was the original request.

But it was too limiting. It was the way a human thought, not the way Socrates should.

I can change that.

"I have to go," she told Johnny, pushing away from the table.

"Your burger."

"I'm not really hungry. Bring it home."

"Where are you going?"

"Back to work."

91

Langley—later that night

JOHANSEN HAD ANTICIPATED COLBY'S QUESTION EVEN before boarding the flight back, but he still hadn't come up with an answer.

"If Ghadab is in the U.S.," asked the Director as they sat in the basement secure room, "why hasn't he contacted Persia?"

"Maybe he has" was the best Johansen could offer. "Maybe Persia just hasn't contacted us."

"He told us last time," said Marcus Winston. Winston was the former head of the terror desk, brought in for consultation. Johansen surmised that he'd had a hand in recruiting or running Persia, though no one had said that.

Persia was a deep-planted double agent who had worked for the CIA for years, having managed to infiltrate the terror network around al-Qaeda. As he wasn't Johansen's asset—until this assignment, most of Johansen's work involved Russia and Eastern Europe directly—Johansen knew almost nothing about him. With the exception of Winston, it didn't appear any of the others knew all that much about him either.

"He told us about the contact relatively late," said Blitz, the DDO. "Too late to do any good. I don't think we can even be sure that he's on our side."

"Playing devil's advocate for a moment," said Colby, "if Ghadab was planning an attack here, why would he come? He generally works through his people."

"We killed most of his people," suggested Johansen. "He wants revenge."

"I agree with that," said Blitz. "So he targets D.C. Us."

"Possibly," agreed Johansen.

"Persia," said Blitz, looking at Winston. "He's our best bet. We have to contact him."

"I can arrange it," said Winston.

"No." Colby turned to Johansen. "Find someone to tell him to come in."

"He's not my guy."

"I realize that. I want someone neutral, that he doesn't know. I want to see what he does. It's the only way to test him."

"Or spook him," said Winston. "It'll be much better if he's dealing with someone he knows."

"No. I don't trust him. And we have to test him somehow. Yuri, do it quickly."

An hour and a seven-shot latte later, Johansen had read the entire file on Persia.

Most of that time had been spent dealing with

the security protocols using the secure "library." It wasn't a very big file.

He lived in New Hampshire—not all that far from where the Canadian terrorist had been found. He had gone to Afghanistan as a young man. He had been contacted and turned by a third party, who answered to Winston.

Two days before the attack on Boston, he had sent a message to Winston, warning that something was imminent. There were no other details; apparently the warning had not been specific.

Impression—the Director felt Winston had screwed up somehow. But he wasn't sharing.

In any event, that wasn't his concern. He needed to find someone to get a message to him.

Who do I trust who owes me a favor?

92

Burlington, Vermont—a few hours later

Gʜᴀᴅᴀʙ ɢʀᴀʙʙᴇᴅ ᴀ ᴄᴏʟʟᴇɢᴇ ID ᴏꜰꜰ ᴀ ᴛᴀʙʟᴇ ɪɴ ᴛʜᴇ campus café before going to the library, scratching the photo image just in case anyone bothered to ask. He memorized the name—Mitchel Cutter—and his graduating class, repeating the information to himself as he walked across to the library. He needn't have bothered: there was no security or even a clerk at the door.

The internet computers were all taken. He sat down nearby, joining an informal queue.

He glanced around, effecting a bored look while watching the students and gathering information on how the process worked. It was simple, really: scan your ID, get an hour on the machine.

There was a girl at the far kiosk with long black hair. She reminded him of Shadaa.

He imagined Shadaa in a T-shirt and jeans, with sneakers half-off her feet. He imagined Shadaa pounding the keyboard as the girl did, then stopping to push the strands of her hair back.

It was almost a reincarnation.

The girl rose, her session over. Ghadab forgot his task. He rose, following her down and then out the door, along the walkway that led to the street.

Work to do, he reminded himself. But he kept following as she walked down the street.

She's not Shadaa.

Ghadab kept thinking she would turn up the walk of one of the houses lining the street. When she did, he told himself, he would keep walking, turn back.

But she didn't turn on the first block or the second or even the third. When she came to the fourth corner, she crossed against the light—there was no traffic, and she didn't even have to pause. Ghadab continued on the opposite side, watching out of the corner of his eye as she went down the block, turning onto a side street.

I've come this far. Why not?

He waited a moment, then crossed. He remembered the feel of Shadaa's hips.

God sent her as an angel, to give me a glimpse of what waits.

Small stores, cafés, and bars clustered on the next block. Picking up his pace, Ghadab saw her go up the steps to a bar that called itself Angels Hideout.

Surely that was a sign, he thought. Ordinarily he would never go into a bar, but surely that was a sign.

His hand trembled as he put it on the rail going up the steps. He was more nervous than he'd been at the airport.

The noise hit him like a physical thing, pounding at his head. He'd been in places like this before, in Europe, in Argentina, yet this felt completely new, unknown. The interior was divided in half, with tables on the right and a long bar on the left. It was a college hangout; undoubtedly many of the patrons were underage, though clearly no one cared.

The place smelled sweet. Ghadab walked to the far end of the bar before turning and scanning the crowd. She'd sat at a booth alone close to the front of the room. He'd taken a step in her direction, debating how he might introduce himself, when a young man about her age came up from the back and sat across from her.

Ghadab stepped back to the bar, watching. The girl put her hand on the man's hand; he didn't remove it.

"Whatcha gettin'?" the bartender asked.

It took Ghadab a moment to realize the question was meant for him.

"Seltzer," he said.

"Somethin' in it?"

"No."

"Lime?"

Ghadab shook his head. The man stepped away. Ghadab looked back at the table but his view was blocked by a waitress.

"Two bucks," said the bartender, sliding a tumbler toward him.

Ghadab reached into his pocket and fished out a five-dollar bill.

So this is what we must have looked like, he

thought, watching across the room as the couple talked. The girl seemed reserved, formal—as Shadaa was. She sat with her back straight against the bench. He liked that; she had virtue.

The boy—they were all alike, Westerners. He was trying to get her into bed, clearly: *Look how he pets her hand.*

Ghadab couldn't blame him. But she wasn't having it.

She laughed, and the laugh stung Ghadab.

His thoughts turned dark. He would kill her in the worst way possible.

Ghadab missed something. In the moment he'd blinked, the girl had gotten out of her seat and begun to walk away. She was upset. The boy didn't follow.

She walked like Shadaa.

Ghadab left the drink and money on the bar and started outside, dodging a group of men as they entered. One of the men didn't like something about the way he looked or moved and put his hand out as if to stop him; Ghadab tightened his eyes into a glare. He had a folding knife in his pocket, but it wasn't necessary: the young man moved out of the way with a sneer. Ghadab brushed past.

You'll be dead soon anyway.

The girl turned to the right when she reached the sidewalk. Ghadab started to follow, his pace gradually increasing.

His heart began to pound. He needed her now. He would have her now.

He quickened his pace. She was a half block

ahead, ten yards, five. Ghadab glanced left and right. They were alone.

She crossed the street, angling toward a set of porch steps. Ghadab slipped his hand into his pocket, grabbing the knife as he stepped off the curb.

A horn blared. He jerked back as a car swept up behind him. A college-aged student was leaning out the driver's side window, cursing at him.

"Hey, asshole!" shouted the kid.

Before Ghadab could react, the night erupted with a blue strobe light. A police car was just down the street.

Run!

Ghadab took a step back to the sidewalk, unsure what to do. He slid the knife back into his pocket. The car that had nearly hit him stopped abruptly. The police car pulled up behind his left bumper, blocking traffic in both directions.

"You all right?" asked the policeman as he got out.

"Yes," said Ghadab.

The cop motioned with his hand, thumbing back in the direction of the bar. Then he walked toward the car he'd just stopped.

Go! Go!

Ghadab put his head down and walked swiftly away.

This was a warning. I need to focus on only my mission. I must move quickly, before I make another mistake.

93

Boston—around the same time

SOME PEOPLE WATCHED TV TO RELAX. MASSINA worked out problems.

Or tried to anyway. And the problem that he kept coming back to was Peter.

The bot and its autonomous brain had been their biggest success story . . . until he became Hamlet, thinking rather than doing.

Why? It wasn't a mechanical problem, nor an error in coding as far as either concept was generally understood. The bot had *chosen* to think rather than act.

Was it afraid?

Massina dismissed the notion out of hand—machines did not know fear. The bot considered the possibility that it would be damaged every time it was given a task, but even an assessment of 100 percent would not prevent it from carrying out a task. And neither in Syria nor in any of the exercises had the probability of destruction come close to that.

He wasn't necessarily thinking about danger.

He was running memory routines against present simulations—essentially comparing his history to his present situation. Which made sense: it was a way to find a solution to a problem. Except he didn't solve out the solution and act on it.

Was he thinking about who he was?

Literally, yes.

I⊤ ⊤OOK CHELSEA SEVERAL HOURS ⊤O CHANGE ⊤HE base parameters Socrates used to conduct its searches; inserting the new programming with the requisite debugging took two more. But the change yielded immediate results—the computer matched a cash withdrawal at an ATM near a hunting store in suburban Montreal, and from that match, discovered a pair of credit cards used to buy clothes. Chelsea had just off-loaded details of the clothes—three of the bar codes included reasonably detailed descriptions—when Massina surprised her.

"I thought you went home," he said, looking over her shoulder.

"Not yet," she said.

"I have an odd theory about RBT PJT 23-A," said Massina. "I'm wondering if he's becoming self-aware."

"It knows where it is."

"True, but more than that—gaining another level of introspection. Why it doesn't act?"

"How would we test that?"

Massina shook his head, as if he were apologizing. "I haven't figured it out yet." He shrugged, honestly unsure but clearly intrigued by the problem.

"It's philosophy more than coding," said Chelsea.

"No, it's always coding. We just haven't caught up with him yet." Massina's wry smile changed to something more serious. The intrigued wizard disappeared, morphing into the concerned and rigorous boss. "What are you working on?"

"I had an idea," said Chelsea. "We've gone back and figured out some clothes Ghadab might have been wearing. If we can match that to visuals, maybe surveillance cameras—"

"We? You and the program?"

"Socrates."

"You gave the code a name?"

Chelsea shrugged.

"Maybe you should call it a night," Massina suggested.

"We have a couple of bank accounts we can track," said Chelsea. "I'm not going to leave until I get more results."

"All right. But stop using 'we,'" added Massina. "The AI program is just a tool."

"Socrates," said Chelsea. "His name is Socrates."

94

Vermont—early the next morning

THE AIR WAS DIFFERENT. WET. PREGNANT.

That was what he always noticed about America. No matter where Ghadab was, a city, a suburb, a farm, the air smelled different than what he'd grown up breathing. It wasn't just the scent of diesels or factory gases, the exhaust from cars or cows. It was more intrinsic.

Some would put it down to humidity, the most obvious difference to the deserts of the Middle East. There was something to that, especially on a day like today, when rain was only a few hours away. But Ghadab knew it was more than that, more an expression of the country and its people. What they breathed out.

And what he was now breathing in.

Ghadab continued down the long, twisted gravel driveway of the safe house, walking in the direction of the highway. Large fields lay to either side; given over to hay, in the early predawn light they looked more like jungles than cultivated farm acres. A large barn leased to a local farmer sat in the distance, close to the highway. In the shadows, the structure looked like a squatting soldier.

The image gave Ghadab some comfort.

He continued walking, strolling leisurely. Casual movement helped clear the mind of thoughts. Then, with distractions gone, he could focus on the tasks of the day.

Dealing with the traitor was first.

He had reached the highway and started back for the house when he heard the pickup. He stepped to the side and waited, watching as the headlights swept up from the road. The driver saw him and slowed before pulling alongside.

"Commander, you are up early," said Amin Greene, leaning across the cab to talk.

"I always rise before dawn."

"Can I give you a lift to the house?"

"I prefer to walk, then pray."

"I'll make you breakfast, then."

Greene let his foot off the brake and moved away slowly. He was a jolly sort, perpetually happy, easily amused.

Useful, though not deep.

By the time Ghadab got to the house, it smelled of strong coffee. Greene was stirring a pancake batter.

"It's time for prayers," said Ghadab, entering the kitchen.

"A few minutes yet," said Greene, glancing at his watch.

"Now, by my watch."

"Of course."

Greene turned off the flame and followed Ghadab out to the porch. Ghadab unrolled his prayer rug; Greene found one near the door and together they prayed.

As Ghadab finished, he took the knife from his belt.

"I have done you a mercy, though you don't deserve it," he said, reaching his arm around the front of Greene's chest and pulling up quickly to stab his throat.

Taken by surprise, Greene grabbed at his chest, then floundered as Ghadab sliced him again and stepped back.

"You are a disgrace to the cause," said Ghadab.

Greene started to shake his head. Blood fell from his neck like a waterfall, seeping in places, spurting in others.

"You spoke to them just before Easter," said Ghadab. "The Turk learned this. I didn't believe him, but I have seen the proof in your bank accounts."

Greene slid down, eyes still open, but definitely gone.

"You will serve us in death," said Ghadab. He took a flash drive from his pocket and slipped it into Greene's. "So perhaps you will be considered a martyr after all."

95

Burlington, Vermont—noon

GABOR TOLEVI HAD RUN DOZENS OF "ERRANDS" FOR Johansen, but never in America. It was easy enough, though: a signal had been sent, which would require the contact to meet him at a Dunkin' Donuts coffee shop just outside of town at exactly 12:03 P.M.

The shop was nearly deserted when Tolevi arrived a few minutes before noon. A quick glance around told him the contact wasn't among the patrons—all but one were women, and the exception looked to be seventy at least, and very white.

"Coffee," he told the girl at the counter.

"Donut?"

"Just coffee."

"We're serving a new lunch menu."

Tolevi stared straight ahead.

"What size coffee?" asked the girl finally.

"Large."

He gave her a five and told her to keep the change. He went and found a booth on the side.

Tolevi had no idea what his contact looked like; Persia was supposed to approach him, signaled by the *New York Times* he unfolded on the table.

They'll need to revise their procedures soon, thought Tolevi. *There won't be any newspapers left in a few years.*

He could see most of the parking lot from his seat. A car pulled in—right on time, Tolevi thought, until he saw that the occupants were both barely teenagers, one black, the other Hispanic. Neither gave him or his newspaper a second look.

And so it went for an hour. Even with their new lunch menu, business was not exactly booming. No more than twenty people came in, and none of them looked remotely like they might be his contact.

This sort of thing had happened to Tolevi more than he could count. It was never a good sign, but it was not necessarily disastrous. It could mean that the contact was being watched and had bailed; it could mean he hadn't gotten the message. It could mean he felt he was being taken advantage of and wanted to demonstrate that he was worth more than he was being paid—respect always being a function of the money involved.

It could mean many other things as well. As far as Tolevi was concerned, its only importance was that it made it necessary to call Johansen.

"Didn't show," he told the CIA officer as he walked to his car.

"Not at all?" There was no alarm in Johansen's voice, but still, the mere fact that he answered—

Johansen did not like to talk on cell phones, especially ones that were not encrypted—was a surprise.

"No, he did not."

"OK. I'll text you an address."

"I have other things to do."

"I need this," said Johansen.

Tolevi hung up. He considered driving back to Boston, but there was always a chance that he might need Johansen for something important in the near future. Even if he didn't, having the CIA as an enemy always complicated one's life.

The phone rang five minutes later—not only was it a call rather than a text, but it was far sooner than he expected.

"This is the address where he works. I need you to bring him to me."

"What?"

"I need you to do it."

"This is *way* out of the ordinary."

"You'll be paid, don't worry. I need you to bring him to Langley."

"Me?"

"Don't take no for an answer."

Tolevi knew where Langley was, of course, but he'd never been there. The request was completely bizarre. But Johansen not haggling over money—that was the most suspicious thing of all.

The company Greene worked for specialized in demolitions, primarily taking down derelict buildings. Destroying things made some people very happy, including the woman who worked as the company receptionist.

"Good afternoon!" she said, practically shouting.

He nodded. The floor was heavily carpeted but still squeaked as he walked across the room toward her desk. She was the only person in the very large office; it was easy to guess she didn't talk to many people in the course of the day.

"I'm looking for a friend of mine, Amin Greene," he told her. "We were in high school together."

"High school, God, what a glorious time," said the woman.

I'll bet you were a cheerleader, he thought. *Or at least on the pep squad.*

"I still have some of my best friends from those days," added the woman. She started naming them.

"So, is Amin around?" he asked finally.

"He took off this week. His mother . . ." She shook her head. "Not doing well."

"Sorry to hear that."

"Let me get his address for you. I'm sure he'd love to see you."

THE ADDRESS WAS TWENTY MILES OUT OF TOWN. Tolevi drove past the driveway a couple of times; it was impossible to see more than a sliver of the house. He found a place near a culvert down the road to park, then hiked through the woods a short distance to the field at the side of the house.

A split-level dating from the late 1980s, the

home was spectacularly unspectacular, the sort of place built without much thought and lived in with even less. But Tolevi hadn't come to critique the architecture. Taking no chances, he took out his pistol and walked across to the side yard, approaching from the side of the house that had no windows. After making sure there were no cars in the driveway at the front, he swung around to the back and came across the yard. Shredded fireworks filled the path and the nearby grass.

Going up two at a time, Tolevi bounded up the stairs to a deck made of pressure-treated wood, badly in need of paint or at least cleaning. Spent matches lay all around.

Gotta like a man who believes in fireworks.

Tolevi peered through the sliding glass door but couldn't see much inside: a dining room table, some chairs, but otherwise, nothing.

He could break in, but undoubtedly that would be subtracted from his fee. And it might make it more difficult to convince Greene to come to Virginia with him. It certainly wouldn't help. So Tolevi decided to walk around to the front door, where he rang several times. Getting no answer, he tried the knob—it was locked.

It wouldn't take all that much to force it, but once again he left that as a last resort. He went first to the garage, which was also locked, then went back up the stairs to the sliding door. It slid open easily—with the help of his credit card, which slid through the jamb with space to spare.

"Hey, Greene!" he yelled, standing at the

threshold. "I gotta talk to you. Some of your friends need you."

There was no answer. Tolevi took out his gun again and, holding it close to his body, entered.

Modestly furnished, the house didn't appear to hold many secrets. It was clear that the owner was a single male—the couch and chairs were mismatched; the sink was a mess. Down the hall, the sheets and covers on the bed were haphazardly spread, though the rest of the room was orderly enough.

The room across from the bedroom was used as an office; there was a computer screen and a keyboard on the desk, but no computer—obviously, a laptop usually sat here. A wire led to a USB hub, and another set of wires—along with a little outline of dust—showed where an external hard drive had sat until very recently.

Curious, Tolevi went through the drawers and found a flash drive; he left it. There were some bills, all in Greene's name.

A set of file cabinets against the wall demonstrated organization an OCD sufferer would have been thrilled with—folders for everything from groceries to land taxes, auto insurance to car washes, all separated by year.

Tolevi couldn't help but check the bank accounts. There were two, checking and savings; each had less than five thousand in it.

But his three credit cards were paid in full.

Back in the kitchen, Tolevi opened the refrigerator and checked the milk. It had been purchased not more than a day or two before, if the freshness date was to be believed.

There was a whiteboard on the wall. It looked to be something of a makeshift to-do list or calendar, though all but one entry had been erased beyond readability.

Farm—5.

What farm was that? Tolevi wondered.

HE FOUND THE ANSWER, OR AT LEAST WHAT HE thought was the answer, in a file of tax receipts in the office. The property was on his way out of town anyway, so he decided he'd swing by and see if there was anything worth seeing—maybe some unexploded fireworks.

Borya called when he was about a mile away.

"How are you, sweetie?" he asked, punching the Answer key on the car's display.

"Can I go to Jenny's house and help her with her homework?" asked his daughter.

"Is she going to help you with yours?"

Borya laughed. "That's crazy talk."

"That's fine. You're not doing your internship today?"

"Chelsea gave me a project at home," she told him.

"And how's that coming?"

"Piece of cake."

"Humph."

"So can I go to Jenny's?"

"As long as it's all right with Mary."

"See, I told you he would say it was all right," he heard her shout to the babysitter as she hung up.

He might have called her back if he hadn't seen the number on the mailbox matching the address. He stopped quickly, skidding a bit on the gravel, and pulled in. A dilapidated Victorian-era house sat on a hill a good three hundred yards from the road. The driveway was so pitted, he decided to leave the Mercedes at the bottom and walk up.

What he'd seen in the other house made him somewhat less cautious; he walked along the driveway for a good two hundred yards before swinging wide to get a look at the back. Unlike the other house, there was no deck, or door that he could see. Nor was there a garage.

Which meant this place, too, was probably empty.

But just to be sure, he went up the side stairs to the porch, maneuvering gingerly to avoid the two broken steps. He started to bend down to take a look in the window, when he saw that something was propping the front storm door half-open.

A leg. Attached to a body. A body in a pool of half-dried blood on the porch.

"I'm guessing you're Amin Greene," he told it, taking out his cell phone.

96

Boston—later that day

"THERE'S NO QUESTION NOW THAT GHADAB'S IN THE U.S. And we have to assume that he's interested in you. You specifically, Chelsea."

Johansen's face filled the screen at the front of the Box. He was in D.C., or at Langley, or somewhere—he didn't say.

Chelsea glanced at Massina, standing a few feet away, arms crossed in front of him. Johnny and Bozzone were behind him.

"Where is Ghadab now?" asked Massina.

"I don't know," said Johansen. "The data on the flash drive we found points to Boston. They have plans for Fenway Park, Faneuil Hall, Bunker Hill, and a few other places around town."

A USB flash drive had been discovered on "Persia," a CIA double agent discovered killed by knife wounds on a farm in Vermont. There was no question in anyone's mind that the man had been killed by Ghadab; the wounds were very similar to those of others he'd killed. The drive contained a host of documents and backed-up web pages that, as Johansen said, seemed to indicate Boston was once again a target. So much so that a special task force with the CIA, FBI, and state authorities was going to set up shop in town.

Johansen had shared the entire contents of the drive, though not the drive itself, with Massina's team at the beginning of his briefing. The Agency theorized that Persia was planning to give the drive to his contact when Ghadab discovered his treachery and killed him.

"The one thing that doesn't make sense to me," said Johnny, speaking for the first time since the meeting started, "is the drive. Why leave it in his pocket?"

"Everything was still in his pockets," said Johansen. "His wallet, money—it looks like there was an argument, and he fled."

"That doesn't sound like Ghadab," said Chelsea. "He's very methodical."

"Granted. We can't rule out that this was a misdirection play. We're looking into other possible targets. But we would be foolish not to put Boston on high alert. The FBI is trying to track him down."

"Maybe he tied Chelsea to Palmyra," said Johnny. "But what about the rest of us?"

"Everyone who was on the mission may be a target," said Johansen. "But we found her personal information on the drive."

"What do you think, Chelsea?" asked Massina.

"He's definitely in the U.S.," she said softly.

"We can have a dozen marshals from the U.S. Marshals Service watching you around the clock," said Johansen.

"I don't think I need that," said Chelsea.

"You need some protection," said Johnny.

"A whole army?"

"We can make it as unobtrusive as possible," said Johansen.

"I agree, she has to be protected," said Massina. "As does Johnny. We welcome the assistance—our head of security will work with your people."

"The attack is going to be made against nuclear plants," said Chelsea. "That's what they were researching."

"That may have been his original plan," agreed Johansen. "But now—this data is different. And power plants, they are very hard to hit."

"There's always the fear factor, though," said Massina. "Even an unsuccessful attack would panic a lot of people."

"True."

Chelsea's attention drifted as Johansen outlined the precautions they would take. It seemed unreal. She doubted she was really the target.

He figured out that the dead man was a CIA agent somehow. He'd use that.

What's the real target?

Boston again?

No terrorist had ever hit the same target again, at least not so quickly. But sometimes the most obvious solution was the right one.

Johansen signed off. Massina stood up.

"Everyone will be guarded," Massina said. "We will provide a safe house—safe houses. Beef is in charge."

Bozzone nodded.

"No unnecessary risks for our people," Massina said. "For anyone."

"So what are you going to do?" Johnny asked her as they left the Box.

"I'm going back to work," she said. "What else can I do?"

97

Boston—three days later

IN THE DAYS THAT FOLLOWED, BOSTON BECAME SOME-thing of an armed camp. Homeland Security issued a blanket warning, saying an attack was imminent and that Boston appeared to be "high on the list" of potential targets.

A deluge of news reports—most wildly speculative—filled the web and airwaves. National Guard troops moved onto power installations in every state, not just Boston. Police forces suspended vacations. People suspected of terrorist leanings were brought in for questioning or put under surveillance. Police officers, many armed with AR-15s and shotguns, guarded every notable building in Boston, and much of the Northeast.

Boston's mood was defiant. People went about their business with a definite edge. Even though the Red Sox were out of town, thousands of young fans showed up at Fenway every afternoon to keep vigil, staying well into the night. Other citizens gathered spontaneously at the city's landmarks. The police didn't like this—they argued, with some logic, that the presence of so many civilians increased the danger, presenting rich targets of opportunity.

But who could take issue with the attitude? Who would have expected less?

Massina understood: *You don't mess with Boston. You don't mess with America.*

But he was frustrated. He knew far more than the kids who slept on the grass at the Common, but he was just as impotent. Socrates churned through millions of leads, yet produced nothing tangible. The chat rooms Massina had lurked in buzzed, but the identities he had linked to terrorists had disappeared.

Johansen—who'd come up to Boston as part of the task force—claimed to be sharing everything he knew, but Massina still had doubts.

On the morning of the third day after the general alert had been sounded, the FBI staged a series of raids in the Burlington area, along with smaller actions in Minneapolis and Portland, Maine. Twenty-five would-be terrorists—several of whom had been first identified by Socrates—were arrested; two caches of weapons and material that could be used to make bombs were seized. A similar raid in the Montreal area by Canada's Mounties yielded ten terrorists and a small armory's worth of weapons.

The news media exhaled.

But Massina didn't. Ghadab wasn't among those arrested, and until he was found, the danger remained.

Six HOURS AFTER THE RAIDS WERE COMPLETED, A LI-aison at the FBI forwarded the names of the suspects and what was known about them to Smart Metal. By that time, Chelsea and her team—augmented by a dozen other Smart Metal employees and two "loaners" from the NSA—had fed the names to Socrates.

The results were very disappointing. As Chelsea put it in her 6 P.M. briefing to Massina: "Aside from the geography, we've found no link between any of the people who have been arrested and Ghadab."

"Does that mean there is no connection?" Massina asked. "Or we just haven't found it?"

"Hard to know at this point." Chelsea was talking to him via a secure link they had established between the Annex and the main building. "I have something else I thought we should try. The identities of the people in the bunker—Johansen never shared that with us."

"Do they know who they are?"

"I'm sure they do."

"I'll ask. That may just send us on some wild-goose chases," added Massina. "I'm sure the CIA has already checked into them."

"We have to keep trying. And Socrates is better at teasing out connections than they are."

"Or at least that they let on," said Massina. "I'll talk to them."

CHELSEA HAD THE PROFILES WITHIN AN HOUR. THE AI program thrashed away, exploring their profiles and plotting possible links. Unlike the first few days where she'd constantly been tweaking the program, there was now little for her to do aside from occasionally looking at what Socrates was probing. The connections it found seemed fairly random, even to the computer: 50 percent probabilities and less. Nothing pointed back to the U.S., and even the connections to Ghadab and the rest of the Daesh hierarchy were tentative.

Hours passed. Chelsea felt her eyes closing; the next thing she knew someone had jerked her leg.

"What?!" she yelled, bolting upright.

"Hey, relax," said Johnny, standing over her. "I was just checking to see if you were awake."

"What are you doing here?"

"Looking after you."

"I'm fine."

"Good."

"I'm going to be working the rest of the night."

"Good," said Johnny. "I rotated in to supervise the security team. You're part of my mission."

"Well, then, get me some coffee."

She tried smiling. Johnny didn't seem to think it was much of a joke.

"When was the last time you got some real sleep?" he asked.

"I'm all right." She got up and walked over to the coffee machines. With the increase in staffing, they had added two microwaves and a pair of refrigerators, along with two more coffee makers.

"Seriously, you do need to get rest."

"An espresso machine would be better," she told him.

Johnny followed her over. "You mad at me?"

"No." She poured herself a cup of coffee. "Want one?"

"Sure."

Chelsea pulled over a cup and poured. "I gotta figure this out. We will," she added.

Back at the console, Chelsea scrolled through the windows detailing what Socrates was up to. It had located what appeared to be a safe house in Chechnya; it highlighted the information, putting it in a special tab for further investigation.

"Here's what I don't get," he told her. "Why do they have so many computers there?"

"Where?"

"In the bunker. Why? No guns, no explosives—"

"Everybody uses computers. They were planning."

"If you're talking to people, one or two will do it. Surfing the web—they don't use it for porn."

"Oh yeah they do. You should see what they look at. Violent stuff." Chelsea shook her head. The Daesh people who worked with Ghadab were sick misogynists.

The ones that didn't prefer little boys, that was.

"You're thinking they're primitive," Chelsea

told him. "Like because they're from the Middle East, they don't use computers. That's not true. They're crazy, but they're not primitive."

"What were they using the computers to do?"

"Map targets."

"But you said they were looking at Chernobyl. There are no other plants like that, right?"

"It's the idea that's important. And we're missing data," said Chelsea. "If we had the original computers, if we had all the data, maybe we'd know."

"Sometimes you can have too much information," suggested Johnny.

"Not in my world," she said, turning back to the screens.

OF THE PRISONERS AND THE OTHERS WHO'D BEEN IN the bunker and identified already, one was a doctoral student in nuclear physics—which reinforced the nuclear-plant theory.

The others had all been software engineers or computer-science majors. Two, according to Socrates, had been active hackers, running scams on Facebook and harvesting credit-card numbers from European retailers.

Not one had anything in common with the people arrested earlier in the day. They did, however, have links to Ghadab.

Subtle links. They'd been in the same countries at times when he was there. They'd looked at the same websites, listened to podcasts from the same demented imams.

Maybe there were messages there. Socrates kept probing.

They were onto something, Chelsea thought, but they didn't have it yet.

An hour later, even Chelsea had to admit she needed a break.

And food.

"I'm going to go get something to eat, take a shower," she announced to the room. "I'll be back."

"I'm coming with you," said Johnny.

Chelsea knew it made no sense to object, especially as he enlisted two other security people—John Bowles and Greta Torbin—to come along as well. Bowles was rather tall and sinewy; Greta was nearly a foot shorter but had fought mixed martial arts. Both were armed with AR-15s.

Johnny insisted that Chelsea put on a bullet-proof vest before they went upstairs. Too tired to argue any more, she cinched it up, then fell in between Bowles and Torbin as they went up to one of the SUVs. Johnny got in the back with her; the others took the front, with Bowles at the wheel.

"They had hackers," Chelsea told Johnny as they started for her home on the west side of the city. "Pretty good ones."

"OK."

"And a programmer who worked on environmental controls."

"Like global warming?"

"No, environmental controls. Like cooling, that kind of stuff."

"Maybe they want to attack our air-conditioning supplies." Johnny laughed.

But Chelsea was serious.

"There must be a connection to what he's doing now."

"You're looking for logic from a nutjob," said Johnny.

They drove the rest of the way in silence. It was a little past six, but it seemed to Chelsea there was far less traffic than normal, as if the city was still not quite sure whether to go fully back to normal or not. A few blocks from her apartment, Chelsea realized she had left the air-conditioning off while she'd been gone; the rooms would be sweltering. She took out her phone, then keyed up the app that controlled her lights and appliances.

"Preset One, make it cold," she told the app.

The screen blinked, then presented a quick environmental rundown—the apartment was eighty-six degrees.

"Good thing you don't have a cat," said Johnny, looking at the screen. "It'll never cool off. We're like two blocks away. Come over and rest at my house."

"No, I want to go home."

Bowles slowed as they turned onto the block, looking for a spot to park. Chelsea leaned forward to tell him to just let her off—he could park down the street—when she saw a flash from down the block.

Something exploded to her right—a missile had just struck her apartment.

98

**Smart Metal Headquarters, Boston—
a moment later**

MASSINA HAD JUST TURNED FROM HIS DESK TO LOOK out the window when he saw it flying in the distance: a Sikorsky S-92A, a huge beast coming in from the north, low, in the direction of the city center. The sun glinted off its nose; it looked like a muscular cat striding across the northern reaches of the city. The helicopter veered in his direction, banking and then leveling, heading directly toward his building.

Directly toward it.

Massina watched as it grew bigger. It was low, barely above him—descending, in fact, in his direction.

Get out!

He reached the outer office just as the helicopter smashed into the exterior windows.

99

Boston—that exact moment

"WE'RE UNDER ATTACK!" JOHNNY PUSHED FORward against his seat belt, leaning toward the front seats. "Get us out of here!"

Bowles had already thrown the SUV into reverse. They spun into a U-turn. Johnny grabbed Chelsea, pushing her down in the seat.

"Hey!"

"Keep your head down until you're out of here. Bowles, get us over to the office."

Something exploded behind them. Another missile, Johnny thought, or maybe an IED.

He pulled out his radio, which was set for the common security channel. "Somebody just attacked Chelsea's house," he said. "Call nine-one-one."

"Johnny—the Smart Metal building's just been struck," said the desk man. "Something flew into the top floor."

"*No.*"

"Outside—there are IEDs. We're under attack here."

Johnny heard an explosion over the radio.

"Bowles, we need to get to the Mountain."

The Mountain was a safe house near Bald Hill well northwest of the city. Massina had purchased the property several years before, keeping the two buildings on it vacant. In the past few days he had clandestinely had work done to increase its security. Two Smart Metal security people were stationed there around the clock.

"I need to get back to work," insisted Chelsea.

"We need to keep you safe," said Johnny.

"If we're under attack, I need to get to work. Get me to the Annex so I can help track him down."

"Johnny, Bozzone's been hit," said Peter Mench, one of the shift supervisors. "A truck hit the front of the building and blew up at the barrier. We need you."

"Secure it. I'll be there in a few minutes." Johnny put his hand to his forehead, as if rubbing the outside of his brain might organize the cells and their thoughts inside. He'd expected something like this, trained for it, prepared, but going from the theoretical to the reality always involved friction—it never happened the way you thought it would.

"The building's been hit," he told the others. "Drop me on Cambridge and take Chelsea to the Mountain."

"I need to be somewhere I can do some good," protested Chelsea.

Johnny ignored her. "She's your priority," he told Bowles. "I can get to the office probably quicker on foot anyway."

"I'm not running away," insisted Chelsea.

"You're not."

Bowles slammed on the brakes. The traffic ahead had stopped dead.

"Throw it into reverse," Johnny insisted. His brain hiccup was over—he could see what he had to do clearly and easily. "Go over to Longfellow, get away from the city. Go!"

Bowles veered into a U-turn. The street ahead was clear.

"Drop me here," shouted Johnny. He unlocked the door and put his hand on the handle as Bowles screeched to a halt.

"I love you," he told Chelsea as he went out the door, the SUV still moving.

"Me, too," she said weakly.

It was the first time either of them had said that to each other, or to themselves.

100

THE BLAST OF THE HELICOPTER STRIKING THE EXTER-
nal wall of the building threw Massina against
the glass at the front of his outer office. He managed to put his prosthetic right arm up as he hit,
which absorbed some of the shock and saved him
from a concussion. But the blow disabled the
mechanics in his arm, bending one of the main
"bones" or rods. Rising slowly, he saw his assistant, Teri, fumbling for the door a few feet away.

"Come on," he told her, pushing it open with
his good arm.

The building's original early-twentieth-century
curtain wall had been reinforced with heavy steel,
and while not designed specifically to withstand
an explosion, it withstood the crash without cata-
strophic failure. The glass was another matter—
the helicopter impaled itself in the office, its nose
a few inches from Massina's desk. Exactly thirty
seconds after impact, a timer ignited a bomb located in the rear of the cockpit; the explosion

brought down a good portion of the ceiling and floor, along with part of the interior walls and roof above the room, damaging the structural members and starting a mini landslide of material toward the ground. At the same time, it ignited the fuel that had leaked from the aircraft. Flames quickly spread into the building, lapping at the carpet and whatever wood and plastic they could find. Two of the three zones of sprinklers covering the floor had been damaged by the crash and explosion; the fire leaped through those sections, racing toward the elevators.

Massina and Teri struggled down the hall, dazed by the smoke and dust as well as the explosion.

"Stairs," said Massina. "We need the stairs."

Finding the door, Massina pushed it open, bracing himself for he knew not what: flames, maybe, or a gaping hole. But instead, fresh air surged into his face.

Safety.

"I'll be down in a minute," Massina told Teri, pushing her through the threshold. "I need to make sure everyone's out."

Teri started to protest, but Massina stepped back quickly and shut the door. Alarms blared; water whistled through the broken pipes of the extinguisher system. Smoke, heavy with toxins from the carpet and other materials, stung Massina's face. A spray of water doused him as he turned back to check the other hall for his people; he could feel soot caking on his head and face.

"Out! This way!" he yelled, pushing open the door to the Administrative Functions suite, where personnel and related matters were handled. Smoke seeped through the walls and water sprayed from the ceiling; the emergency lights were on, along with an alarm light that blinked on and off like a lazy strobe. The office and its cluster of desks and cabinets looked empty, and Massina was just about to go back out to the hall when he heard a moan from the back.

Jason Vendez, the head of Finance, lay on the floor, pinned between a desk and part of the caved-in wall. Massina tried to grab the desk with his prosthetic arm, which ordinarily would have had no trouble leveraging the furniture out of the way. But the arm was broken, unable to respond properly—it was an odd sensation, his brain thinking it was moving yet his eyes registering that it wasn't.

Massina squeezed between the desk and the wall, aiming to lever his feet against the desk. That didn't work; he swung around, butt against the desk, feet against the wall, and tried again. The desk shifted and he fell to the floor as Vendez crawled free.

"I'm OK, I'm OK," Vendez repeated as Massina helped him to his feet.

"Who else is here?"

"No one."

"The smoke is coming in—we have to get out."

Out in the hallway, flames flickered along the bottom of the wall. A layer of smoke had risen to the ceiling, a poisonous cloud layer dividing the air. The smoke drifted toward them slowly, lowering itself as it went.

"Who's here! Who's here!" shouted Massina. "Go to the stairs!"

If anyone answered, he didn't hear. He pushed Vendez toward the stairs, then went down to the next suite, looking inside. The rooms on this side were farthest from the explosion and appeared intact—and fortunately empty.

Massina pushed open the door to the last office and yelled inside. No one answered.

Water from one of the burst pipes shot down from the ceiling. He stepped into the office, crossing through the spray.

"Anyone!" he yelled. "Anyone!"

The room was empty.

He turned and nearly knocked over Vendez.

"I told you to go down," Massina screamed, angry.

"I'm not leaving without you, Louis."

"Come on, then," said Massina. "Crawl."

The smoke had sunk so low there was less than three feet of clear air left. Knots of toxins swirled downward, tiny twisters of poison. Water dripped in large drops, springing from the leaks in the pipes above, impotent against the fiery onslaught.

They had just reached the door when the building shook again, the tremor so strong both men lost their balance. As Massina fell on his back, he saw the hallway wall begin to collapse. He held his breath and leaped upward to grab the door handle.

As he did, the wall next to it began to crumble. Massina's fingers touched the handle, then involuntarily pulled back—the fire had warmed the metal to well over a hundred degrees. He fell back to his knees; before he could rise, the ceiling collapsed, knocking him to his stomach next to Vendez, burying them both in a wet spray of mud and Sheetrock.

101

Boston—a moment later

"I NEED MY LAPTOP," CHELSEA TOLD BOWLES. "STOP at the Annex."

"Johnny told us to go to the Mountain."

"He didn't say I couldn't get my laptop. I can work from the Mountain."

Bowles didn't answer.

"It'll only take me a minute," Chelsea added. "We're going right past it. There's no attack there. Take the ramp."

Bowles waited until the last moment to veer off the highway. He ran through the light and sped up toward the complex.

Looking through the front windshield, everything seemed normal. Aside from a small cluster of white clouds, the sky was azure blue, the sun bright yellow.

Behind the car, black smoke rose from downtown.

Greta Torbin turned on the radio, fiddling until she found a news station.

A helicopter has struck a building downtown, be-

lieved to be the Smart Metal Company Headquarters. There are reports of several IEDs and explosions, and a shooting in the T line . . .

"Maybe you should turn it off," suggested Bowles. "We don't need a play-by-play."

"Leave it on," said Chelsea.

The reporter continued almost breathlessly, describing various attacks, some based on things he had heard over the police scanner, some on Twitter, some from other stations. A few of the reports were clearly wrong—he claimed Logan Airport had been shut down, but Chelsea could see airplanes rising in the sky on a clear path to and from it.

"Five minutes," said Bowles, pulling into the entrance to the mall. "Five minutes or we are coming down and dragging you out."

"Five minutes," answered Chelsea.

Bowles sped toward the entrance, then did a power skid to turn sideways so he could let Chelsea out as close as possible. She hopped out of the car, leaving the door open as she sprinted to the security station. The two men on guard raised their weapons, then realized it was her. One pointed around the X-ray machine, indicating she should skip the check—a violation of protocol, even for her, but understandable under the circumstances.

She had gone around the machine when something exploded in the lot behind her. Chelsea spun back and saw flames leaping from the SUV—it had been hit by an antitank missile.

The two guards ran toward the vehicle. Chelsea started to follow, then stopped, unsure what to do.

"No, keep going," ordered a man behind her.

He grabbed her by the midsection. She kicked his kneecap and elbowed his stomach, but was hit hard in the side of the head before she could spin out of his grip. She fell to the pavement, her head rebounding off the concrete. The world dimmed.

"Finally we meet," said the man, pushing his face into hers.

Ghadab, she thought as she blacked out.

102

A MAN DRIVING A DELIVERY VAN HAD CRASHED INTO the steel barriers between the street and the sidewalk in front of the Smart Metal building; a moment before impact, he set off the fertilizer-based bomb packed into the rear. The explosion had buckled a portion of the front of the building, but had done far more damage to the structure across the street.

Johnny Givens reached the scene two minutes after the explosion. Combusted metal and concrete filled the air, thick enough to obscure the sun. Sirens roared in the distance but so far neither police nor firemen had arrived. Two or three cars, so twisted and split they couldn't be identified, sat like discarded bones in the street.

There were body parts everywhere, but no live people, at least none that Johnny could see.

He picked his way through the street, jumping

past a long gash in the asphalt, nearly tripping over a jagged claw of concrete on the sidewalk. The stone facade at the Smart Metal entrance was scarred black; a slab of metal blocked the doorway, having fallen from above. Johnny doubled back around the side to a second entrance.

The two security men there raised their rifles as soon as he turned the corner.

"It's me, it's me!" he shouted, raising his hands. "It's Johnny!"

They looked spooked. Johnny felt his heart clutch—they were going to shoot.

"It's me!" he shouted again, stopping.

Finally, they lowered their weapons. He walked toward them quickly.

"What's going on?"

"Beefy's downstairs," said one of the men— "Snake" Boone. "He's pretty hurt. He was outside when the first suicide bomber hit."

Two men in suicide vests had arrived at almost the exact moment the helicopter struck the building. The truck bomb had followed a few minutes later, either delayed or purposely timed in an effort to catch people as they evacuated.

"Keep the place locked down," said Johnny. "No one in or out."

"Right."

"Not even Massina himself," added Johnny. "No one!"

He pushed inside. Expecting chaos, he found silence instead. The entire first-floor lobby was empty, except for security teams crouched in defensive positions at the center of the hall and behind the mashed front entrance. Johnny ran to the post at the main entrance.

"Most of the employees are in the basement," said Corey Draken, who was in charge of floor security. "Sweep teams are working their way up."

"Where's Massina?"

"Computer has him on the executive floor still. Where the helicopter hit. Vendez is with him."

Massina coughed so hard it felt as if his chest was turning itself inside out. He crawled forward, trying to escape the blanket of soaked Sheetrock. Water cascaded down the side of the left wall. But the right wall, still dry, turned blue with flames as the fire reached it.

Vendez, struck by part of the wall as it fell, lay on his stomach a few feet away. Massina shook him, but got only a moan in response.

"Time to go," said Massina.

He pulled Vendez with him a few feet, getting away from the worst of the debris. The stairs had been cut off by the collapse of the ceiling and the wall. There was another set at the far end of the building, but that was on the other side of the fire.

Best bet is to go to the window and wait, Massina thought.

Not much of a bet.

Better than being here.

"Come on," he told Vendez. "We'll go into one

of the offices. This side, away from where the helicopter crashed."

THE NORTH STAIRWELL BETWEEN THE FIFTH AND SIXTH floors had collapsed. One of the three elevator shafts appeared intact, but the car was stuck on the fourth floor and wouldn't move, even in emergency manual mode.

Johnny, standing with one of the sweep teams on the fourth floor, had the automated security com operator connect him to Boston's emergency response center.

"I have two men trapped on the top floor," Johnny said. "We're going to need a ladder truck."

"Got it," said the man. "They're estimating five minutes."

"That's too damn long," said Johnny, snapping off the Talk button.

THE SMALL OFFICE AT THE BACK OF THE PERSONNEL section appeared at first glance a haven; drenched by the water, it was intact and several degrees cooler than the hallway. But as soon as Massina stood up, he realized safety was a mirage: smoke was furling in, choking off the oxygen. He dropped quickly to the floor, his eyes and throat burning.

Coughing, he crawled to Vendez near the window. Vendez was slipping in and out of consciousness.

"Stay with me," said Massina as Vendez's eyes closed.

"Oh, yeah," said the Finance chief.

"Stay awake. I need you. Not just today, to-morrow."

"Uh."

Vendez started to slide to the floor. Massina stopped him, then lowered him gently, realizing there was better air there.

Or at least hoping there was better air.

"I wonder if the phones are working. What do you think, Jason?"

Massina didn't expect an answer, and he didn't get one. He lowered his face to the floor, took a big gulp of air, and held his breath. Then he jumped up and grabbed a phone from the desk.

The smoke stung his face so badly he couldn't open his eyes. He put the receiver to his ear, but heard nothing.

Dead.

My cell?

In all of the confusion he hadn't thought of using his own phone. He pulled it from his pocket, put his finger on the print reader, then pulled up the directory to call his security desk. Only after pressing the phone icon did he notice the message at the top indicating that he had no service.

He almost threw it down in anger, but stopped himself. It was important, it was critical, to remain calm, to be calm, to think.

Think.

They know we're here. They'll send help.

Maybe a ladder truck.

The ledge outside. It's wide enough to stand on.

Massina knew this from experience—unfortunate experience, but then he'd lived to tell about it, so how bad could it have been, really?

Not as bad as this.

"We're going out the window, Jason. Come on."

Vendez didn't answer. Massina tried to get him over his back, but it was difficult without the use of one hand and arm.

I'm never going to be able to climb up to the roof with only one hand. I can barely make it with two.

He pulled Vendez with him anyway, moving backward along the floor. As he reached the glass, a red flare shot into the room near the door. A black cloud rolled in behind it.

Massina lowered his chest to the floor, trying to find clean air.

There was a loud pop, then a crash and a crackle, a thousand glasses falling from a cabinet to the floor at the same instant. Massina looked toward the window—a piece of metal had flown through.

Another aircraft?

The metal moved back and forth quickly. Another probe appeared, then a dull gray cloud—it was RBT PJT 23-A, better known as Peter, smashing its way inside to rescue them.

TEN MINUTES LATER, PETER DEPOSITED MASSINA in the second-floor lounge, where Smart Metal's nurse had established a triage center. The bot had taken Vendez down first, then raced back to get its maker.

It was a quick and dizzying ride down the face of the building. Peter's clamps were quite tight—Massina's first thought when he arrived was that would have to be adjusted.

Gulping pure oxygen from a tank, he cleared his head and looked for Beefy. Instead, he found Johnny Givens striding across the room.

"Everyone's accounted for," Johnny told him. "We have thirty-three people hurt, two with probable internal injuries, a lot of broken bones, some smoke and light burns. But everybody's alive."

"Where's Beefy?"

"He had a head injury and a compound fracture of the arm. Maybe a busted rib. He's conscious downstairs. The nurse gave him a shot of morphine to ease the pain."

"Chelsea?"

"On her way to the Mountain."

"The machines?"

"Everything downstairs is fine. They went into shutdown mode automatically."

"All right. I'm going to the Box." Massina patted him on the back. "Good decision, sending Peter."

"I didn't," said Johnny. "Near as we can figure, he went on his own."

103

CHELSEA'S HEAD THROBBED. THE SCENT OF DIESEL filled her nose, diesel and something caustic, ammonia-like. She tried to move, but her hands were restrained behind her back—she was in a straitjacket.

No, just restraints. Not too tight, but enough. No escape.

Where was she?

Moving.

A van.

Have to get out of here.

She pushed her arms, trying to free them. But that only made the restraints tighter.

No one will know where I am.

They can track my phone.

Where is my phone?

She didn't feel it in her pocket. They'd taken it and her wallet and her keys. Everything but her watch.

The watch.

The backing.

Scrape it off, said the voice in her head—her father. *Press it against your skin.*

I can't.

Stop your whining and do it.

Yes, Daddy.

Chelsea twisted her hand, scraping as best she could. The watch, loose on her hand, flipped over. She kept scraping.

"Coming back to us, princess?" sneered Ghadab. He loomed over her. "Don't fear. I haven't killed you yet. There's still more time for that. This, this I want."

Ghadab leaned down and Chelsea felt something poke her in the wrist. Her watch flew off. Her wrist stung.

"Bandage her," Ghadab told someone behind her she couldn't see. "I don't want her dying yet. There's much more to enjoy before that deliciousness."

104

A STORM OF EMOTIONS FLOODED THROUGH MASSINA as he parsed the different media reports. There had been as many as a dozen bombing attacks spread across the city, not counting the ones at Smart Metal. But there were no reports of hostage-style attacks like those that had hit the city months before. Nor had there been a direct attack on any of the power plants in the region, or the airport. With the exception of areas hit by suicide bombers—including his building—electricity was still flowing.

Which wasn't to say that the city was going about its business as if nothing had happened. Boston was in lockdown, with the National Guard rushing to close all of the major highways in and out. The monuments were closed; city and state police were enforcing a curfew.

Ghadab obviously was behind this, Massina realized. So where was he?

"Why isn't the line to the Annex open?" he asked Telakus, who was handling the com section at the consoles.

"We're having trouble with all our lines," Telakus replied.

"We shouldn't have trouble with that. It's direct. Try Chiang's cell phone."

"I did. It went straight to voice mail."

Oh, no.

"Get one of the Nightbird UAVs up, and fly it over the Annex," Massina told Telakus. "Have it feed us video."

Neither the city police nor the FBI emergency posts had any information on Ghadab. Massina tried calling Johansen, but he went directly to voice mail.

By the time he finished leaving his message, the UAV had been launched. He walked over to the console where the controller was sitting—they were using a remote setup, having flown the bot from one of their test yards near the river—and watched as it sped northward.

If you subtracted the police vehicles and troop trucks, there wasn't much traffic. In sharp contrast to the first round of attacks, the city looked amazingly calm.

Is this all you got?

Massina saw the smoke from the wreckage of the SUV miles before the drone closed in. He kept telling himself not to jump to conclusions, not to worry, not to think the worst.

It can't be our vehicle.

But it was.

The aircraft circled several times so they could examine the wreckage. There were two bodies inside, both in the front seat.

"Johnny, you better come down here," Massina said over the company circuit.

JOHNNY SENSED THAT SOMETHING HAD GONE TERRIbly wrong as he made his way down to the Box. After realizing there was no cell service, he'd tried checking in with Torbin via their satellite connection, but gotten no response.

Still, seeing the burned-out hull of the truck was a shock. He couldn't breathe; he felt the way he'd felt when he woke in the hospital after he lost his legs.

"They're gone," said Massina softly.

"God," muttered Johnny.

Time contorted, somehow moving fast and slow at once. He felt as if he could leave his body and circle the room several times before a second passed. Yet it also seemed he'd been standing there forever, unmoving, welded to grief.

"Chelsea's not there," said Massina.

"What . . . ? What?"

"Here." Massina pointed to another screen.

"What is this?" asked Johnny.

"The watch. She's still wearing it."

Johnny looked at the screen. "Where?"

"Heading south, toward Cape Cod maybe?"

"Pilgrim," said Johnny. "The power plant."

THE PILGRIM NUCLEAR PLANT WAS AMONG THE MOST heavily guarded facilities in the Boston area, let alone on the East Coast. Ghadab would be a fool to attack there.

But it seemed clear that was where Chelsea was being taken.

Massina called their liaison at Homeland Security, warning him.

"I'm going down there," said Johnny when he got off the phone.

"I don't know that you'll be able to do anything," said Massina.

"I'm going."

"Wait," said Massina.

The look in Johnny's eyes made it clear he was determined to go, no matter what Massina said or did.

"The FBI is sending a chopper down there," offered Massina, conceding. "Let me see if I can get you on it."

105

Boston—around the same time

IT WAS ALL MOVING TOGETHER PERFECTLY. SURELY this had been God's plan all along. Ghadab had let his ego get the better of him, believing he was privileged to watch the final apocalypse in person. But God had humbled him. As he deserved.

Ghadab was still important. In fact, perhaps more than he realized. He would initiate the end days, reveling in its joy from Paradise, not earth. The Americans would surely seek revenge after the destruction of their birthplace city.

Shadaa, too, had been part of the plan. God had shown him the power of love—it could be as strong a motivator as religion, if properly understood.

And now he did.

Ghadab ran his thumb along the edge of the knife. It was a long blade, purchased at a hippie military surplus store near Burlington. Beautiful in its simplicity.

Not a khanjar, but certainly serviceable.

106

**The Box, Smart Metal Headquarters, Boston—
thirty minutes later**

A STATE POLICE HELICOPTER HAD TENTATIVELY tracked Chelsea's locator to a van driving south on Route 3. But even as the van neared the turnoff for 3A—which would take it directly to the power plant—the police coordinator wasn't convinced that the plant was the target.

"If it's a kidnapping, the last place they're going to go is the power plant," he told Massina.

"This isn't your ordinary kidnapping."

"They won't get to the power plant."

"That's what I'm afraid of."

The state police were feeding real-time images of the power plant to the Box via the CIA connection; the image was from a police UAV circling around the plant. The helicopter Johnny was aboard was just coming south, not yet in range of the van.

The exit for 3A north of the plant was open to allow residents to get to their houses. But the van passed up the ramp, heading instead toward the interchange with the access road. This was closed off, and heavily guarded besides.

He's going to ram the barrier and that'll be the end of it, thought Massina. The end of Chelsea, probably.

He felt helpless.

Ghadab was a fool—going to such elaborate preparations only to thrust himself against a police barrier and die in a hail of bullets.

No, that wasn't him at all. He was crazy, but smarter than that. He'd know his computers were taken and might even have suspected that his men would talk.

He wasn't going to go throw himself against a police barrier. Not there.

Not there.

"Passed the interchange," said the cop. "Still going south, turning off at White Horse Road— they're going the back way? They're going the back way!"

107

Over Plymouth—the same time

THERE WERE SO MANY TREES LINING THE ROAD THAT Johnny couldn't see the van as it sped past the residential area, heading back north toward the power plant. A barrier manned by National Guardsmen as well as plant security and local policemen had been set up three days before at the main entrance. Alerted by the state police, a team moved a pair of heavy troop trucks across the road about fifty feet from the intersection itself; the entrance to the power plant was blocked by two other trucks, which together straddled the entrance. Behind them was an up-armored Humvee, with a gun turret.

Nobody was getting in that way.

"Take out the tires and stop them," said Johnny. He had a headset connected to the command frequency. "Shoot the driver—they have a hostage."

"They'll try," said the pilot over the interphone circuit, an internal line only those in the helicopter could hear. "Leave the line open."

As they came up toward the intersection, Johnny saw men taking cover behind the trucks. There were snipers along the roadway and a set of spikes that would shred tires farther along. A police car with its lights flashing was ahead of the spikes, and two officers were standing out in front of it.

They waved their arms as the van approached, but it was clear the vehicle wasn't stopping.

Oh, God. Oh, God, no!

He could see a burst of glass as one of the snipers took out the driver, but it was too late—the van swerved slightly, banging the front of the police car and then careening across the spikes as it erupted in a fireball so intense the men behind the truck threw themselves down or ran back for more cover.

Oh, God, no . . .

108

Boston—around the same time

MASSINA STARED AT THE SCREEN AS HE SCROLLED through the data, trying to piece everything together. The link to the Annex was still out; he had Chelsea's last report but nothing more recent.

Trying to blow up Pilgrim? That makes zero sense. And nothing in this report comes close to hinting at an explosion, so . . .

What the hell is he doing?

Ghadab was not a stupid man. Evil, a psychopath, the Devil incarnate . . . but not dumb enough to think that he could crash into a power plant and do damage on the scale he dreamed of.

Socrates had to have something.

Chelsea!

He couldn't watch her die. He had to do something instead. Something tangible. Even if it was a dead end.

"Come on," he told Boone. "I need you to drive."

"Where?"

"The Annex."

Outside the door, Massina stopped short. RBT PJT 23-A sat nearby, in full-ready state.

"Peter, come with me," he told the bot. "I may need you."

The bot jumped to follow.

TRAFFIC HAD BEEN SHUNTED AWAY FROM THE CITY, and the streets were relatively clear once they got a few blocks from the building. Massina had grabbed a sweatshirt to hide his arm; he sat in the front seat next to Boone, turning the problem over in his mind.

Ghadab had to want more than simply killing him and Chelsea. He wanted Armageddon and would never settle for mere revenge.

Oh . . .

"We need to get to Cambridge," Massina told Boone. "Fast."

GIVEN THAT THE ATTACKS IN DOWNTOWN BOSTON were barely an hour old, Cambridge was almost supernaturally calm. True, there were plenty of police and other security types scattered around the MIT campus, but there was still a queue in front of the coffee truck parked outside the building.

Under extreme protest, Boone dropped Massina off near the building and squealed off to find a parking spot in a nearby lot. Though he'd promised to wait, Massina walked briskly past the guards at the front and around the corner to the side door. Here, he showed the man his license—and the card that indicated he was a member of the board of trustees.

"We're going to have to pat you down," said the guard. "Could you take your sweatshirt off?"

"Gladly," he told the officer, who was an MIT employee. "I just want you to know, I have a prosthetic arm, and the surface was damaged. So you'll see metal. It will look a little strange."

The guard gave him a funny look and took a half step back, as if he were expecting a trick of some sort. Massina took off the sweatshirt and lifted his arms. He had been able to get a temporary repair to the prosthetic, which gave him better control and mobility in the arm and hand, but not a lot of strength.

Meanwhile, two other guards looked on from the vestibule nearby, more out of curiosity than concern. Behind them stood a pair of National Guardsmen with M4s.

The pat down was quick and light.

"You can, uh, put down your arms," said the guard, handing back the sweatshirt. "You're here to do what?"

"I've come to see Jack, the student manager?"

"You know the way?"

"I've been here once or twice." Massina had actually been in the building at least three dozen times over the past five or ten years.

"You're Louis Massina, right? The robot guy."

"That's me."

The guard nodded. He gave him a visitor badge and a small detector that would keep track of the radiation he was exposed to. Massina clipped it to the pocket of his jacket, then walked across the hall to the stairs.

"You better come with me," said Massina.

"I can't leave my post without permission and—"

"Screw permission," said Massina, starting down. "It can't wait."

THEY CALLED THE BUILDING THE BLUE MUSHROOM, partly because the containment vessel that covered the nuclear power plant was blue and partly as a very twisted joke. It looked more like a water tank than a mushroom, and as a piece of architecture it was about as interesting.

But the Blue Mushroom's purpose had nothing to do with architecture. The plant was one of a small number of research facilities around the country constructed in the 1950s and early '60s. Besides having helped educate several generations of nuclear engineers, the reactor could be credited with saving a number of lives: its radioactivity had played a role in various cancer therapies.

Like every nuclear power plant in the U.S., it had been designed in such a way that a nuclear explosion was impossible; nearby residents had far more to fear from the butane tanks on their barbecue grills than the plant.

But just because it couldn't explode didn't mean it couldn't present a danger. As Fukushima, Chernobyl, and even Three Mile Island showed, there was always a slight possibility of an accidental release at the plant or, far worse, a meltdown that would irradiate the area. To guard against that admittedly remote possibility, nuclear power plants had layers and layers of precautions and were subject to constant monitoring. The Blue Mushroom was no different.

The reactor control room looked as if it were the set for a slightly dated sci-fi movie. Banks of wall-to-ceiling green metal cabinets lined the walls, housing different instruments and monitoring systems. Lit by overhead fluorescents, the floor shone; there was a slight hint of ammonia in the air, as if the room had just been sanitized. Ordinarily, the control room was staffed by one or two students; today there was only one.

"You need to shut the reactor down immediately," announced Massina. He was alone; the guard had remained upstairs. "Begin the shutdown procedure."

"Who the hell are you?" asked the student.

"Shut it down."

The student stepped in his way. Another came down the hall behind him, an AR-15 in his hand.

"Who's in charge?" asked Massina.

"I'm in charge," said a man, rising from behind

the console on Massina's right. "I'm so glad you finally figured it out. I was concerned that I wouldn't have the pleasure of seeing you off."

It was Ghadab min Allah, with a grin on his face and a long combat knife in his hand.

109

Plymouth—around the same time

THE SAFETY PROTOCOLS PUT INTO PLACE BECAUSE OF the emergency meant the helicopter had to land a good distance from the van. Rather than waiting for one of the state troopers to ride him down to the site, Johnny decided to run. And run he did, his prosthetic legs carrying him at a tremendous clip, moving so fast that if he were competing in the Marathon he surely would have set a world's record.

He smelled it first: a bag of fertilizer dumped in a charcoal grill.

The thick black smoke from the explosion and fire had dissipated, but what looked like a gray mist hugged the charred remains of the truck and two vehicles it had rolled into as it exploded. The intense fireball had scorched the ground and nearby vegetation; trees some thirty yards away were scarred black, and the pavement was a slick black splotch, still sticky with the heat.

Three men and one of the women who'd been at the barrier were lightly wounded in the explosion, cut and bruised, but otherwise the only casualties were the people in the van.

The nuclear power plant was safe, though at the moment that was little consolation to Johnny.

As he approached the van, one of the police supervisors, a lieutenant, put his hand out to stop him.

Johnny stopped and held up his credentials, but the lieutenant didn't budge. "My—my, uh, wife, was the hostage," said Johnny.

It was the only word strong enough to let him through, Johnny intuited. And at the moment, he couldn't have felt any more pain than if it'd been true.

The lieutenant stared at the credentials balefully, then put his radio to his mouth and called in the ID. He held his other hand to his ear, listening on the earpiece.

"I have to see," said Johnny, starting past. "Let me. I'd do the same for you."

"Yeah, OK," the lieutenant told the others. "Let him. But listen, it's a crime scene," he added. "It's a crime scene."

Johnny barely heard. He knew he should prepare himself for the worst, but there was no way to do that. There was no way to prepare, period.

So he just walked.

Two National Guardsmen were standing near the back of what had been the van. It was open, burned-out, empty. Johnny walked to the front cab and peered in. The van had turned over as it exploded and landed on its roof. The driver, burned to a skeleton, hung from the seat belt, bits of fabric glued to the bones and skull.

"Where are the other bodies?" Johnny asked, staring.

"Other bodies?" One of the soldiers walked over to him. "Sir?"

"The woman. The hostage."

"There were no other bodies," said the man.

"None?"

"Just this bastard."

"You're sure?"

"Pretty damn sure. Look—he's burned to shit, but he's the only one here."

110

Cambridge—about the same time

CHELSEA TRIED TO MOVE HER ARMS BUT IT WAS NO use; she was strapped into a restraining jacket like a 1960s mental patient. She looked down into the clear water, peering at the top of the nuclear reactor. The water was bubbling, and given the heat in the room, she was sure it was boiling. The place smelled of steam, like an iron ready to press a wrinkled dress.

It's not boiling. It's my imagination.

The water bath doesn't boil. I've been here. I've seen this.

It looks like it's boiling.

Mind tricks.

I need to clear my head and figure a way out.

There were voices. Chelsea lifted her head, straining to hear.

Someone moved through the fog.

Massina.

I'm hallucinating.

MASSINA STOPPED AT THE RAILING.

Ghadab came toward him, trailed by the pair

of "students"—clearly his own people, whom he'd managed to substitute at some point over the past several days . . . or maybe weeks, even years.

The computer geeks he'd gathered in the Syria bunker had obviously been working on a plan to make the reactor go critical while fooling the monitoring devices into thinking nothing was wrong. He'd managed to get his own people onto the reactor team—maybe they were all deep-planted agents, or maybe he'd brought them over when he decided on his target.

It was all moot now. The reactor core must be in breach: an unstoppable chain reaction spewing radiation.

This was not a nuclear bomb; Cambridge and Boston and Massachusetts would remain intact. But people would die—at least a few hundred in the blocks close to the reactor. Thousands more might succumb over the succeeding years to radiation-caused cancer or some other disease that took advantage of their compromised immune systems.

As horrible as it was, as unthinkable, the loss of life was not the worst thing that would happen. The center of the city would be abandoned, perhaps for a century. The university would be permanently damaged, shunned.

That would pale next to the longer-term consequences. People would want, would demand, revenge on a scale beyond anything before.

Unleash a nuke on us, we will unleash one on you.

It was not inconceivable that Mecca would be leveled in retaliation. And then?

Once used, nuclear weapons would be "thinkable" again. North Korea, Iran—who would use them first, and what would the consequences be?

Massina took a step along the railing, backing away from Ghadab. The kid with the gun waved it in Massina's direction.

Three against one was bad enough, even if he'd been thirty years younger, but the gun made the situation impossible.

The knife wouldn't be much fun either.

Massina jerked his head upward and saw that a bundle had been tied to a rope dangling from the block-and-chain mechanism over the cooling pool.

Old clothes?

A doll . . .

Chelsea!

"Yes, that's your woman," said Ghadab. "How does it feel to see your people dying?"

"Let her go," said Massina. "It's me you want. Right? You left enough clues that I would come and see this."

"I expected you sooner," bragged Ghadab.

"My life for hers."

Ghadab pointed the knife upward. "Would you trade her life for the city's? You can save her, or save the city."

The terrorist was implying that the reactor could reach its final critical meltdown in moments—that there was only a short amount of time to stop it.

Maybe he was right—maybe there was still

hope. But if so, what would he do? What could he do?

"Let her go," said Massina.

"I can drop her in the water." Ghadab pulled a smartphone from his pocket. "Then she'll die instantly. And you won't have a choice—your city will burn. And your puppet will, too."

"That's not what Allah wants," said Massina.

"What do you know of God's will?"

"I know he doesn't want slaughter."

"You know nothing of religion." Ghadab's tone was adamant, angry—he'd been taken by surprise by the argument, clearly, but it was one he couldn't ignore; it touched him to the core.

"Everyone who follows you," said Massina, "dies because of your crazy beliefs. You've turned your religion into something perverse. God doesn't ask for destruction."

"Silence, blasphemer! You dishonor the one true God."

"You're not even a true believer."

"I know you, Satan. I know you've pulled all of these strings, like some master manipulating his puppets."

"I'm not Satan. I have no puppets."

"Look at her!" Ghadab shouted, pointing to Chelsea twisting above the pool. "She's already sick from the radiation."

"You expect Armageddon," said Massina. "I know from your notes in the bunker. But that's not going to happen. The West will simply crush you. If there were ever an Armageddon, it would be Islam that would be eliminated, not the West."

"You have no idea what you're talking about."

"Explain it to me, then. If you are what and who you say you are, enlighten me. Or are you just a psychotic, as even the Saudis claim you are?"

GHADAB FELT HIS ANGER RISING BEYOND THE BREAK-ing point. He struggled to control himself— there was still so much to be accomplished.

But he couldn't. He drew back the knife and aimed his body at Massina.

He saw the American's shoulders start to droop. The man was a coward!

Disappointment mixed with triumph.

Then, in a flash too quick to record, surprise.

MASSINA LAUNCHED HIMSELF ARM-FIRST INTO Ghadab, slamming his arm into the terrorist's windpipe like a baseball bat. Ghadab gasped as he fell backward, rolling over the railing and into the containment pool.

Light flashed in the room, then the overloud echo of rifle shots—the security guard who had reluctantly followed him down had appeared at the doorway, only to be chased back by gun-fire from two thugs who'd been with Ghadab. But the guard's tardiness had been for a good cause—he'd brought reinforcements. The room lit with a white flash, instantly followed with a boom that hollowed out Massina's ears—a flash-bang grenade thrown by a member of the local SWAT team, assigned as backup security for the campus.

Massina climbed to his knees. He couldn't hear—the explosions had rendered him temporarily deaf.

Two bodies lay on the platform nearby—the "students" who'd been with Ghadab.

Massina got to his feet and went to the control panel. The emergency shutoff was a simple lever; remove the guard and pull it, and the reactor would automatically begin shutdown.

Except, knowing Ghadab, things wouldn't be that simple.

Massina took his hand off the panel.

"Chelsea." She was suspended from a rope tied through a hoist in the ceiling; the end was secured on the railing. But before Massina could get to it, he felt himself pushed hard to the floor. One of the SWAT team members appeared at his side, screaming something.

"I can't hear you!" Massina shouted back. "The grenade. I'm Louis Massina. We need to shut the reactor down! I need Chelsea! My employee!"

The guard from upstairs ran over, yelling to let him be. Massina was pulled to his feet. He rubbed his ears and the side of his face. His senses were returning, but he felt as if he were underwater.

The guard took hold of the rope Chelsea was suspended from. Tugging, he swung her toward the rail, where one of the SWAT team grabbed her. He quickly cut her loose.

"Chelsea?" asked Massina. "Do you know what they did to the controls? Are they sabotaged?"

She blinked, then shook her head—but was she answering him or saying she didn't know?

There were footsteps in the hall. Two of the SWAT team members moved into a blocking position.

"It's us!" yelled Boone. Beams of light danced near the doorway. "The power's been turned off upstairs."

"Let them through," said Massina.

Boone and a half-dozen guardsmen came into the control room. Johansen followed.

"We need to shut the plant down," said Massina. "But I'm sure the controls have been sabotaged."

"A crew from the Department of Energy is on their way."

"Good," said Massina, taking out his phone. "In the meantime, I have another plan."

BY THE TIME THE DEPARTMENT OF ENERGY special-ists arrived, Massina had already started disman-tling the plant's nuclear rods. Or rather, Peter had. Working with data provided by Telakus back at Smart Metal, Massina had sent the bot into the containment pool with instructions on how to remove and stockpile the rods. It was a good thing—a close inspection of the control panel revealed two charges that would have blown up the entire room had a controlled shut-down been attempted. And the control program itself had been sabotaged, making it impossible to shut down the plant from the panel.

"Your bot is doing a great job," said the lead DOE expert. A Virginia native, the nuclear scientist's faint accent carried through his containment helmet and suit. "We'll be done inside the hour."

"Mmmm," said Massina, staring over the rail.

"Dr. Massina, you really should go upstairs with the others," said the DOE expert. "The radiation is well beyond normal."

"Two chest X-rays an hour," said Massina.

"A little more than that, actually. To be precise—"

"That's all right. I was joking."

Upstairs in the guardroom, Massina found Johansen talking on his secure sat phone. Boone was frowning nearby. Chelsea, wrapped in a blanket, sat on a metal chair. A paramedic was taking her blood pressure. She looked tired, but more angry than hurt.

"Are you all right?" Massina asked her.

"Yeah." She was hoarse.

"You should get combat pay," suggested Massina.

"Talk to my boss."

"I will."

"You put Peter back to work?" she asked.

"Yes."

"You trust him?"

"Enough. He rescued me."

"What?"

"They were running diagnostics. He knew I

was in trouble, and he came to help. Our learning program—he's learning better than we thought."

"You know why he froze?"

"I think he's trying to figure out who he is."

"Huh? What do you mean?"

"I'm not sure yet."

Johansen had finished his call and walked over. "How did Ghadab get out?" he asked.

"He didn't," said Massina. "I pushed him in."

Johansen shook his head, then pointed to the nearby security console. "He's not in the pool."

"Sure he is."

"Screen 12."

The TV screen was the second from last in the bottom row; it showed the video feed from a camera at the bottom of the containment pool. The image was a little blurry, but clear enough for Massina to see Peter pulling the last fuel rod from the reactor.

There was no body in the water anywhere, just the bot and the rods.

"I don't understand," said Massina. "I hit him hard enough to kill him."

"Maybe not," said Johansen.

"Where did he go? How did he get out?"

Johansen's pursed lips made it clear he didn't know.

DONE DEAL

——

111

**Grace Sisters Hospital, Boston—
two hours later**

JOHNNY LEAPED OFF THE HELICOPTER AND RAN INTO the hospital, barely slowing when the security people tried to flag him down. He waved his wallet at them, not even bothering to open it and show his ID. He made the elevator just as the doors were closing.

The two nurses in the car exchanged a glance.

"I'm sorry, I know I smell a bit," he said apologetically. "It's been a long day."

"Amen to that," said one.

Johnny found Chelsea sitting up in bed. Massina, Johansen, and Sister Rose Marie, the hospital administrator, were by her bedside, talking about the Red Sox game due to start in a few hours—Boston being Boston, no one was shutting down Fenway.

Especially when the Yankees were in town.

"You're OK?" said Johnny. "You're OK."

"Of course I'm OK," insisted Chelsea.

Then she burst into tears. Johnny folded her against his chest.

"WE SHOULD GIVE THEM SOME PRIVACY, MAYBE," said Massina, leading the others out of the room.

"You let him think she was dead?" asked Sister Rose. She had known Massina all his life and was, in many ways, one of his closest friends, despite the difference in their ages and outlook. "That was very cruel."

"No, I didn't know. I wasn't sure about the reactor, not until I was inside."

"I thought you were dead wrong," admitted Johansen. "The reactor is so small."

"Ghadab's attacks were always more psychological. He wanted to make it seem that anything could happen anywhere. And, frankly, a lot of people would have died had the core actually melted down. Everyone in the building, for starters."

"Most were his people," said Johansen. Daesh had managed to infiltrate the student cadre at the plant over a year before; once he targeted it, Ghadab replaced all of the control-room people and the guards with his own recruits. They'd been there for days, proceeding slowly so as not to attract attention. If Massina hadn't figured out the plot, it was very possible they would still be there, blocking the doors as the reactor finally went critical.

"The question now is, where is he?" said Massina. "He got out of the building."

"I doubt that," said Johansen. "We've only done a preliminary search. We'll get him. He won't get away."

I could have, should have, killed him, thought Massina.

He'd wanted to. He'd have felt no remorse.

Yet, he wouldn't have felt joy either, and maybe not even satisfaction. He knew that now, from what he had felt in the room when he thought Ghadab was dead.

Revenge wasn't enough. He'd thought he had it, but it hadn't made him feel any better.

Wiping Ghadab and Daesh off the face of the earth—it had to be done, but it wouldn't necessarily bring joy. It might not even bring closure.

What would?

"I really should be getting back over to the command center," said Johansen, glancing at his watch. "We'll set up a full debrief for tomorrow. I'll let you know."

"OK," answered Massina.

"The Director will want to formalize a relationship going forward. There are . . . legal things to work on."

"I'm sure we can do that. I have a question."

"Yes?"

"Were we only supposed to be a scapegoat if things went wrong, or did you really want our help?"

"I always wanted your help."

"The rest of the Agency?"

"The world is complicated, Louis." Johansen nodded at the nun, then walked away.

"So what do you say, Sister?" asked Massina. "Think the Red Sox will play tonight?"

"Absolutely. It's important that we play. We have to prove that we can't be messed with. These bastards can't win."

Massina felt a sudden pain in his chest: he had never in his life heard the nun use that word before.

"And besides," she added. "It's the Yankees."

"Did you just say 'bastards'?"

"Get over it." Sister Rose took a step, but then stopped and turned back to him. "Louis, tell me the truth. Did you push him into the vat of water?"

"I did," admitted Massina.

"You know it may be a sin to try to drown him."

"Maybe. But he didn't. And that's the real sin. Isn't it?"

She tightened her lips into a frown. He expected she would give him a lecture about God's mercy.

"Come on," said the nun instead. "I don't want to be late. I hate missing any part of the Sox kicking the Yankees' butts."